*LENIN IN ZURICH*
ALEXANDER SOLZHENITSYN

D1409974

Bantam Books by Alexander Solzhenitsyn
Ask your bookseller for the books you have missed

# LENIN IN ZURICH

CHAPTERS

# ALEXANDER SOLZHENITSYN

TRANSLATED BY H. T. WILLETTS

LENIN IN ZURICH

*A Bantam Book / published by arrangement with
Farrar, Straus and Giroux, Inc.*

*PRINTING HISTORY*
*Russian text first published by YMCA Press,
under the title*

Ленин в Цюрихе

*Farrar, Straus and Giroux edition published April 1976
Book-of-the-Month Club edition published August 1976
Conservative Book Club edition published September 1976
Macmillan Book Club edition published October 1976
Bantam edition / March 1977*

ISBN 0–553–10079–3

*Published simultaneously in the United States and Canada*

PRINTED IN THE UNITED STATES OF AMERICA

# Contents

## Author's Preface

Chapter 22 of Knot I, which was omitted from the published version of that work (August 1914), and the chapters from Knots II and III [October 1916 and March 1917] on Lenin in Zurich during the First World War, were written or begun while I was still in the U.S.S.R. Unexpectedly finding myself in Zurich, I came across much important additional material. As a result, the scope of these chapters has been considerably enlarged, and there seemed to be some point in publishing them as a separate book, rather than making them wait for publication of the Knots themselves, which will not be in the very near future.

FROM KNOT I

# AUGUST 1914

Yes, yes, yes, yes! It's a vice, this habit of plunging recklessly, of rushing full steam ahead, intent only on your goal, blind and deaf to all around, so that you fail to see the childishly obvious danger beside you! Like when he and Yuli Martov (the moment their three years of Siberian tedium were over and they were on their way abroad at last), carrying a basket of subversive literature and a letter with the plan for *Iskra* in invisible ink, chose that of all times to be too clever, too conspiratorial. The rule is to change trains en route, but they had forgotten that the other train would pass through Tsarskoye Selo, and were detained by the gendarmes as suspicious persons. Luckily the police with their salutary Russian sluggishness gave them time to get rid of the basket, and took the letter at its face value because they could not be bothered to hold it over a flame—and that was how *Iskra* was saved!

Later there was a year of tense struggle between the "majority" of 21 and the "minority" of 22, when the whole party had let the Japanese war slip by almost unnoticed.

This other war he had neither written nor thought about. He had not responded to Jaurès's appeal. Why? Because the *reunion movement* had spread like a plague, until in the last few years it had infected the whole of Russian Social Democracy. Nothing could be more dangerous and damaging to the proletariat than this epidemic: "conciliation," "reunification"—cretinous nonsense, the ruin of the party! Then the leaders of the drooling International seized the initiative. Let them make peace between us! Let them unify us! They summoned us to their sordid little unification conference in Brussels.[1] How to wangle out of it? How to dodge it? Engrossed in this problem, he had hardly heard the pistol shot at Sarajevo! When Austria declared war on Serbia—he had hardly noticed. Even Germany's declaration of war on Russia had meant nothing to him. Reports were put about that the German Social Democrats had voted for war credits. Obviously a trick. Take more than that to fool us. Just trying to create confusion in the socialist ranks. Yes, yes—once you get up steam, you are carried helplessly along. It is difficult to stop, to collect your wits. Yes, yes, yes, he had had ten days to consider the ambiguity of his situation, right on the Russian frontier, to get clear of Poronin now that the damned place was no good to anybody, to escape altogether from the Austro-Hungarian trap. What work could he do in a country at war? He should have made a dash for the blessed haven of Switzerland—a neutral country, a safe country where there were no restrictions, policemen were intelligent, and laws were laws. But no! He hadn't stirred. His mind was still on old prewar problems. Suddenly Russia was at war with Austria, and the very next evening, in pouring rain, a sergeant of gendarmes was knocking at his door.

In a general way, of course, he had known that war must come! He had foreseen it, foretold it. But not at this precise moment, not this year. So he had missed his chance. And landed in a mess.

Hanecki's clean-shaven, pleasant, rather delicate face is calm enough now, but how he had raged at the judge in Nowy Targ! How he had thundered about in that old cart! Hanecki didn't abandon me in my time of trouble.

Along the platform to the engine and back. To the engine and back again.

Still a hellish long time before the train was due to

leave. Almost half an hour. Anything might happen yet. Although there at the station, with a gendarme reassuringly pacing the platform, nobody was likely to attack him.

Looked at dialectically, a gendarme is sometimes a bad thing and sometimes a good thing.

The engine had a big red wheel, almost the height of a man.

However wary you are, however circumspect, however suspicious, in seven long years the abominable tranquillity of an essentially petit-bourgeois existence will make you drowsy. In the shadow of something big, you lean against a massive iron wall, without looking at it carefully—and suddenly it moves, it turns out to be a big red engine wheel, driven by a long, naked piston rod, your spine is twisted and you are underneath! With your head banging against the rails, you belatedly realize that yet again some stupid danger has taken you unawares.

But why had it happened to him, the moment the war began? At first he had laughed. What could they suspect him of? As far as the Austrian police were concerned, he was immaculate. (He had moved to Cracow only because he had heard from Hanecki that the Austrian government would support all anti-Tsarist forces.) Then his lodgings were searched. He had Russian addresses, and conspiratorial notes (they were a nuisance, always getting into the wrong hands), but these the blockhead sergeant had missed altogether, pouncing instead on a manuscript about the agrarian problem. Too many figures! Must be in code! He had confiscated the manuscript. A pity, but never mind. The police always rub the wrong way and find a pimple on the smoothest back. Lenin's only worry was the Russian addresses, but the sergeant poked and pried till he finally found a Browning and some cartridges! Lenin looked at Nadya in amazement. He didn't recognize the loathsome revolver, had no memory of it, had never handled it, didn't know how to fire it, nor would it ever have occurred to him to use such a crude weapon. Where had it come from? (It turned out that some overzealous Russian comrade—silly fool—had showed up with it, and Nadya, like a nitwit, had accepted it.)

You live your own life, never seeing yourself as others see you. Then suddenly in the eyes of a policeman you are someone who has taken up residence near the Russian frontier, has visitors from Russia, receives money from Russia, and large sums at that, does a lot of walking in the mountains, no doubt sketching out plans. Everyone in Nowy Targ had been warned to detain suspicious persons, who might be making road maps or poisoning the wells. A spy! And with a revolver yet! Please report on time for the morning train, we're going to Nowy Targ.

An endless chain of stupidities! A wall of stupidity! The silliest, most elementary, blindest of oversights—just like that time at Tsarskoye Selo. (Or that other time in 1895—when they were all ready to publish their paper but came to grief before they could get out the first issue.) Yes, yes, yes, yes! A revolutionary must always be ready to go to prison. (Though it's cleverer to stay out.) But not for such a silly reason! Not in this humiliating way! Don't let them tie your hands just at the wrong moment! That stinking cell in the Nowy Targ police station! Moldy old Austria-Hungary! Perhaps he would be c o u r t - m a r t i a l e d ?[2]

No accidental setback, no defeat, no dirty, underhand trick on the part of your enemies is ever as galling as your own miscalculation, however slight. It nags at you day and night, especially in a prison cell. Because it is *your own* mistake, you cannot be objective about it, cannot live it down or forget it, cannot get away from the thought that it need never have happened! It need never have happened! But it has happened be-

cause of your own bungling! The blunder is all *yours!*
Pace the flagged floor from wall to wall, toss on your
creaking wire bed for eleven long days and eleven long
nights—you won't get away from it, you won't sleep it
off. It nags and burns like an ulcer. It need never have
happened! It need never have happened! You brought
it on yourself! You put your foot in it!

Still twenty-three minutes until the train leaves,
only the first bell has sounded. If only we could be off!

Hanecki—Kuba to his party comrades—looks
very much at ease, every inch the businessman, with his
ingeniously trained wisp of a moustache and his cool,
steady stare—an irresistible charmer. In that critical
situation he had not backed away, not gone soft or surrendered, but behaved like a bulldog sinking its teeth
in a policeman's trousers. The minute the search was
over, Lenin had bicycled straight over to see him, not
Grishka Zinoviev, and he had not been mistaken. So as
not to lose face, he had tried to make light of it, turn it
into an amusing if tiresome little story. (But inside he
felt stunned. After all, there was a war on, who was
going to waste time on inquiries? They would just shoot
him! There was nothing to stop them from polishing
him off—and because of one silly slip the whole party
would go down the drain, and the socialist world revolution with it!) But Kuba had seen the danger at once!
He hadn't encouraged Lenin's show of unconcern,
hadn't tried to reassure him, but had showered him
with names. Social Democrats! Members of Parliament! Public figures! People who must be written to immediately, told the facts, pestered! Urged to intervene!

That same evening, from Poronin, Hanecki had
sent his first telegrams and Ulyanov had wired the
Cracow police, requesting confirmation of his unquali-
fied loyalty to the Austro-Hungarian Empire. In the
morning, Lenin had still not returned from Nowy Targ,
and Hanecki—since there was no train in the middle

of the day—had jumped into a cart and raced off to see the police chief and the investigating magistrate (at some risk to himself; he might easily have been arrested, as Grishka was shortly afterward). He had dispatched letters by the dozen in all directions, gone immediately to see people in Cracow (he could spin any bureaucrat a yarn at a moment's notice), and then wired Vienna. In his place any Slav would have wearied, relaxed his efforts, given up, but Hanecki was indefatigable, he could not have gone to more trouble for his own brother, he had not relaxed for a moment. On his return from Cracow, he had even forced his way into the prison to visit Lenin, who had given him one further commission: to obtain for him permission to leave for Switzerland.

Spurred on by Hanecki's urgent telegrams, the Social Democratic deputies Viktor Adler and Diamand had appealed to the Chancellor and the Ministry of the Interior, giving written guarantees that the Social Democrat Ulyanov was a worse enemy of the Russian government than the Chancellor of Austria-Hungary himself. The Cracow police had been given their instructions: "In the present circumstances Ulyanov may be of great service to us." Even so, they had taken eleven days—until August 6—to release him. How they hated letting go!

Even after his release, the week in Poronin had not been at all quiet. What you could drum into the Chancellor and other aristocratic Austrian imbeciles was less readily understood by Galician peasants, who were as obtuse as peasants the world over, in Europe, in Asia, or in Alakayevka. To the thick-headed inhabitants of Poronin, this foreigner, although now at large, remained just what he had been—a spy! It was staggering! Beyond all comprehension! Peasant women coming out of church, whether or not they had seen Nadya and were doing it for her benefit, had deafened the whole street with their din: the authorities might have let him go, but they would poke out his eyes for him! Cut out his tongue! Nadya had come home pale and trembling all over. Her fright was contagious. They might very well poke out his eyes, he wouldn't be a bit surprised! There was nothing to stop them from cutting his tongue out! Nothing could be simpler: they would come along with their pitchforks and knives . . . Never in his life had Lenin been exposed to such enormous danger. Nobody had ever treated him like this . . . But history records many such obscene outbursts of mob fury! There are no guarantees against it even in civilized countries. You are safer in prison than in the middle of an ignorant rabble.

To feel alarm in the face of threats means that you are prepared, not that you are panicky.

So his last days and hours in Poronin had been darkened and troubled. For two years this safe, peaceful little town had been crouched to spring. They had kept to the house, been unable to eat or sleep, started packing feverishly. Lenin had tried to pick out his most important papers and books, but he had no control over himself, he could not concentrate, and besides he had amassed tons and tons of paper. (It was only that spring that they had moved there from Cracow to settle once and for all.)

How could he have been so slow, lingered so close to the Russian frontier? Cossack raiders could have carried him off in a flash.

Here on the platform by the neat green train, in the presence of the gendarme and the station personnel, there could be no mob violence, and at last he felt at ease. They were all more cheerful on this cheerful, sunny, cloudless morning. No military freight was being loaded, no newly mobilized soldiers were on the move, the platform and the train looked just as they always did in the summer holiday season. But tickets were freely available only as far as Nowy Targ, and passengers for Cracow needed a police permit.

For this reason the carriages were half empty. Nadya and his mother-in-law had already taken their seats and were looking out of the window. A few comrades had come to see them off and stood looking up at them. Vladimir Ilyich had taken Kuba's arm and they were walking back and forth along the platform, both of them short men, both of them broad, but Lenin was big-boned and Kuba merely fat.

When a man displays such remarkable abilities you must listen carefully to what he says, however visionary it may seem to be. He had known Kuba a long time, ever since the Second Congress, but solely in connection with Polish affairs. It was only that summer that Kuba had shown a new side of himself and become indispensable. He was worth his weight in gold: extraordinarily efficient, and tight-lipped in all serious matters—no outsider would ever get a word out of him. They had spent the months of June and July walking about the plateau near Poronin, discussing Kuba's pyrotechnic schemes for making money. Possibly because of his bourgeois origins, Hanecki had a remarkable financial flair, an extraordinary grasp of money matters—a quality as valuable as it was rare in a revolutionary. He had argued, correctly, that money was the party's arms and legs; without money any party was helpless, just a lot of hot air. If even parliamentary parties needed a great deal of money—for their electoral campaigns—it was infinitely more important to an underground, revolutionary party, which had to organize hiding places, safe meeting places, transportation, *literature,* and weapons, train its fighters, support its professionals, and when the time was right carry out a revolution.

He was preaching to the converted! These were things all Bolsheviks had understood ever since the Second Congress and their first steps as an independent party: without money you can't move an inch, money is all-important. They had started by squeezing donations out of fatheaded Russian merchants like Mamontov, or "give them a sweet roll" Konovalov, and Savva Morozov had kicked in a thousand a month to pay the expenses of the Petersburg committee, but others had shelled out irregularly, in a fit of businessman's benevolence or "intellectual" sympathy. (Garin-Mikhailovsky had just once given ten thousand.) Then you had to start begging again. A surer way was to take it yourself. Perhaps screw a legacy out of somebody, as they had from Schmidt, the factory owner, or marry off party members to heiresses, or swindle the Lbov gang out in the Urals by taking their money and not delivering the promised weapons. Or you could be more systematic about it and develop military techniques: they had planned to print false money in Finland, and Krassin had obtained the watermarked paper. Krassin, again, had made bombs for the expropriations. The "exes" had gone off extraordinarily well: then because of Plekhanov's and Martov's squeamishness the Fifth Congress had banned them, but it was impossible to call a halt, and Kamo and Koba had triumphantly grabbed another 340,000 from the Treasury in Tiflis. But success had gone to their heads, and they had started changing crisp Tsarist five-hundred-ruble notes in Berlin, in Paris, in Stockholm. They should have been content with less. The Tsarist ministry had circulated the serial numbers, and Litvinov was caught. Also Sarah Ravich, in Munich, and a note she was trying to smuggle out of prison was intercepted. After an investigation, thirteen Geneva Bolsheviks had been picked up, and Karpinsky and Semashko would have been put away for a spell if the liberals in Parliament hadn't helped. But worst of all, obscenest of all, Kautsky, with his false, hypocritical, sneaking devotion to principle, had started squawking like an old hen. What a vile trick: setting up a "socialist court" to try the Russian Bolsheviks and, like a half-wit, ordering them to burn the all-powerful five-hundred-ruble notes! (Just looking at a picture of that hoary-headed holy man in his goggling glasses made Lenin retch as though he'd been swallowing a frog.) It's all right for you, the German workers are well-off, they pay large dues, your party is legal, but what about us? (Of course they hadn't been such fools as to burn all of them.) Then they had done another stupid thing: making the malicious old man financial arbiter between Bolsheviks and Mensheviks. (They had to make a tactical pretense of accepting reunion, which meant pooling their funds—but the Mensheviks hadn't a bean. Since it was impossible to conceal the whole Schmidt inheritance, they had given part of it to Kautsky as arbitrator—and later on, when the new split came, he would not hand it back to the Bolsheviks.)

This last summer Hanecki had captured Lenin's imagination with his plans to found a trading company of his own in Europe, or become a partner in some existing firm, and make guaranteed monthly remittances to the party out of his profits. This was not a Russian pipe dream: every move had been worked out with impressive precision. Kuba hadn't thought of it himself; it was the brainchild of the elephantine genius Parvus, who had been writing to him from Constantinople. Parvus, once as poor as any other Social Democrat, had gone to Turkey to organize strikes, and now wrote frankly that he had all the money he needed (if rumor was right, he was fabulously wealthy) and that the time had come for the party too to get rich. He had put it neatly: their best hope of overthrowing capitalism was to become capitalists themselves. Socialists must start by becoming capitalists! The socialists had laughed at him. Rosa, Clara, and Liebknecht had let him know that they despised him. But perhaps they had been in too much of a hurry. Sarcasm wilted in the face of Parvus's solid financial power.

It was partly because of Hanecki's schemes that the war had caught them napping.

They discussed them further in these last few minutes and made arrangements to keep in touch. They would in any case be seeing each other soon. Zinoviev would follow after Lenin, and then Hanecki, as soon as he obtained an exemption from Austrian military service.

. . . There went the second bell. Lenin hopped nimbly onto the step. Hatless, almost completely bald, in his shabby suit, with his sharp features, his habit of looking uneasily over his shoulder, and his neglected beard, he really did look like a spy. Hanecki wanted to tease him about it, but he knew that Lenin couldn't take a joke, and refrained.

But with his sad, wary eyes and the shiny suit that did not go with his businessman's face, what did he look like himself if not a spy?

The stationmaster stood stern and stiff in his tall red-and-black cap. There were three rings on the bell. The guard sounded his horn and started running.

People waved goodbye, and they waved back through the open window.

All in all, life in Poronin hadn't been too bad. A quiet, steady life, not like the mad rush of Paris. For all his homeless wanderings around Europe, he had never become a European. He found it easier to act if his surroundings were simple and narrow. They had lived through so many anxious moments here. So many joys.

So many disillusionments.

Malinovsky . . .

The platform, the station, and those left behind were snatched from sight. Even Hanecki, admirable and reliable comrade though he was, would be missing from the next stage of his life. At some point in the future he might very well become again the most important and useful of men, and desperately urgent letters with double and treble underlining would be dashed off in the small hours, but for the time being he had done a splendid job and ceased to exist.

There was an infallible law of revolutionary struggle, or perhaps of human life in general, which no one had yet put into words but which Lenin had often noticed at work. At any given time one or two people emerged to take their place at his side, people who for the moment were intellectually closer to him, more interesting, important, and useful than anyone else, people who particularly stimulated him to confide in them, to discuss things with them, to act together with them. But hardly any of them retained this position for long, because situations change every day, and we must change dialectically with them, change instantly, or, rather, anticipate change—that is what political genius is. It was natural that one after another, encountering the whirlwind that was Lenin, should be drawn instantly into his activities, should carry out his instructions as the prescribed moment and with the prescribed speed, by whatever means and at whatever personal sacrifice. Natural, because all this was done not for Vladimir Ilyich but for the compelling power whch manifested itself through him, and of which he was only the infallible interpreter, who always knew precisely what was right just for today—and indeed by evening it was not always what it had been in the morning. Once one of these transitional people grew obstinate, ceased to understand why his duties were essential and urgent, began to mention his mixed feelings or his own unique destiny, then it was just as natural to remove him from the main road, dismiss him, forget him, abuse and anathematize him if necessary—but even when he dismissed or damned someone, Lenin was acting in obedience to the power which drew him on.

The exiles on the Yenisei had held such a position of intellectual intimacy for a long, long time, but only because there was no one geographically nearer. From afar he had imagined that Plekhanov would take their place—but after a few short meetings a cold, cruel lesson had put an abrupt end to that. Martov had been close, indeed dangerously, undesirably close, for years on end. But he too had given way. (From his bitter experience with Martov he had learned once and for all that there can be no such relationship between human beings as simple friendship transcending political, class, and material ties.) Krassin had been a close friend while he was making his bombs. So had Bogdanov while he was raising funds for the party, but when this abruptly ended, he had misjudged the sharp slope before him, yet had wanted to set the course, and had come crashing down. Meanwhile, new loyal followers were sucked into the whirlwind—Kamenev, Zinoviev ... Malinovsky ...

Only those who saw the party's needs in the right perspective could hold their places and march at his side. But when the urgent need of the moment changed, the perspective usually changed too, so that all those recent collaborators remained helplessly rooted in the dull, stationary ground, like so many signposts, receding from view until they vanished and were forgotten, though sometimes they loomed sharply at a new turning in the road, this time as enemies. There had been fellow spirits who were close for a week, a day, an hour, for the space of a single conversation, a single report, a single errand—and Lenin openheartedly lavished all his fervor and impressed them with his own sense of urgency, so that each one felt himself to be the most important person in the world; then an hour later they were already receding, and he would soon clean forget who they were and why he had needed them. Thus, Valentinov had seemed close when he first arrived from Russia, though he had aroused misgivings with his stupid remark that when he was working in a factory some piece of metal-work he had made meant more to him than the political struggle. He had soon shown his true nature: he had lacked the stamina to stand up to Martov and had become no better than a Menshevik himself.

The train was rolling down the incline, struggling around the mountain turns. Paths and cart tracks ran down the slopes, and higher up, beyond farmhouses, ricks, and standing crops, the mountain road was still visible. You could run up it with your eyes. In all his walks around Poronin he had never been there.

He sat down at last. He should be thinking, or working, not sentimentalizing.

His womenfolk, correctly reading his looks and movements, did not pester him with trifles or fidget unnecessarily, but sat quietly in their seats.

All those exhausting years, from 1908 on, after the defeat of the revolution, had been one long story of desertions and dismissals. One after another they had left: the *Vperyod* group, the Recallists, the Ultimatists, the Machists, the God Builders . . . Lunacharsky, Bazarov, Alexinsky, Brilliant, Rozhkov, Krassin, Liadov, Menzhinsky, Lozovsky, Manuilsky, Gorky . . . The whole old guard, knocked together during the split with the Mensheviks. So that there were moments when it seemed there would be no one left, that the whole Bolshevik Party would consist of himself, a couple of women, and a dozen third-raters and washouts who used to come to Bolshevik meetings back in the Paris days; that if he got up to speak at a general meeting he would not have a single friend there and would be shoved off the platform. They went away, one after another—and what iron certainty was needed not to start doubting himself, not to waver, not to run after them and make up, but, with clear prophetic insight, to stand firm and wait for them to return of their own accord, to come to their senses ... and those who didn't could go to hell.

In 1906 and 1907 defeat was not yet total, society was still on the boil, milling about on the rim of the maelstrom. Lenin had sat in Kuokkala, waiting in vain for the second wave. But from 1908, when the reactionary rabble had tightened its grip on the whole country, the underground had shriveled to nothing, the workers had swarmed like ants out of their holes and into legal bodies—trade unions and mutual-aid societies —and the decline of the underground had sapped the vitality of the emigration too, reduced it to a hothouse existence. . . . B a c k  t h e r e was the Duma, a legal press—and every émigré was eager to publish there. . . .

That was why the outbreak of war was such a marvelous thing! He was overjoyed by it! B a c k t h e r e, all those liquidators would be suppressed immediately, the importance of legal activity would sink sharply, whereas the importance of the emigration, and its strength, would increase! The center of gravity of Russian political life was shifting back abroad!

Lenin had sized up the situation while he was still in prison at Nowy Targ. (Nadya! Have we gone through Nowy Targ yet? I must have missed it.) There in his cell, fighting down his anxiety, trying not to let a personal mishap overshadow the general good fortune, he had absorbed and begun processing the fact that all Europe was at war. The result of this process in Lenin's brain was always the birth of slogans ready for use: the creation of slogans for present needs was the ultimate purpose of all his thinking. That, and the translation of his arguments into the Marxist vernacular: his supporters and followers would not understand him in any other language.

What emerged he had revealed, after his release, to Hanecki before anyone else: the thing to realize was that now that the war had begun they should not wish it away or try to stop it but should take advantage of it. They must rise above the sanctimonious notion, sometimes insinuated even into proletarian heads, that war was a disaster or a sin. The slogan "Peace at any price" was for psalm-singing hypocrites! What line should revolutionary democrats everywhere follow in the present situation? The first need was to refute the fairy tale that the Central Powers were to blame for starting the war! The Entente would cover itself with the story that "they were innocent victims of aggression." They would even pretend that the rentiers' republic must be defended in the interests of democracy. These excuses must be crushed, trampled underfoot! The propaganda line must be that *all governments* were equally to blame. What mattered was not who was to blame but how to turn the war to the best advantage. "They're all to blame"— only if that was accepted could they go on working to bring down the Tsar's government.

This is a lucky war! It will greatly benefit international socialism; with one sharp jolt it will cleanse the workers' movement of the accumulated filth of peacetime! Instead of the previous division of socialists into opportunists and revolutionaries—an ambiguous distinction which leaves loopholes for enemies—it will make unmistakably clear the real line of cleavage in the international movement—that between patriots and anti-patriots. We are the anti-patriots!

It means the end of the International's shabby schemes for reuniting Bolsheviks and Mensheviks. They had planned a further attempt at reconciliation—at the Vienna Congress in August—but by July five fronts were ablaze! There wouldn't be another peep out of them. The rift now yawned so wide that there could be no thought of reconciliation! Yet earlier in July they had

had him by the throat: We see no differences sufficient to justify a split! Send a delegation to talk peace! Talk peace with the Menshevik scum! Ah, but now, now that you've voted war credits, your International is dead! It will never get on its feet again, it's a corpse! You'll keep up your skeleton's dance for a long time yet, but we must declare for all to hear: you're dead! Inessa's trip to Brussels was our last meeting with you, we've had enough!

At this point, his mother-in-law suddenly realized that they had left a suitcase behind! They hastily checked and counted the baggage under the seats and on the overhead racks. It wasn't there! How disgraceful! They might have been escaping from a burning building! Vladimir Ilyich was upset. Without order in the family and the home, work was impossible. It might sound comic, but an orderly household was itself a contribution to the party cause. He didn't dare tell the older woman off. She could give as good as she got, and anyway, they respected each other—he even gave her little presents to stay on her good side. But he reprimanded Nadya. What could you expect from her, though, when she couldn't sew on a button or remove a stain properly? He could do better himself. She wouldn't even give him a clean handkerchief unless he asked.

He never forgave a mistake. No matter who made it, he would remember as long as he lived.

He turned his head to the window.

The train was gradually winding its way down from the mountains. Engine smoke, sometimes gray, sometimes white, swept past the windows. He was sick of mountains too, after all these years of emigration.

With Nadya, it was like water off a duck's back. All right, we've forgotten a suitcase. We can't go back for it, can we? We'll write from Cracow, and they'll send it on.

Nadya had a firm rule, often applied in the past. If

she took Volodya's share of the blame on herself, he would cool off and come around. What vexed him most was to be found equally at fault.

He looked his age as he sat there gloomily, with his untrimmed beard and moustache, and his anxiously arched ginger eyebrows, staring absently, unseeingly, through the window. Nadya knew his changes of expression so well. Just now, she must be careful not to cross him, not even to speak to him, or distract him by exchanging a word with her mother. She must just let him sit there, sink into himself, bathe his hurts in soothing silence, recover from the frantic days in Nowy Targ, the threats in Poronin, the lost suitcase. At such times, whether he took a solitary walk or sat silently thinking, after half an hour or an hour of meditation his brow would clear and the angry little wrinkles would be smoothed from around his eyes, leaving long deep creases.

A split in the international socialist movement was long overdue, but only the war had brought it into the open and made it unavoidable. It was absolutely marvelous! It might seem that the proletarian front had been weakened by the mass betrayal of socialists: not so—it was *good* that they had betrayed! It would now be so much easier to insist on his own distinct line.

Whereas a month ago he hadn't known what to say, how to wriggle out of it! An inspiration—instead of going to Brussels himself he would send Inessa, leading a delegation!! Inessa!!! With her excellent French! With her incomparable poise—cool, calm, slightly disdainful. (The Frenchmen in the Presidium will be at your feet immediately. And the Germans won't understand you too well—which is just fine! Every time a German speaks, call for a translation!) What a clever move! They would be at their wits' end, those ultra-socialist donkeys! . . . Get on with it at once! Write and ask her. Will she go? Can she go? A holiday with the children on the Adriatic? Rubbish, find somebody to look after the children, we'll pay the expenses out of party funds. Writing an article on free love? Not to be rude (a woman can never give herself a hundred percent to the party, she's always up to some nonsense), but your manuscript can wait. I'm sure you're one of those who are at their best and bravest doing a responsible job single-handed. Rubbish, rubbish, I don't listen to pessimists! . . . You'll cope magnificently! . . . I'm sure you have cheek enough for it . . . They'll all be furious I'm not there (that makes me happy) and they'll probably want to revenge themselves on you, but I'm sure you'll show your claws the best you can! . . . We'll call you . . . let's see . . . Petrova. Why reveal your real name to liquidators? (I'm Petrov too—you should remember, if nobody else does. So, through our pseudonyms, we shall face the public united in one person—openly yet secretly. You will actually be me.) My dear friend! I do beg you to say yes! Will you go? . . . Of course you will! . . . Of course you will! . . . Yes indeed, we must rehearse thoroughly. And be mighty quick about it. You must simply lie to the liquidators: promise them that *maybe,* later on, we'll accept a majority resolution. (But *of course* we shall never really accept anything! *Not a single one* of their proposals!) Then tell some fib about the children being ill, and say that you can't stay on any longer. We must convince the European socialists, petit-bourgeois scum that they are, that the Bolsheviks are the most serious of the Russian parties. Slip them the bit about trade unions and mutual-aid societies—that has a tremendous effect on them. When they ask questions—cut them short, avoid answering, fight them off! At all times—take the offensive! Get Rosa talking, show them that she has no real party behind her, that Hanecki's opposition is the real party. You've got it now! You'll go! . . . Warmest best wishes! Very truly[3] . . . Your own . . .

Then Hanecki had spoiled things. He'd delivered an ultimatum (not altogether unreasonable): 250 crowns for the Brussels trip, or he wouldn't go. But party funds must be used carefully. (Hanecki isn't the only one! There are plenty of people we could make use of, but we can't throw our money around . . .) So, in Hanecki's absence, the lousy Polish opposition had betrayed, and voted with Rosa and Plekhanov for the rotten, idiotic conciliation scheme.

. . . All the same, you saw it through better than I could. Apart from the fact that I don't know the language, I would certainly have blown up! I couldn't have stood that farce! I would have called them scoundrels. But you carried it off calmly, firmly, you foiled all their tricks. You have done the party a great service! I'm sending you 150 francs. (Probably not enough? Let me know how much more you spent, and I'll send it.) Write to me. Are you very tired? Are you very angry with me? Why is it "extremely unpleasant" for you to write about the conference? Maybe you are ill? What is wrong with you? Do reply, or I shall have no peace.

Inessa was the only human being whose moods he sensed and responded to even at a distance. Indeed, at a distance the pull was stronger.

One thing to remember: with wartime censorship he must adopt a less intimate tone. It might provide grounds for blackmail. Socialists must be prudent.

Their correspondence had been interrupted by the war, and now her letters would go to Poronin. Still, there was every reason to believe that once she had sent her children off to Russia, Inessa would return to Switzerland. Perhaps she was there already.

The women were quietly discussing how they were going to manage in Cracow. Nadya suggested that her mother and Volodya should stay with the luggage while she called on Inessa's old landlady. It would save trouble if they could move in that very day.

As she said it, her eyes traveled to the window, brushing Volodya's cheek. He remained impassive, didn't turn his head, made no comment, but all the same the tightening of his temples and the lowering of his eyelids assured Nadya that he had heard and approved.

It was convenient and quick, it would save them having to look, true enough. But still, there was no particular need for them to stay in Inessa's room. It was just that Volodya disliked the unfamiliar, and anyway it was only for a short time. These were the best excuses she could offer her mother.

She had always felt humiliated in her mother's eyes. The feeling was less painful now than it had been. But it was still there.

However, Nadya had schooled herself to follow rigid rules. Volodya must not be deflected from his path by so much as a hairbreadth. She must do everything to make his life easier, and never hinder his work. She must always be there, but ready at any moment to efface herself when she was unwanted.

She had made her choice, and she must stick to it. She had shouldered the burden, and must bear it. She must not permit herself a single hard word about her rival, although there was plenty she could say. She must always welcome her warmly, like a girlhood friend—so as not to spoil Volodya's good humor, or his standing with his comrades. She must join in their rambles, and their reading sessions—*à trois*.

When it had all started—indeed, earlier, when Inessa, then a Sorbonne student with a red feather in her hat (no Russian woman revolutionary would have had the nerve to wear it), although she had two husbands and five children behind her, when she had first walked into their Paris apartment, and before Volodya was half out of his chair, Nadya had seen clearly what was to come. Seen, too, her powerlessness to prevent it. And that it was her duty not to try.

Nadya had volunteered to remove herself. She would not be an obstacle in the life of such a man— there were obstacles enough already. More than once she had been on the verge of leaving him. But Volodya, after some thought, had told her to stay. He had made up his mind. Once and for all.

She was needed, then. Certainly, nobody else would get on so well with him. Resignation was made easier by the realization that no woman could claim such a man all to herself. It was enough of a vocation that she, among others, was useful to him. No less than the other one. Indeed, in many ways she was closer to him.

So she had stayed, determined never to stand in his way. Never to show her hurt. To train herself not to feel it. So that the hurt would burn itself out and die down. Instead of treating it gently, she had prodded and inflamed the wound so as to cauterize it. So that, if there was some practical advantage in staying in what not so long ago had been Inessa's room, then that was where she would stay, without fretting about all the time Volodya had spent there in the past.

But with her mother there to see it . . .

It would soon be Cracow. Volodya was brightening up. Obviously, he had made some headway in his thinking.

No, the trip to Brussels went off splendidly, you mustn't regret it. My one regret is that you had no time to strike up a correspondence with Kautsky, as I told you to . . . (You would have written under your own name, but I would have discreetly drafted the letters for you.) What a low character he is! I hate and despise him more than anyone on earth. What a filthy, rotten hypocrite! . . . It really is a pity we couldn't get that game going, we'd have had some sport with him!

Volodya had cheered up, and even whistled a little tune. Completely forgetting the lost suitcase, he suggested eating. And took out the pocketknife he always carried.

They spread out a napkin and produced a chicken, hard-boiled eggs, a bottle of milk, Galician bread, butter in grease-proof paper, salt in a little box.

Volodya even made a bit of a joke about his mother-in-law being a capitalist and a blot on his revolutionary biography.

Seriously, though, they must get their financial affairs settled, and swiftly. They had a lot of money in a Cracow bank—who could have expected war so soon?—a legacy from Nadya's aunt in Novocherkassk, her mother's sister, more than four thousand rubles. And now it was bound to be confiscated, as enemy-alien property. What a blunder! At all costs, he must find someone smart enough to squeeze the money out of them, then convert it into something safe—into gold, or maybe some of it into Swiss francs. And they must take it with them.

Then—to Vienna without delay. They must hurry the visas and guarantees for Switzerland, and get there quickly. Austria-Hungary was a belligerent, anything might happen. His mother-in-law had a legal Russian passport, and so had Nadya, except that hers had expired. But Lenin had none at all.

One thing to be said for the opportunists' International was that it never refused help to anyone in difficulties. And in every country it had what amounted to ministers of its own. On this occasion, Kuba had insisted that he pay courtesy calls on Adler and Diamand, thank them all over again in person for obtaining his release (although he had already telegraphed his heartfelt gratitude), and, whatever happened, keep a civil tongue . . . Volodya smiled wryly, with specks of white and yolk around his mouth. It was certainly a tricky corner for him—having to go and make himself agreeable to moldy old revisionists, petit-bourgeois scum. After all, it was only fair: if loyalty to principles was beyond them, they could at least help him to live. That provided a concrete, practical platform for a temporary tactical understanding with them. Even in Switzerland he wouldn't be able to do without this bunch. He wouldn't be admitted without sponsors—and who else would sponsor him? (Robert Grimm is an overgrown schoolboy—I met him in Bern last year, when you, Inessa, were in the hospital.)

Ridicule left not a scratch on Lenin, no humiliation could get him down, he never felt ashamed—but all the same it was not easy for a man of forty-four to humble himself to younger men, to be so dependent on other people, to have no strength of his own.

If they hadn't left Geneva for Paris in 1908, they would not now have to fight their way into Switzerland, they would have been firmly and safely established there—with their own printing press, with connections, with all they needed. What had possessed them to move to Paris?

(If they hadn't gone to Paris—he would not have met Inessa.)

Only last year, when you went to Kocher for treatment, Inessa, and we discovered what a good doctor is (Volodya had read up on goiter himself and checked the treatment), we should have had the sense to stay in Bern right then. Why not? If a revolutionary has to outlive Tsarism, and he is no longer twenty-five, his health counts as one of his weapons. It is also party property. The party's funds should be used ungrudgingly for its maintenance. He should live where there are excellent doctors, indeed as close as possible to the most eminent men in the profession—and that could only mean Switzerland. You wouldn't go to Semashko for treatment —that would be too silly! . . . As doctors, our revolutionary comrades are a lot of donkeys. You wouldn't trust one of them to poke around inside you.

You're still far from well, Inessa. You ought to be closer to Kocher.

Yes, but, Volodya, the atmosphere in Switzerland is dreadfully petit bourgeois. Remember how stuffy we always found it! Remember how they all shied away from us after the Tiflis "ex"? In their country, you see, the law is sacrosanct, and they will not stand for crimes against property! . . . And they call themselves Social Democrats!

All very true, but in Switzerland you'll never be in a fix like mine in Nowy Targ. Getting Semashko and Karpinsky out was child's play.

And what libraries they have! What a pleasure it always is to work there—and now, with a war on . . . ! No other place is so civilized and so comfortable.

A clean, well-scrubbed country, pleasant mountains, friendly pensions, limpid lakes with waterfowl on them.

The settling tank of the Russian revolution.

And because it was a neutral country, the only place from which he could keep up his international contacts.

He must think. He must think. What a joy it was —all Europe involved in a war such as it had never known before! The war which Marx and Engels had expected but had not lived to see. Such a war was the surest way to world revolution. The spark which they had fanned in vain in 1905 would burst unaided into conflagration! There would never be a more propitious moment!

A presentiment quickened within him; this is it, the event you have lived to interpret and complete! Twenty-seven years of political self-education, books, pamphlets, party squabbles. An apathetic and ineffectual spectator during the First Revolution. Regarded by everyone in the International as a disturber of the peace, an impertinent sectarian, leading a feeble, constantly dwindling little group, that called itself a party. All the time, without knowing it, you were waiting for this moment, and now the moment has come! The heavy wheel turns, gathering speed—like the red wheel of the engine—and you must keep up with its mighty rush. He who had never yet stood before the crowd, directing the movement of the masses, how was he to harness them to that wheel, to his own racing heart, check their impetus and put them into reverse?

Cracow.

They put their coats on and collected their things.

Lenin got ready absentmindedly, only vaguely aware of their arrival and of what must be done.

They carried the baggage themselves, without a porter.

They were deafened by the noise. They had grown unused to crowds. And this was a different, a wartime crowd. There were five times as many people on the platform as there should have been on a working day, and they were five times more worried, and all in a hurry. Nuns, who shouldn't have been there at all, elbowed the travelers, thrusting holy pictures and printed prayers at them. Lenin hastily drew back his hand as though from something dirty. A truck stood incongruously on a passenger platform, and people were carrying into it an endless succession of large boxes labeled "flea powder." Soldiers, civilians, railwaymen, and passengers jostled each other. Slowly and with difficulty they elbowed their way along the densely thronged platform. There was a banner on the station wall, with a slogan in red letters on yellow fabric:

*Jedem Russ—ein Schuss!*[4]

This had nothing at all to do with them, but he couldn't suppress a shudder.

The station hall was packed and stifling. They

found a shady spot, on a raised place against the side wall, at an angle to the square. The crowd there was denser than ever, and there were a lot of women. They settled Nadya's mother on a bench, with the luggage all around her. Nadya went off to see Inessa's landlady. Vladimir Ilyich ran to buy newspapers and came back reading them as he walked, bumping into people, then perched himself on a hard suitcase, gripping the pile of papers between his elbows and his knees.

There was nothing particularly cheerful in the news. Reports on the battle in Galicia and on East Prussia were equally evasive, which meant the Russians weren't doing too badly. But there were battles in France! War in Serbia! Who among the older generation of socialists would ever have dreamed of such a thing?

The socialists would be completely at a loss. They couldn't rise above their calls for peace. Those who weren't "defenders of the fatherland" could think of nothing better than blathering and yapping about "stopping the war."

As though anyone could. As though anyone had the strength to seize the racing engine wheel with his bare hands.

Piss-poor, slobbering pseudo-socialists with the petit-bourgeois worm in them would try to capture the masses by jabbering away "for peace" and even "against annexations." And everybody would find it quite natural: against war means "for peace," doesn't it? . . . They must be hit first and hit hard.

Which of them had the vision to see and the strength of mind to embrace the great decision ahead: not to try to stop the war, but to step it up! To transfer it—*to your own country!*

We won't openly say so, but we are *for* the war!

"Peace" is a slogan for fatheads and traitors! What is the point of a hollow peace that nobody needs, un-

less you can convert it immediately into c i v i l
w a r  w i t h  n o  q u a r t e r  g i v e n? Anyone who
does *not* come out in favor of civil war must be branded
a traitor!

The main thing is a sober grasp of the balance of
forces, a sober assessment of alliances. It is no good
standing like silly priests between the embattled armies,
arms raised, sleeves flapping. Germany must be seen
from the start not as just another imperialist country but
as a mighty ally. To make a revolution you need weapons, troops, money, so you must look for someone with
an interest in giving them to you. You must find chan-
nels for negotiation, covertly reassure yourself that if
difficulties arise in Russia and she starts suing for peace,
Germany will not agree to peace talks, will not abandon
the Russian revolutionaries to the whim of fate.

Germany! What power! What weapons! And
what determination she had shown in striking through
Belgium! The Germans knew there would be whines of
indignation, but that didn't worry them. If fight they
must, then fight they would. How resolute were the orders of their High Command! Not a hint of Russian
vacillation there. (They had shown the same decisive-
ness in grabbing him and slinging him into the cell in
Nowy Targ. And still more in releasing him.)

Germany will undoubtedly win this war. And so
she is the best, the natural ally against the Tsar.

The carrion crow in the Russian coat of arms is
trapped at last. You're caught by the foot, you'll never
pull free! This war was of your own choosing. Now
you'll be cut down to size. Shorn of everything as far as
Kiev, as far as Kharkov, as far as Riga. We'll thrash the
imperial spirit out of you! Die, damn you, die! All
you're good for is oppressing others. Russia will be
completely dismembered. Poland and Finland must be
detached. And the Baltic lands. And the Ukraine. And
the Caucasus. Die, damn you!

There was a hubbub on the square and the crowd surged in their direction, as far as the platform barrier, where the police held them back. What was going on? A train had pulled in. A hospital train. Perhaps the first such train, after the first major battle. A path was cleared through the crowd, to give the row of waiting ambulances room to turn around. Hefty, grim-looking orderlies quickly passed stretcher after stretcher from the train to the ambulances. Women pressed forward from every side, struggling to get through the crowd, eagerly, fearfully craning to catch a glimpse of gray faces barely visible among bandages and sheets, dreading to discover their men. There were shrieks of recognition or relief, and the crowd closed in tighter and pulsed like a single being.

Though the raised place where the Ulyanovs were sitting was some distance away, they could see it all. But Lenin, to get a better view, got up and went nearer to the parapet.

There weren't enough ambulances and stretchers, and instead of waiting, some of the wounded, supported by nurses, were leaving the platform on their own feet—white figures in gray hospital smocks or blue greatcoats, with heavily bandaged heads, necks, shoulders, arms, some walking haltingly, some firmer on their feet. And now the waiting crowd would not be held, but swarmed toward them, shrilly, joyfully yelling, embracing and kissing dear ones and strangers alike, taking them from the nurses, carrying their kit bags, while above them, over all those heads, borne aloft by male hands, mugs of frothy beer and white plates of roast meat floated out from the restaurant.

By the parapet, refreshed and excited, stood the man in the black bowler, his reddish beard untrimmed, his brows knitted in concentration, his eyes sharp and eager, and he too had one hand raised, the fingers splayed as though holding a great beer mug, he too swallowed painfully as though he'd been in the trenches and was parched for want of that drink. His probing gaze widened and contracted, widened and contracted as he seized on every detail in the scene which might be turned to use.

A joyful inspiration took shape in his dynamic mind—one of the most powerful, swiftest, surest decisions of his life. The smell of printer's ink from the newspapers, the smell of blood and medications from the station hall evaporate—and suddenly, like a soaring eagle following the movements of a tiny golden lizard, you only have eyes for the one truth that matters, your heart pounds, like an eagle you swoop down on it, seize it by its trembling tail as it is about to vanish into a crevice in the rock—and you tug and tug and rise up into the air unfurling it like a ribbon, like a banner bearing the slogan: CONVERT THE WAR INTO CIVIL WAR! . . . and this war, this war will bring all the governments of Europe down in ruins!!!

He stood by the parapet, looking down on the square with his hand raised, as though he had taken his place for a speech but was not quite ready to begin.

Daily, hourly, wherever you may be—*protest* angrily and uncompromisingly against this war! But . . . !

(The dialectic essence of the situation.) But . . . will it to continue! See that it does not stop short! That it drags on and is *transformed!* A war *like this one* must not be fumbled, must not be wasted.

Such a war is a gift from history!

Their meetings in the Stüssihof restaurant were known as the Skittle Club, although there was no skittle alley.

". . . The Swiss government is the executive committee of the bourgeoisie."

"Skittle Club" was somebody's idea of a joke: their politics made no sense, but plenty of noise.

". . . The Swiss government is a pawn in the hands of the military clique."

But they had cheerfully adopted the name. We'll knock the capitalists down like ninepins!

(He had educated them. He had cured them of religion. He had implanted in them an appreciation of the historical role of violence.)

". . . The Swiss government is shamelessly selling out the masses to the financial magnates."

It was some years now since Nobs had started the discussion table in the restaurant on the Stüssihof square. He had brought together the younger people, the activists. After a while, Lenin had started coming.

(How many humiliations he had had to endure in this conceited country. The Social Democrats in Bern had always looked down on him. When he moved to Zurich last spring he had tried to get the Russian émigrés together for lectures—but the few who came at all soon drifted away. Then he had transferred his attentions to the young Swiss. Some men of forty-seven might think it beneath their dignity—fishing for baby-faced supporters and working them up one by one, but if you could wrest a single one of them from the opportunist Grimm, it was time well spent.)

". . . The Swiss government is toadying to European reactionaries and encroaching on the democratic rights of the people."

Across the table sits simpleminded, broad-faced Platten, the fitter (since he had broken his arm he had become a draftsman, but "fitter" sounded more proletarian). His big face is trying to absorb what is said—it is all so difficult. His brow is knotted and his soft ripe lips pursed with effort, helping his eyes and ears not to miss a word.

". . . Swiss Social Democrats must show complete lack of confidence in their government."

The table has been made longer, for a gay Swiss gathering. No cloth covers its planed surface, pitted with knotholes and polished by a century of elbows and plates. The nine of them have arranged themselves on two benches, giving themselves plenty of room, and one place is blocked by a pillar. Some have ordered snacks, others beer, to keep up appearances, and because the Swiss always do—everyone pays for himself. A lantern hangs from the pillar.

That elongated, triangular face under the unruly lick of hair, the keenest face there, belongs to Willi Münzenberg, the German from Erfurt. He is very quick to catch on and, in fact, it's all much too slow for him. His long, restless hands reach out for more. These are the clichés he calls out himself in public meetings.

(He'd had luck with the younger people in Zurich. There were half a dozen of them here—all youth leaders. Not like in 1914, when he had sent Inessa to see the Swiss leftists: Naine was fishing, Graber helping his wife hang out the wash—and nobody wanted to know anything.)

". . . We must learn not to trust our governments."

Lenin is at the corner of the table by the pillar, which conceals him on one side. Nobs, watchful, ingratiating, catlike, is at the far end, diagonally opposite, as far from danger as possible. He started it all; does he now regret it? In years he is one of them (they are all around thirty) but in party status, in self-importance, and even in girth, he has ceased or is ceasing to belong.

Over every table hangs a lamp of a different color. The one over the Skittle Club is red. A reddish light plays on every face—Platten's broad open features; the black forelock and starched collar of the self-assured and foppish Mimiola; the unkempt, tousled curls of Radek, with his irremovable pipe and slightly parted wet lips.

". . . In every country, stir up hatred of your own government! This is the only work worthy of a socialist."

(Working with the young was the only thing worth doing. There was nothing humiliating about it. It was simply taking the long view. Actually, Grimm wasn't so very old—he was eleven years Lenin's junior—yet he had already gotten a grip on power. He wasn't stupid, but theory was over his head. He didn't want an armed rising, yet he had leftish sympathies. When Lenin came to Switzerland in 1914, mentioning Greulich's name, and established himself here with Grimm as his sponsor, they had met and talked far into the night. Grimm had asked: "What do you think the Swiss Social Democrats should do in the present situation?" To see how far he would go, Lenin had answered in a flash: "I would immediately declare *civil war!*" For a moment Grimm was scared. But then he had decided that it was a joke.)

". . . The neutrality of Switzerland is a bourgeois fraud and means submission to the imperialist war."

Platten's brow is convulsed, his eyes strained and bewildered. How difficult, how terribly difficult it is to master the lofty science of socialism! These grandiose formulas somehow refuse to fit in with your own poor limited experience. War is a fraud, and neutrality is a fraud, so neutrality is just as bad as war? . . . But a side glance at your comrades shows you they understand it all, and you are ashamed to admit that you don't, so you pretend.

(It was not just facile phrase mongering. He had thought up these ideas in a fit of inspiration on his journey across Austria, written a definitive summary of them when he reached Bern, introduced them into a Central Committee manifesto, then defended them in his skirmish with Plekhanov at Lausanne. You could know your Marxism inside out and still not find an answer when a real crisis burst upon you: the man who finds that makes an original discovery. In the autumn of 1914, when four fifths of Europe's socialists had taken a stand in defense of the fatherland, while one fifth timidly bleated "For peace," Lenin alone in the ranks of world socialism had pointed the way for the others: f o r   w a r !—but a *different* war!—and immediately!!)

Lenin, too, has a mug of beer in front of him. It's a type he can't endure—the Swiss politician at the tavern table—but this is the ritual. Bronski looks sleepy and imperturbable as always. But Radek, with the black whiskers that run from ear to ear under his chin, with his horn-rimmed glassses, his quick glance, and his buck teeth, restlessly switching his eternally smoking black pipe from corner to corner of his mouth—Radek has heard it all before, and now finds it too elementary, too tame, and too slow.

". . . The petty ambition of petty states to stand apart from the great battles of world history . . ."

Platten is quietly floundering, trying not to give himself away. The idea of world revolution is easy to understand, but it is so difficult to apply to his Switzerland. His mind consents: since they have avoided the universal bloodbath, they cannot sit calmly by, they must summon the people to class battles. But his heart is unreasonable: it's good that in those houses clinging to the mountain ledges the peasants live at peace, that the men are all at home, that grass is mown in the meadows four times in a summer, however steep the slopes may be, that the tall barns are filled to the roof with the store of hay, that the tinkling of hundreds of little bells, sheep bells and cow bells, sounds from spur to spur, as though the mountains themselves are ringing.

". . . The narrow-minded egoism of privileged small nations . . ."

The plodding walk of herdsmen. Now and then, the deafening crack of a stock whip on the stony road, echoing through the folds in the hills. Water troughs at mountain springs, long enough for twenty cows to drink. Shifting winds over swaying grass, shifting mists steaming over wooded gorges, and when sunlight breaks through the rain there may be no room for the rainbow's arc and it will stand upright like a pillar on the mountain. The quiet inscription on a hostel in the high wilderness . . .

*The motherland shelters her children*
*with her forest cloak*

". . . Industry tied to tourism . . . Your bourgeoisie trades in the beauties of the Alps, and your opportunists help them do it."

Platten gives up his attempt at concealment, and innocently, trustingly, his face reflects his doubts.

Lenin notices! From where he sits at the corner of the table—the only older man among all those youngsters, looking well over fifty—he strikes home with a swift, shrewd, side thrust.

". . . A r e p u b l i c  o f  l a c k e y s !  That's what Switzerland is!"

The keynote of his harangue.

Radek guffaws happily, deftly switches his pipe (the fingering is different every time) and sucks in impressive quantities of damp smoke. Willi mischievously tries to catch his teacher's eye, his long hands writhing impatiently: *encore! encore!*

Platten isn't arguing. Platten is merely puzzled. Perhaps his country is like an ornate hotel, but lackeys are obsequious, fussing and fawning, while the Swiss are staid and dignified. Even ministers' wives don't keep lackeys, they beat their own carpets.

(But it had never been known for a letter to go astray in Switzerland, and the libraries were magnificently run: books were sent without charge and immediately to remote pensions in the mountains.)

". . . Bribes for docile workers in the guise of social reforms—to persuade them not to overthrow the bourgeoisie . . ."

It had taken three weeks of effort to arrange this meeting and they had finally got them all together on the evening of Friday, the twenty-first—the eve of the party congress. Radek had been a great help, made himself highly useful.

When Radek is nice he is very nice, a super-pal. At present, there is no living without him. And how well he speaks and writes German! He takes the sharpest curves with ease—there is no need to waste time explaining. A scoundrel, but a brilliant one—such people are most valuable. But at times he is loathsome. In Bern they had avoided meeting, communicated by mail, and in February had broken off forever. At Kienthal he had spoken like an out-and-out provocateur.

". . . The Swiss people are more cruelly hungry every day, and risk being drawn into the war and killed in the interests of capitalism."

Nobs's skeptical amber cigarette holder balances unaided on his lower lip.

(What a business it had been, starting, without a single supporter in Europe, the struggle for the renewal of the International, or rather its razing and the construction of a new, Third International. One minute, scraping together any of the Bolshevik émigrés who would agree to come. The next, rallying with Grimm's help three dozen women, the International Conference of Socialist Women—and since he could hardly attend in person to give them the guidance they needed, sitting for three days in the café of the Volkshaus while Inessa, Nadya, and Zinka Lilina ran in to report and receive instructions.)

". . . Will you go to the slaughter for interests foreign to your own? Or will you instead make great sacrifices for socialism, for the interests of nine tenths of mankind?"

(Then there was the International Socialist Youth Conference. They had mustered fewer than a score, mostly those who had evaded the draft and were sure to be against the war, and again he had sat in the same café for three days while Inessa and Safarov trotted to him for instructions. This was when Willi had appeared on the scene.)

If you're twenty-seven, with ten turbulent years of the youth movement behind you—meetings, organizations, conferences, demonstrations . . . and if, among your peers, you discover that you have a voice, courage, luck, that people listen to you—you rise step by step as though to a platform where you can be seen better, and suddenly you find yourself in demand as a public speaker, delegate, secretary . . . And the party leaders immediately try to draw you into their orbit, and urge you not to listen to that Asiatic with his wild ideas, but it is from him and from the incendiary Trotsky that you always learn what is right and what matters!

". . . 'Defense of the fatherland' is a fraud on the people and can never be 'war for democracy.' And Switzerland is no different."

Twenty-seven! The things he'd been through! His mother's early death, beatings from his stepmother, beatings from his father, service in his father's tavern, playing cards and talking politics with the customers, at the washtub under his stepmother's eye, always suffering because his clothes were ragged and his boots the wrong size, drawn into propaganda work while apprenticed to a shoemaker, emigration to Zurich when only twenty, to work as a pharmacist's assistant and join in all the class battles . . .

In the reddish light from the lamp Münzenberg's devoted and determined face is trustful and expectant. The tempered strength of his will shows in the sharp jut of his narrow chin. His brows are knit in an eager frown of welcome for revolutionary ideas. Already he has often done as Lenin said, and the results have been good. He has rallied more than two thousand people for a "youth day" on the Zürichberg and led them through the city singing the "Internationale," waving red flags, and shouting, "Down with the war." He earned an invitation to Kienthal, and joined Lenin in signing the resolution of the left.

". . . In Switzerland, too, 'defense of the fatherland' is a hypocritical phrase. It opens the way for the massacre of workers and small peasants."

Schmidt from Winterthur, an ungainly figure at the far end of the bench, is puzzled and peers past his neighbors to say: "The war can't affect our country, we're neutral."

"Ah, but Switzerland may enter the war at any moment!"

Nobs is chewing his amber holder under his fluffy blond moustache. Although he smiles like an amiable cat, his eyes are mistrustful and a tuft of hair stands up like a question mark.

"Of course, refusal to defend the fatherland makes exceptionally high demands on revolutionary consciousness!"

(All his life he had been the leader of a minority, pitting himself with a handful of followers against all the rest, and aggressive tactics had been essential. His tactic was to whittle down the majority resolution as far as he could—and then still not accept it. Either you record our opinion in the minutes or we leave! . . . But you're in the minority, why are you dictating to us? . . . Right—we're leaving! A breakdown! A public brawl! A disgrace! . . . That was how it had been at all those conferences, and there had never been a majority that hadn't weakened. *The wind always blows from the far left!* No socialist in the world could afford to ignore that fact. That was why Grimm was so unsure of himself, and why he had hurriedly called the Zimmerwald Conference.)

". . . Not a single penny for a regular army, not even in Switzerland!"

"Not even in peacetime?"

"Even in peacetime socialists must vote against war credits for the bourgeois state!"

(Lenin had had to wait a long time for his invitation to Zimmerwald, and had been very depressed. Grimm might not summon him, and it would be improper to force himself on them. What sort of conference would it be, anyway? A bunch of silly shits would get together and declare themselves "for peace and against annexations." *For peace*—he couldn't bear to hear those words! . . . Meanwhile, he discreetly used his influence to insinuate as many of his supporters as he could into the list of delegates. Those who were against *their own* governments—they would be the nucleus of

the left International! . . . But they could only muster
eight: himself, Grishka, and Radek—that was three—
Platten, one Latvian, and three Scandinavians. Still, the
*whole* of the "old" International, fifty years after it was
founded, barely filled the four wagons that carried the
participants into the mountains so as not to attract the
attention of the authorities, who in fact noticed neither
the arrival of the delegates in Switzerland nor their dis-
persal. They learned of it only from the foreign press.)

"But the special character of Switzerland . . ."

"Special character nothing! Switzerland is just another imperialist country!"

Platten recoils. His brow is an open book. He
struggles to bring the creases of astonishment under control. His unregenerate heart rebels: our Switzerland may
be a tiny country, but surely it is a very special one.
Since the three cantons were first united, have we ever
annexed anybody? With intense mental effort he strives
to accept these advanced ideas. His big, strong, helpless
hands lie palm up on the table.

(Platten was good material to work on. Through
Platten alone, he could bring the whole Zurich organization into line. If only he would work harder at edu-
cating himself.)

"And so we, the Zimmerwald left, are now completely unanimous: we r e j e c t defense of the fatherland!"

Some of the dunces still don't understand.

"But if we reject defense of the fatherland, are
we to leave the country defenseless?"

"A radically incorrect formulation! The right way
to put it is this: either we let ourselves be killed in the
interests of the world imperialist bourgeoisie, or at the
cost of fewer casualties we carry out a socialist revolution in Switzerland—the only way to deliver the Swiss
masses from rising prices and hunger!"

(In Zimmerwald he had scarcely spoken at all, but had directed his left-wing supporters from the shadows. That was the most effective way to deploy his forces. The speechmaking could be safely left to Radek —he'd be witty, resourceful, relaxed, self-confident. His own duty as leader was to weld his small group more firmly together. An ordinary enemy is only half an enemy. But the man who used to be with you and suddenly wobbles off the line is doubly your enemy. You must hit him first of all. But it is better to anticipate trouble and prime your followers in caucus between sessions.)

". . . The disgusting thing about pacifists is that they dream of peace without a socialist revolution."

Radek is always cheerfully ready for marching orders. His pockets bulge with newspapers, books, all he needs for a day: if he has to hurry off to a revolution, he can go as he is. How interesting he finds it all!

(But the rogue needed watching. He might change sides, might betray them, any minute. And he sometimes got things wrong—trying to reconcile Grimm and Platten, for instance, when it was important to keep them quarreling.)

". . . Revolution is absolutely essential for the elimination of all wars."

Just look at Bronski, dozing again. He might as well not be here at all. He is only needed to make the number. When his vote is wanted, it will be there. And when required, he will say what is required.

(Yes, he is stupid. But there are so few of us that each one may count.)

". . . Only a socialist system can deliver mankind from war."

Difficult to say whether Nobs really approves. His eyes and his lips sympathize, but his ears are still and his brow unruffled. But he is editor in chief of the main left-wing paper, and effortlessly advancing to the highest levels of the party. They all have great need of him.

He needs them too, though. Nobs knows perfectly well that the wind always blows from the left. Small as their group is, it may change the course of the whole Swiss party. Only, he doesn't want them to be a millstone around his neck.

". . . It is illogical for anyone whose aim is to bring the war to an end to reject socialist revolution."

(When Liebknecht's letter was read to the Zimmerwald Conference, Lenin had sprung to his feet, shouting: "CIVIL WAR IS A SPLENDID THING!" Caution is all very well nine times out of ten, but the tenth time you must overstep the mark. Take the proletarian slogan —"Fraternization"—to the trenches! Preach class struggle to the troops. Tell them to turn their bayonets against their fellow countrymen! THE AGE OF THE BAYONET IS AT HAND! It was risky, of course, for an émigré in a neutral country to carry on like this, but he had always gotten away with it. At Zimmerwald, though, that foul German crook Ledebour had said, "You can put your name to it here, because you're safe—why don't you go to Russia and *send* your signature?" That was the level of debate with such people!)

". . . The Swiss party is obstinately stuck in the rut of strict legality and makes no preparation for revolutionary mass struggle."

From the counter with its two potbellied old barrels and its dozens of colorful bottles a waiter with blunt Swiss features is slowly carrying golden tankards and dark-red glasses and tumblers to the tables. From the serving window, another waiter brings yellow trays with thin brown slices of smoked sausage and plates of roast meat or fish. Swiss bellies are unhurriedly packing away inordinately lavish Swiss helpings, each enough for four. And at every glutton's elbow a second helping is keeping warm over a little flame.

". . . The socialist reorganization of Switzerland is perfectly feasible and urgently needed. Capitalism is absolutely ripe for transformation into socialism—here and now."

(At the last session of the Zimmerwald Conference, from midday on and throughout the night, the left had raised a storm over each amendment, demanded at every juncture that its dissenting opinion be recorded, and by these means shifted the resolution considerably in their favor. They hadn't of course succeeded in putting through either the "Civil War" or the "New International" resolution. Still, the Zimmerwald left had emerged as a new wing of the international movement, and Lenin was no longer a mere Russian sectarian but its chief. The official leadership, however, had remained with the centrists, and the hero of the conference, in newspapers throughout the world, was Grimm. Though barely thirty, he was already on the Executive Committee of the International, because he was hand in glove with the opportunists. Lenin had been visiting or living in Switzerland for twenty years on and off, long before Grimm was ever heard of.)

Willi's thin, eager face. He agrees, agrees completely; but it is essential for him to understand exactly what must be done, and where to start.

". . . In Switzerland it will be necessary to expropriate . . . a maximum of . . . thirty thousand bourgeois at the very most. And of course to seize all the banks right away. And Switzerland will then be a proletarian country."

From his place by the pillar, Lenin observes them obliquely, his domed brow inclined, bringing the full pressure of his mind and his hard gaze to bear on them, skillfully checking how much each of them has taken in. His thinning hair is a richer red in the light from the lantern.

". . . Strike at the roots of the present social order *by concrete action.* And *now!*"

That is the step which socialists everywhere find so difficult. Nobs screws up his eyes as though in pain. Even the proletarian from Winterthur looks a bit down in the mouth. And Mimiola's high starched collar is choking him.

A fine fellow, our Ulyanov, but much too extreme. Nowhere on earth, let alone in Switzerland or Italy, will you find anyone so extreme.

It is hard, so hard for them. Lenin's gaze slides rapidly, restlessly over all those heads, so different, yet all so nearly his for the taking.

They all dread his lethal sarcasm.

(When you can't force something through a narrow opening, it often helps to add extra weight.)

He addresses the entire table, simultaneously pursuing each of the six Swiss into his thoughts. His voice is tense, but lacking in resonance—it seems always to get lost in his chest, his larynx, or his mouth, and it slurs the *r*'s.

"The only way to do it is to s p l i t t h e p a r t y! It's a bourgeois affectation to pretend that 'civil peace' can reign in Swiss Social Democracy!"

They shudder. They freeze.

But he goes on: "The bourgeoisie has reared the social chauvinists to serve it as watchdogs! How can you speak of *unity* with them?"

(Keep hitting the same spot, over and over again, varying the words just slightly—that's the first rule for propagandists and preachers.)

"It's a disease that affects Social Democrats not only in Switzerland, not only in Russia, but all over the world—this maudlin craving for 'reconciliation'! They're all ready to renounce their principles for the sake of a bogus 'unity'! Yet short of a complete organizational break with the social patriots, it's impossible to advance a single step toward socialism!!"

However unresponsive they are, whatever they may be thinking, he has the assurance of a teacher confronting his class: the whole class may disagree, but the teacher is right just the same. His voice becomes still more guttural, more impatient, more excited.

"The question of a split is of fundamental importance. Any concession here is a crime. All those who vacillate on this are e n e m i e s o f t h e p r o-l e t a r i a t. True revolutionaries are never afraid of a split!"

(Split, split, and split again! Split at all stages of the movement! Go on splitting until you find yourselves a tiny clique—but nonetheless the Central Committee. Those left in it may be the most mediocre, the most insignificant people, but if they are united in a common obedience you can achieve anything!)

"It is high time for a split at the international level! We have excellent reports on the split in the German Socialist Party. The time has come to break with the Kautskyites in your own and all other countries! B r e a k with the Second International—and start building the Third!"

(A method tried and proven at the very dawn of the century. He had pierced and slain the Economists with the death ray of *What Is to Be Done?*—his scheme for a band of professional conspirators. He had shaken off the clammy clinging incubus of Menshevism with his *One Step Forward, Two Steps Back*. He did not want power for its own sake, but how could he help taking control when all the rest managed so incompetently? He could not let his incomparable qualities of leadership atrophy and go to waste.)

Yet the idea might have been born there and then, at the table, might have been an instantaneous and irresistible revelation: s p l i t your party—and thereby insure the victory or the revolution!

Nobs, stiff with delicious fear, doesn't even murmur. If you refuse, who knows, you might be the loser. Perhaps the smartest place to be is right here, at this table.

Platten's paw has frozen on the handle of his beer tankard. The path of a socialist is hard—and will be harder.

Mimiola triumphs over his contricting collar, rises clear of it. But he looks gloomy.

Willi wears a little smile of startled enlightenment. He is ready. And he will carry the young with him. He will repeat every word of it from the platform.

The heavy brow batters away at the breached wall.

"My book *Imperialism* proves conclusively that revolution is imminent and inevitable in all the industrialized countries of Europe."

There are still a couple of them who want to believe but can't quite see it. There you are, living in a room you've grown used to, and one morning you go ou into the street, with familiar buildings all around you, and you start a revolution. B u t  h o w ?  . . . Who would show you how? There had never been anything quite like it.

"Yes, but this is Switzerland . . ."

"What of it? That was a glorious strike in Zurich in 1912! And what about this summer? Willi's marvelous demonstration on the Bahnhofstrasse! A baptism of blood!"

Yes, this is Willi's proudest boast: "All those casualties!"

Even the first of August hadn't been as good as the third, in defense of the fallen.

They hem and haw . . . In Switzerland? . . .

How can they disbelieve him? He treats every

youngster as his equal, with perfect seriousness. Not like those leaders who snub their juniors once they get one foot on the ladder. He never begrudges the effort spent on conversation with the young, wearing them down with questions, questions, questions, until he can slip a noose on them.

"Yes, but in Switzerland . . ."

While they clear this little matter up, Radek finds time to read two of the newspapers from his bulging pocket and leaf through a book. And still they don't understand!

Radek pokes the stem of his pipe at them. "Your own party congress last year . . . adopted a resolution on revolutionary action by the masses! What about that?"

Well, what about it? . . . All sorts of resolutions were passed. Passing resolutions was easy enough.

"Then there's Kienthal!"

Five of those present had been at Kienthal, including Nobs and Münzenberg. Of the forty-five delegates they had been among the minority of twelve. They had threatened once more to disrupt the meeting by walking out, had in fact left the hall and returned. So the majority had given way to the minority, and they had pushed the resolution further and further to the left: *Only the conquest of political power by the proletariat can insure peace!*

True enough, but you can say anything in a resolution . . .

"No, but here in Switzerland . . ."

The most patient of men couldn't listen to these numskulls without exploding! Then—he amazes himself with a fresh revelation, which comes out in a hoarse cracked whisper. "Don't you realize that S w i t-z e r l a n d  i s  t h e  m o s t  r e v o l u t i o n a r y  c o u n t r y  i n  t h e  w o r l d ??!"

They all rock back in their seats, clutching tan-

kards, plates, forks . . . The lantern on the pillar sways
in the wind of his voice. Nobs grabs at his cigarette
holder as it falls from his mouth.

? ? ? ? ? ? ? ? ? ?

(He saw it all. Saw the barricades that would
soon rise in Zurich, not perhaps on the Bahnhofstrasse,
where all the banks were, but over toward the working-
class district by the Volkshaus on the Helvetia-Platz!)

And with a caustic flash of his Mongol eyes, in a
voice without depth or resonance, but with the cutting
edge of a Kalmuck saber (catching only on the *r*'s):
"Because Switzerland is the only country in the world
where soldiers are given weapons and ammunition to
take home!"

So . . . ?

"D o   y o u   k n o w   w h a t   r e v o l u t i o n
m e a n s ? It means seizing the banks! The railway station! The post office and telegraph! The big enterprises!
And that's all! Once you've done that, the revolution is
victorious. And what do you need to do it? O n l y
w e a p o n s. And the weapons are there."

The things Fritz Platten heard from this man, who
was his fate and his doom! Sometimes his blood
froze . . .

Lenin abandons persuasion and raps out orders
to these recalcitrants, these incompetent muddlers.

"So what are you waiting for? What more do you
need? Universal military training? Well then, the time
has come to demand it!"

He is improvising, thinking between sentences,
picking his way among his thoughts, but his voice never
falters.

"Officers must be elected by the people. Any
group of . . . a hundred can demand military training!
With instructors paid out of the public purse. It is *precisely* the civic freedom of Switzerland, its effective
democracy, that makes revolution immensely easier!"

Bracing himself against the table, he looks as if he is about to spread his wings, fly up from the little hall of the Stüssihof restaurant, and soar above the five-cornered, enclosed medieval square, itself no bigger than a good-sized hall, glide over the comic flag-bearing soldier on the fountain, spiral past the jutting balconies, past the fresco of the two cobblers hammering away on their stools three floors up, past the coats of arms on the pediments five floors up, and over the tiled roofs of old Zurich, over the mountain pensions and the overdecorated chalets of the lackeys' republic.

"Begin propaganda in the army *immediately*. Make the troops and the young men of recruiting age see that it is right and inevitable for them to use their arms to free themselves from the slavery of hirelings! ... Distribute leaflets calling for an *immediate* socialist revolution in Switzerland!"

(Rather rash words for a foreigner without a passport—but this was the one time in ten which made the difference between victory and defeat.)

"Take executive control of all working-class associations immediately! Insist that the party's parliamentary representatives publicly preach socialist revolution! The compulsory take-over of factories, mills, and agricultural landholdings!"

What? Go and take people's property away from them, just like that? Without enacting a law? The Swiss dunces couldn't blink fast enough.

"To reinforce the revolutionary elements in the country, all foreigners should be naturalized without charge. If the government makes the slightest move toward war—create underground workers' organizations! And in the event of war ..."

Full of daring, Münzenberg and Mimiola, the leaders of youth, finish it for him "... refuse to perform military service!"

(Luckily, Münzenberg and Radek, deserters from

the German and Austro-Hungarian armies, respectively, could not be deported, under Swiss law.)

Not one little thing do they understand! A mocking smile, but not unfriendly, passes over Lenin's face. There is nothing else to do but—down, down he comes, past the cobblers hammering away at their work with slavish diligence, over the blue shaft of the fountain, to alight with a rush in his old place in the restaurant.

"In no circumstances must you refuse. What can you be thinking of?! In Switzerland, especially! When they give you arms, take them! Demand demobilization—yes, but don't give up your arms. Keep your arms and get out into the streets! Not a single hour of civic peace! Strikes! Demonstrations! Form squads of armed workers! And then an a r m e d  u p r i s- i n g !!!"

Broad-browed Platten is bowled over as though by a blow on the head:

"But with all Europe at war . . . will the neighboring powers . . . tolerate a revolution in Switzerland? They'll intervene."

This is the nub of Lenin's plan—the utter, unreproduceable uniqueness of Switzerland.

"That's what's so splendid! While all Europe is at war—barricades in Switzerland! A revolution in Switzerland! Switzerland speaks three major European languages! And through those three languages the revolution will spill over in three directions and flood all Europe! The alliance of revolutionary elements will expand to include the proletariat of all Europe! A sense of class solidarity will be aroused in the three neighboring countries! If there is any intervention, revolution will flare up t h r o u g h o u t  E u r o p e !! That is why SWITZERLAND IS THE CENTER OF WORLD REVOLUTION TODAY!!!"

Singed by the red light, the members of the Skittle

Club sit transfixed as the words chance to find them.
The narrow triangle of Münzenberg's intrepid face is
thrust forward into the glow. Nobs's fluffy moustache is
also touched with the flame. Mimiola looks as if he is
about to pull his tie off and lead his hotblooded Italians
over the ruins of Europe. Bronski in his sad, sly way is
trying to look ready for battle. Radek wriggles, licks his
lips, and excitement flashes behind his glasses: if that
was the way of it, what fun he would have!

(The Skittle Club is the Third International in
embryo!)

"You are the best part of the Swiss proletariat!"

Radek has a resolution ready and waiting for tomorrow's congress of the Swiss party. If only Nobs will
print it . . .

Hmmmmm . . .

But who will put it to the congress?

Hmmmmm . . .


Since the restaurant would soon be closing, the
group broke up.

There were three streetlamps on the Stüssihof
square, and lights shone from the windows of houses all
around. You could easily read the plaque telling how
in 1443 Burgomaster Stüssi fell in battle not far from
here. His family home, in the wind's eye, had stood for
sixty years before that. That must be Stüssi too, the
comic Swiss soldier in armor and blue hose in the middle
of the fountain. You could hear the thin jets of water
splashing into the bluish basin. The air was dry, and
cold for this part of the world.

They were still talking as they took leave of one
another and walked away over the cobbled square. The
square seemed completely enclosed, and unless you
knew where to look for the crevices that were streets,

you might wonder whether you would ever get out. Some of the company went off down a bumpy cobbled slope and took the side street that led to the embankment. Others turned off at the beerhouse called the Franciscan. Willi, however, accompanied his teacher along the same street in the opposite direction, past the Voltaire cabaret on the next corner, where the bohemians raved the night away, and on the narrow sidewalk they encountered prostitutes still waiting for customers. Past the Voltaire they walked steeply uphill, under an antiquated lamp on an iron post, along a street like a stairway, so narrow that with arms outstretched you could almost touch both walls at once, and there was scarcely room to walk two abreast, up and up they went.

The heels of Lenin's stout mountain boots clattered on the cobbles.

Willi wanted his teacher to reassure him over and over again. He had not forgotten the fight on the Bahnhofstrasse that summer, but every trace had been washed and swept away, the shop windows were as dazzling as ever, the bourgeoisie strolled around as comfortably as before, and the workers placidly obeyed their accommodating leaders.

"Yes, but the people, are they really ready for it . . ."

At a sharp turning in the alley, in the dim light of someone's sleepless upper windows, the voice from under the dark cap was quiet but as sharp-edged as ever. "Of course the *people* aren't ready. But that doesn't give us the right to postpone the *beginning*."

In spite of the platform victories behind him, the shouts of assembled youth in his ears, Willi persisted. "But we are such a small minority!"

Lenin stopped and out of the darkness came something not disclosed even to the select gathering at the Skittle Club. "The majority is always stupid, and we

cannot wait for it. A resolute minority must act—and
then it becomes the majority."

\*

The congress opened the following morning, across
the river in the Merchants' Hall. Lenin, as leader of a
foreign party, was invited to greet the assembly. Radek
was also there, ostensibly representing the Polish party.
Two from "our side," speaking one after the other.

On that first morning, not all the delegates had
arrived, and the audience was no larger than for a
good lecture. (Lenin, in fact, was not used to large
audiences; he had never known what it was like to
address a thousand people at a time—except just once,
at a mass meeting in Petersburg, when he had lost his
tongue.)

As soon as he looked out over the hall, caution
overcame him. Just as at Zimmerwald, just as at Kienthal, he had no overwhelming urge to speak his mind
fully—no, the full fervor of his conviction was reserved
for a closed meeting of his supporters. Here, of course,
he did not call for action either against the government
or against the banks. Standing before this nominally
Social Democratic but in fact bourgeois mass of self-
satisfied, fat-faced Swiss lounging at their little tables,
Lenin sensed at once that they did not and would not
understand him, and that he had practically nothing to
say to them. Somehow he couldn't even bring himself to
remind them of the highly revolutionary resolution
which they themselves had adopted last year—and anyway, it might spoil everything.

So that his salutations would have been quite
short, if he had not become painfully entangled in the
Adler affair. (Two weeks earlier, Fritz Adler, secretary
of the Austrian Social Democratic Party, had shot
and killed the Prime Minister of Austria-Hungary—

killed the head of the Imperial government in time of war!) This assassination had captured everyone's imagination, there was a lot of talk about it, and before making up his own mind about it Lenin had inquired carefully into the circumstances. Who had influenced Adler? (His Russian S.R. wife, perhaps?) Because he was secretly preoccupied with this problem (his eternal argument with the S.R.'s), here, at the congress, he devoted half his speech to an irrelevant discussion of terrorism ... He said that the greetings sent to the terrorist by the Central Committee of the Italian party *deserved full sympathy,* if the assassination was understood as a signal to Social Democrats to abandon opportunist tactics. And he defended at length the opposition of the Russian Bolsheviks to individual terror: it was only because terror ought to be a mass activity.

Meanwhile, the Swiss munched and swigged and mooed—there was no understanding them.

But still, the Saturday session went well, and raised his hopes. Platten was applauded by the majority, and Papa Greulich, a seventy-five-year-old with a luxurious gray mop of hair, started joking about the party "adopting new favorites." (Nothing to the Schweizer curses we'll heap on you when the time comes! When we come to power, we'll hang you!) It had worked, it had gone off beautifully! Lenin cheered up and felt like an old war horse in the swirl of battle. Moreover, the circumspect Nobs had not refused to put forward the Skittle Club's (that is, Radek's) resolution: that the congress should adhere to the Kienthal decisions. (The stupid Swiss might vote for it just to follow the fashion, without really knowing what the Kienthal decisions were—and then they'd be caught! After that, you could bait your hook with their own resolution and catch the lot of them. Grimm as well!)

Trivialities? No! That is how history is made—from one hard-won resolution to the next, through pressure by the minority, you push and push every resolution—left! ever left!

Then the next step. That Saturday evening, on the Skittle Club's initiative, by individual invitation, a separate, secret, private meeting of all young delegates was held away from the congress building; they gambled on the normal sympathy of the young for the *left*. The plan was simple: to work out, with their help, a resolution (or, rather, submit a ready-made one brought along by Radek) for them to present and force through the congress on the following day, Sunday.

At this private conference of young delegates, Willi, of course, was chairman—making lavish use of his commanding gestures, his bold, cheerful voice, and his tumbling hair—and Radek was at his side, smothered in curls, wearing his merrily militant spectacles, reading his resolution, explaining it, answering questions. (He was a good speaker too—but his pen was beyond price.) Lenin, as he always preferred, sat inconspicuously among the others, and contented himself with listening attentively.

All might have gone well. The young delegates listened closely to their Russo-Polish comrade and seemed to agree.

All might have gone well, if something extremely unpleasant hadn't happened. They had not had the sense to lock the door. And through the unlocked door, unnoticed at first, came two malicious tattletales, two horrid old bags: Mme Blok, who was Grimm's friend, no less, and Martov's lady friend, Dimka Smidovich. Once these wretched females were in, there was no turning them out: they'd scream and make a scene. And the entire meeting could hardly move elsewhere! Anyway, they'd already seen and heard Radek speaking, and realized, of course, that a resolution for the Swiss congress was being drafted by Russians.

What an infernal nuisance! What a colossal fiasco!

Loathsome creatures with their filthy little intrigues! Of course, they rushed off to Grimm and whispered in his ear. And he, the brute, the scum, the utter swine, believed the silly bitches! And tried to start a vulgar brawl by printing vile innuendos in his *Berner Tagwacht,* which were absolutely incomprehensible to ninety-nine percent of its readers: *A certain small group of foreigners,* who look at our workers' movement through spectacles of their own, and are utterly indifferent to Swiss affairs, are trying in a fit of impatience to provoke an artificial revolution in our country! . . .

Rubbish! Unmitigated hogwash! And that is what they call a working-class leader?

Then at the congress they'd laughed down Nobs's resolution. When he proposed making it a rule that, in the future, only those opposed to national self-defense should be put up for Parliament, Greulich had been greatly amused: if we elect such deputies, he said, their hotheadedness may land them in the *skittle alley.*

The congress had roared with laughter.

Consideration of the Kienthal resolution had also been postponed—until February 1917.


What a tragedy it all was! So much effort, so many evenings, so much conviction, lucid thought, and revolutionary dynamite had gone into it! And the result was a heap of opportunist debris, banal and stupid, like dingy cotton wool, like the dust of a junk room.

In moldy old Switzerland the bacillus of petit-bourgeois cretinism reigned triumphant.

And the bourgeois world still stood, unexploded.

The Ulyanovs lived exactly halfway between the cantonal and city libraries, and it was only slightly farther to the Center for Socialist Literature: all were between five and seven minutes away at average walking speed. They all opened at nine o'clock, but today he was driven out of the house forty minutes earlier: stupidly, humiliatingly fleeing from that shaggy-headed ragamuffin, Zemlyachka's nephew, so as to spare himself, to avoid impertinent chatter which might enrage him and ruin his whole day.

Objectively speaking, there was no avoiding such figures in émigré revolutionary circles—slovenly, vacant-looking young men with unformed minds, but ever ready to make a pronouncement on any subject, just to show that they had opinions. They were everlastingly hungry and penniless. You might think that they would try to earn something by copying (copyists were in short supply in Zurich, think of all the trouble he'd had getting his lost *Imperialism* copied), but no, they could neither spell nor write legibly—and anyway, they all wanted to be editors, and immediately! Their constant preoccupation was where to find a free meal. On the Ulyanovs' budget, this was an intolerable imposition: Zemlyachka's nephew could wolf down two eggs, and four sandwiches for good measure. They had firmly forbidden him the dinner table, so he started appearing early in the morning, always with some flimsy excuse—returning or borrowing a book or a newspaper, but really with an eye to breakfast. ("Whatever you do, don't feed him," he had told Nadya as he left the house just now. "He'll soon stop coming.") It wouldn't be so bad if he ate meekly and then went away, but no, he thought it necessary to show his gratitude with a gush of pseudo-intellectual drivel, to elucidate fundamental questions, and always in the same aggressive, know-it-all fashion.

These visits, that knowing, superior smile on the face of a milksop, made Vladimir Ilyich ill for the day. In general, any unexpected upset to his daily routine, especially an uninvited and untimely guest, any pointless waste of time, so exasperated and unsettled him that he was incapable of work. Nothing was more vexatious than expending his nervous energy and his cogency in argument not at a conference, in a pamphlet, in debate with an important party opponent, but, for no good reason, on a lout who didn't even mean what he was saying. Most émigrés had to count their pennies, but a whole day frittered away was no loss to them. A single wasted hour made Lenin ill! Even if, in retrospect, some unforeseen meeting, conversation, or piece of business proved important and necessary, the unexpected always irritated him at the time.

But the émigré world has its own code of behavior and you are defenseless against such visitors, you cannot simply show them the door or refuse to let them in: it would set malicious tongues wagging among the émigrés and seriously damage your reputation. You would instantly be accused of arrogance, lordliness, overweening conceit, "leaderism," dictatorial pretensions . . . the émigré community was a nest of vicious snakes, endlessly writhing and hissing. So that whenever one of these impudent rogues saw fit to leave Russia—and even escaping from Siberia was the easiest thing in the world, which meant everybody fled abroad, expecting to be kept at the party's expense—you must not only welcome him but invent something for him to do. And within a year you might find the swine actually working on some journal, though probably only one issue would ever appear.

Take that born troublemaker Yevgenia Bosch. Why didn't she go to Russia, as she was supposed to? There was absolutely nothing for her to do *here,* but she would try to invent something, and expect others to invent something for her. One of the plagues of émigré life was having to invent occupations for émigrés.

Of course, once the revolution began, its ramifications would provide work for every one of these little boys and girls; indeed, each of them would be indispensable, there would be only too few of them. But while there was no revolution, cramped and poor as everyone was, these brats were unbearable.

It was an exhausting state of affairs. How long had it existed? Was it nine years since they had fled from Russia, fled from defeat? Sixteen since that first unhappy meeting and clash with Plekhanov? Twenty-one since that stupid bungle in Petersburg? That tormenting state of mind when every sinew craves action, when you feel you could move mountains or continents with the energy pent up and tense inside you, but there is nothing to exert your powers on, no contact between the tips of your fingers and other people, when parties, crowds, and continents will not bow to your will but chaotically, senselessly whirl and collide, not knowing where they are bound—you alone know that!—but all your energy, all your plans are burned out converting half a dozen Swiss youngsters in the Skittle Club. Still, even they were something. Earlier, when no one came to meetings except two Swiss, two Germans, one Pole, one Jew, and one Russian, who sat telling each other jokes —things were really bad, it was pathetic, he was ready to abandon the game!

Now that he had got down onto the Limmat embankment without meeting Zemlyachka's nephew, he could assume that he was safe. His self-defensive irritation gradually subsided.

Ragged gray clouds with whitish edges gave the day a cold, severe light.

Big plate-glass windows encroached upon the lakefront, blatantly displaying on a background of silk and velvet all the ingenious handiwork of idleness—jewelry, perfumes, haberdashery, linen. The lackeys' republic was flaunting its luxury, untouched by the war, as provocatively as it knew how.

Moving away in disgust from these perverse fantasies in gold, satin, and lace—he hated the things themselves, and still more the people who loved them —Lenin waited for a trolley to pass—a dog ran right in front of it but reached the other side unhurt—then crossed the road and set out along the riverbank.

By the Fraumünster Bridge he let a car, a hansom, and a cyclist with a long basket on his back go by. The city library was then right in front of him, and he would have liked to go in at once, but it was still closed.

If he went on, he would have to make a detour: there was no passage between the library and the water. The library building was the former Wasser-Kirche, so called because it jutted out into the water. Four hundred years ago, the resolute Zwingli had taken it away from the priests and handed it over for civic use.

There he himself stood before the requisitioned church, on a black marble pedestal several steps high, with his snub nose, his book, and the point of his sword resting between his feet. Lenin always spared him an approving glance. True, his book was the Bible, but all the same, for the sixteenth century, he had shown splendid resoluteness, today's socialists could learn a lesson from him. An excellent combination, the book and the sword. The book, with the sword as its extension.

Clausewitz: war is politics, with the pen finally exchanged for the sword. All politics leads to war, and that is its only value.

The river added dampness to the cold of the morning air. They said it never froze. Somehow he always associated Russia with winter, and emigration with perpetual winterlessness. He leaned over the railings. Here, where the river mouth widened, there was an array of boats several rows deep along both banks—boats masted and unmasted, boats with cabins and boats with tarpaulin covers. The masts were swaying.

Kesküla was complaining that someone close to the Central Committee had stolen money intended to pay for the printing of a pamphlet. It would have to be raised again. Outrageous!

The water was dark, but quite clear. Gray stones could be seen on the bottom.

The three aspects of war according to Clausewitz: the operations of reason belong to the government, free spiritual activity belongs to the commanders, and hatred belongs to the people.

The neat square stones of the embankment sidewalk were thickly strewn with maple leaves (it was the custom not to sweep them). That tree there—what was it?—had not yet lost its spiked cones.

Everything was becoming dreadfully expensive. They would soon have nothing to live on. The price of paper was rising faster than anything! Shliapnikov was no good at all at extracting money from Gorky and from Bonch. He should wrench it out of them with pincers! Let them pay up and pay handsomely.

All his life his mother had helped him out from family funds. On his foreign travels or in Petersburg, however much he overspent he never had to think of earning money, he had been able to afford a balanced diet in prison, to shorten his journey to Siberia, to avoid transit prisons. In emigration he could ask for money at any time, and by some miracle she had always managed to send it. But since the summer he had had no mother, and he would never be able to ask again.

A flock of black ducks with white heads bobbed on the lake, suddenly took off, scuffing the water, flew low over the surface, and settled down. Then they flocked together again and swam sedately back to their old place.

But although Clausewitz seemed to have explained the basic laws of war in general, it was impossible to understand the law of the war now in progress. Or that of the war which must be started.

Surely the Swedes at least could give him a loan? Shliapnikov must drop Branting a hint: it would come more naturally from him, as Russia's representative.

A professional revolutionary should be relieved of the need to worry about his livelihood. Party funds should guarantee the leading members of the Central Committee a maintenance allowance for some time ahead.

The wives of solid Swiss burghers were crumbling bread and dropping it from the big bridge. The ducks gathered quickly, and others—with green heads and yellow beaks—joined them. And still others, with blue-gray plumage.

If we are to publish in *Letopis,* the alliance between the Machists and the Orgkom must be split. People around Gorky are intriguing against us.

Two or three ducks skimmed the lake, chasing each other, churning the water with wings and feet.

To think that he must look to Gorky for money, and what was more, humble himself before that incredibly spineless calf—*beg* his forgiveness for attacking Kautsky, cut out the most telling and enjoyable blows in the whole book just to please him.

It would be nice now to go for a brisk row. They'd often talked about it, never got around to it.

Now it would have to wait till spring. Walking and scrambling about in the mountains and tramping the streets of Zurich were the only ways Lenin had of soothing and dispelling the ache of unused muscles. But he still felt it in his shoulders, and the best thing for that was rowing.

Another great worry was the loss of his *Imperialism,* sent off in manuscript last summer. The most mysterious thing about it was that a responsible post office could find no clue as to how it had vanished. The British censorship had become ridiculous, and the French had lost all shame, so it would not be surprising if *Imperialism* had attracted attention—its author no longer an ordinary émigré, one of the thousands here in Switzerland whom the police ignored. Perhaps he was already under surveillance. Perhaps he was being watched at this very moment, here on the embankment. His situation was precarious. At the first—or anyway the second—hint from the Russian or the French ambassador he might be hauled before a military court or deported from Switzerland for infringing its neutrality. They would only have to listen in from a neighboring table to one speech at the Skittle Club.

He stretched himself and trudged on downstream, along the railings near the water's edge, looking like the neediest of Zurich's inhabitants with his shabby bowler hat, his threadbare coat, and his waterproof shopping bag (but his held notebooks, abstracts, clippings). Reaching the big bridge, he patiently let pass someone's opulent phaeton, a slow, four-horse dray, and a one-horse trolley with three big windows and a uniformed driver up front.

He would therefore have to burn dangerous drafts, give all important documents to respectable Swiss citizens for safekeeping, start signing himself "Frey" again, or something like that, and on occasion use invisible ink even for letters between Zurich, Bern, and Geneva. All this in a neutral country! Just like home, under the noses of the gendarmes . . . And *Imperialism,* written out all over again, must be put between book covers so that it would get through.

He crossed the big bridge and came out on the broad paved avenue along the lake, which was also unswept and carpeted with brown maple leaves.

The air from this wider part of the lake was stronger, fresher, colder.

Swans, white and gray, floated there. Or rather, sat statuesquely on the water. In the shallows, now one, now another of them dipped its head to peck at something, its white behind sticking up, its feet treading air. Then it lengthily shook the water from its snaky neck.

Behind, to the left, a pale sun was peering from beyond the Opera House. But it was a cold sun, its light held no warmth.

It was soothing, all this water. All this space. The pressure in his chest eased. It was only when it eased and released him that he realized how hard-pressed and harassed he normally was.

The broad expanse of the lake. Scattered about it, fishing boats rode at anchor. On the other side, and to the left, the elongated, gently sloping wooded bulk of the Uetliberg stretched to the far end of the lake. There were white spots on it in places: a light snow had fallen on the higher ground and had not melted.

A spacious lake, reminding him of Geneva.

The fresh, lapping waves of Lake Geneva would stay in his memory as long as he lived. That was where he had suffered the greatest disaster of his life: the shattering of his idol.

How young he had been, how full of youthful rapture, how infatuated when he had gone to Switzerland for that first meeting with Plekhanov, to seek his recognition. It was then, sending "Volgin" (Plekhanov) his declaration of friendship before leaving Munich, that he had first thought of signing himself "Lenin." All that was needed was that the old man should control his vanity, that one great river should acknowledge the other, so that together they could encompass all Russia.

Young men full of vigor, who had served their time in Siberia, survived great dangers, and broken out of Russia, they were bringing these elderly distinguished revolutionaries their plans for *Iskra,* for a journal, for working side by side together to fan the flames of revolution! It was incredible in retrospect, but he had still believed in a general reunification, to include even the Economists, had even defended Kautsky against Plekhanov. It sounded like a bad joke! They had naïvely supposed that all Marxists stood for the same things, and could work in harmony. They would be greeted as bearers of glad tidings; we, the young, are continuing what you began.

They had run up against something else: a calculating concern to retain power, to remain in command. The *Iskra* plan, and the fanning of flames in Russia, was a matter of complete indifference to Plekhanov: all he wanted was to be sole leader. So he had cunningly represented Lenin as a comic conciliator, an opportunist, and himself as a rock-hard revolutionary. And he had taught Lenin where the advantage lies in a schism: the one who calls for the split is always on firmer ground.

How could he ever forget that night in the village of Vésenaz when he and Potresov had disembarked from the Geneva steamer like whipped schoolboys, smarting and humiliated, when they had paced the village from end to end in the darkness, shouting their resentment, seething, ashamed of themselves—and all around them, over the mountains and the lake, an electric storm had walked the night sky, without breaking out in rain. They were so outraged that at times they almost burst into tears. And an infernal chill had descended on his heart.

On that bitter night Vladimir Ulyanov was born again. Only since that night had he become what he was, become his true self.

Lenin took this harsh lesson to heart, never to forget it: he would never believe anyone again, never let sentiment tinge his dealings with others.

Somebody began to feed the gulls, and they shot up from the water, greedily, impatiently swooping and wheeling, catching the bread in mid-air, screaming, fighting, even venturing onto the parapet, flying almost into the faces of Lenin and others nearby.

He waved one of them away and walked on.

How memory catches at coincidences, sentimental associations. Lake Geneva again, nothing more, had been between them, before they had known each other, when he was beginning to come into his own, receiving delegates to the Second Congress, carefully studying each one, feeling him out, making a bid for his support, and she—was bearing her fifth child, to a husband *younger than herself,* and reading for the first time *The Development of Capitalism in Russia,* by somebody called Ilin, with no idea of what lay ahead.

Five years had gone by, and they still did not know each other, although she had been in Geneva several times. It was in Geneva too, at an unforgettable performance of *La Dame aux Camélias,* that he had been pierced with anguish, had first doubted the meaning of his life. At that very time her husband lay dying in Davos. Then, only a few months later, in Paris, she had come to him.

The wind, noticeably chillier here, crinkled the waters in a frown.

He put his bag down by the embankment railing, raised his collar, and stood there peering down at the lake. It was quite cold. According to the stupid Russian calendar it was October 25, which meant November 7

European-style. And Inessa was still freezing at her Sörenberg villa, doing her best to catch a chill. Or to make him angry.

Or to punish him.

She hadn't even written promptly. She was denying him news of herself. Either she didn't answer at all or else she delayed writing. So he had to choose his words carefully: of course, if you don't feel like answering . . . or if you feel like not answering . . . I won't pester you with questions . . .

In all his personal relationships Lenin was careful to assert his superiority, was always on his dignity. But here it was impossible: he could find no vantage point. He could only hide his embarrassment in jokes. Only beg.

He must learn to meet silence with silence. To wait for her answer. But nothing could be more difficult: it was when you didn't see each other that you needed most of all to write, to share your thoughts! And anyway, there was business which could not wait.

It would be quite simple, here and now, without waiting for her answer, to write a few affectionate, unresentful lines. (No, they mustn't be affectionate, there must not be the slightest breath of affection, all letters in wartime were subject to censorship, and you had to write as though you were making a statement in a police station. Mustn't give them a weapon against you.)

Yes, he was at her mercy if she chose to punish him. He acknowledged dependence on no one in the world except Inessa. He felt it least when he was smarting from one of their fights. Most of all, when they were together.

No, when they were not . . .

Everything he had ever had in life—food, drink, clothes, house and home—had been not *for him;* indeed, he had wanted nothing of all this except as a means to keep himself going for the sake of the cause. His month off in summer, his mountain walks in the Carpathians or from Sörenberg up the Rothorn, the Alpine view before his eyes, the bar of chocolate eaten stretched out on the slopes of the Zürichberg, the smoked Volga sturgeon sent by his mother—none of that was self-indulgence, mere gratification of the flesh, it was a way of making himself mentally fit for his work. Good health was a revolutionary's main asset.

Only his meetings with Inessa, even their business meetings, were just for himself, for the sake of the foolishly happy, free and easy, lighthearted state of animal contentment in which they left him, although they could be a time-wasting and debilitating distraction.

All the men and women Lenin had ever met in his life he had valued only if, and as long as, they were useful to the cause. Only Inessa, although she had entered his life by way of the cause—and there was no other means, no outsider could have come near him— existed as if for him alone, complementing his existence with her own.

Inessa showed him things he would never have thought of, never imagined, and might have lived his life without discovering. In their arguments about free love he had an unbreakable net of logic for her vague ideas. Slip through it if you can! But it was hopeless. The dark water from the depths of the lake runs unimpeded through the fisherman's net, and Inessa with her concept of free love was not to be caught in the net of class analysis. Slowed down for a moment, she slipped easily through the mesh. Her arguments were defeated but she was invincible.

Long ago when the whole world was carefully measured, appraised, and regulated, she had shaken his certainties, bidding him break all bounds and follow her through a world which, though it was the same, was yet unlike anything he had imagined, and he had gone with her, like a timid but delighted schoolboy, anxiously clinging to her guiding hand, full of childlike, doglike gratitude toward her, worshipping her down to the blue veins of her slender foot, for all that she had revealed and given to him for as long as their love lasted.

From where she was, from Sörenberg in the southwest, over the frowning autumn waters, even in the whistling November wind, he felt her love calling to him. He seemed to see the flutter of eyelids over half-closed eyes, the quick gleam of her white teeth.

Why was she punishing him? Why hadn't she come down to Clarens, where it was warmer? Last year the first snow had fallen on Sörenberg at the beginning of October. It had been very cold.

Over the roof of the theater, which was scattered with mythological winged trumpeters, the sun suddenly shone full-strength. The sunlight was cold here, and orange-colored where it had encroached on the heights of the Uetliberg. The lower slopes, where buildings towered around a gray-green dome with a belfry, were still in gloom.

Those were happy days—in Longjumeau, Brussels, Copenhagen, Cracow. In Bern too. Happy years. Seven of them.

He, who was incapable of wasting five minutes without finding idleness an exasperating burden, had spent hours on end with Inessa. He had not despised himself for it, not been in any hurry to pull himself together, but had abandoned himself completely to his weakness. It had reached the point where he confided everything to her, wanted to tell her everything—much more than he would tell any man. How quick and fresh was her response and her advice! And how he had missed them in the last six months. Since April. Since Kienthal.

Had something snapped at Kienthal? He hadn't felt it at the time.

He had been forced to leave Bern: Grimm was the dominant influence there, and he would never have been able to gather a circle of sympathizers. He had been right to go away. But how could he imagine when he left that they would never meet again?

In Kienthal he had noticed nothing. In the thick of that wonderful six-day battle.

The one person whose feelings he could not afford to hurt: he might lose her forever. This fear of upsetting a delicate equilibrium, which he had experienced with no one else, sometimes put him in a comic position. He had to humor her unfortunate passion for writing theoretical articles. Frank criticism was impossible, and he had to choose his words carefully, or sometimes simply lie. "What could I possibly have against publishing your article? Of course I'm for it." Then, afterward, he would pretend that unforeseen circumstances prevented it. Rebukes, and even political correction, had to be softened until they almost became praise. He had to endure her arbitrariness as a translator: at times, instead of translating his text, she would amend the sense! Or even censor it, rejecting ideas which were not to her liking. No one could be allowed to do that! But to Inessa, his reproaches were mild and courteous. His courtesy was a way of ingratiating himself. If he wrote a longer letter than usual, he would immediately apologize: I shouldn't be rambling on like this.

But even his eagerness to please did not make him feel small. With Inessa, nothing was humiliating.

This was her way of punishing him, not writing. Not answering his letters.

Once she dug her heels in, there was no persuading her.

A white steamer moved away from the pier, sending waves toward him. Two white swans, immune to the cold, their necks gracefully arched, seemingly set in their pose forever, were rocked by the waves.

He felt cold. He took his bag and walked on along the railing.

With Inessa beside him, he had painfully bent his will to hers, but now that she was far away he could attain almost complete freedom from her.

There in the severe light of an autumn morning, with sunshine chasing shadow over the cold lake.

For as long as he could remember, he had been aware of a safety device in himself. Any setback, any waste of time, any display of weakness depressed the catch further and further, until suddenly it sprang back, flinging him into action with a force that nothing could withstand.

You must economize on idle sentiment or your work will stagnate.

With Inessa far away, his natural caution was coming back to him. Caution forbade any additional stress in his life. A permanent union with Inessa? Life would be chaotic. She was too mercurial, too much a person in her own right, too distracting. Then there were her children—and a way of life altogether strange to him. He could not, he had no right to let himself be slowed down or diverted by those children.

The best solution was to live with Nadya, and he had been right to adopt it all those years ago. Yakubova had been more vivacious, and better-looking, but could never have helped him as Nadya had. Nadya was much more than a fellow spirit: on the most trivial of subjects, her thoughts and feelings never differed from his own. She knew how the whole world frayed and fretted and irritated him, and she herself not only did not irritate but soothed and protected him, took all his worries upon herself. However sharp his revulsions of feeling, however sudden his outbursts, she was there to share and soften them. And how quick she was to take her cue! When Radek was behaving like a swine, she was curt and hard with him, and if he made some excuse to call, she stopped him at the door. But when Radek became a model comrade, a congenial adviser, how warmly she welcomed him. If she had had to rehearse, to make an effort, she might sometimes have gone wrong, but she merely felt for Ilyich with unwavering loyalty. Living with her made no excessive demands on his nerves.

Then again—and this was not to be ignored—Inessa was not economical, not capable of living sensibly and modestly. She often behaved erratically. She would suddenly, for instance, take it into her head to dress in the latest fashion. Whereas Nadya had no equal for orderliness and economy. She understood instinctively that every extra franc in hand meant extra time for thinking and working. What was more, she never let her tongue run off with her—a rare thing in a woman—never boasted, never said a word to outsiders when she had been warned not to. For that matter, she knew when to keep quiet without being told.

In view of all this, it would ill become a revolutionary to be ashamed in company that his wife was far from beautiful, not outstandingly intelligent, and a year older than himself. To succeed in the world, he must be as free as possible from inner doubts and outside distractions, must narrowly concentrate all his efforts on his goal. For Lenin the politician, the union with Nadya was all that reason could require.

True, there had always been the three of them. Leaving their homes in adjoining streets to meet in the forest around Bern; going for mountain rambles on Sörenberg to pick Alpine roses or mushrooms (sometimes he and Inessa had gone off by themselves to remote mountain refuges); at some pension, where he and Nadya had sat reading in the shade, while Inessa spent hours at the piano; sitting on tree stumps on the warm slopes, he and Nadya at their books as always, and Inessa gracefully sunning herself like a little girl out with her elders; best of all, those long hours when he had talked to both of them about his ideas, his plans, his future articles. How often he had taken in at a glance and marveled at his imcomparable, incredible, impossible good luck, wished that it would last for years. And it had lasted! If Nadya ever wrote a long, detailed, friendly letter, it was to Inessa. If there was one person whom she tirelessly praised to all their comrades, it was Inessa. Only in letters to Volodya's mother (her own mother saw how things were), in letters from daughter-in-law to mother-in-law, describing their life together and their walks, did she write as though there were just the two of them. Very tactfully.

Now both mothers had died within a short time: hers last spring in Bern after an attack of influenza, his that summer in Petersburg. The mail reached their mountain pension at Flums by pack mule, the telegram announcing his mother's death was late, had come on the second anniversary of the outbreak of war, which was also Swiss Union Day. One of those innumerable, chaotic Swiss festivals when bonfires were lit, skyrockets were let off, and guns fired from every mountaintop. They had sat together that evening looking at the bonfires, and paid their last respects to his mother to the sound of those salvos. It was probably easier like that, at a distance.

If you are both getting on fifty, and your mothers, yours and hers, both die, it makes you older still. And brings you closer. Besides, you are both revolutionaries. So that perhaps . . .

A motorboat was traveling diagonally across the

lake, from that very direction, from Sörenberg, tossing its prow as it swiftly plowed the water, leaving behind a triangular patch of foam, and shattering the silence with its metallic coughing.

There was something about it, as it sped on, cutting a swift furrow through the water, pointing its merciless beak, harshly chattering, which broke his train of thought, jolted his mind—and forgetting social analysis, forgetting logical argument, he suddenly saw very, very simply what he had never seen before.

If she stood for free love in theory, and could not be dissuaded, what reason was there to think that she did not practice it . . . ?

He had mentally reviewed, anticipated, and enumerated for her benefit every point that could be made about relations between bourgeois and proletarians, but he had overlooked just one little thing: if they had not seen each other since Kienthal—and they were so near —if for half a year she had neither come nor called him, and had now almost stopped writing—

perhaps this summer she had been with someone else?

Why had he invariably pictured her alone, and never imagined that it could be otherwise?

On this side of the lake there was still wan sunlight, but on the other side thick gray clouds were streaming over the Uetliberg, packing the valley with mist. The mountain, the lower slopes, the bell tower were quickly swathed, and the mist crept on toward the Zurich shore.

What could be simpler? And how was it that he had examined the question from every angle—except this?

No, it was impossible! His comrade and friend! After their glorious fight against the centrists at Kienthal!

He gripped the cold railing and felt like howling—

through the railing, across the lake, over the Uetliberg, over all the mountains between them. Inessa! Don't leave me! Inessa! ...

He must write, immediately, swallowing his pride, write anything so long as it brought an answer. Of course, the post office opened earlier than the library, why hadn't he thought of it before? It opened at eight: he should have gone there and written a letter. Now it was too late.

Yes, it was too late now. They were banging and clanging their bells like madmen, like idiots! As though every bit of old iron in the city was under repair. The bells of the Fraumünster clanged out over the post office, the double-belfried Grossmünster crashed out the hour up above the shop signs on every floor of Bellevue ... how many more churches there were in Zurich!

The mist and clouds had rolled over to his side of the lake and it was suddenly gray and cheerless.

He drew his watch from his vest pocket with numb fingers. If they were banging on their buckets, it must be nine o'clock. He hadn't been to the post office, he'd lost track of time, he'd come too far—however briskly he walked now, he would reach the cantonal library well after opening time. A bad start. And he had set out with such good intentions.

Very well. The letter must wait. He must work now.

He rolled along, a short, stocky figure, scarcely troubling to avoid those in his path. There, close by, was the city library. He could go there, but he had the journals and books for today's work on call at the cantonal. He hurried as fast as he could along the loathsome bourgeois embankment, where the smells of delicatessen and pastry wafted from doorways to tickle jaded appetites, where the shopkeepers had performed miracles of ingenuity to offer their customers a twenty-first version of sausage and a hundred and first variety of *pâtisserie*. Windows full of chocolates, smokers' supplies, dinner services, clocks, antiques flashed by . . . It was so difficult on this smart embankment to imagine a mob with axes and firebrands someday smashing all that plate glass to smithereens.

But—it must be done!

Everything here looked too solid and permanent —the houses, doors, doorbells, locks.

Yet—it must be done!

From every corner of the city came the clanging of bells, frenzied and hollow.

## 45

Here, too, Zwingli had swung his arm with almost proletarian boldness, setting a good example by bisecting the Prediger-Kirche midway between its spires. Half of it had been occupied for centuries by a library. It was a source of particular satisfaction that both the main libraries of Zurich had triumphed over religion.

He went into the hushed room. Nine windows with pointed arches rose to a height of five or six stories. At a still dizzier height, the ribs of the vaulted roof met in knots.

All this soaring space was entirely wasted, except for a two-storied wooden gallery attached to the walls. On the walls, between bookcases, hung many somber portraits—haughty municipal councilors and burgomasters in doublets and frilled shirts. He had never had time to look at them carefully, or read the inscriptions.

As he passed through the heavy doors, Lenin saw that his favorite place in the gallery, by the central window, and another which he found convenient, were both occupied. He was late. The day had begun awkwardly.

He signed the visitors' book, but the librarian with the glasses and the ex officio smile could not figure out what had become of one of his three piles on reserve.

These petty vexations, one on top of another, could rob him of hours of working time.

The success or failure of a working day may depend on trivial events at its outset. Now he had started late. There was less than half a day, only three hours in

81

fact, between opening time and the lunch break, and part of that was already wasted.

*Imperialism* had been drafted in full in twenty notebooks, written up, lost, and rewritten—but Lenin had taken out still another pile of materials on the same subject. He felt that something more was needed. Yet it was difficult to see what. He had all his findings clearly in mind long before he had filled his twenty notebooks. His foresight had become so acute of late that he knew remarkably early, before he sat down to write, what his conclusions would be.

Now it looked as though he must take out the sweetest blows in the whole book. Stinking, slimy, sanctimonious old creature! Nowhere, in the whole history of Social Democracy, had there been a more loathsome and despicable hypocrite.

The missing pile was on Persia. He had already started making précis. Nobody had thought about socialism's eastern front properly, and it needed study.

Never mind, his swipes at Kautsky would not go to waste—he would put them in somewhere else.

He was also drafting an important and detailed summary of policy for the Swiss leftists, so that they could systematically correct their failures at the congress. But this could be more conveniently done in the Center for Socialist Literature than here.

No, she had always helped, always translated for him. Any day now, she would leave the mountains for Clarens, and might come to him. Why imagine the worst? He had not been thinking straight.

He had arrived feeling he had left something undone, overlooked something, in his article against disarmament. He had finished it (it was there in his bag), but something nagged at the back of his mind. The main ideas were all there: disarmament is a counsel of despair; disarmament means renouncing any idea of revolution; those who look for socialism without revolution and dictatorship are no socialists; we will have women and children of thirteen and up fighting for us in the coming civil war. All true enough, but he still had the feeling that some statements were inadequately phrased. You must be super-cautious, never give your enemies a thing to quote against you. You must equip all dangerous sentences with defensive subsidiary clauses, make sure that every sentence is defended at all points, hedged with qualifications, carefully balanced, so that no one can find a vulnerable spot.

The article, then, could stand reexamination—and in fact he had already started. Here, for example, was something written in the heat of the moment: "We support the use of violence by the masses." They'd pounce on that! Tack something on: ". . . against their oppressors."

But, this was something he could do somewhere else, and time was going by.

He started looking over the theses for the Swiss leftists. Still a lot of work there. Everything had to be chewed up very small for them. House-to-house distribution of leaflets—to whom? To the poorest peasants and the farm laborers. Which collective plots are subject to forcible expropriation? Let's say those with over fifteen hectares. After what period of residence should foreigners qualify for Swiss citizenship? Let's say three months—and gratis, that's important. What is meant by "revolutionary rates of taxation"? Too general. Must compile a table showing concretely what percentage is to be paid on property over 20,000 francs, property over 50,000 francs, and so on. How should people in pensions be assessed? Draw up a precise scale for them, too—nobody ever seems to get down to practical details. A guest paying five francs a day is one of us—one percent is enough—but anyone paying ten francs should be charged twenty percent immediately.

His gorge rose as he thought of Grimm and

Greulich's latest dirty trick. Filthy opportunists, sneaking scoundrels—just wait, we'll have you in the pillory!

He seemed unable to escape these vexations and distractions. It's always the same: let them get out of hand and it's impossible to concentrate, to work methodically, or even to sit still.

Then there was that frantic and still unsettled argument with the "Japanese," which had wasted so much of his energy and was still interfering with his work. He had thought that after several articles and a couple of dozen letters the conflict was resolved, but it was still not dead!

He could never manage to concentrate all his efforts on a single major objective. He was forever discovering enemies in secondary sectors which might at present look quite unimportant; but no front was ever unimportant—at some future time these secondary fronts might be decisive. So you must furiously turn on those snapping at your flanks and show them your teeth. It wasn't just the "Japanese" (Piatakov and that Bosch woman of his, who had escaped from Siberia via Japan). Bukharin was siding with them, too. They, who hadn't an ounce of brains among them, had reduced themselves with Radek's assistance to a state of collective stupidity, to the ultimate in cretinism—if it wasn't "imperialist economics" it was the self-determination of nations, or democracy. These little piglets, this younger generation of party members, were so self-satisfied, so very sure of themselves, so ready to take over leadership at any moment, and yet they were thrown by every sharp turn, not one of them had the trained skill and flexibility to swerve instantly to left or right, anticipating every fall with which the tortuous road of revolution threatened them.

Take democracy. Bukharin undervalued it in a primitive, adolescent fashion. He wrote openly: "We shall have to dispense with democracy in the period of

the seizure of power." Not at all! *In a general way,*
socialist revolution was impossible without a struggle
for democracy, and the piglets should have their little
pink snouts rubbed in this truth. But, of course, it must
always be remembered that this was true only in a particular situation, in a certain sense, for a certain period.
A different time would come when democratic aims
*of any kind* would only be a *hindrance* to socialist revolution. (Double underlining here!) Suppose, for instance, when the battle is raging, when the revolution is
under way, we must s e i z e  t h e  b a n k s—and they
call on us to wait, to put the republic on a legal basis
first?

Lenin had explained it over and over again, in
letters many pages long, but they had turned up their
noses. He had taken so much time with these trouble-
makers and intriguers only because the "Japanese" had
money for a journal. *Kommunist* could not have been
started without their help. All the same, the alliance
made sense only as long as Lenin had a majority on the
editorial board. (Equality with such fools was unthink-
able. To hell with them! It would be idiocy, it would
ruin everything!) It was better to drag the fatheads
through the mud. You wouldn't accept a peaceful solution, so we'll bash your ugly faces in!

He had confined his argument with Bukharin to
letters, and had not let it come out into the open. But
he had been too furious to answer the letter Bukharin
had written before his departure. Now he had gone off
to America—probably he had taken offense.

To himself, Lenin acknowledged that Bukharin
was very clever. But his constant resistance was exasperating.

All opposition exasperated him—especially on
theoretical questions, where it implied a claim to leadership.

Radek was another matter, and it would be well

worth while to thrash the little shit as a lesson to the rest. Radek's lowest trick yet was to surreptitiously egg on the piglets while hiding behind the Zimmerwald left. (At Kienthal he had tried to make Lenin quarrel with the leftists, and had caused him to fall out with Rosa.) Radek's political behavior was that of a barefaced, impudent Tyszka-type mercenary—the only politics such snotty-nosed guttersnipes had ever known. After the way he had pushed Lenin and Zinoviev off the board of *Vorbote,* the only thing to do was punch him in the nose, or snub him. If you forgive this sort of thing in politics, people regard you as a fool or a scoundrel.

In the present case, the right thing was to snub him. Especially as there was no disagreement on general matters, only on Russo-Polish problems. Where Switzerland was concerned, Radek had no choice. Since he opposed Grimm, he was forced into alliance with Lenin—and what an ally he was!

Zinoviev, too, had acted like a scoundrel in this business of the "Japanese," and urged him to give in. They were all unstable. You couldn't even rely on those closest to you.

To put a stop to Bukharin's capers, it was necessary to carry the argument to Russia too, and finish off the "Japanese" on Russian soil. Shliapnikov had been ordered to do so. But Shliapnikov was another muddlehead, and his girl friend Kollontai was worse. (Incidentally, he mustn't forget that it would be a good idea to sneak her into the Scandinavian Conference of Neutrals, perhaps as interpreter to one of the delegates, and sniff out their plans!)

There were so many of them everywhere, these pseudo-socialist muddlers—in the warring countries, among the neutrals, in Russia. Was Trotsky any better, though, with his pious fatuities—"neither victors nor vanquished"? What nonsense. No, of course he was seeking cheap popularity—but let's see to it that Tsarism is nevertheless vanquished, don't let it wriggle out of the present free-for-all! You can't be "against all wars" and remain a socialist.

Where Shliapnikov was right now, he didn't know. Still in Stockholm? Or had he already gone to Russia? Letters reached Sweden through Kesküla and his people as occasion offered—but did they get any farther? There was nobody with any sense there, no system. There was no end to Shliapnikov's delays, he went to Russia only rarely, and once there, always stayed too long, the sluggard. If you said anything to him, he took offense. And if he didn't go, there was nobody else. So, to make him look important, they had had to co-opt him to the Central Committee.

At this point the librarian came up to Lenin's desk, and with a whispered apology, and an apologetic bow, placed the pile of materials on Persia before him.

Many thanks. Half an hour or so to the lunch break, and along comes Persia! Should he make a start, or not?

Of course, Shliapnikov was not yet ripe for membership on the Central Committee, he lacked Malinovsky's maturity. But he had taken Malinovsky's place, and the titles "member of the C.C.," "chairman of the Russia Bureau" had turned his head, given him a taste for power. First he was shouldering Litvinov aside to get in on talks with foreign socialists, then he started giving idiotic advice in practically every letter he wrote: "Why don't you move to Sweden?" He was sickeningly sure of himself, but he couldn't be cut adrift, he was doing a serious job, and he had to be answered, formally at least, with respect.

Somehow he couldn't settle down to his work. His brain was in too much of a whirl. He couldn't concentrate, couldn't adjust to the leisurely movement of Persia's feudal economy.

Malinovsky, Malinovsky! The Russian Bebel

manqué. How he could work! How well he handled the masses! What a remarkable type, what a personality! A natural leader of workingmen, a collective symbol of the Russian proletariat. Lenin had long felt the lack of such a working-class leader in the party, at his right hand, to complement him, to convert his ideas into mass action. What Lenin particularly liked in him was that he molded himself to his allotted place, carried out orders with alacrity and without demur—but brilliantly and effectively. He had what is known in bourgeois terms as a criminal record, a few thefts, but this only set off his proletarian intolerance of private property and the colorfulness of his character. So that, when excessively suspicious comrades began casting aspersions, Lenin's confidence in him grew stronger all the time. Imagine him as a provocateur? Impossible! (And it was still impossible.) After his inflammatory speeches in the Duma, and his skillful management of the split between Bolsheviks and Mensheviks in the Duma group, Lenin not only had been glad to introduce Malinovsky into the Central Committee himself but brought in others solely on the strength of Malinovsky's recommendation —Stalin, for instance. When they were living in Poronin, no guest from Russia was more welcome than Malinovsky. Except on that last, dreadful night in May, when he had appeared unexpectedly after his sudden and unauthorized withdrawal from the Duma. But still, he had put in an appearance and not run away. Would he have dared to do so if his hands were not clean? . . . Their discussion had gone on all night. It was in any case impossible to *prove* anything against Malinovsky. (And what good could it do?) Who could believe the stupid tale that the secret police themselves had found it "embarrassing" that one of their informers was among the best orators in the Duma and had ordered him to withdraw? What rot. Were the secret police stupid enough to work against themselves? He,

Kuba, and Grishka had constituted themselves a sort of party tribunal, found Roman Malinovsky not guilty, and vouched for his innocence before the International Socialist Bureau.

Nonetheless, they had quietly parted company for the time being. For personal reasons.

Lenin would never have another such helper! . . . Shliapnikov? No, no.

Now the lunch break was upon him. How on earth did these Swiss manage to work up an appetite for lunch by twelve o'clock?

However, Lenin had noticed that the librarian on duty today did not always go to lunch. He went over and inquired. No, he wasn't going. Was it at all possible to stay through the lunch break? It was.

Here was a bit of luck. Lunch wasn't worth the disturbance it would involve. It was easier to work on an empty stomach. And he would gain time.

He needn't hurry now. The best thing, in fact, would be to stock up with newspapers right away. To save money, Lenin never bought them, never took out subscriptions, though he needed to read thirty or forty of them—all the various *Arbeiters* and *Stimmes*.

He collected all there were and carried them to his desk.

Reading the papers was one of his most important daily tasks, his access to the outside world. Reading the papers heightened his sense of responsibility, his firmness of purpose, his militancy, helped him to feel that his enemies were alive and real. Socialists, social patriots, and centrists from every spot on the face of the earth, not to mention all the bourgeois donkeys, seemed to crowd around you in the reading room, gesturing, babbling, all speaking loudly at once, and you seized your opportunity to strike back, to note their weak points, and hit out at them. Reading the papers meant making abstracts at the same time. By analogy, by association, by contradiction, sparks of thought were continually struck off, flying at a tangent to left or right, onto scraps of paper, onto the lined pages of notebooks, into blank margins, and every thought must be stitched to paper with a fiery thread before it could fade, to smolder there until it was wanted, in an abstract or else in a letter begun right then so that he could forge his sentences red-hot. Some of these thoughts were intended to clear his own mind, others for use in arguments, to sting or to stun, others as a more effective rehash of things which the stupid found difficult; others still to keep distant comrades, perhaps as far away as Russia, attuned to his theories.

Vandervelde and Branting, Huysmans and Jouhaux, Plekhanov and Potresov, Ledebour and Haase, Bauer and Bernstein, the two Adlers, even Pannekoek and Roland-Holst—Lenin felt as though all these exasperating opponents were close enough to touch. No matter where their nests were, in Holland, England, France, Scandinavia, Austria, or Petersburg—he felt them to be within sight, within hearing, he was connected with all of them in a single complex of throbbing nerves—asleep or awake, at his books, at the table, or out walking.

There were no readers left. Evidently the lunch break had begun. The librarian went through a glass door into the depths of the bookstacks. All the desk lamps were extinguished and the reading room was lost in the soaring dimness, the tomblike silence of the church it once was. Taking advantage of this rare opportunity to discharge his excess nervous tension, Lenin began briskly pacing the longest straight walk in the building, the central aisle from the entrance under the wooden gallery to the two long transverse steps before what had once been the altar. A distance of fifty paces unobstructed by bookshelves or desks.

He was used to walking in city streets, or in the

mountains, and he had always lived in dark little places with no room to move around. Now, pacing faster and faster, with his hunter's stride, brushing aside the Hilferdings, Martovs, Greulichs, Longuets, Pressemanes, and Chkheidzes, abruptly choking them off in midsentence, pulling them up short, routing them—in this frenzied pendulum-like oscillation he beat off wave after wave of enemies.

He was liberating himself from his enemies.

And he felt more and more ready for methodical work.

And then, halfway along the aisle, he suddenly felt that it was enough.

And sat down to work.

He had been wrong to think like that about Inessa. He had nothing at all to go on.

No! He had been sitting at the wrong desk. Now he would have to move everything—books, newspapers, notebooks—into the gallery, to his usual desk. He had to make two journeys.

The steps creaked slightly in the gray Gothic hush.

And suddenly he felt very weary. He almost collapsed onto his chair.

His head was . . .

Although he had missed lunch, he did not feel at all hungry. He could make do with very little food: he generated energy almost without eating.

Right by the window, without lamplight for the time being. But it was a gloomy day.

He started reading the newspapers. He read about the general military situation. There was nothing there to cheer him.

Not so bad, of course, as in August, at that terrible moment when a still fresh Roumania had suddenly joined in, enormously reinforcing her allies, and it had seemed that Russia would extricate herself after all. But Germany had proved strong enough to smash Roumania almost effortlessly. It was astonishing—no one could have prophesied it two months earlier. Nevertheless, and contrary to all predictions, Germany was not winning the war in Europe. On the Western Front there was an unbreakable and hopeless impasse. On the Eastern Front, too—and this was the greatest shock—1916 had brought no victory. A year ago, Tsarism had been close to collapse, was *already* shaken to its foundations, yet now it was on its feet again and holding its own. The greatest hope, the greatest victory, had ebbed, seeped away, vanished.

In one corner of his head, just in that one tiny spot near his left temple, it was as though a vacuum had formed. That was bad. He had let himself get too excited.

In no country did it seem that even the third year of this bloody war had awakened the people to reality. The Russians as always were the most hopeless of all. It was they who were bearing the most extravagant losses, they whose stacked bodies barred the way to German efficiency and German technology. Reporting on the Eastern Front was generally vague and inaccurate, there were no war correspondents there, people knew and cared little about it, and of course the press in the Entente countries tried not to say much about an ally it was ashamed of. But the newspapers often gave figures of Russian casualties. Lenin always looked for these figures and made a nail mark by them—with surprise and satisfaction. The bigger the figures, the happier they made him: all these soldiers killed, wounded, or taken prisoner were stakes falling out of absolutism's fence, leaving the monarchy weaker. But at the same time these figures drove him to despair: no people on earth were so long-suffering and so devoid of sense as the Russians. Their patience knew no bounds. Any abomination, any filth dished out to them they would lap up with nothing but reverent gratitude toward their beloved benefactor.

Should he put the lights on after all? The words seemed to swim before his eyes.

This damp Russian firewood refused to catch fire! The best blazes were all ancient history—the salt riots, the cholera riots, the copper-coin riots, the Razin rebellion, the Pugachev rebellion. Except perhaps to seize the estate of a neighboring landowner, which was there before their eyes, neither proletariat nor professional revolutionaries would ever set the dark peasant mass in motion. Corrupted and emasculated by Orthodoxy, the peasants seemed to have lost their passion for the ax and the torch. If a people could endure such a war without rebelling, what could be done with it?

The game was lost. There would be no revolution in Russia.

He covered his eyes with his hands and sat still.

Whether from tiredness or from depression, something seemed to have sagged inside him.

The readers were reassembling. Chairs were moved. A book fell. Lamps were turned on.

There might be worse to come. Was Tsarism already wriggling out of the trap? By making a s e p a r a t e  p e a c e ? ? (Treble underlining.) And what else could Germany do, when she couldn't win a war on two fronts?

That was really frightening. The worst thing possible. All would be lost. The world revolution. Revolution in Russia. Lenin's whole life, two decades of ceaseless effort.

A report that a separate peace was in the making, that secret negotiations between Germany and Russia had already *officially* begun, and that the two powers were agreed on the main points, had recently been published by Grimm in the *Berner Tagwacht*. It was signed

K.R. Without asking the rascally Radek, you could safely guess that it was he. (But how had he managed to persuade Grimm?!) And if you knew his gift for sparkling improvisation, you could safely assume that he had not eavesdropped on diplomats, sneaked a look at secret documents, or even picked up a stray rumor, but that as he idled away the morning in bed, with newspapers over and under the blankets and books on the floor, he occasionally composed such items "from our own correspondent" in Norway or Argentina.

What mattered was not where this *particular report* had originated. Or that the Russian ambassador in Bern had denied it—what else could he do? . . . What did matter was that it had the piercing ring of truth: for the Tsar this r e a l l y   w a s   t h e   r i g h t   w a y   o u t! Just what he should do. Just what Lenin would do in his place.

So they must strike and strike again at this weak point. Raise the alarm. Put a stop to it. Forestall him. Not let him wrest his feet out of the trap untouched.

Of course, you could expect only utter stupidity from Nicholas II and his government. You wouldn't have expected them to start this war if they had any sense at all. But they did start it—and what a wonderful gift they've given us!

So perhaps it was still possible to frighten them with publicity and avert the danger?

A separate peace! It would of course be a remarkably neat way out. But still, they weren't clever enough for it.

In any case, there was nothing to be done in Russia for the present. Nobody there read the *Sozialdemokrat*. All eyes were on the Miliukovs and Shingarevs. All anyone ever heard of was the Kadets. And just look how their delegation had been received in the West. The Tsar might take it into his head to move over a little, let Guchkov and the Kadets have ministries—

and then you'd never get them, never break through.

How could you knead sad Russian dough into any sort of shape! Why was he born in that uncouth country? Just because a quarter of his blood was Russian, fate had hitched him to the ramshackle Russian rattle-trap. A quarter of his blood, but nothing in his character, his will, his inclinations made him kin to that slovenly, slapdash, eternally drunken country. Lenin knew of nothing more revolting than back-slapping Russian hearties, tearful tavern penitents, self-styled geniuses bewailing their ruined lives. Lenin was a bowstring, or an arrow from the bow. Lenin could size up a situation, and the best or only means to an end, at half a glance. What, then, tied him to that country? With a little more work he could have mastered three European languages, as he had mastered that semi-Tatar tongue. He was tied, you say, to Russia by twenty years as a practicing revolutionary? Yes, but by nothing else. Now, after the creation of the Zimmerwald left, he was sufficiently well known in international socialist circles to cross over. Socialism made no distinctions of nationality. Trotsky, for instance, had left for America. He had made the right choice. Bukharin was on his way there. Perhaps that was the place to go.

No, there was something wrong with him today. The day had started wrong and had never got going right. It was as though the working of his mind was too fast for his body, his physical frame, his breast. And there was that little pocket of emptiness near his left temple. He felt hollow with fatigue, and the tissues of his body seemed to sag around the cavity within him.

Too much had happened at once, and he suddenly felt that he would not get through a good day's work, but would roll on downhill, enervated, ineffectual, dejected.

A true politician is not at the mercy of his years,

his feelings, circumstances, but brings to bear at all seasons and times of day an unvarying mechanical efficiency in his actions, his speeches, his battles. Lenin, too, was an excellent, smooth-functioning machine, with inexhaustible drive, but even he experienced one or two days in a year when his drive slackened, leaving him despondent, exhausted, prostrate. On such a day there was nothing to do but go to bed early and sleep soundly.

Lenin might seem completely in control of his mind and his will, but even he was helpless against these attacks of despair. His certainties, his firm perspective, his proven tactics would suddenly become blurred, indistinct, elusive. The world would turn its stupid gray backside on him.

And the disease which sat inside him, ever watchful, would suddenly make its sharp corners felt, like a stone in a sack.

He felt it in his temple.

Yes, he had always followed the path of refusal to compromise, to smooth over differences, and by doing so had created a conquering force. He had a prophetic certainty that it would conquer. That it was important to preserve a strictly centralized group, no matter how small, no matter who its members. The conciliation and unification movements had long ago shown that they spelled ruin for a workers' party. Reconciliation with disarmers? Reconciliation with the *Nashe Slovo* gang? Reconciliation with the Russian Kautskyites? With the swine in the Menshevik Organizing Committee? Become a flunky to social chauvinists? Embrace the village idiots of socialism? No, to hell with that! Give him a tiny minority which was firm, sure, his own!

However, he had gradually found himself almost isolated—betrayed and deserted—while all manner of unifiers and disarmers, liquidators and defensists, chauvinists and anti-statists, trashy scribblers and mangy timeserving petit-bourgeois riffraff had gathered elsewhere in a tight group. Sometimes he was reduced to such a small minority that nobody at all remained at his side, as in 1908, the year of loneliness and misery after all his defeats, and most dreadful, the hardest year of his life—also spent in Switzerland. The intellectuals had abandoned the Bolshevik ranks in a panic: so much the better, at least the party was rid of that petit-bourgeois scum. Among those foul, caricature intellectuals Lenin had felt particularly humiliated, insignificant, lost. It filled him with despair to feel himself sinking into their mire. It would have been idiotic to become like them. In every gesture, every word, every oath even, he was determined not to resemble them! . . . But soon it looked as though there would be no one left at all. It reached the point where he was desperately clinging to his last ten or fifteen supporters! And simply in order to capture fifteen Bolsheviks, and to deny them to the Machists, he had dashed off to London for materials and written a philosophical work three hundred pages long, which no one had ever read, but he had discredited Bogdanov and dislodged him from the leadership! Then throughout the damp autumn those endless chilly walks by Lake Geneva, endlessly assuring themselves that they were not downhearted, and were on the road to victory.

Even with the cleverest of them, like Trotsky and Bukharin, he could find no common language. He could never be sure of the few who stayed near for more than a month ahead—Zinoviev, for instance, with his weak nerves and his precarious beliefs. (Grishka really had no beliefs at all.)

So that no "conquering force" had been created after all. His whole career, twenty-three years of uninterrupted militant campaigning against political stupidity, vulgarity, opportunism, his whole grim life under a constant hail of hatred, had brought him—what?

Only isolation. The force of inertia carried him on along the same line—splitting with one, branding another. disassociating himself from a third, but he warily realized that he was in a rut, that he could no longer look forward to real success.

The loneliness.

If only there was someone to tell, someone to share it with, so that he would hear his own voice.

What a day . . . Everything had come to pieces in his hands. He had sat away the hours to no purpose.

Piles of books. Piles of newspapers . . . The reams, stacks, pillars of paper he had read, scanned, written in his years as an émigré.

When he was young, the scent of imminent revolution was fresh in the air. The path to it seemed simple and short. He told everyone, again and again, that "the universal belief in revolution is in itself the beginning of revolution"! A time of happy expectancy.

But these last ten years, since his second emigration, had been filled, stuffed, packed tight with—what? Nothing but paper—envelopes, packets, newspaper wrappers, routine letters, express letters. So much time went on correspondence alone (not to mention the cost of postage, but that came from party funds). Almost his whole life, half of every day, went into these endless letters. Nobody lived near him, his sympathizers were scattered to the four corners of the earth, and from a distance he had to keep their loyalty, rally, direct, advise, interrogate, beg, and thank them, coordinate resolutions (all this with his friends, at the same time never interrupting for a moment the fierce struggle with his enemies), and nothing was ever more urgent and important than the letter of the moment (though tomorrow it might seem trivial, and too late, and anyway wrong). You exchanged articles in outline, proofs, criticisms, corrections, reviews, abstracts, points for discussion, excerpts from the press, newspapers by the cartload, sometimes issues of your own journals, which never got beyond the first few numbers—and all the time you felt that none of it was serious, you couldn't believe, couldn't imagine, that a social movement could force its way up through the mounds of paper and newspaper wrappers littering the earth, to the cherished goal of state power—where you would need qualities quite different from those required during your dozen years in reading rooms.

He was nearing the end of his forty-seventh year, in an anxious, monotonous life of nothing but ink on paper, enmities and alliances, quarrels and agreements that sprang up and faded in a day or a week, all extremely important, all requiring enormous tact and skill, and always with politicians so much inferior to himself, all of it water into a bottomless bucket, instantly lost and forgotten, labor in vain. In a life of constant agitation, twisting and turning, his whole achievement was to fight his way into an impassable rubbish heap.

His arms dangled limply, his back would not straighten, he felt utterly played out.

While his disease grew heavier, fitfully stirring and nagging inside him. It made not a sound, entered into no disputes, but no opponent was more powerful.

An evil which now would never leave him.

His vocation—he knew no other—was to change the course of history, and fulfillment had been denied him.

All his incomparable abilities (appreciated now by everyone in the party, but he set a truer and still higher value on them), all his quick-wittedness, his penetration, his grasp, his uselessly clear understanding of world events, had failed to bring him not only political victory but even the position of a member of Parliament in toyland, like Grimm. Or that of a successful lawyer (though he would hate to be a lawyer—he had lost every case in Samara). Or even that of a journalist.

Just because he had been born in accursed Russia.

It was his habit to carry out even the most laborious and thankless tasks conscientiously, and he was still trying to draft his detailed theses for the education of the Swiss left Zimmerwaldists. On the cost of living, on the intolerable economic position of the masses. What should be the maximum salary for office workers and bureaucrats. What to watch for in the party press. How to rid the party of Rütlian reformists . . .

It was no good. His work would not take shape. The heart had gone out of his routine and left a hollow. His head was beginning to ache. Breathing was difficult. The very sight of his papers sickened him. By tomorrow morning the attack would be over, but at present he felt such a loathing for everything that he could have lain down and died.

Guiltily deciding not to sit through the working day (not that there was much of it left), he bundled the notebooks and manuscripts into his shopping bag as best he could, slammed the books shut and stacked them, made a neat bundle of the newspapers, put some things on their shelves and took the rest back to the librarian, treading carefully on the steps so as not to come crashing down with his great load.

At the door he pulled on his heavy overcoat, carelessly crammed on his bowler hat, and shuffled off.

Walking the same route, day in and day out, gave neither legs nor eyes enough to do: it had become automatic.

It was beginning to get dark, and there was some mist, too. Electric lights were already lit in the windows of shops and restaurants.

A huge barrel was being rolled along the narrow

side street, and behind it came a wheelbarrow. There was no way around them.

It would be easy, very easy, never to escape from this cramped, apathetic, petit-bourgeois Switzerland, but to end his days here with the Skittle Club.

Through the window of a food shop he could see a nickel-plated machine rhythmically cutting an appetizing ham into even slices. The grocer, looking as smug as all Swiss, came out on the threshold of his establishment and—whether he knew them or not—presented a *"Grötzi"* free of charge to one passer-by after another. In the third year of war the shops still importunately flaunted their plenty, though prices had risen by leaps and bounds because of the submarines. The bourgeois could still pick and choose.

Luckily, it was too cold to put café tables out on the sidewalk, or they would be sitting, lounging, sprawling there, goggling at the passers-by, making you step around them with a curse. Throughout all his years as an émigré Lenin had hated cafés, those smoke-filled dens of logorrhea, where nine tenths of the compulsive revolutionary windbags were in permanent session. During the war, Zurich had drawn in another dubious crowd from its belligerent neighbors. It was because of them that rents had gone up—this mob of adventurers, shady businessmen, profiteers, draft-dodging students, and chattering intellectuals, with their philosophical manifestos and artistic demonstrations, in revolt against they knew not what. And they were all there—in the cafés.

America was no doubt just as prosperous. The upper stratum of the working class everywhere would sooner get rich than make a revolution. No one, either here or there, needed his dynamite, the sweep of his ax.

He who was capable of taking the world apart, of blowing it up, and then rebuilding it, he had been born too soon, born merely to be a torment to himself.

At its mid-point the Spiegelgasse rose in a hump, riding over a little hill of its own. Leaving home, wherever bound, he half ran down. Coming back, wherever he had been, he faced a steep hill. If he had got into his stride, or was in a good humor, he thought nothing of it. But now he could scarcely drag himself along. He seemed not to be walking but scraping the ground with his feet.

The steep, narrow staircase of the old house held the smells of many years. It was dark now, the lamps had not been lit, and he had to tread cautiously.

Third floor. A polyglot babble, the oppressive smells of the apartment.

His room was like a prison cell for two. Two beds, a table, chairs. An iron stove, with its pipe running through the wall, no fire in it (although it was getting cold enough). An upturned crate that had once held books served as a dresser. (Because they were forever on the move, they bought no furniture.)

In the last rays of daylight, Nadya was still writing at the table. She turned around. She was surprised.

But her eyes were used to the poor light, and when she saw his yellow-gray face, his fixed dead gaze, saw him looking sixty, she did not ask why he was so early.

She had some experience with these attacks, which could prostrate him for days or sometimes for weeks— when he was burned out with excitement, or the strain of battle was too much even for his iron body. He had suffered nervous attacks of this kind after 1903, again after *One Step Forward, Two Steps Back,* and more than once after the Fifth Congress.

The bowler hat weighed heavy on his head, the overcoat on his shoulders. It was a struggle to rid himself of them . . . Nadya helped him . . . He dragged his feet and the shopping bag of books across the room.

He found strength to look at what Nadya had been writing and raised it to his eyes. Their accounts.

A depressingly long column of figures.

Though 1908 had been gloomy and lonely, they had been rolling in money after the Tiflis expropriation. They had an account with the Crédit Lyonnais. To escape from their misery, they went to concerts in the evenings, had a holiday in Nice, traveled, lived in hotels, took cabs, rented a Paris apartment, with a mirror over the fireplace, for a thousand francs.

He sat down on the bed.

Sat, slumped, shrank. His body sank into the mattress, his head sank onto his shoulders, his neck disappeared: his chin rested on his chest, the back of his head on his spine.

With one hand he held on to the edge of the table in front of him.

One eye was half closed. His mouth was half open. A tough untidy stubble bristled on his upper lip. The flattened tip of his nose was thrust forward.

He sat like that for one minute, two, three.

"Do you want to lie down? Get undressed?" Nadya asked in her soft, toneless voice.

He was silent.

"Why didn't you come to lunch? Were you working too hard?"

He nodded, with an effort.

"Will you eat now?" But her voice held no promise of carnivorous delights. She had never learned to cook.

How different from Shushenskoye! Where there was always fire in the stove, pots on it, a roast in the oven (a whole sheep was one week's meat), barrels of pickles, snipe, blackcocks, you could bathe in milk if you felt like it. And everything was washed sparkling clean by a little servant girl.

His dome was completely bald now. He had kept

only his back hair, and that was thinning (They themselves had made things worse in 1902: they had begrudged the money for a good doctor, and a half-trained Russian medical student prescribed iodine for a rash on his head, which caused his hair to fall out.)

Nadya came closer. Gently, timidly stroked his head.

Several long, deep lines furrowed his brow from temple to temple.

Ilyich sighed loudly, jerkily—more like a man pulling a heavy load than a desk-bound intellectual. Without raising his submerged head, looking not at his wife but straight ahead, over the table, he said wearily, oh so wearily: "When the war ends, we'll go to America."

She couldn't believe her ears.

"But what about the Zimmerwald left? The new International?" She stood there, forlorn and frumpish.

Ilyich sighed, and answered in a hoarse, flat, weak voice. "It's obvious which way things are going in Russia. The Tsar will make a deal with the Kadets, and they will form a government. Then we will have twenty or thirty years of boring, vulgar, bourgeois evolution. With no hope at all for revolutionaries. We won't live to see the day."

Very well, then. They would go. She stroked the thin hair on the back of his head.

Suddenly the landlady knocked at the door. Someone had come to see them.

This was all they needed. Whoever it was had chosen a fine time! Without even asking, Nadya went to send the visitor away.

She came back looking bewildered. "Volodya! It's Sklarz! From Berlin . . ."

# [47]

To establish regular secret contact with anyone you please, without ever meeting face to face, you need only set up a chain of regular intermediaries—at least two, but preferably three. Your immediate contact habitually meets twenty people besides yourself, only one of whom is the next link in the chain, and each of these meets twenty others. This gives four hundred possible combinations, and no secret police, no Burtsev, can ever investigate them all.

The ultra-cautious Lenin had several such lines of communication.

The previous summer, after meeting Parvus in Bern, Lenin had released Hanecki to join him in Scandinavia, as director of his agency for trade and revolution. Thus the tirelessly questing Hanecki was able to display his commercial talents, while a direct and ever-warm line of communication was open to Parvus. However, the line between Copenhagen and Zurich was down, so they had chosen a new intermediary—Sklarz, a Berlin businessman, who also had shares in Parvus's agency and could travel freely both to Denmark and to Switzerland. They had, however, agreed that when he came to Zurich he should follow the rule about intermediate links, and not meet Lenin personally but use Bronski's lady friend, Dora Dolina, as his go-between. The fact that he had come to Lenin's lodgings in person meant either a breach of conspiratorial discipline or that something extraordinarily important had happened.

How untimely it was, though! Lenin was exhausted, he could not think clearly, his heartbeat was irregular. But since he had come, since he had been seen in the street, on the stairs, at the door, it was too late to turn him away.

To greet Sklarz, he not only had to rise from the bed but with his enfeebled legs had to project his hollow body upward from the bottom of a well. And only then, with his head thrust forward, could he see the energetic little Jew from the southwest.

Very conscious of his own importance he was too, more expensively dressed than ever: that overcoat, that hat (he had placed it on the one and only desk-*cum*-dining-table, but still there was nowhere else); and he was holding a light commercial traveler's case of crocodile skin or maybe hippopotamus hide.

At least he refrained from the ritual German *"Wie geht's?"* and the forced how-nice-to-see-you smile. He gave a businesslike bow and extended his small hand with dignity. He looked around to see that it was safe, that there were no witnesses. Nadya had gone out, and they were alone.

Why, though, had he come straight there and in person?

Here it came. From a deep inner pocket he produced an envelope.

Expensive pale-green paper, with an embossed crest. A fat envelope, obese.

How shamelessly Parvus displayed his wealth even in little things! This envelope, for instance. And on his visits to Zurich he stayed at the most expensive hotel, Bauer au Lac. In Bern he had ambled about a cheap student canteen (dinner, 65 rappen) in search of Lenin, puffing the most expensive of cigars.

To think that this was the man he had started *Iskra* with in Munich long ago.

All right, he had a letter. But why couldn't he have sent it with Dora? These fleeting visits had to be explained to *comrades*.

Sklarz was surprised to find Mr. Ulyanov so ill educated. That was no way to do *business*. He had been told to destroy the letter before leaving.

His fingers went through the motions of striking a match and holding it to the envelope.

Tell me something I don't know! What do you think *we* do? The letters we've burned in our time! . . .

Right, let's read it. A familiar situation for anyone in the underground. Lenin, too, would have to insure that his reply, once read, was not preserved. One such scrap of paper could destroy a whole political career.

Neither knife nor scissors handy. The table was bare. And Nadya was in the kitchen. Tearing off one corner, Lenin inserted his thick index finger and used it as a paper knife. Like a dog's teeth it left jagged edges on both sides of the tear. So much for you and your blasted money! How much pleasanter to handle the cheapest of envelopes, to write on the cheapest paper.

He took out the letter. That's why it was so fat, because the paper was even thicker and more opulent than the envelope. And the letter was written in bold capitals, with wide spaces between the lines, and on one side only. Now here was the way not to do *business*. Parvus had forgotten how they used to send *Iskra* into Russia on super-thin paper.

Careful. He must pull himself together, clear his mind. (He had eaten nothing since breakfast.) Must examine it thoroughly.

Sklarz made himself unobtrusive. He was not troublesomely familiar. Without superfluous talk, without even removing his coat, he went over to the other chair, by the window. Leaving, however, his soft gray hat, with its elegantly dented crown, on the table.

His case, too, he did not carry over to the window but put down on the floor in the middle of the room.

Polite of him, of course, but on an overcast day the best place for reading was over by the window. Sklarz had already occupied the other chair, however, taken a crumpled picture magazine out of his pocket and solemnly unfolded it.

Should he light the lamp? No matches in sight. And Nadya was in the kitchen.

Oh—the lamp was already lit! It was half hidden by the hat, and its wick was turned down low. Had Nadya lit it? He didn't remember her doing so. Perhaps Sklarz really had struck a match? Could he have . . . ? Strange.

Thick vellum, crested. Three sheets of writing, altogether. And a fourth, bare except for one line.

There was nothing special about Parvus's handwriting; it was not noticeably hostile, or imperious, or impertinent, and his signature, "Dr. Helphand," was unrevealing.

But Parvus's hippopotamus blood spurted from the letter into Lenin's feverish hands, poured into his veins, swirled threateningly in his bloodstream. To prevent it from rising above his elbows, Lenin dropped the letter on the table as though it were heavy. And flopped down helplessly in his chair.

In twenty years of life and struggle, Lenin had experienced every kind of opponent—the haughtily ironical, the sarcastic, the sly, the base, the obstinate, the stalwart, not to mention the spluttering-rhetorical, the quixotic, the effete, the slow-witted, the lachrymose, and other miscellaneous shits. With some of them he had wrestled for many years, and not all of them had he overcome, flattened with one blow, but he had always been aware of the immeasurable superiority given him by his clear view of the situation, his firm grip, his ability sooner or later to down any of them.

With this man alone he felt unsure of himself. He did not know whether he could stand up to Parvus as an enemy.

But there had scarcely been a day of enmity between them. He was Lenin's natural ally, had offered an alliance many times in his life, insistently, importunately, last year in particular, and now of course was doing it again.

But alliance with Parvus was something Lenin had hardly ever been able to accept.

He read. His eyes moved along the lines, but somehow his head would not take in the meaning. He was too unwell.

Lenin knew the key to every Social Democrat in the world, knew the shelf to put him on. But Parvus would not open, would not be put anywhere, and he stood across Lenin's path. Parvus did not fit into any classification. He had never joined either Bolsheviks or Mensheviks (had even naïvely attempted to reconcile them). He was a Russian revolutionary, but at nineteen he had come here to Switzerland from Odessa, and immediately chosen the Western way, decided to become a Western socialist and never return to Russia. He had said jokingly: "I'm looking for a homeland which doesn't cost too much." All the same, he hadn't found himself a cheap one, but had knocked around Europe for twenty-five years like the Wandering Jew, never acquiring citizenship. It was only this year that he had finally become a German subject—but at too high a price.

His eyes happened to fall on Sklarz's case. It was heavy, so tightly packed. How did he lug it around? He was so small himself. Why did he need it?

Ah, that was why he didn't seem to be able to read—there wasn't enough light. He moved the lamp right up to the letter.

Two points at the end were clear enough. Both complaints. One against Bukharin and Piatakov for their overzealous investigation of the German network in Sweden: these silly little boys must not be allowed to get out of hand. The other against Shliapnikov: he is

willful, refuses to collaborate, goes his own way
though unity is essential to our forces in Petersburg.
Write and tell him not to rebuff our representatives.

He called himself Parvus—"small"—but was in-
disputably big. He had become one of the outstanding
publicists in the German Social Democratic movement.
His capacity for work was no less than Lenin's. He had
written brilliant Marxist articles which had delighted
Bebel, Kautsky, Liebknecht, Rosa, and Lenin himself
(how he had lambasted Bernstein!), and had brought
the young Trotsky under his sway. Then he had suddenly abandoned his newspapers, and the position he
had won for himself in the journalistic world, and fled,
first to peddle Gorky's plays (and of course rob him),
then to sink out of sight altogether. His vision was
keen and far-reaching. He had been the first, back in
the nineteenth century, to fight for the eight-hour day.
The first to hail the general strike as the chief means of
struggle for the proletariat. But it could hardly be said
that any proposal of his had started a movement, won
him followers: instead of organizing them, he would
detach himself and drop out after a while. He had to
be first, and alone, on the road he followed.

Lenin had now read the letter right through, without even noticing whether it was written in Russian or
in German. It alternated between the two from sentence
to sentence. There were spelling mistakes in the Russian.

Parvus was full of contradictions. A desperate revolutionary whose hand would not tremble in the act of
overthrowing an empire; and a passionate trader
whose hand trembled as it counted out money. At one
time he went around in torn shoes and shiny trousers,
but back in Munich in 1901 he was forever dinning into
Lenin the need to get rich, the immense power of money. Earlier still, in Odessa, while Alexander III was
still on the throne, he had come to the conclusion that

the liberation of the Jews in Russia was impossible unless Tsardom was overthrown—and immediately lost all interest in Russian affairs, left for the West, returning clandestinely only once, as the companion of a doctor specializing in the study of famine, after which he had published *Starving Russia: A Traveler's Impressions*. Then he seemed to have immersed himself completely in German Social Democracy. But at the very beginning of the Japanese war, which was almost ignored in Geneva émigré circles, Parvus had been the first to declare it "the bloody dawn of great events."

There was not enough light. He kept screwing up the wick, but it only smoldered and smoked. Of course, the lamp was empty, she'd forgotten to put kerosene in it.

There and then, in 1904, Parvus had prophesied that the industrial states would come to a *world* war. Parvus invariably leaped, or rather, with his unwieldy bulk, stepped forward to prophesy earlier, and further into the future, than anyone else. Sometimes his predictions were very accurate, as, for instance, that industry would do away with national boundaries. Or that, in the future, revolution would be the inseparable companion of war, and world revolution of world war. He had, in essence, said before Lenin all that there was to be said about imperialism. Sometimes, though, he talked the wildest nonsense: about Europe as a whole declining and getting caught in a vise between America and Russia; about Russia needing only schools and freedom to become a second America. Another time, showing scant respect for the central tenets of Marxism, he had suggested that private industry should not be nationalized, because it might prove unprofitable. Then there was his grotesque fantasy about the possibility of a socialist party winning power only to turn it against the majority of the people and suppress the trade unions. But, right or wrong, his massive, elephantine figure always moved to a position so distinctive that he half blocked the Social Democratic horizon: though he had never wholly blocked the true path, he had always been so much in Lenin's way that there was no passing him without collision. Never an opponent, always an ally, but one who, if you were not careful, might crush your ribs. He was, uniquely, incomparably, Lenin's rival—and more often than not, successful, always ahead. In no way his enemy, always extending the hand of an ally—which it was quite impossible to take.

What did Sklarz want with that case? It looked as big as a boar.

Things might have gone very differently between them but for 1905. Lenin had taken no part at all in the 1905 Revolution, done absolutely nothing—entirely because of Parvus: Parvus with his heavy and unerring tread, never straying for a moment, had filled the road ahead, and robbed Lenin of the will to go forward, of all initiative. At the first thunderclap of Bloody Sunday, Parvus had made his proclamation: S e t  u p  a  w o r k e r s ' g o v e r n m e n t ! His quick-sightedness, his impetuosity had taken even Lenin's breath away: surely decisions could not be taken so quickly and simply! And he had retorted in *Vperyod* that Parvus's slogan was premature and dangerous, that they must act in alliance with the petit bourgeoisie, with the revolutionary democrats, because the proletariat was too weak! But Parvus and Trotsky had scrawled a hasty pamphlet and flung it at the Geneva émigrés, Bolsheviks and Mensheviks alike, as a challenge: Russia had no experience of parliaments, the bourgeoisie was feeble, the bureaucratic hierarchy was insignificant, the peasantry was ignorant and unorganized, so that the proletariat had no alternative but to take command of the revolution. While those Social Democrats who recoiled from the initiative of the proletariat would become an insignificant sect.

The whole Geneva émigré world, however, had stayed lethargically where it was, as though to make this prophecy come true—all except Trotsky, who rushed to Kiev, then to Finland, drawing closer to make his jump; and Parvus, who charged in at the first signal of the October general strike, which, once again, he had been prophesying back in the last century. Neither Bolsheviks nor Mensheviks, these two were free of all discipline, and fellows in audacity.

Yes, it was the size of a large boar. Its swelling bulk blocked the entire room. While Sklarz, by the window, seemed to have grown smaller?

It's not something I could put on paper, or say at the most restricted conference—but yes, I did make a mistake. Belief in yourself, political maturity, skill in assessing situations all come to you gradually, with age and experience. (Though Parvus was only three years older.) Yes, I made a mistake, I was shortsighted, I wasn't bold enough. (But you must not talk like that even to your closest supporter, or you may rob him of his faith in his leader.) Yet, how could he help making this mistake? The months had dragged by in that year of turmoil and confusion, everything was in ferment, there was thunder in the air, but real revolution never looked like it was going to break out. There in Geneva, still unable to travel, he was filled with indignation: couldn't those dolts back home move, couldn't they start a proper revolution? He wrote letter after letter to Russia: Energy is what is needed, frantic energy! You've been babbling about bombs for six months now and haven't made a single one! Let everyone arm himself at once as best he can—with a revolver, a knife, a kerosene-soaked rag for starting fires, anything! The combat groups should not wait, there will be no regular training. Let each group begin training itself—if only by beating up policemen! Or by killing a plainclothesman! Or blowing up a police station! Or raiding a bank! These attacks, of course, may degenerate into reckless extremism, but never mind! A few dozen casualties will be handsomely made up for if the party gains hundreds of experienced fighters.

No, his tired mind would not take in this untimely letter. He read on, understanding nothing.

. . . It had all seemed so obvious. Brass knuckles! Clubs! Kerosene rags! Spades! Guncotton! Barbed wire! Nails (for use against mounted police)! These are all weapons, and good ones. If one Cossack is accidentally cut off from the rest, attack and take his sword. Climb to the upper stories of buildings, and rain stones on the troops! Pour boiling water on them! Keep acid up there to pour on the police!

Parvus and Trotsky had done none of these things, but merely arrived in Petersburg, issued a proclamation, and convened a new organ of government: the Soviet of Workers' Deputies. They asked no one's permission, and nobody stood in their way. A pure workers' government. Already in session. Although they arrived a mere two weeks before the others, they had taken control of everything. The chairman of the Soviet was their man of straw, Nosar; its outstanding orator and general favorite, Trotsky; while its inventor, Parvus, directed it from behind the scenes. They had taken over the struggling *Russkaya Gazeta,* which sold for one kopeck and had a popular style and tone, and suddenly its sales rose to half a million and the ideas of the two friends flowed out to the masses.

Over by the window, Sklarz had slid lower in his chair, shrunk till he looked like a little bird with its beak buried in a picture magazine.

During those last days in Geneva, Lenin's pen had raced to spell out the whole theory and practice of

revolution, as he had learned it in libraries from the best
French authorities. He had kept up a rapid fire of letters to Russia, telling them how large a combat group
should be (from three to thirty people), how to main-
tain communication with party military committees,
how to choose the best places for street fighting, where
to store bombs and stones. They must find out where
the arsenals are, familiarize themselves with the routine
of government offices and banks, get to know people
who could help them infiltrate and take over . . . To
begin an attack under favorable conditions was not just
the right but the duty of any revolutionary. Fighting the
Black Hundreds would be a splendid baptism of fire:
beat them up, kill them, blow up their headquarters!

He had gone to Russia on the heels of his last letter. And found things there very different. No combat
groups were being formed, no one was storing up acid,
bombs, stones. He found instead that even the bourgeois came to listen to the Soviet, with Trotsky on the
platform, spinning and whirling and coruscating like a
Catherine wheel. He and Parvus, as though born for a
life in the public eye, dazzled all Petersburg—the editorial offices, the political salons; they were invited
everywhere and received with applause. There was even
a group who called themselves "Parvusists." Instead of
sneaking around corners with kerosene-soaked rags,
Parvus was preparing a collected edition of his works,
Parvus was buying up tickets for satirical shows and distributing them to friends. A fine revolution, if in the
evening there was no measured tread of patrols on deserted streets and theater doors were open wide . . .

He couldn't run over to the window and back—
the swollen black case stood big as a trunk in the way.
And there was no strength in his legs.

In that revolution Lenin had been bruised by
Parvus, as though he had stood too near to an elephant. He had sat at meetings of the Soviet, listening to

the hero of the day, with his head in his hands. Parvus's slogans, repeated and read out over and over again, were perfectly correct: after the victory of the revolution, the proletariat *must not give up its weapons,* but *prepare for civil war! It must regard its liberal allies as enemies!* Excellent slogans, and he himself was left with nothing to say from the platform of the Soviet. Everything was going almost as it should, indeed so well that there was no room for the Bolshevik leader. His whole life had been adapted to the demands of the underground, and his legs would not carry him up into the broad daylight. He had not gone to Moscow when the rising began, no longer caring whether the insurgents were following his instructions, from Geneva, or someone else's. His self-confidence had failed him, and Lenin had skulked through the revolution in a daze, sitting it out in Kuokkala, forty miles from Petersburg and across the Finnish border, where he was safe from arrest—while Krupskaya traveled to the capital every day to get the news. He couldn't understand it himself: all his life he had done nothing but prepare for revolution, and when it came, his strength had ebbed and left him.

Next, from the shadows (he always tried to operate behind the scenes, not to get in front of cameras, not to feed biographers), Parvus had fathered an anonymous resolution in the congress—its Financial Manifesto. What looked like a set of rough-hewn, primitive demands from the illiterate masses was really the program of a clever and experienced financier striking at the foundations of the hated Russian state, to bring it down in ruins at a single blow. Give Parvus his due—it was a superb, a most instructive revolutionary document. (But the government, too, had seen its significance and arrested the whole Petersburg Soviet on the following day. As it happened, Parvus was not there, and had survived to set up a second

Soviet, at once, with a different membership. They came to arrest this new body, and again Parvus escaped.)

There was no kerosene in the lamp, yet it had been burning for an hour, giving no less light than before.

It took years for the ribs dented by Parvus to straighten out again, for Lenin to regain his assurance that he, too, was of some use in the world. What had helped most was seeing Parvus's mistakes and his failures, seeing this hippopotamus, this elephant, crashing blindly through the thickets, its hide punctured by broken branches, seeing it stumble into holes in its headlong charge. He had been expelled from the party for misappropriation of funds, had become a ruthless profiteer, boozed with his bosomy blondes in public—and ended by openly supporting German imperialism: he had expressed his views frankly in print, and in speeches, and defiantly left for Berlin.

The hat behind the lamp shifted and revealed its satin lining.

No, it was lying quietly, just as Sklarz had left it.

Rumors had already reached Lenin, through Christian Rakovsky in Roumania and David Riazanov in Vienna, that Parvus would be coming to him with *interesting proposals*—so careless was he about covering his tracks. But Parvus's reputation as an undisguised ally of the Kaiser had preceded him, while he was boozing in Zurich on the way. They were all used to poverty, year in and year out, and suddenly their former comrade turned up in the role of an Oriental pasha, something of a shock to the émigré mind, but also a source of largessse. When he found Lenin in the canteen at Bern, wedged his enormous belly behind the table, and loudly declared in the presence of a dozen comrades that they must have a talk, Lenin, without hesitation, without even thinking about it, replied with a curt rebuff. He had come from warring Germany to chat, like a peacetime tourist, had he? (Lenin was no less eager for a talk!) Well then, Lenin must again ask him to t a k e  h i m s e l f  a w a y! (It was the only possible thing to do!)

The handle of the big case flopped to one side.

But they had to see each other, of course! They couldn't keep putting things on paper, in case one of their letters fell into the hands of an enemy. So Lenin whispered to Siefeldt, who ran after the fat man and gave him the address. (Lenin told Siefeldt afterward that he had sent the shark away unfed.) And in the Ulyanovs' Spartan room the broad-beamed Parvus, with diamond studs in his dazzlingly displayed cuffs, had with some difficulty seated himself on the bed next to Lenin, lolling against him and pushing him toward the pillow and the iron bedstead.

Snap! The suitcase had finally burst open . . . and freeing his elbows, straightening his back, he unfolded, rose to his full height and girth, in his dark-blue three-piece suit, with his diamond cuff-links, and stretching his cramped legs, came one step, two steps closer.

There he stood, life-sized, in the flesh, with his ungovernable belly, the elongated dome of his head, the flashy bulldog features, the little imperial—looking at Lenin with pale watchful eyes. Amicably, as ever.

True, true—they should have had a talk long ago. They had always talked in hasty snatches, been out of touch or at odds, and it was so difficult for them to meet: with enemies, and friends too, on the watch. The utmost secrecy was necessary! But now that he had found his way here, this was better than writing letters. The critical moment for an eye-to-eye talk had arrived.

"Israel Lazarevich! You surprise me! Whatever has become of your remarkable intelligence? Why are you so indiscreet? Why have you put yourself in such a vulnerable position? You yourself are making it quite impossible for us to collaborate."

No hello, no proffered hand (and it was just as well, because Lenin lacked the strength to rise and greet him, his hand seemed paralyzed, and a hello would have stuck in his throat), he simply slumped, not of course on the chair, but on the bed again, his unwieldy bulk sprawling against Lenin and squeezing him into the corner.

Training his protuberant, colorless eyes directly on his companion's face, he spoke with casual irony, teasing a friend, not addressing an audience.

"I'm surprised too, Vladimir Ilyich. Have you still nothing to occupy you but agitation and protests? What's the use of all this childish prattle? All these so-called conferences—thirty silly women in the Volkshaus one day, a dozen deserters the next?"

He unceremoniously pushed Lenin farther along the bed, and his unhealthily enlarged head loomed close.

"Since when have you sided with those who want to change the world with a broad-nibbed pen? What children all these socialists are, with their eternal indignation. But you mustn't be like them! If you want serious a c t i o n, should you really be hiding in holes and corners, not letting it be known where your sympathies lie in this war?"

Although speech was still difficult, his head was clearer, as though he had drunk strong tea. Even without words they understood each other perfectly.

Well, of course this was no pathetic Kautsky demonstrating "for peace," refusing to meddle in the war.

"Neither of us looks at war like a sister of mercy. Casualties, bloodshed, suffering are inevitable. What matters is the outcome."

Well, of course Parvus was utterly right. If Russia was to be shattered, Germany must be victorious, and they must seek German support. So far, so good. But Parvus overstepped the mark. Not for the first time.

"Israel Lazarevich, if a socialist has one real asset, it is his honor. If we forfeit our honor, we forfeit everything. Between ourselves, the closeness of our positions naturally makes us allies. And of course we'll need each other and help each other. But these days you are politically in such bad odor . . . It would take just one Burtsev to ruin everything. So we'll have to make a show of disagreement, attack each other in the press. Not a full-time controversy, of course . . . just from time to time . . . so if I should call you . . ." (Even face to face, Lenin never moderated his language: the more harshly you speak, the better you understand each other.) "If I should call you, for instance . . . Hindenburg's morally degenerate toady . . . that renegade, that filthy lackey . . . you can see for yourself that you leave me no alternative . . ."

"By all means, it doesn't matter a bit." A bitter smile creased Parvus's puffy face. "In Berlin last spring I was given a million marks, some of which I sent at once to Rakovsky, to Trotsky and Martov, and to you here in Switzerland—did you get it? What? You weren't aware of it? Do please check with your treasurer, maybe he's pocketed it . . . Trotsky took the money . . . although he'd already publicly disowned me— 'Falstaff in politics,' he called me . . . He's written my obituary before I'm dead. I say nothing, it's all right, of course I understand."

A fixed glassy stare from under the faint raised brows.

Parvus and Trotsky had parted company earlier,

over the theory of permanent revolution. He had loved
Trotsky like a younger brother.

But now he had high hopes for Lenin, and leaned
on him with all his pudgy immensity, forcing him farther and farther along the bed, until he was sitting on
the pillow and could feel the bedstead against his elbow.

"Aren't you afraid that mere slogans will be useless without money? With money in your hands—
power will be yours. How else will you seize power?
That's the unpleasant question. And, if you don't
mind my saying so, I seem to remember you in 1904
taking what looked very much like Japanese money
for the Third Congress and *Vperyod*. That was all
right, wasn't it? And now I'm Hindenburg's lackey,
am I?" He did his best to laugh.

It was just like last time. Perhaps it *was* last time?
. . . In Bern, in the room he had rented from a
housewife? Or was he in his room in the Zurich cob-
bler's house? Or not in a room at all? He seemed to
be hearing it all for the second time. No table, no
Sklarz. Just a massive Swiss iron bed, with the two of
them upon it, great men both, floating above a world
pregnant with revolution, a world which looked up to
them expectantly, as they sat with their legs dangling,
and the bed sped again around its dark orbit. There
was just enough light from some invisible source for
him to see his companion, just enough sound for him
to hear.

"Never mind . . . It's all right . . . I understand."

Parvus despised the world. That world, far below,
under the bed.

"As I see it, if you want to *turn the war into a
civil war,* one ally is as good as another. At present
you have—how much?" He was being funny. "I won't
ask you, it isn't done. But I have . . . not for myself,
but for the *cause*—well, I got a million last spring,

and I'll get another five million this summer. And there's plenty more to come. What do you say to that?"

Both he and Parvus had always despised the émigré world for its unreality, its ineffectualness, its driveling intellectualism—it was all talk, nothing but talk. But money was something more serious. Oh, yes.

Lenin was sickened by his self-assurance but fascinated by the reality of his power.

Parvus opened his pale eyes wide and smacked his lips under the straggly moustache.

"The Plan! I've produced a Master Plan. I've submitted it to the German government. And, let me tell you, I can get as much as twenty million to carry it out. Only I have reserved the most important place in my Plan for *you*. What are you . . ."

A gust of marshy breath, right in his face.

". . . going to do? . . . Go on waiting? . . . Well, I . . ."

His dome was no smaller than Lenin's, half his face was bare brow, half his head a thinly covered backward slope. Ruthless, inhuman intelligence in his eyes, as he said it.

"I AM SETTING THE DATE OF THE RUSSIAN REVOLUTION FOR THE NINTH OF JANUARY[1] NEXT YEAR!"

## 48

How are great yet simple plans born? Ideas are conceived and grow in the subconscious before you have any definite purpose for them. Then, suddenly, elements perhaps long familiar to others as well as yourself spontaneously converge, and it is in your head that they fuse to form a single plan, a plan so clear and simple that you wonder why no one has arrived at it before.

Why had it not taken shape earlier, in the minds of the German General Staff, who should have been the first to think of it?

True, they did not understand Russia very well. From autumn 1914 and the battle on the Marne, when they realized that their plans for a quick victory had failed, to autumn 1915 they had continued to hope for a separate peace with Russia, busily putting out feelers, never imagining that the Romanovs would rebuff them. This was what had distracted them.

Parvus, isolated from the main events, stranded in bronze and blue Constantinople, in possession of the riches he had so desired, and with them every imaginable carnal delight—the East knows how to sate the male soul and slake male desire—remote from the great battle ("in the socialist army of reserve," as Trotsky had advised), and in no danger of experiencing its consequences—had never, even at his most jaded and dissipated, abandoned the quest which had begun in his youth on the diagonally opposite shore of the Black Sea.

He had not abandoned it when, earlier, he went

to the Balkans, where he was more widely read than Marx and Engels. He had not forgotten it when he was earning his bread in the low dives of Constantinople and rallying the dockside beggars for a May Day demonstration. He had been still more mindful of it when he rose in the world through his work for the Young Turks and converted his financial genius from an ax hacking at the Russian trunk to a gardener's spade mulching the Turkish sapling. The millions which so mysteriously flooded in to him and carried him along on their tide had not dazed him or made him forgetful. And he did not forget while he was founding banks and trading with mother Odessa or stepmother Germany. The shot at Sarajevo had stung him like the stroke of a whip. Parvus had a seismographic sense of movement in the depths, he knew at once that the rock bed was slipping. That the stupid old bear would be trapped. At last it had come, the Great War, the World War. He had long foretold it, described it, invoked it—the most powerful locomotive of history. The first chariot of socialism! While back there, all over Europe, socialist parties were in an uproar over war credits, Parvus made not a single speech, Parvus published not a single line. He wasted no time, there was not a minute to lose, but scurried about his secret passages, trying to persuade Turkey's rulers that only by siding with Germany could their country break loose from the endless chain of capitulations. He speeded up the delivery of equipment and spare parts for Turkish railways and flour mills, to supply the towns with grain and put Turkey in a position not only to declare war in the autumn but to begin serious military operations in the Caucasus as soon as possible. (He was working just as busily in Bulgaria, which he also succeeded in preparing for war.) Only after these essential tasks could Parvus allow himself to settle back comfortably into his favorite and long neglected occupation—propaganda: this time, in the Balkan press, with the slogan "FOR DEMOCRACY! AGAINST TSARISM!"

This needed explanation, careful argument, to convince as many as possible—and the sparks rained merrily from his unblunted pen: Why ask who bears the "war guilt," "who attacked first," when world imperialism has been preparing for this fight for decades? —somebody had to attack first, and it might have been anyone. Don't look for meaningless causes but think like socialists: how are we, the world proletariat, to make use of the war, or, in other words, on which side should we fight? Germany has the most powerful Social Democratic Party in the world, Germany is the stronghold of socialism, and so for Germany this is a war of self-defense. If socialism is smashed in Germany, it will be defeated everywhere. The road to the victory of world socialism lies through the reinforcement of German military power. While the fact that Tsarism is on the same side as the Entente reveals even more clearly where the true enemies of socialism are: the victory of the Entente would bring a new age of oppression to the whole world. So workers' parties throughout the world must fight a g a i n s t  R u s s i a n  T s a r i s m. Advising the proletariat to adopt neutrality (as Trotsky does) means opting out from history, it is revolutionary cretinism. So the object of world socialism is the crushing defeat of Russia and a revolution in that country! Unless Russia is decentralized and democratized, the whole world is in danger. And since Germany bears the main burden of struggle against Muscovite imperialism, the revolutionary movement there must be suspended for the time being. At a later stage, victory in war will bring class victories to the proletariat. THE VICTORY OF GERMANY IS THE VICTORY OF SOCIALISM!

The first to come and consult Parvus in response

to this publication was the League for the Liberation of the Ukraine, based in Vienna (including old acquaintances from *Iskra* days), then the Armenian and Georgian nationalists. His door in Constantinople was open to all engaged in fighting Russia.

Thus Parvus's dynamism magnetically attracted people of different experience, and from this explosive combination of socialist and nationalist experience the Plan was born. Until then, socialist programs had always babbled about autonomy. But no! Only the disruption and dismemberment of Russia could bring down absolutism, and give the nations freedom and socialism simultaneously.

While the first Ukrainian and Caucasian expeditionary groups were collapsing (in their haste they had recruited all sorts of braggarts and adventurers, the conspiratorial scheme was suddenly made public in the émigré press, and Enver Pasha had had to stop the expeditions), the magnetic combination of iron components into a single Plan was gradually perfected in Parvus's grotesquely capacious head. Just as engineers prefer triangular supports because of their resistance to deformation, so Parvus found that the nationalist and socialist components lacked a third partner—the German government. The aims of all three very closely coincided!

Parvus's past life might have been deliberately designed for the faultless creation of this Plan. It now only remained for him—happy amalgam of theorist, operator, and politician that he was—to formulate the Plan point by point in December 1914, give the German ambassador a hint of it in January, receive a hospitable summons to Berlin, and stagger the higherups at a personal interview in the ministry. (In nineteen years that country had not even tossed him a set of naturalization papers, it had closed down all his journals, hounded him from city to city, contemplated handing him over to the Russian secret police, and now the highest in the government gazed deferentially into his prophetic eyes.) In March 1915, on presentation of a definitive and detailed memorandum, he received his first advance of a million marks.

The Plan was to concentrate all their potential, all their forces, all their resources under a single command, to control from a single headquarters the activities of the Central Powers, the Russian revolutionaries, and the border peoples. (He knew the strength of this bull, and had chosen his ax to match it.) No uncoordinated, private improvisations. The Plan asserted that German victory could never be final without a revolution in Russia: until it was carved up, Russia would remain an unabated menace. The Russian fortress, however, could not be destroyed by any one of these forces in isolation, but only by a single-minded union of all three. There must be simultaneous explosions of social revolution and national revolution, with German financial and material support. Experience of the 1905 Revolution (and the author should know! What induced the Imperial government to treat their adviser seriously was that he was no mere footloose businessman but the Father of the First Revolution) enables us to see that all the symptoms are recurring, that all the conditions for revolution are still in existence, and that it will indeed proceed more quickly in conditions of world war, but only if it is given a skillful push, only if the catastrophe is speeded up by action from outside. The Putilov, Obukhov, and Baltic factories in Petersburg and the shipyards at Nikolayev will be made ready to serve as centers of s o c i a l revolution (the author had particularly strong links with southern Russia). The date is set—one which already has a painful significance in Russia, the anniversary of Bloody Sunday—for a one-day strike in memory of the victims, and a single street demonstration in favor of the eight-hour day and a democratic republic. But when the police begin to disperse the demonstrators they will resist, and if there is the slightest bloodshed —the flame will race along all the fuses. The one-day strike will merge into a general strike "for freedom and peace." Leaflets will be distributed in the biggest factories—and weapons will be ready for use in Petersburg and Moscow. Within twenty-four hours a hundred thousand men will be set in motion. The railwaymen (also primed in advance) will join them, and all traffic will be halted on the Petersburg–Moscow, Petersburg–Warsaw, Moscow–Warsaw, and south-western lines. To ensure a total and simultaneous stoppage, several bridges will be blown up, as in 1905. Bridges should also be blown up at several points along the Trans-Siberian trunk line, and a team of skilled agents should be dispatched for this purpose. Siberia is dealt with in a separate section of the Plan. The forces stationed there are extremely weak, and the towns, under the influence of political exiles, are in a revolutionary mood. This makes it easier to organize sabotage, and once the disorders begin, the exiles should be transferred en masse to Petersburg, to inject thousands of experienced agitators into the capital and bring millions of conscripts within range of propaganda. Propaganda will be carried on by the entire Russian left-wing press and reinforced by a flood of defeatist émigré leaflets. (It will be easy enough to get them printed in bulk in Switzerland, for instance.) Any publication which saps the Russian will to resist, and points to social revolution as the way out of the war, will be useful. The main target for propaganda will be the army in the field. (He also envisaged a mutiny in the Black Sea fleet. Parvus had established links with the Odessa sailors on his way through Bulgaria long ago. He had always strongly suspected that the Japanese were responsible for the *Potemkin* mutiny.) Experienced agents will also be sent to set fire to the Baku oil wells, which presented no difficulty since they were so inadequately guarded. The pace of social revolution must be further accelerated by financial means: counterfeit rubles will be showered on the Russian population from German planes, while bank notes with identical serial numbers will be put into simultaneous circulation abroad, in Petersburg, and in Moscow, to undermine the exchange rate of the ruble and create panic in the capitals.

For all their Clausewitzes, Moltke Seniors, and Moltke Juniors, for all their self-confident strategy, for all the haughty precision of their staff work, these limited Prussian brains had never risen to a concept of such grandeur!

Germany had never had such an adviser on Russia and its weaknesses. (Even now she did not fully appreciate him.)

And that is by no means all! The national revolutions will begin simultaneously. Our most important lever is the Ukrainian movement. Without the Ukraine to buttress it, the Russian edifice will soon topple over. The Ukrainian movement will spread to the Kuban Cossacks, and the Don Cossacks too may prove shaky. There will naturally be collaboration with the Finns, who are the most mature of the Empire's peoples, and almost free already. It will be easy to send weapons to them, and through them to Russia. Poland is always just five minutes away from rebellion against Russia and only awaits a signal. With Poland and Finland in revolt, the Baltic lands in between will be stirred to action. (In another version of the Plan, Parvus provided for the voluntary union of the Baltic provinces with Germany.) The Georgian and Armenian nationalists are already actively collaborating with the governments of the Central Powers and are in their pay. The Caucasus is fragmented, and will be more difficult to rouse, but with Turkey's help, by means of Moslem agitation, we'll stir them up to a Gazavat, a Holy War. And with that all around them the Terek Cossacks will scarcely want to lay down their lives for the Tsar rather than break away themselves.

So the highly centralized Russian Empire will collapse, never to rise again. Internal struggles will shake Russia to its foundations. Peasants will start taking the land from its owners. Soldiers will desert the trenches in droves to make sure of their share when the land is divided up. (They will mutiny against their officers, shoot all the generals. But this part of the Plan must be tactfully concealed—it might stir unpleasant forebodings in Prussian breasts.)

Wait a minute, though (catching his breath), that's not all. That's not the end of it. Shaken by destructive propaganda within, Russia must also be besieged by a hostile world press. An anti-Tsarist campaign will be mounted by socialist newspapers in various countries, and the excitement of Tsar baiting will spread to their neighbors on the right, the liberals —that is to say, to the dominant section of the press throughout the world. A newspaper crusade against the Tsar! In this connection it is particularly important to win public opinion in the United States. And by exposing Tsarism we will simultaneously unmask and undermine the whole Entente!

This, then, was Parvus's proposal to Germany: instead of the desperate butchery of infantry and of artillery warfare—a single injection of German money and, with no German losses, the most populous member of the Entente would be torn away in the space of a few months! Not surprisingly, the German government jumped at the program!

Parvus, indeed, had never doubted that they would. He was, however, anxious about the reaction of others in Berlin: the socialists. How would his project be received by his stepmother party? His ideas had always been too profound for use in their mass agitation, and too far in advance of the times to seem practical even to the leaders of the party in which he had been knocking his head against the wall for nineteen years now, without ever holding office or voting rights at a single congress. He had, for a short time, been one of its heroes—when he had just returned from Siberia, and everyone was devouring his memoirs, *In the Russian Bastille.* Then he had dirtied his hands in the unfortunate Gorky affair, a secret party commission had condemned him to expulsion, and five years of excommunication still had not wiped out the stain. Worst of all, though, was his legendary and inexplicable rise to wealth, in a single year—something people in general, and Social Democrats in particular, are too narrow-minded to forgive. (It was a psychological puzzle: had his wealth been inherited, no one would ever have reproached him with it.) His wealth alone was bound to make them hate and reject him, but they had found nobler grounds for indignation: he had become a henchman of imperialism! Clara and Liebknecht he could understand, but Rosa! Rosa, with whom he had once been on intimate terms (though even then she had been ashamed of him—because of his appearance perhaps—and always concealed their relationship), Rosa too had shown him the door. In the meantime, Bebel had died, Kautsky and Bernstein had split up and impaired their authority, and a complacent new leadership tried to find weaknesses in the position of this socialist drifter. How, they asked, would the Prussian government behave after victory? Why should revolution in Russia make Prussia look more tolerantly and kindly on socialism? Would it not see its chance to put the lid on English and French democracy?

Of course, there was some truth in their objections, there were grounds for doubt—but there was nothing of that bold and perfect vision that can shake and remake a world! No one, or hardly anyone, in Europe could lift himself far enough out of his rut to see that *the destruction of Russia now held the key to the future history of the world!* All else was secondary.

Meanwhile, the socialists of the Entente were mounting a campaign to expose Parvus.

The bitterness of their reproaches poisoned the pleasure that his success should have given him, although the majority of European socialists were neither well versed in theory nor effective in practice. They could not rise to an overall view of the terrain, they lacked the skill to match each turn of events with a tactical twist. They were merely bureaucrats of socialism, stuck fast, coffined in the corridors of dogma: they no longer moved, no longer crawled along those corridors, but lay down in them, not even daring to imagine a turn ahead. When Parvus first openly called on them to help Germany he had filled them with virginal horror. How nice it would be for them to sit the war out as innocent neutrals, salving their consciences with moral indignation, both against war and against those who dared to interfere with it.

But the decisive role belonged to the Russian socialists, and they were the subject of careful analysis in the Plan submitted to the German government. They were broken up into scattered groups, and therefore impotent—but not one of these groups must be neglected, each must be used. It was necessary to lead them along the road to unity—arrange a unification congress, for which Geneva would be most suitable. Some groups, such as the Bund, the Spilka, the Poles, the Finns, would certainly support the Plan. But unity could not be achieved without reconciling the Bolsheviks and Mensheviks. And that would depend entirely on the Bolshevik leader, who was presently in Switzerland.

Various difficulties might arise, and it might even turn out that some Russian socialists were patriots who would not want to see the Russian Empire dismembered. But there were grounds for confidence: these beggarly émigrés had been short of money for decades, both for everyday needs—they had never known where their next meal was coming from, and they were quite incapable of earning a living—and for their incessant journeys and congresses, their endless scribbling of pamphlets and articles. They would not be able to resist if a fat purse were held out to them. Why, even the strong, legal Western parties and trade unions readily accepted offers of financial help, for their workers, of course, but still—who in this world does not want to eat well, be better dressed, live in a warmer and more spacious house? (Discreet help for leaders who live modestly also greatly reinforces our friendship with them.) How could the émigrés refuse?

On his way to Switzerland, Parvus had anticipated with particular relish a successful meeting with Lenin. Their collaboration in Munich was a thing of the past, they had not seen each other in years, but Parvus's keen eye had never lost sight of this unique socialist, who had no equal in all Europe: uninhibited, free from prejudice and squeamishness, ready in any new situation to adopt whatever methods promised success. The only hard-faced realist, never carried away by illusions, the greatest realist in the socialist movement except for Parvus himself. All that Lenin lacked was breadth. The savage, intolerant narrowness of the natural schismatic harnessed his tremendous energy to futilities—fragmenting this group, dissociating himself from that, yapping at intruders, petty bickering, dogfights, needling newspaper articles—wasted his strength in meaningless struggles, with nothing to show except mounds of scribbled paper. This schismatic narrowness doomed him to sterility in Europe, left him no future except in Russia—but also made him indispensable for any activity there. Indispensable now!

Now that Parvus's younger comrade-in-arms, Trotsky, whom he had so dearly loved, had abdicated once and for all, now that Trotsky's vitality and clarity of vision had deserted him—the cruel gleam of Lenin's star summoned him irresistibly to Switzerland. Quite spontaneously, Lenin had been saying the same things as Parvus: that it did not matter who was the aggressor, that Tsarism was the stronghold of reaction and must be shattered first, that . . . Nuances in parenthetical remarks, buried in subsidiary clauses and barely noticed by anyone else, told Parvus that Lenin had not changed, that he was still as demanding in some matters and as undemanding in others as he had always been, that he would not balk at an alliance with the Kaiser or the devil himself if it helped to crush the Tsar. Parvus had therefore warned him in advance to expect interesting proposals: there was no reason to doubt that an alliance would be concluded. The only trouble was those miserable artificial disagreements with the Mensheviks, about which Lenin was particularly stupid and stubborn. Still, a million marks in subsidies should carry some weight. In his memorandum to the German government Parvus had specifically mentioned Lenin, with his underground organization throughout Russia, as his main support. With Lenin at his right hand, as Trotsky had been in the other revolution, success was assured.

Sure of success, Parvus had traveled to Bern, had paced the student canteen, cigar in mouth, and been surprised at first by Lenin's resounding refusal, but quickly appreciated his prudence and tact. Later, sitting on the cramped bed, he had used his bulk to squeeze the lightweight Lenin into a corner. "But you must have c a p i t a l ! W h a t will you use to seize power? That's the unpleasant question."

Tha-a-a-a-at was something Lenin understood very well! That bare ideas will get you no further forward, that you cannot make a revolution without power, that in our time the primary source of power is money, and that all other forms of power—organization, weapons, people capable of using those weapons to kill—are begotten of money. Very true, nobody would deny it!

With his incomparable mental agility which made reflection unnecessary, with his expression changing from one moment to the next—Parvus even glimpsed a smiling hint of complicity—Lenin coolly shifted his ground and answered in his burring voice. "Why unpleasant? When people take the right party attitude toward money, the party is pleased. It is displeased when money is turned into a weapon *against* the party."

"That's all very well, but you can't help giving yourself away." Parvus spoke with friendly irony. "The *Sozialdemokrat* costs something to publish. Or maybe"—his Falstaffian belly shook with laughter— "maybe you tell the Swiss tax inspectors that, on the contrary, you live on your fees from the *Sozialdemokrat?*"

Lenin often wore a mocking look, but very rarely smiled: instead, he screwed up his naturally deep-set eyes, hiding them completely. He chose his words carefully. "Philanthropic donations keep coming from somewhere. It is perfectly correct from the party's point of view to accept charity—why shouldn't it be?"

(Money, in fact, was not so short as all that, they could all live more easily if they were as shameless as some of those through whose hands it flowed.

Bagocki threw money around in a scandalous fashion, and nobody would think of checking the Austrian money held by Weiss. It made no sense to put pressure on them, that might spoil everything. But it ran through their hands like water.)

Parvus's eye found no comfort anywhere—not in Lenin's frayed jacket, or in his patched collar, or in the worn-out tablecloth, or in the bare room, where two boxes, one on top of the other, served as a bookcase. But Parvus did not feel at all apologetic about his diamonds, his cheviot coat, his English shoes: this parade of poverty on Lenin's part was a game, the party line, intended to set the tone and provide an example of a "leader beyond reproach." In this adopted role, faithfully performed for years on end, could be seen the narrowness and drabness of his mind. But this could be corrected, and even Lenin could be taught to cut a figure.

(But no! No! A deep antipathy, an instinctive protest made Lenin *spontaneously* and on all occasions forbid himself any luxury, however easily available. To have enough was a different matter, that was reasonable. But luxury was the beginning of degeneracy, and Parvus had been caught that way. Let the money pour in by the million, but for the revolution, while he himself kept within the limits of the necessary, proudly counting every rappen. It was not at all a pose, and only partly by way of example to those whom he could not coerce.)

Glancing swiftly sideways and up, Lenin spoke without hostility or resentment. "Israel Lazarevich! Your undying faith in the omnipotence of money is what has let you down. You know what I mean."

(If your expenses are small, it is like being in a locked room, your secrets are safe: nothing leaks, you feel secure, you will never recklessly let yourself go, all is firm and fast. But riches are like uncontrolled chatter. No! There must be discipline in this as in everything. Only self-limitation makes it possible to build up a powerful drive. Thus, although he could afford to put down the 1,200 francs security for permission to reside in Switzerland—which was essential to his safety and his work—he wouldn't just pay, but chose instead to make a fuss, write letters, declare himself destitute, beg for a discretionary reduction to one tenth, waste precious time calling on the chief of police, sometimes accompanied by Karl Moor, who had a well-stuffed wallet in his pocket, so that he need only hold his hand out and extract a bank note from him. When he was finally granted a reduction to 300 francs, he still paid only a hundred, and continued haggling, and then when he moved to Zurich he wouldn't pay at all, but begged to be excused, and corresponded with Bern, requesting the transfer of his hundred francs to his present canton. Lenin was good at this: good at lacing himself tight: only tight-laced did he breathe freely.)

The purpose of any conversation is to understand your partner fully without unnecessarily exposing yourself.

With a sharp, probing look and a skeptical grin, he asked: "Why do you need wealth of your own? Come on, tell me! Explain yourself."

A child's question. One of those "whys" which it is ridiculous to answer. So that every wish can become reality, of course. The feeling it gives you is probably like that which a physical giant gets from the play of his muscles. An affirmation of his rights on earth. The meaning of life. He sighed. "It's only human, to like being rich. Surely you understand, Vladimir Ilyich?"

But looking at his bald brow, at the aging skin of his temples, at the too sharp, too tense vee of his eyebrows, Parvus suddenly suspected that he really didn't understand, that he wasn't pretending. His all-penetrating gaze only saw what was in front of him.

Parvus spoke again, more gently. "How shall I put it? . . . It's pleasant to have perfect sight or perfect hearing, and it's just the same with wealth . . ."

But was his decision to get rich really the result of conscious thought, of a theoretical belief? No, it was an innate necessity, and his commercial impulses, his flair for *Geschäft,* his reluctance to let slip any profit which loomed in his field of vision, were not a matter of plans and programs, but almost a biological function, which proceeded almost unconsciously, yet unerringly. It was a matter of instinct with him: always to feel the movement of economic life around him, the emergence of disproportions, imbalances, gaps which begged him, cried out to him to insert his hand and extract a profit. This was so much a part of his innermost nature that he conducted his multifarious business transactions, which by now were scattered over ten European countries, without a single ledger, keeping all the figures in his head.

(Lenin, of course, accepted that in the final analysis personal wealth was a *Privatsache,* a private matter. But his eyes bored into Parvus, probing for an answer: was he or was he not a socialist? That was the problem. Twenty-five years of socialist journalism—but was he a socialist? . . .)

Parvus hurriedly returned to the point. "Let me tell you—wealth means *power*. Power is what the proletariat aspires to, isn't it? I was a big name for twenty-five years, better known than you, and it did nothing for me. But wealth clears all paths. Take these negotiations, for instance. What government would believe a beggar, and give him millions for a project? Whereas a rich man obviously won't take it for himself, he has his own millions."

The inordinately large, asymmetrical head tilted trustfully, and the colorless, philosophical eyes looked amicably and peacefully at Lenin. "Don't miss your chance, Vladimir Ilyich. Life offers you opportunities like this just once."

Yes, this he understood. At the beginning of the war he had enjoyed an unaccustomed luxury; a friendly eagle (Austrian in this case) had taken him on its wing and carried him in a twinkling where it was bidden. (There was no passenger transportation to Switzerland, and the Ulyanovs had traveled in a troop train.) Lenin had discovered with a thrill that it might be better not to hover helplessly, to drift on a sea of words and ideas, but to abandon, once and for all, his helpless and uneasy émigré existence, and cling instead to real material forces, move in concert with them. As always, and in everything, Parvus had been ahead of him.

"To make a revolution takes a lot of money," Parvus insisted, his friendly shoulder pressing against Lenin. "But to hold on to power when you get there will take even more."

An odd way of putting it, but strikingly true.

Seen from the summit of Parvus's philosophy— Parvus was undoubtedly correct.

And seen from the summit of Lenin's philosophy —so was Lenin.

"Just think, if only we combined your capacities with mine. And with such powerful support! With your incomparable talent for revolution. How much longer do you want to go on lounging about in these émigré holes? How much longer can you go on waiting for a revolution somewhere ahead—and refusing to recognize it when it arrives and grabs you by the shoulder? . . ."

Oh, no! Nothing, neither shared joy, nor fervent hope, and still less, flattery, could dim Lenin's vigilant gaze. He had a quicker and keener eye for the narrowest chink of disagreement than for the broad expanse of converging platforms. He might be an outcast, and a failure, but he had invariably known that Parvus in all his successes, all his prophecies, was wrong, or, at least, not altogether right! Although he himself had achieved nothing—right was on his side!

Now Parvus was amused. Laughter was shaking that unwieldy body, which so loved its bottle of champagne before breakfast, its leisurely bath, its little suppers with the ladies—when it was not chained to its couch by rheumatism.

"Do you intend to go on in the same way, raising money by bank raids? What are you going to do next—rob the Crédit Lyonnais? You'll be deported to New Caledonia, comrades! To the galleys!"

He was overcome with laughter.

Lenin's brows twitched slightly in disagreement. But his searching gaze considered the problem dispassionately.

There was no theoretical objection to raiding a bank before general expropriation was legalized—it was, so to speak, borrowing against your future. But, in practice, it might or might not be worthwhile. If there was one thing the Bolsheviks had undoubtedly been good at in the revolutionary years, it was the "exes." They had begun with raids on ticket offices and trains. The first 200,000 from Georgia had simply transformed the life of the party. And if only they had succeeded in taking that 15 million from Mendelssohn's Bank in Berlin in 1907 . . . ! (Kamo was arrested en route, and it fell through.) It was a risky method, but very effective, and in any case it dirtied the party's hands less than dealings with the general staffs of foreign countries.

"Don't like dirtying your hands? Afraid of being found out?" Parvus, too, narrowed his eyes to slits, deliberately, contemptuously, shaming and reproving him. "You can rely on my experience: in *big* enterprises you'll never be found out. It's those who balk at small ones who get caught."

What a pachyderm! He didn't give a damn what people said, just clumped about the world on his great flat feet, crushing everything in his path.

Lenin's right eye darted an angry glance at him.

Parvus became sympathetic. He took both of Lenin's hands in his own jellied paws (an unpleasant habit of his) and spoke like the closest of friends. (At one time they had almost been on a first-name basis.) "Vladimir Ilyich, you must not neglect to analyze the reasons for your failure in one revolution already. Perhaps the fault lies in you? It is important to know that for the future. Be careful you don't lose next time."

Where did he get his brazen self-assurance? What the hell did he mean by setting himself up as a teacher? Was this another attempt to impose his leadership? Self-infatuation must have blinded him.

Lenin wrenched his hands free, and spoke with a savage grin, one of those grins of spontaneous mockery that forced up his eyebrows and brought a flush of joy to his face as he savored his triumphant retort. "Israel Lazarevich! It's you who should be analyzing *your own* failings! I didn't lose last time, because I wasn't running the revolution! You were the one who lost! How did *you* come to grief?"

So far, he had said nothing irreparable. Just a businesslike argument. He could still stop in time. But all those years of gasping for breath, with that great hulk crushing his ribs, and an irrepressible urge to tease, made him go further than he had to. (And was there anything to the man except ambition? Except the thirst for power? Except wealth?)

"Why did you lose heart so quickly in the Peter

and Paul fortress—was it the solitary confinement, the damp? Why such tender concern for your miserable carcass? How do you explain that diary full of cheap pathos for German philistines? All that gibberish about amnesties? How you came within an inch of petitioning the Tsar? Is that the behavior of a revolutionary leader? A fine revolutionary leader you are!"

And he himself? A bald-headed, spiky-browed, flinty-eyed little man with fussy, fidgety movements?

Yet, except for the two of them, there was no one left for the job.

Parvus never blushed, as though the fluid coursing in his veins were not the usual red, but watery green, like the color of his skin. There was no reason at all for him to lose his temper, but when Lenin thrust that sarcastic grin in his face, and shook with mocking laughter, and went on shaking, Parvus suddenly forgot his great strengths and foolishly retorted: "Anybody would think you had fought on the barricades! Or that you had marched just once in a street demonstration with Cossack whips waiting for you! At least I escaped from a transit prison on the way to Siberia! But why should you run away, when you had a false medical certificate and got yourself sent to the Siberian Riviera instead of the North."

(There were plenty of other things on the tip of his tongue. All very well for you, he thought, to call for war from neutral Switzerland, especially when you've avoided military service all your life!)

If anyone insults you like that in public, you have to commit political murder, fatally blacken his reputation, but when it happens in private you have a choice. You can even suppose that this criticism is not completely unsympathetic. Or admit that you have been unnecessarily rough yourself, as you often are in discussions.

No, thought Parvus, it was foolish of me to speak like that! I didn't come to Switzerland just to quarrel.

Parvus—thought Lenin—may be very useful. He is in a unique position. Why quarrel with him?

Lenin is the pillar on which the whole Plan rests. If he deserts me, who will make the revolution?

Another grin from Lenin, but a different one, not at all caustic, but infinitely knowing, a grin to be shared between the cleverest people in the world. His hand fell on Parvus's shoulder, and he spoke in a half whisper. "I tell you what. Do you know what your main mistake was in 1905? Why the revolution was a failure?"

Parvus responded with selfless objectivity, like a scientist ready to admit error, however painful it might be. "The Financial Manifesto? Was I in too much of a hurry?"

Lenin wagged his finger in the little space left between their heads, and smiled like a Kalmuck extolling a melon in an Astrakhan bazaar. "No, no, no. The Financial Manifesto was a stroke of genius. But those Soviets of yours . . ."

"My Soviets united the whole working class instead of splitting it up the way the Social Democrats do. My Soviets were gradually becoming the center of power. If only we'd succeeded in getting the eight-hour day— that and nothing else—there would have been risings like ours throughout Europe, and there you would have had your *permanent revolution!*"

Slyly, slit-eyed, Lenin watched Parvus erecting defenses for his vanity, and was in no hurry to interrupt. This damned muddle over permanent revolution was another reason why he, Parvus, and Trotsky had quarreled. As though they rode behind each other on a merry-go-round, they had all at different times moved to this position, and as each of them emerged from its shadow he had insisted that the other two were wrong. The other two were always somewhere ahead or still far behind.

Lenin parried in a confidential whisper, with the same slyly good-natured Asiatic grin. "Not at all. As you yourself so rightly said at the time: there must be uninterrupted civil war! The proletariat must not lay down its weapons! Where *were* your weapons, though?"

Parvus frowned. Nobody likes to remember his blunders.

Lenin had thought so much about it, had never thought so much about anything, and now, still gripping his companion by the shoulder, bending toward him, narrowing his eyes to a piercing squint, he was in the mood to share his thoughts.

"You shouldn't have waited for a national assembly, other than the Soviets. Once you convened the Petersburg Soviet, you had your proletarian national assembly. What you should have done . . ." He leaned forward as though sharpening the focus of his gaze, his mind, his words, and spoke still more confidentially. "What you should have done the very next day was set up an armed punitive organization under the Soviet. That would have been your *weapon!*"

Then he sat silent, with Parvus fixed in his searchlight beam. Nothing seemed so important to him.

A typical armchair philosopher, a dreamer. After years of thought he had made his discovery, and although it was a decade late he considered it incomparably important. The crippling frustrations of émigré existence, remote from the scene of action, from the real forces—what a miserable fate! All his energy for years and years had gone into quarrels and wrangles, and schisms and squabbles, and now Parvus had flung wide the gates into the world arena! But all he did was sit curled up on his bed like a gopher and grin.

The second most powerful mind in European socialism was going to waste in an émigré hole. He must be saved—for his own sake.

But also for the cause.

For the Plan.

"Well, then, do you understand my P l a n ? Do you accept it?"

How to break through that frozen stiffness? Had he dozed off? Was he in a trance? He wasn't taking anything in.

Parvus moved still nearer, and spoke right into his ear, so that he could not help hearing. "Vladimir Ilyich! Will you join our a l l i a n c e ?"

Like a man deaf and dumb. His eyes were unreadable. His tongue did not answer.

Hooking a hand to his shoulder, Parvus tried again. "Vladimir Ilyich! Your hour has come! The time has come for your underground to work and conquer! In the past you had no strength—I mean, no money—but now I'll pump in as much as you like. Just open the pipes for it to flow in. Tell us in which towns we should give money, and to whom. Give us names. Who is to receive leaflets and literature? Transporting weapons is more difficult, but we'll take weapons in too. And how are we going to coordinate our actions? I can't imagine how you manage from here, from Switzerland. Shall I arrange a move to Stockholm? It's very simple . . ."


On and on. Pushing. Pumping in his hippopotamus blood!

Lenin wriggled his shoulders and shook off Parvus's hand.

## 49

He had heard and understood it all perfectly. But a candid answer would not have passed the barrier of distrust and distaste in his breast.

His frankness about 1905 was quite enough.

Of course he saw the merits of Parvus's Plan. If he couldn't, who could? A splendid program—a *sound* program! The offensive tactics were practical, the means chosen reliable, the forces enlisted adequate.

Now he would admit it: there was no third thinker of such power, such penetrating vision in the International. Just the two of them.

And that was why he must be immensely circumspect. In political negotiations, always suspect a trap where the ground looks smoothest.

Was Parvus ahead once again? No. Theoretically and in a more general way Lenin had formulated the same ideas when war first broke out. But what was impressive in Parvus was his businesslike attention to concrete detail. Parvus the financier.

Faced with this grandiose program, Lenin could question neither its soundness nor its desirability.

It was all quite right. On the simple calculation that my worst enemy's worst enemy is my friend, the Kaiser's government was the best ally in the world. That such an alliance was permissible he agreed without a moment's hesitation: only an utter fool disdains serious assistance in a serious struggle.

An alliance—yes. But the dictates of caution must come first. Caution not as a merely negative measure, but as the condition of any effective action. With-

out super-super-caution, to hell with your alliance and
to hell with your Plan! We don't want the chorus of
Social Democratic grannies all over Europe indignantly
spluttering! Lenin, too, admitted—cautiously—that no
one need have qualms about France—the rentiers' republic. But he always knew where to stop, what to
leave unsaid, where to keep an emergency exit open.
Whereas Parvus paraded his wild views, and irre-
deemably compromised his political reputation.

This was when Lenin realized the other man's
weakness and his own superiority. Parvus had always
been the first to discover new ground, and had
tramped on ahead, blocking the way. But he lacked the
stamina for a long race. He had been unable to lead
the Soviets more than two months. Twenty years and
more of trying to reeducate the German socialists was
too much for him—he had broken loose, fallen by
the wayside. Whereas Lenin felt that he had the stamina
to run forever, without ever losing his breath, to run
as long as he remained conscious—if need be, he
would collapse into the grave with his race unfinished.
But he would never drop out.

An alliance—certainly, with pleasure. But in this
alliance he would be the coy bride, not the eager
bridegroom. Let them run after *you*. Behave in such a
way that even when you are weak you keep the upper
hand and your independence. In fact, Lenin had already done something of the sort in Bern. He had,
of course, not gone knocking on the German ambassador Romberg's door, like Parvus in Constantinople.
But when he had made his theses public he knew very
well whose ears they would please—and the theses
had reached the right ears. Romberg himself had sent
the Estonian revolutionary Kesküla to discuss things
with him and discover his intentions. And, of course,
while remaining within the limits of his actual program
—the overthrow of Tsarism, a separate peace with

Germany, secession of the non-Russian peoples, renunciation of the Turkish straits—he felt entitled to offer a slightly juicier bribe: without being untrue to himself, or distorting the line, he could and did promise Romberg the invasion of India by a Russian revolutionary army. In this there was no betrayal of *principles:* an assault on British imperialism was necessary, and who if not Russia could mount it? One of these days we will invade. Of course, it was a concession, a bribe, a swerve, a skid, but there was no danger in it. True, Kesküla had a wolfish look and wolfish ways, and he was stronger-minded and more effective than any wishy-washy Russian Social Democrat, but here too Lenin sensed no danger. Since Estonia must in any case be released, like all the subject peoples, from the Russian prison house, there was no distortion of the line: each of them used the other, without fear of stumbling. They introduced Artur Siefeldt and Moisei Kharitonov into the chain of contacts, and Kesküla went off to Scandinavia, where he was most helpful, especially with publications, found money for pamphlets, and helped organize contacts with Shliapnikov, and so with Russia.

All this lacked the grandeur of Parvus's Plan, but in its quiet little way was politically sound. And Lenin had kept his nose clean.

Parvus had now begun to show impatience. (Another of his faults.) Seeing that the conversation was not going as he wished, that he was letting his candidate slip, he said bitterly and contemptuously (which could do no good at all): "So you are like all the rest? Afraid of getting a smudge on your nose? Waiting for something?"

He had set such hopes on Lenin! He at least, he'd thought, is with me! If I can't get together with him, who else is there?

In some agitation, losing his millionaire's complacency altogether, he haltingly produced his last arguments. "Vladimir Ilyich, you must not fall behind the times. With other people it doesn't matter, but with you it would be unforgivable. Surely you must see that the age of revolutionaries with parcels of illegal literature and homemade bombs has gone, never to return. The new type of revolutionary is a giant, like you and me. He counts everything in millions—people and money alike—and he must be able to get his hands on the levers by which states are overthrown or established. Getting at those levers is not easy, and at times it is even necessary to join the chauvinists."

Also true. True enough. But . . .

(Should he ask what price the Russian revolution would have to pay for German help? He refrained from doing so, but kept the question in mind for the future. It would be naïve to expect such help for nothing.)

When you enter into an alliance, the first rule is not to trust your ally. On the treacherous ground of diplomacy, always see every ally as above all a potential cheat.

Lenin had not been dozing at all. He had been weighing things up. If anyone had been dozing, it was probably Parvus in his Berlin negotiations. Lenin finally opened his eyes and radiated anxious inquiry. He rattled off his questions like a drum roll. "Will Wilhelm's government really want to overthrow the Russian monarchy? Why should they? All they need is peace with Russia. They would happily go on living in friendship with the Russian monarchy. They only need our strikes to scare the Tsar and force him to make peace, that's all."

As though Parvus needed to be told! No one should be deceived by the way he looked—rich, well fed, with a carefully groomed imperial on his pendulous double chin. To speak frankly (and sometimes, with some people, he would go that far), the shadow of a separate peace had troubled all his negotiations with the German government. Peace between Russia and Germany would be the graveyard of the Great Idea. All the time there was a suspicion that, although they were giving money for revolution, in their hearts they thought only of a separate peace with the Tsar, and were surreptitiously sending people to make contact. These muffled secret tunnelings must be detected, and frustrated by timely ridicule: The Tsar is *no longer* in a position to make peace. If he suddenly decides to make peace with you, power in Russia may pass to a strong right-wing nationalist government, which will not respect the Tsar's undertakings—and you will only have reinforced their position. . . . It must be drilled into Prussian skulls that only a government having the people's confidence could sign a *real* peace with Germany. Let "peace" be the revolution's first slogan, the first concern of the new government! That government would find it easier to make concessions: because it would bear no guilt for the war. From such a government Germany could expect m u c h m o r e . . .

He could already see the treaty, and was ready to sign it himself in advance.

And he caught a gleam in Lenin's eyes which meant that he could see it too.

You couldn't go into every detail. (Nor should you.) There were various schools of thought among the Germans. The majority were inclined to view England as the main enemy, and were prepared to make peace with Russia. And unfortunately Secretary of State Jagow, the most Prussian of Prussians, although he considered the onslaught of Slavdom a greater danger than England, did not, you know, favor the plan to fragment Russia by revolution. (It was impossible to understand him fully: with his aristocratic mannerisms

and his effete skepticism, he did not conceal his distaste
for the diplomacy of secret agents, *hommes de confi-
ance,* dubious middlemen. It was, of course, a great hindrance that such a man should be the head of the German Foreign Ministry.)

Parvus, however, in spite of his exquisite ugliness,
could be captivating. The German ambassador in Copenhagen, Count Brockdorff-Rantzau, enchanted by
Parvus's incomparable intelligence, was his already.

All arguments must be used to prevent the catastrophe of a separate peace. They must strenuously try
to convince the Germans that revolution in Russia was
inevitable, that the whole country, and the army with it,
was in ferment, that educated society was seething with
discontent, not to mention the workers, including those
in arms production—a single match would be enough to
blow everything up. Why, it was even possible to set an
exact date—and keep to it.

But the sharp little man with the big head, the bald
brow, and the grin which hardly ever left his lips,
seemed even less convinced than Jagow, and showed no
mercy. "So you have in fact no agreement with them?
Just the semblance of one? Still just talking?"

The eternal privilege of those who never act themselves: to interrogate, be dissatisfied, find fault.

Rowing with both hands, Parvus straightened up
to prevent his body from collapsing backward like an
overstuffed sack. "Not on crested paper, of course! It's
all very fluid. And you have to keep its contours in sight
at every moment and determine its direction."

Try even to determine the direction of strategic
offensives. Explaining, urging, insistently advising
that whatever happened, they should not advance on
Petersburg! That would cause an upsurge of patriotism,
Russia would unite, and the revolution would subside.
At the same time, the Tsar must be denied any success
in the field, and in particular must not be allowed to

reach the Dardanelles, which would irreversibly reinforce his prestige. The best place to strike was on the
southern flank: make the Ukraine your ally, detach the
Donets coalfields, and Russia is finished.

Then again, they were afraid the earthquake
might set up tremors in Berlin. So that he also had to
persuade them that revolution in Russia would not
spread to Germany.

The little man jumped. "What's that? What did
you say?" Steadily pushing his obese companion away,
and winning more room for himself on the bed. "What
do you mean? Have you reconciled yourself to the idea
that the revolution will not go beyond Russia? Do you
really think that?" His eyes were hard and inquisitorial.
Suddenly—he would never mince his words when a
principle was threatened—he burst out indignantly:
"Why, that's treason!"

(No, Parvus was simply not a socialist. He was
something quite different.)

He, who never ventured outside Switzerland, never
set his hand to anything *practical,* had been proved
right again, must attack, must denounce. "How shortsighted! What poverty of vision! How could the revolution survive in a single country?"

It was the same old *permanent revolution* all over
again, the enchanted merry-go-round on which they
were doomed to circle forever, eternally following and
fleeing, hurling yesterday's or tomorrow's reproaches at
each other, not one of them ever in the right.

Didn't he want revolution in Germany? Was it
really not his aim? Was it true what they wrote about
him, that he had become a German patriot?

Parvus, though, was no longer a child, riding
that merry-go-round. A revolutionary of the new type,
a millionaire revolutionary, a financier and industrialist,
can afford to express himself more frankly. "World
revolution is not at present feasible, but a socialist

revolution in Russia is. Tsarism is the enemy against which *all* workers' parties everywhere must unite!"

More frankly does not mean frankly. It was a ticklish problem, one which you could not put into so many words in public discussions among socialists. Even tête-à-tête you wouldn't mention it to every fellow socialist.

You never knew where you had him—this mercurial creature with the bullet head and the sharp tongue. You could hardly ever tell what his next slogan would be—he always surprised everybody. You could never discover at all what he was thinking. Didn't he understand that Russian socialism had special tasks to perform? Didn't he accept them? Had his specific interest in Russia declined?

It was easier to discuss this problem with Brockdorff, even. (Indeed, Parvus had noticed that you could always discuss things more straightforwardly and simply with diplomats than with socialists.)

All he could do now was emphasize the elementary. "It is Tsarism which must be destroyed here and now, by any means possible, and that's all we must think of!"

And so to the main question—how do you destroy it? The whole point of his visit and of this conversation was to find out what underground organizations in the capitals and in the provinces Lenin was willing to assign immediately to the preparation of an uprising. Who and where were these people, with their ironclad unity and their invincible battle-readiness? Parvus knew what he was doing when he recommended this man to the German government as the most fanatical of Russian revolutionaries. He knew why he had come now to enlist him as an ally. For decades, Lenin had seemed merely a mad sectarian. He had cast off all allies, fragmented all his forces, refused to hear of a party of professors, would have nothing to do with smooth economic development, cared for nothing but the underground, always the underground, and his party of professional revolutionaries! In peacetime Parvus and everyone else had thought this absurd, but now that there was a war on they began at last to see clearly how provident, how farsighted, and how clever he was! The time had finally come to use his powerful, well-trained secret army! Now at last it would prove its worth. Parvus had been counting on this army in his negotiations in Berlin, he had been counting on it when he drew up his Plan.

But Lenin was not to be diverted, not to be thrown out of his stride like that. He had his own end in view and stubbornly pursued it. "And how can you equate the revolutionary situation of 1905 with the present situation in such a primitive fashion?"

Well, obviously this war was more destructive and more protracted, the masses incomparably more exhausted and embittered, the revolutionary organizations stronger, the liberals also stronger, while Tsarism had utterly failed to reinforce itself.

Lenin, however, persisted. His eyes seemed never to look directly at the other man, but to zigzag around him. "Very well. But how can you set a starting date so confidently *from outside?*"

"Well, Vladimir Ilyich, we must have some date to aim at, if we are to unite our activities. Suggest a different one, if you like. But January 9 is best, because it is symbolic, everybody remembers it, and many will begin without any signal from us. It will be easier to bring them out into the streets. And once the first few are out, there'll be no stopping it!"

Lenin was being very difficult. Understandable, though: to uncover his beloved underground would be like handing it over to someone else. Of course he didn't like the idea.

If Parvus was so ardently persistent, it meant that he was trying to take advantage of him.

"So what do you say, Vladimir Ilyich? The time has come to act!"

(Oh yes, I understand your Plan! You will emerge as the unifier of all the party groups. Add to that your financial power and your theoretical talent, and there you are—leader of a united party and of the Second Revolution? Not again?!)

From the inscrutable eyes, from the set lips, through the impenetrable bald dome, Parvus, himself extraordinarily perspicacious, seized Lenin's thoughts, opened them out, read them, and answered at a tangent. "My reason for suggesting that you go to Stockholm is so that you can be in charge from beginning to end. You need give me no names, tell me no secrets— just take the money, the leaflets, the weapons, and send them on! I'm not, you know"—Parvus sighed weakly; so exhausting, these political discussions—"I'm not the man I was ten years ago. I will not go to Russia. I consider myself German these days."

(All the more suspicious. Why in that case could he think of nothing but Russia?)

"I only want to see the Plan carried out."

. . . But perhaps we see the Plan in different ways?

Elusive as quicksilver, he slipped through Parvus's grip.

"You mean that I too should be seen dirtying my hands, like you, on the German General Staff? A revolutionary internationalist can't afford that."

Two more pulls at his invisible oars brought him alongside his armor-plated companion.

"You needn't get dirty! Why should you? I'll take all the dirty work on myself—I already have. The millions I give you will be clean. Just show me how to pipe them in. Once we've tied in your subterranean, submarine, secret connections with mine, we'll t o u c h o f f the Second Russian Revolution! Well?"

The eyes, which at the expense of color in the irises, lashes, and brows were pellucid concentrations of pure intelligence, tried to understand. Why this refusal?

But Lenin's own eyes were piercing gimlets. There was no way into them.

With his gimlet eyes and his crooked little grin—suspicious, shrewd, derisory—Lenin resisted these enticements.

"And for this purpose, you say, we need a conciliation conference in Geneva?" His voice was silky and venomous. "We must make peace? With the Mensheviks?" And he recoiled as though from a shock, as far as the bedstead would permit. "What are you thinking of? What does *making peace* mean? G i v i n g i n t o t h e M e n s h e v i k s ?" He tossed his head violently, as though he were butting someone. "Ne-ver! Not for anything! Peace with the Mensheviks? I would sooner see Tsarism survive another thousand years than give an inch to the Mensheviks!"

And anyway—was he or wasn't he a socialist?!

Lenin went on butting the air after he had stopped speaking, as though he were finishing someone off. As though he were finishing what he had to say soundlessly, in a frenzied pantomime.

Not a thing did Parvus understand. This, after all, was not what he had come for. The greatest, most indefatigable, and most extreme of revolutionaries in the most favorable of situations, with assistance lavished upon him—would not make a revolution?

Parvus, losing hope by now, asked point-blank: "So why have you spent twenty years on theoretical battles and border disputes? Where is your logic? You built up an underground, didn't you? Here is the best possible occasion for using it, there'll never be another like it as long as you live! Surely you weren't just playing a part?"

Lenin was never stuck for an answer. "If we're going to accuse each other of inconsistency . . . You used to say that a handful of people cannot revolutionize the masses. Do you still say so?"

Parvus's chin was suddenly too heavy for his head, his head for his neck, and his neck for his body, his hands drooped between his knees.

"We-e-ell . . ."

With Lenin's refusal, the Great Plan was almost in ruins.

"All right then . . . Good . . . or not so good . . . there's so little time . . . I will have to create my own organization."

Lenin has miscalculated! He'll be sorry someday.

"You might at least let me have one of your men, our mutual friend perhaps?"

(No good burning bridges, no good quarreling, Parvus may come in useful someday.)

"Who do you mean?"

"Hanecki."

"He's yours."

"I've already got Chudnovsky and Uritsky. What about Bukharin?"

"No, this is not for him."

"All right. But you yourself, will you go to Scandivania? I can get you there quickly."

Lenin's eyes were gimlets.

"No, no, no!"

Parvus was helpless under the burden of his own weight. He heaved a deep sigh.

"Ah, well . . . There's one other thing I've dreamed of all my life and can now afford: a socialist journal of my own." He tried to throw back his swollen head proudly, in imitation of the bold and ardent spirit who had first thought of the name. "I'll call it *The Bell*."

Four feet felt a jarring bump as the bed landed on the shoemaker's floor.

## 50

The revolutionary who succeeds underground is not the one who hides like a mouse under the floorboards, shunning the light of day and social involvement. The successful and resourceful underground worker takes a very active part in the everyday life of those around him, he shares their weaknesses and passions, he is in the public eye, in the hurly-burly, with an occupation which everyone understands, and he may spend much of his time and strength on his daily routine—but his main, his secret activity goes on side by side with his overt daily round, and all the more successfully if they are organically connected. The wisest way is also the simplest: to combine your secret and your overt activity easily and naturally.

This was how Parvus saw it. (His experience in underground work was slight—the few months in 1905, between the suppression of the Soviet and his arrest, then between his return from banishment and his departure abroad.) He understood still better that a man's natural occupation is one for which he has a vocation and talent. So, in May 1915, as he prepared to carry on alone after Lenin's disastrous refusal to join him in making a revolution, he decided, with as little conscious thought as he gave to breathing, that he and his collaborators would make commerce their first and chief occupation, and that revolution would be run in tandem with business.

That same summer he set up in neutral Denmark —which retained the main prerogative of all free Western countries, the right to trade without impediment—

an import-export agency, which in present circumstances would naturally be ready to deal with firms in any country at all—Germany, Russia, England, Sweden, the Netherlands—buying and selling where prices were most favorable. With Lenin's agreement, Hanecki at once became business manager of Parvus's new concern. The combination of two such ardent commercial spirits does not merely double their power, but increases it many times over. Then they were joined by a third, who was very nearly their equal—Georg Sklarz. (Not, it must be said, blown along by a whim of fate, but obligingly sent to cooperate with them by the Intelligence branch of the German General Staff.) This Sklarz (who achieved notoriety in postwar Germany, among other things for a succession of court cases in which he showed himself to be a remarkable actor) became an indispensable member of the trio—a business genius like his partners, resourceful, quick-thinking, reacting silently and quickly to any assignment or any twist of events, and always emerging successful. (He had brought with him two other Sklarz brothers: Waldemar, who went to work in the trade-and-revolution agency itself, and Henryk, who, under the pseudonym of Pundik, and in partnership with Romanovich and Dolgopolsky, already ran a secret office in Copenhagen, investigating illicit exports from Germany on behalf of the German General Staff.) The idea of combining business with political activity soon proved its value: *Geschäft* served politics, and politics smoothed the path of *Geschäft*. Support from the General Staff made the agency's transactions easier and its profits greater.

Within a few months of its founding, the import-export agency was a flourishing business, buying, selling, and shipping, with no thought of narrow specialization, copper, chrome, nickel, and rubber, transferring from Russia to Germany mainly grain and produce, from Germany to Russia mainly technical equipment, chemicals, medicines, but the range of goods supplied also included stockings, contraceptives, Salvarsan, caviar, cognac, and used motor vehicles (in Russia, they were able to stipulate that these should not be commandeered for military purposes). In trade with Western countries this was one of many such agencies uncomfortably jostling each other, but in trade with Russia, which for him mattered most, Parvus's agency had a monopoly. Some goods were shipped openly, with legal export licenses; others were shipped under false bills of lading, or even smuggled. This required ingenuity in packing and loading, and there had to be someone to take responsibility if caught, but it was Hanecki and Sklarz who involved themselves in all this, letting Parvus remain quietly in the shade, his favorite place, to deal with matters of high policy.

What made the combination of commercial and revolutionary activity an idea of genius was that revolutionary agents posing as business representatives, with the Petersburg lawyer Kozlovsky playing the main part, could travel quite legally to Russia, inside Russia, and back again to Parvus. But Parvus's brilliance was seen still more clearly in his arrangements for sending money. To pass money from the German government quickly and without hindrance into the hands of Russian revolutionaries might seem an impossible task, but the import-export agency performed it with ease. It sent goods and only goods to Russia, but always in excess of what it bought there. The earnings of collaborating firms, such as Fabian Klingsland, were banked in the normal way (in the Petersburg branch of the Bank of Siberia), and it was then entirely up to the agency to decide whether or not to withdraw the money from Russia—in fact, it was to Russia's advantage that it should stay there. Hanecki's intermediary in Petersburg, Yevgenia Sumenson, could withdraw any sum at any time and hand it over to revolutionaries.

This was where Parvus showed his genius: the importing of goods which Russia badly needed to wage war provided funds for knocking Russia out of the war!

Parvus's method of selecting the agency's revolutionary staff showed the same insistence on combining the overt and the covert. For this purpose, he set up yet another subsidiary organization in Copenhagen—the Institute for Research into the Consequences of War. To recruit its personnel he frequently and openly sought the acquaintance of socialists and met them for discussions. Whenever a candidate was eager, and qualified, to plunge into the depths, he did so and became a secret agent. Those who proved unsuitable or intractable were kept in the dark, the conversation followed its natural course, and they might be taken on as overt members of a legal institute. The institute itself was not fictitious, but gratified Parvus's long-cherished passion for economic research, just as the heavily subsidized *Bell,* published in Germany, gratified his passion for socialism. (One who longed to join the institute was Bukharin—and there could have been no better place for him, nor could the institute have found a more useful member—but the fastidious and puritanical Lenin forbade his young comrade to associate with the shady Parvus, just as he forbade Shliapnikov to go near the dubious Hanecki.)

All this Parvus managed brilliantly, because here he was in his element. But what came next was more difficult. To *whom* should this money be given in Russia? And *how* could you bring about a revolution in that huge country with a dozen business representatives and a few Western socialists like Kruse? It was easiest in Petersburg, where he had many contacts, where the lawyer Kozlovsky could receive clients without arousing

suspicion and recruit the necessary people in the factories, and where the zealots of the Inter-District group
were active—following what had always been Parvus's
own line, recognizing neither Bolsheviks nor Mensheviks, and readily accessible to him through one of their
members, Uritsky. Although the socialist forces in
Petersburg were split, Parvus had put together a strong
group of activists, especially in the Putilov factory. But
while it has been truly said that revolution in any state
succeeds or fails in the capital, there was no assurance
that the initial shock would be effective in such a large
country without disturbances in the provinces. Parvus,
however, had live connections of his own only in Odessa, and through Odessa with Nikolayev. There was no
one to stir up this inert, mute country as a whole. A
handful of agents, however freely they spent, could not
create a network in the few remaining months. Whereas Lenin had a ready-made network—and had treacher-
ously concealed it.

But Parvus, from his memories of 1905, understood very well how disturbances begin. To start a
strike, or a riot, to bring the people out in the streets,
you do not need the unanimous consent of the
majority, or even one in four—indeed, it is wasted effort to try and prepare even a tenth of them for action.
A single shrill cry from the thick of the crowd, a
single orator at the factory gates, two or three toughs
brandishing fists or sticks are often enough to keep a
whole shift from their benches or bring them out into
the streets. Then there are neighborly conversations
condemning the government, the transmission of alarm-
ing rumors (which with no further effort can be left to
strike at a distance like a charge of electricity), the
scattering of leaflets in factory lavatories and smoking
rooms, under workbenches—for each and any of these
preliminary blows you need no more than five men to a

factory, and if you cannot find five who will do it out of conviction, you can buy help in the nearest tavern—what tavern scrounger refuses money?

In any other circumstances, sporadic trouble-making in factories would not have been enough, but now, in the second year of a war which had already devoured so many, with hunger suddenly threatening, with the army losing battle after battle, with the whole country in ferment, with revolution still fresh in the minds of the present generation, a few such jolts—Parvus was convinced of it—could set off a landslide. That was his strategy—to start an avalanche with a few light snowfalls. Without Lenin's help, in the remaining months he could do no more. But the date itself was fraught with menace for Tsarism: even if there were no agents at work, if Yevgenia Sumenson spent not a single ruble, January 9 still could not pass quietly. All the same, it would be good to give a helping hand.

So Parvus, who had Count von Brockdorff-Rantzau completely under his spell, and practically dictated his dispatches from Copenhagen to the Foreign Ministry, confidently promised revolution in Russia on January 9, 1916.

He hoped, at least, that it would be so. Overgenerously endowed with the gift of far-reaching and penetrating prophecy, he was nonetheless a creature of earth and could not always distinguish a flash of prophetic insight from the rushes of desire. He longed so violently for a devastating revolution in Russia that he could be forgiven for misinterpreting his emotion.

This was not, however, something which the German government, and especially Secretary of State Gottlieb von Jagow, would readily forgive. Always the ironist, always contemptuous of this grubby socialist millionaire, Jagow now concluded that Parvus had been deceiving the German Reich all along, that he had never seriously tried to bring about a revolution, that he had most probably simply pocketed the millions given to him. Intelligence services have a rule that such expenditure is not subject to audit. But for the rest of 1916 the Ministry of Foreign Affairs paid Parvus not a pfennig more.

This didn't mean total defeat, and outwardly it was not a defeat at all. The wheels of the import-export agency went on turning, and making money. The General Staff compassionately filled the gap left by the Foreign Ministry. The Research Institute continued collecting information and studying it. Parvus took an active hand in supplying Denmark with cheap coal, won over the Danish trade unions, was treated as their friend and equal by Danish and later by German socialist leaders. He finally obtained German citizenship, which he had been begging for since 1891, and there seemed to be no doubt that at the first postwar elections he would take his place among the leaders of the socialist group in Parliament. His *Bell* continued to appear, exhorting Germany to patriotic socialism. His excessive personal wealth grew and grew, and he had holdings in almost all neutral countries, as well as in Turkey and Bulgaria of course, where he had first begun to make his fortune. His house in the aristocratic quarter of Copenhagen was furnished with the flamboyance of the nouveau riche, guarded by savage dogs, and an elegant Adler carried him from his door. He even managed to preserve intact his influence on Count von Brockdorff-Rantzau, and to impress on this constant conversation partner the full complexity of the revolutionary's task, the intricate mechanics of his difficulties. Through Brockdorff, too, as far as tact allowed, he tried to obstruct the renewed German quest for a separate peace with Russia.

You might suppose that the long procession of successes which came to this man would have more than satisfied him. Not so! His uneasy consciousness of a mission unfulfilled—although he no longer had any intentions of returning to *that* country—secretly teased and tormented him. During his leisurely suppers with the Prussian aristocrat he expounded a variant, adapted to the German outlook, of what was now not so much a program as his political testament, a hazy outline of the future. How the revolution, once begun, must quickly broaden its scope, like the great French Revolution, by trying and executing the Tsar: only such an inaugural sacrifice could show the revolution that it need recognize no boundaries for itself. How the peasants must feel free to take the redistribution of land into their own hands—which alone would open the floodgates of anarchy. And when anarchy was at its height, in full flood, that was the very moment when Germany, by military intervention, with minimal losses and enormous advantages, could rid itself forever of the threat from the East: sink Russia's fleet, take away its arms, raze its fortifications, forbid it ever again to form an army or establish war industries, or, better still, any industry at all, cripple it by amputating all that could be amputated—leave it, in short, a *tabula rasa,* so that it could forget its ten centuries of meanness and begin its history all over again.

Parvus never forgot an injury.

But today he did not see what more he could do.

Meanwhile, the government of the German Empire was disgracing itself by seeking a separate peace with this still undestroyed power.

But Secretary of State Jagow's health was steadily declining, and in the late autumn of 1916 he was happy to retire, giving up his post to the more active Zimmermann, who did not take over with it his predecessor's Old World distaste for secret agents and political brokers.

New plans of action soared into view. And Parvus's old reproach to Lenin raised its head. *Why* had he done it? What did he mean by it?

The bed hit the shoemaker's floor with all four feet and Parvus was catapulted upright on his pedestal legs. Painfully stretching, he shuffled across the room, carrying his pampered body like a heavy sack. He went around and sat on the other side of the table, no longer caring about soiling his snow-white cuffs on the Ulyanovs' dirty oilcloth.

Now his smile was not for a man of power, and an equal, but for a pathetic little animal in a hole.

"That's it, then, is it? Zimmerwald? . . . Kienthal? . . . Getting the leftists to vote correctly? . . . And what has the great party done at home in Russia these past two years? . . . Why isn't there a single bubble to be seen on the surface?"

Lenin just sat there, sinking into the bed, and bent his heavy head without answering.

"Didn't you say you had no need of money?"

Lenin's answer was lost, almost inaudible. "We never said that, Israel Lazarevich. We need money very, very badly. Desperately."

"But I offered you money! And you refused!"

Lenin's voice was parched and strained. "What do you mean, refused? A reasonable offer of help, without strings, we never refuse. We're only too glad . . ."

"You're just playing children's games here in Switzerland." The great hulk would have liked to gloat, but there was nothing to gloat over. Russia was not losing the war, Germany was not winning it; Germany's main ally, and his own, was giving up the fight.

Lenin's words seemed to stick in his throat. "For serious games you have to pay a serious price."

He looked sick. His eyes, less secretive than usual,

were full of pain, and his next words were spoken without vehemence, with no other motive, it seemed, than to distract himself from his pain. "After all, Israel Lazarevich, your revolution, too, was a will-o'-the-wisp, a soap bubble. It was naïve to expect anything else."

Parvus began to heave indignantly, and the lamp flame flickered, leaped, and smoked as his breath played on it. "We had f o r t y - f i v e   t h o u - s a n d on strike in Petersburg! Do you think you, sitting here, could bring out forty-five?"

He forestalled Lenin's retort that the forty-five thousand included some of his people. "The Putilov workers got the date wrong—but they were marvelous! What a fracas they kicked up! But the Nevskaya Zastava let me down—why didn't you bring them out? I staged a splendid strike in Nikolayev—ten thousand came out! With impossible demands, so that an uprising was certain! But they, too, were four days late. It's not so easy from this distance to tie them all to the same day. But how is it that Moscow never stirred? What was your Moscow committee doing?"

(Lenin only wished that he knew!)

Parvus warmed to his theme, crooking a finger for each of his successes, as though he were boasting about his wealth. "I brought out the Yekaterinoslav Ironworks! And the Tula Copperworks! And the Tula Cartridge Factory! . . ."

All these strikes had indeed broken out in January, though not on the ninth—but who had started them, who had led them, there on the spot? It was not clear at this distance, and everybody claimed credit, including the Mensheviks.

"We came very close—but where were *your* people? The Inter-District group gave me wholehearted support, they've got fire in their bellies, but they're a mere handful. While you and the Mensheviks are still tossing balls to each other? Russia is flooded with leaflets—are you going to tell me they're yours? I was the one who blew up the *Empress Maria*—or didn't you notice it?" Parvus thundered on, his eyes staring wildly. "The battleship on the Black Sea—didn't you notice it?!"

He threw up his manicured white hands—look at the hands that blew up a battleship!

"Why wouldn't you join us, Vladimir Ilyich? Where are *your* strikes? Where are your riots? Which factories can you bring to a standstill on a prearranged date? . . . Which of the nationalist organizations are you working with?"

Does he really not understand? . . . For all his cleverness? My disguise is a success, then! I must keep it up!

Why hadn't he joined in! . . . Of course, he could have gotten around the Mensheviks somehow. Made some arrangement to share the leadership (although this, yes, this, was the most painful and difficult thing of all). Only . . .

Only—everyone's abilities are limited. Lenin was —a writer of articles. And pamphlets. He gave lectures. He made speeches. He carried on agitation among young leftists. He trounced opportunists everywhere in Europe. He believed that he had acquired a thorough knowledge of problems connected with industry, agriculture, the strike movement, trade unions. And now, after reading Clausewitz, of military matters, too. He understood now what war was, and how an armed uprising should be carried out. And he could explain it all, with tireless clarity, to any audience.

There was only one thing he was incapable of— *action*. The one thing he could not do was—blow up a battleship.

"But all is not yet lost, Vladimir Ilyich," said Parvus, consoling, encouraging, from across the table. He took his gold watch from his vest pocket and nodded at it approvingly. "We'll postpone the revolution until January 9, 1917! But let's do it together! Shall we be together this time?"

Why on earth shouldn't they? The perspicacious Parvus simply couldn't understand.

Lenin could not keep up his end of this conversation. He was lost for an answer. How could he talk about entering or not entering into an alliance, when his position was so ridiculously weak? Dignified concealment of his impotence was what he must aim at: hiding the fact that he had no functioning organization in Russia, no underground. If it existed at all, it was a law unto itself, and he had no control over its motions or timing. He simply did not know what *was* there—he was not in constant communication with Russia, had no means of sending instructions or receiving a reply. He was only too glad if Shliapnikov, who was all by himself, managed to pitch some copies of *Sozialdemokrat* over the frontier. He had corresponded with his sister Anya in invisible ink, but even this link had snapped. How could *he* stir up rebellion among the national minorities? If would be something if he could preserve a fragment of his own party . . .

Parvus, flabbily draped over his creaking chair, had not exhausted his generosity. "How do your collaborators cross the Russian front? Surely not on their own feet, or in rowboats? That's all out of date, nineteenth-century stuff. It's time you forgot all that! If you like, we'll provide them with documents and they can travel first-class, like my people . . ."

Parvus, no doubt, was ugly—as seen by women, or a public meeting. But his colorless, watery eyes were irresistibly clever—and cleverness was something Lenin appreciated.

If only he could get away from them. Parvus must not guess the truth.

Must not guess that a c t i o n was just what

Lenin could not manage. All the rest he knew how to do. But one thing he could not do: bring the great moment nearer, make it happen.

Parvus, with his millions, with his weapons probably already in the ports, with his conspiratorial skill, with the Putilov factory already securely in his grip—Parvus clapped his hands, the hands of a man of action, white and pudgy though they were, and continued his interrogation. "What are you waiting for, Vladimir Ilyich? Why don't you give the signal? How long do you intend to wait?"

Lenin was waiting for—for *something* to happen. For some favorable tide of affairs to carry his little boat home—to a *fait accompli*.

Ludicrously, all the ideas Lenin had based his life on could neither change the course of the war nor transform it into a civil war nor force Russia to lose.

The little boat lay like a toy on the sand, and there was no tide to float it ...

All this time the letter on expensive greenish paper lay there asking him: What do you say then, Vladimir Ilyich? Will y o u r people cooperate or won't they? Where are your meeting points? Who takes delivery of weapons? Tell me what you have there of any real use.

Just the question which Lenin could not answer, since he had nothing. Switzerland was on one planet, Russia on another. What he had was ... a tiny group, calling itself a party, and he could not account for all its members—some might have split off. What he had was ... *What Is to Be Done?, One Step Forward, Two Steps Back, Two Tactics, Materialism and Empirico-Criticism, Imperialism.* What he had was—a head, capable at any moment of providing a centralized organization with decisions, each individual revolutionary with detailed instructions, and the masses with stirring slogans. And nothing more, no more today than he had eighteen months ago. So that tactical caution and simple pride alike kept him from exposing his weak spot to Parvus, any more than he had eighteen months ago.

But Parvus hung over the table, his fishy eyes full of mockery, his brow no less steeply terraced than Lenin's, and awaited, demanded an answer.

He had very cleverly seized the initiative, asking question after question so that he need do no explaining himself. But he must have his own reasons for this approach at this particular time, after eighteen months of silence.

Avoiding the puzzled, hovering gaze from under Parvus's upturned, hairless eyebrows, rolling his head as he perused the letter, Lenin tried to think how he could refuse help without giving offense, without losing an ally, how to conceal his own secret while divining that of his companion. Skipping what was in the letter and looking for what was not there.

Lenin was always eager, above all, to seize on weaknesses which offset his own.

If there was no chink in Parvus's armor—why was he making this second approach, and so insistently? Had his strength failed him? Or his funds, perhaps? Had his network broken down? Or perhaps the German government was no longer paying so well? They made you work for your money, once they had you hooked.

How good it was to be independent! Oh no, we're not so weak as you think! Not nearly as weak as some!

His right hand as usual made pencil marks in preparation for his reply—straight lines, wavy lines, squiggles, question marks, exclamation marks . . . While his left hand restlessly rubbed his forehead, and his forehead gathered in the points he would make.

Trotsky's complaints against his former mentor —that he was frivolous, lacked stamina, and abandoned his friends in time of trouble—were so much sentimental nonsense. These were all pardonable faults, and need not stand in the way of an alliance. If only Parvus had not committed gross political errors. He should not have exposed himself publicly by rushing at a mirage of revolution. He should not have made *The Bell* a cesspool of German chauvinism. The hippo had wallowed in the mire with Hindenburg—and destroyed his reputation. Destroyed himself as a socialist once and for all.

It was sad. There were not many socialists like him!

(But although he had destroyed himself, there was no sense in quarreling. Parvus might still be enormously helpful.)

Regaining his confidence, Lenin raised his eyes from the letter, from the edge of the table, and looked at his indefatigable rival. The contours of his head, shapeless enough at the best of times, and of his pudgy shoulders, blurred and trembled.

Trembled as though they were shaking with grief. Grief that even with Lenin he could not make himself fully understood.

His features faded, till he was no more than a lengthening streak of bluish mist. He bowed, drifted across the room, and seeped through the window.

But while there was still time Lenin shouted after him, not crowing over him, but just so that the truth would not go untold: "Let myself be tied to someone else's policy? Not for anything in the world! That's where you made your mistake, Israel Lazarevich! I'll take what I need from others—of course! But tie my *own* hands? No!!! It would be absurd to speak of an alliance that would mean tying our own hands!"

The whole scene vanished like smoke, leaving no trace of Sklarz or of his case. His hat, too, belatedly whisked off the table and flung itself after him.

Lenin had proved the more farsighted of the two.

Though he had made no revolution, though he was helpless and ineffectual, he knew that he was right, he had not let himself be misled: ideas are more durable than all those millions, I can go on without them. Never fear, even the conferences for women and deserters will prove to have been worthwhile. Under the crimson flag of the International I can wait another thirty years if need be.

He had preserved his greatest treasure—his honor as a socialist.


No, it's too soon to think of surrender! Too soon to abandon Switzerland. A few more months of persistent work and the Swiss party will be split.

Soon after that—we will start the revolution here!

And from Switzerland the flame of revolution will be kindled throughout Europe.

FROM KNOT III

# MARCH 1917

# [1]

That past winter had seen an unbroken series of dramatic struggles which might have culminated in a proletarian revolution spreading from Switzerland throughout Europe but for the base betrayal of a gang of leaders who had defiled, polluted, debauched the whole Swiss party, foremost and vilest among them the scoundrelly intriguer and political prostitute Grimm. And that old ruin Greulich. And other filthy villains.

The superficial, Philistine eye—that of most people, and even most revolutionaries—cannot discern the tiny cracks in a huge mountain, cannot understand that if you know how to widen them you can bring the whole mass crashing down. The terrified man in the street, observing all Europe at war, armies numbering millions, millions of shell bursts, could not believe that it was in the power of a tiny group of highly resolute men to stop this iron hurricane (or change its direction). True, an enormous event must first take place—a revolution, like the war, involving all Europe. But revolution in Switzerland, which though small and neutral was trilingual and at the heart of Europe, might suffice to set it off. To this end, it was necessary to gain control of the Swiss Social Democratic Party, or if that proved impossible, to split it and detach its battle-worthy section. And all that was needed to split such a party— though opportunists and armchair theorists would hardly believe it—was some five resolute members together with three foreigners capable of providing the local comrades with a program, drafting texts or theses for their speeches, and writing pamphlets for them.

Thus, fewer than a dozen skillful and steadfast socialists were enough to turn Europe upside down! The Skittle Club!

They had thought it all out in the autumn, and now they set to work. At first, merely to repair the psychological damage caused by their failure at the party congress in November, Lenin drafted outline instructions for the young leftists, summarizing their practical tasks in the struggle. Many months of absorption in the subject, and even the reading of insignificant Swiss newspapers, now came in handy. Next he started holding meetings to explain his theses in detail. The theses were allowed to leak throughout the country. The idea was that if even one tiny local party organization *adopted* the theses, it would be legitimate to demand their publication in the socialist press, and broaden the discussion. They explored the possibility of publishing the theses in leaflet form, and distributing several thousand copies. (Nobody was any good at distribution: they were all talk and no action, all depressives or malingerers.)

Perhaps they should start publishing leaflets independently? Münzenberg, leader of the young, and Lenin's main support, grumbled that there was plenty of *literature* already. (As if they had ever had literature *like this*.) They were weak, the Swiss leftists, infernally weak.

The impatient gaze of the revolutionary noticed another welcome crack, which promised more, and sooner: another Swiss party congress was due to be held soon, at the beginning of February,[1] and the leadership had been forced to promise that it would be especially devoted to the party's *attitude toward war*. This provided a marvelous opportunity to badger and batter the whole opportunist leadership, to bombard them in full view of the Swiss masses with vitally important questions which they could not evade. Was it

right that Switzerland should be brought to the brink of
war? Was it right that descendants of William Tell
should die for the international banks? Was this right,
was that right? . . . You could go on like that forever.
Another reason why such a congress was particularly
dangerous for the opportunists was that parliamentary
elections were due in September 1917—next year—and
whether the congress now decided *for* or *against* the
fatherland, the party would undoubtedly split during
the elections, or even cease to exist. (And that is exactly
what we want!)

The opportunists got the point and began maneu-
vering: could they perhaps postpone the rashly promised congress altogether, avoid making any decision at
all on the war question, as long as Switzerland itself was
not at war, or leave the decision until all wars came
to an end?

They still did not know how the blow would be
struck, how the question would be put: not in terms
of "support for the fatherland" or "opposition to mili-
tarism," but with relentless straightforwardness: the
struggle against war is impossible without socialist revolution! The vote, in effect, would be not about war
but for or against the immediate expropriation of the
banks and industry. The Skittle Club busily prepared a
resolution for the congress: Platten wrote a feeble version, and Lenin redrafted it in his name. (No easy
work, but worthwhile. The Swiss left must be given all
possible help by their foreign comrades.) They must
attack heavily on all fronts. Demobilize the Swiss army
immediately! Defense of Switzerland is a hypocritical
phrase! *Switzerland's* peace policy is criminal! The result could be a colossal success: a resolution of this sort
adopted by the Swiss congress would win the enthusias-
tic support of the working class in all civilized countries.

But the opportunists bestirred themselves. It was
learned confidentially that the people at the top were

preparing to *postpone* the congress—shameless wretches! In cases like this, you must get your blow in first. Rob them of the initiative. So they instructed Bronski to put forward a resolution at a meeting of the Zurich organization "against agitation behind the scenes for the adjournment of the congress and condemning symptoms of a lapse into social chauvinism." It had been possible to demand a recount, and they managed to get the resolution carried! This was hitting the centrists where it hurt—they dreaded being thought of as chauvinists.

But the opportunist gang were so shameless by now that even this didn't deter them! They called a meeting of the Presidium for the following day, and threw off their masks. (Platten, Nobs, and Münzenberg were present, so that all this was reliably reported.) Old Greulich stooped to defamation of the whole Zurich party organization: it includes many deserters, he said, people vouched for by us, and it is only to be expected that their views on the question of national self-defense . . . Somebody else shouted out that if the party was going to be insulted, as it had been by Bronski's resolution, "we, from St. Gall, shall be forced to withdraw from it!" "These comrades," he said, "have a poor opinion of the Swiss workers" (hinting that it was *foreigners* who were muddying the waters) . . . Another of them had an attack of chauvinist hysteria: Go, and take the formulas of your international congresses with you! Discussing the war question in wartime is madness! At such moments any nation is united by recognition of its common destiny. (United with its capitalists . . .) How can we demobilize the army, when it is defending our frontiers? Why, if Switzerland is in danger, the working class will rise to its defense! (Hear, hear!) But Grimm behaved even more shamelessly than the others. What a political crook he was, the chairman of the Zimmerwald and Kienthal conferences: Think of it, he said, if war begins we are supposed to raise a rebellion! . . . He made vile innuendos against *foreigners* and the young. He, the centrist, sided with the chauvinists, and his vote decided the issue: by an insignificant majority—7 to 5—they agreed to postpone the congress *indefinitely* (i.e., till the end of the war . . . A uniquely disgraceful decision!) Grimm was an out-and-out traitor.

The scoundrel, the treacherous swine! Enough to drive you insane! It was all the more necessary now to intensify the war within the party as never before. The only thing left to them was to cut the ground from under Grimm's feet. He blocked their way completely: it was urgently necessary to ruin his reputation, expose him, strip off his mask. Just as in a fight the hand feels for the most suitable object to grip and to strike with, so the brain of an embattled politician chooses among moves as deviously swift as lightning. His first thought was—Naine! Naine was not very far to the left, and it was unusual for him to vote with them. So that it would be particularly advantageous to overthrow Grimm with Naine's help. How, exactly? By writing an open letter to Naine's newspaper *publicly* calling Grimm a scoundrel and saying that it was henceforth impossible to remain in the Zimmerwald organization with him! . . . Better still, let's get e v e r y o n e we can to write to Naine's paper—and bury Grimm forever under an avalanche of open letters and votes of protest. Every minute is precious. We must rally the left everywhere, and set them on Grimm.

A dramatic moment. At La Chaux-de-Fonds the faithful Abramovich supported the move. In Geneva, Brilliant and Guilbeaux were undecided.

While, in Zurich, the leftists and the young met night after night to work out their plan of attack. It became clear that open letters were not enough. They must commit *political murder,* make sure that Grimm would never get on his feet again.

This was the plan: All supporters in Zurich at the time were quickly called in, and Lenin, Krupskaya, Zinoviev, Radek, and Levi walked over to Münzenberg's lodgings, several blocks away. Then, when all the militants were assembled, Willi summoned Platten by telephone, giving no reasons, but saying that it was urgent. They had to set a trap for him. For some time he had obviously been afraid—of Grimm and of a split—and had been reluctant to learn from international experience, to show himself too Swiss, too parochial—and so, for that matter, had Nobs. (Where, come to think of it, had they sprung from? They had merely *enrolled* with the left at Zimmerwald . . .) So Platten had to be taken unawares, and by the throat.

In he came—and when he saw not just Münzenberg, as he had expected, but six of them in a tight huddle in the little room, three squashed together on the bed, and all of them looking somber, his big-browed, candid face, which was not equipped to dissemble, expressed bewilderment and alarm. If there had been just one to whom he could turn for support or encouragement! There was no one. They shoved him into a corner seat—away from the door, behind a chest of drawers—and all six of them bore down on him, shifting their chairs closer, or leaning forward on the bed. Then Münzenberg (cast for the part) announced in his insolent, ringing voice: "We, our whole group, I mean, have decided to break immediately and finally with Grimm, and to discredit him in the eyes of the whole world." Platten must choose: "Either you're with us, or you're with Grimm." Platten didn't know what to do with himself, he gazed around that ring of faces in agitation, looking for a hint of kindness, but even

Nadya wore the frozen stare of a witch. Platten mopped his brow, kneaded his weak chin, pleaded for time to think, but while he talked the six remained motionless, grimly silent, looking at him as though he was their enemy (all this was the joker Radek's idea), and nothing could have frightened him more. Platten lost his head and began to give way, but suggested that perhaps it needn't be done so abruptly! They could warn Grimm, call him to order . . . No!!! It was all over! All decided! All Platten could do was choose: you're either with us, in an honorable international alliance, or with your Swiss traitor, and we shall disgrace the pair of you! And we want your answer now!

Platten seized his head with both hands. Sat still for a while.

Surrendered.

Writing a pamphlet to discredit Grimm was to be Radek's task. He could easily have done it, puffing away at his pipe, before the night was out. But the lazy creature wrote nothing. Lenin had to spend hour after hour walking around Zurich with him, coaxing and scolding, urging him to write and to make it really scathing, as he alone could. Whatever else, he was an incomparable journalist.

The next step was to attack Grimm at a session of the International Socialist Commission. Lenin stayed away, not wishing to make himself conspicuous, and Zinoviev, Radek, Münzenberg, and Levi were the accusers; Grimm's activities in Switzerland were criminal, outrageous, depraved—and he should therefore be expelled from the Zimmerwald leadership. (Dethroned.) A simultaneous attack was mounted in Münzenberg's Youth International. Their next idea was to press for a referendum in the party, to decide whether a congress should be organized immediately, in March. The argument for the referendum (Lenin had to write it himself) was the best thing in the whole campaign: the postponement of the congress was called a *defeat for socialism!*

What an uproar there was. What a dust storm! It was m-m-marvelous!!! The party leaders howled with indignation, rushed to refute the charges. No socialist can stand up to a bold, harsh indictment from the left. One accusing voice can lay low a thousand opportunists.

M-m-marvelous! It had come off! Just what was needed.

At the cantonal congress they managed to collect a sixth of the votes for the left's resolution. This was a major victory!

It was also the high point of the campaign. After that, it began to peter out.

Grimm attacked the referendum furiously—and frightened the youngsters.

Nobs, foxily cautious, publicly dissociated himself from the referendum.

While Platten, the weakling, said nothing . . . Some good planning a battle around him! He was hopeless. He didn't want to learn how to organize a revolutionary party.

Nor was anyone willing to publish Radek's pamphlet: "If we do, we will be hounded out of the party." There are your leftists for you! There are your fireeaters!

Sensing their weakness, Grimm called an ultraprivate conference and invited the leftists. Münzenberg and Bronski of course did not go. But Nobs and Platten came to heel.

No, they were already three quarters of the way down the slope to social patriotism. The Swiss left were a thoroughly worthless lot, people without backbone.

Instead of sharpening disagreements, they blurred them, glossed over them. Mean, sneaking creatures!

Next came the scandalous Bronski affair. At a general meeting of the city party organization, some of those elected to the executive refused to serve. Substitutes were taken from among the runners-up, and luckily Bronski was high enough on the list to be included. Suddenly Bronski was in. Whereupon the rightists, by now utterly without shame, declared that they would not be able to work with him, and would stand down. Unfortunately, Nobs was in the chair—and agreed to annul the election.

As for Platten, he meekly accepted this slap in the face.

Lenin was at the meeting, saying nothing, but beside himself with rage. And he had not a minute's sleep that night.

These daily meetings always had the same effect: they played hell with his nerves, gave him headaches, ruined his sleep.

The whole Swiss party was opportunist through and through, an almshouse for petit bourgeois. It consisted of bureaucrats, future bureaucrats, and a handful of people terrorized by bureaucrats.

The leftists fled from his offers of help, both in Zurich and in Bern. Only Abramovich was doing well, but he was too far away. While Guilbeaux and Brilliant still wavered.

The leaders of the young—even bold, tough, inflexible Münzenberg—were inclined to compromise. Even Münzenberg turned Radek's pamphlet down! (And Radek went off to Davos for his health—he, too, was worn out from it all.)

It would be funny, if it were not so disgusting. Evidently, his labors with the Zurich left were at an end . . .

But he had nothing to regret, though he had lost. He had always known how rotten European socialist parties were. Now he had personal experience of it.

He had nothing to regret. What had been done would not vanish without trace. Others will take over from us, and create a party of the left in Switzerland!

A meeting of the left was called for March 8—and never took place. They simply didn't come, no one wanted it. Lenin had intended to deliver a report, but went down there for nothing and came back in a rage. Rage kept him awake all night.

He envied Inessa and Grishka Zinoviev, who were traveling around, addressing meetings—in places where you saw in front of you, not socialist petit bourgeois, but unspoiled people, workers, the crowd, and you could directly influence the masses.

There were many other things to disturb him. He and Radek—who was unbearable when he put on his professorial airs—were friends one day and quarreling the next, and Inessa and Grishka were distressed by the discord between them. Then there was his quarrel with Usievich. (With Bukharin he had never stopped quarreling—the one good thing was that they had not made it public.) Then Shklovsky had misappropriated party funds. Then Inessa had taken it into her head to "reconsider" the question of national self-defense, and he had wasted far too much time on superfluous argument.

In letters. She had never once come to Zurich.

It would soon be a year . . .

Then there was a spine-chilling rumor that Switzerland would shortly be drawn into the war, and he had quickly calculated that it would be best for Nadya and himself to remain in the German occupation zone, while Inessa went to Geneva, where the French would seize her—in this way they could improve communications with Russia. To his relief, it turned out that there would be no war. Then Nadya was ill with bronchitis and a high temperature, he had to run for the doctor several times, and his life was completely disorganized.

All the same, he could not sit with folded arms.

What if they left the Swiss socialists out of it, and themselves provoked a mutiny in the Swiss army? The scheme that grew out of this was to write a leaflet ("Let us spread the flames of revolutionary propaganda in the army! Let us turn the stale civil peace into revolutionary class action!"), keep its origin absolutely secret (you could suffer severely for this sort of thing and even be expelled from Switzerland), sign it "the Swiss section of the Zimmerwald left" (let the authorities suspect one of the group, Platten for instance), and distribute it by a circuitous route, to conceal their connection with it. Inessa would quickly translate it into French. But the rough drafts must be burned to insure absolute secrecy. (They had satisfied themselves that the post office did not check letters.)

They set to work. But this scheme gave rise to another. Perhaps they should write, and sign with someone else's name, a leaflet to bring the w h o l e E u r o p e a n  p r o l e t a r i a t out on strike on May Day? Why not? Could there by any doubt that the proletariat would respond? What a show of strength that would be at the height of the war. Mass revolutionary actions might easily spring from the strike spontaneously. One good leaflet and all Europe would rise in revolt. What about that?! Only, they must hurry, May Day was not far away—the leaflet must be quickly translated into French, and quickly printed and distributed. (And all this in absolute secrecy.)

But before the European general strike could be properly thought out, before the translations of the leaflet were finished, a letter suddenly arrived from the Kollontai woman, now back from America and in Scandinavia. Another fuse was lit under the powder keg! The congress of the Swedish party, as it turned out, had ended in a s p l i t .

What an unexpected piece of good luck! Yet how could he have forgotten his loyal Zimmerwald comrades-in-arms? What chaos, what infernal confusion there must now be in those Swedish heads.

How could he influence them? How could he help them? Sudden illumination: *this* was what he had been waiting for, the greatest and noblest of tasks—to bring about revolution not in Switzerland but in Sweden! To begin it all f r o m  t h e r e !

Kollontai wrote further that the younger Swedes had decided to hold a congress on May 12 and to found a new party "on Zimmerwald principles." Innocent fledglings, so sincere and so inexperienced—who will explain to you that the principles of Zimmerwald and Kienthal have been b e t r a y e d ! Betrayed and tramped in the mire by nearly every socialist party in Europe. Zimmerwald is bankrupt, Zimmerwald is dead. But you are sincere and unsullied, and at all costs someone must help you to understand the shoddiness of Kautskyism, the vileness of the Zimmerwald majority. (Oh, why am I not there with you?!) The time has come to trim Branting's claws! I must help you by sending my theses. We all have a moral and political responsibility toward you. This is the crucial moment for the Scandinavian workers' movement!

The momentary pessimism and helplessness which had taken possession of him after his setbacks with the useless, spineless, hopeless Swiss leftists was swept away by an upsurge of joyous impatience to s e t  E u-r o p e  a b l a z e  f r o m  t h e  N o r t h !!! But there was little time left, and a great deal to be done, and sending correspondence through Germany was fraught with difficulties. No matter—life had begun all over again! A life of vigorous, active, purposeful struggle! The gloomy vaults of the reading rooms in the old Zurich churches, the stacked newspapers and well-thumbed pamphlets in the Center for Socialist Literature were suffused with a new light. By May Day there must be a leaflet! By May 12—a set of theses, and an agreed plan! All forces must be concentrated on the European general strike and on the Swedish split! Only the young were worth working on! *We* shall never do anything, never see anything. But the crimson sun of revolution will yet rise on *them!*

On March 15 he was at home and just finishing lunch when there was a sudden knock. Bronski. A somewhat untimely visit. (He had banked heavily on Bronski in his unsatisfactory dealings with the leftists, and then there was the electoral fiasco, so that seeing him was no pleasure just now. And he was not yet fitted into the latest plans.) In he came, and without sitting down, in his usual languid, somewhat melancholy manner, asked: "Haven't you heard?"

"Heard what?"

"About Russia . . . been a revolution . . . so they say . . . it's in the papers."

As was his way, he spoke without emphasis, in a hesitant drawl. Ilyich raised his eyes from the boiled beef on his plate—he had finished the broth—and looked at the soft-spoken Bronski, as calmly as though he had announced that the price of meat had gone down five rappen a kilo. A revolution in Russia?

"What rubbish. Who says so?"

He went on eating, cutting crosswise, to get lean and fat together. It made no sense. The nonsense people came out with. He dipped the bits of meat in the mustard on the rim of his plate. It annoyed him when people interrupted his meals and wouldn't let him eat in peace.

But Bronski stood there without taking his overcoat off, crumpling the damp felt hat which he always took such good care of. For him this was a sign of great excitement.

Nadya ran her hands down her checkered gray

frock as though she were wiping them, and asked: "What do you mean, Moisei? In which papers? Where did you see it?"

"Dispatches. In the German papers."

"Is that all! German newspapers writing about Russia! It's all lies."

He calmly continued his meal.

News about Russia in the European press was scanty and always garbled. With no reliable information of your own, it was hard work sifting the true from the false. And letters from Russia hardly ever came. Two new Russians, escaped prisoners of war from Germany, had come to Zurich—he had rushed to look at them and talk to them, out of interest. He occasionally mentioned Russia in addresses, but no more often than the Paris Commune, long vanished.

"What exactly do they say, then?"

Bronski tried to repeat it. Like most other people —though a revolutionary should be ashamed of it—he was incapable of reproducing the exact sense, let alone the exact words, of what he had read.

"Disturbances in Petersburg . . . crowds in the streets . . . police . . . the revolution . . . is victorious . . ."

"And what exactly does its victory amount to?"

"The ministers . . . have resigned or something, I can't remember . . ."

"I thought you'd read it for yourself? What about the Tsar?"

"There's nothing about the Tsar."

"Nothing about the Tsar? So where's the victory?"

Such drivel. Perhaps it wasn't Bronski's fault, perhaps the news item itself had been just as vague.

Nadya's hands hovered at her breast, puckering her dress, which looked shabbier than ever in the dimness of their room—a steady drizzle had been falling since early morning.

"Maybe there is something in it, though, Volodya? Where would such a report come from?"

Where from! It was an ordinary bourgeois journalist's canard, another petty failure in the enemy camp blown up out of all proportion, like so many they had seen in the course of the war.

"If there was a revolution, is this how we would hear of it? Remember Geneva and the Lunacharskys."

Walking along the street one January evening, he and Nadya had met the Lunacharskys, radiantly happy. "Yesterday, the ninth of January, troops fired on the crowd in Petersburg! Many people were killed!!" How could he forget that evening of triumphant celebration among the Russian émigrés! They had darted into a Russian restaurant, where the whole colony was assembled and sat talking excitedly, singing songs . . . Everyone was suddenly young, vigorous, alive again . . . Trotsky, his outstretched arms making him look longer than ever, busily proposed toasts, congratulated everybody, kept saying that he was going home at once. (And he had gone.)

"All right. Give me some tea."

Or should he not bother?

It would probably be no good going back to the reading room and carrying on with his routine work: in spite of himself, he was caught, disturbed. He must see what it was all about. There might be some obstacle to his plans.

But the newspapers with today's dispatches would not be in the reading rooms until tomorrow.

Yes, but late news flashes were pinned up in the *Neue Zürcher Zeitung*'s window at Bellevue.

Right, let's go down there.

Nadya was still not going out very much after

her bronchitis in February, and wanted to stay at home. So Ilyich pulled on his heavy, well-worn, much-mended overcoat, planted his old bowler on his head as though it were a hat block, and set off with Bronski.

"Here lived the poet Georg Büchner," said a plaque on the house next door. Along the damp, narrow alley, where loose slushy snow still lay unmelted beside the walls, they walked quickly, almost rolled, down the hill. They took shortcuts along back streets to reach Bellevue as quickly as possible.

As usual, the Swiss were all carrying umbrellas, passing each other with difficulty in the narrow streets and in danger of poking each other's eyes out. But Lenin didn't like dragging an umbrella around: sometimes it was useful, sometimes not. Anyway, his clothes were all old, no need to worry about them. Bronski, too, did without.

In the newspaper office windows they found things more or less as Bronski had said. Except that the ministers were supposed to have been arrested. Arrested? . . . And further, that power had passed to— members of the Duma. But what of the Tsar? There was not a word about the Tsar. So obviously the Tsar was at liberty, with his army, and would soon give it to them hot and strong.

If, of course, the whole thing wasn't a pack of lies.

No, no, *that sort of thing* couldn't possibly happen in Russia today.

Nor was there any crowd around the windows, no one, in fact, except the two of them.

A fine drizzle was falling on the square and on the lake. The sky over the lake was monotonously overcast, and the Uetliberg on the other shore was swathed in a milky gray mist. Hansom cabs with dark roofs went by, and there was a monotonous procession of dark umbrellas. No, no, there was no revolution! . . .

All the same, he must get to the bottom of it.

They went to the newspaper kiosk at the Heimplatz, hoping to find something there. Lenin never bought newspapers, but on such an occasion he could allow himself to do so, out of party funds.

The artless news vendor, however, admitted that there was nothing of the kind in any of his papers, so they bought none.

He must cut out this nonsense and go to the reading room to work. But Bronski, shaken and confused, seemed determined to keep it up, to trail around the streets or wait in the rain by the windows for the next dispatches—drifting with the current, like all rudderless people. Lenin reproved him, and went his own way. Once again, once again, along streets he had walked a thousand times, with eyes neither for houses nor for shopwindows nor for people, he set out for the cantonal reading room.

Then, with its pointed windows before him, he hesitated.

Something would not let him enter. It was as though he was meant to get stuck in the doorway. As though something had swelled up inside him in the last half hour, something which would not let him through.

Meanwhile, it had stopped raining.

He stood there, angry with himself. He could, of course, force himself, and sit there till evening, but . . . A clear and immediate task summoned him—his work for the Swedes, but . . . This distraction could not have come at a worse time. Then there were his notes on Marxism and the state . . . But still he could not go in.

Instead, an uncharacteristic, alien, even criminal thought surfaced in his mind: he would go to the Russian reading room. That den of S.R.'s, anarchists, Mensheviks, and every kind of Russian riffraff. Like a nest of snakes—he always tried to avoid it, not to walk along Culmannstrasse, not to breathe the same air, not to meet or even see any of them. But now he thought: That's where they'll all be gathering, if they aren't there already . . . They may know nothing, but they can be relied on to talk. Might hear something. Tell them none of my business, but try to get something out of them.

He broke all his rules and let himself be drawn to that loathsome place.

Culmannstrasse was not at all near, and he would have to go quite a way uphill. He went.

As he had expected, he found that about twenty people had come in from the cold and wet to pack the overheated little room in their damp clothes, some of them sitting, some with no thought of sitting—but not one of them silent, all talking at once, babbling and bawling, so that the general din swept across the room in waves. Nothing surprising in that! The Russian loves to pour out his heart.

He had been mistaken in one respect only: he had thought that they would go for him, be surprised to see him, show hostility. But no. Some did not even notice his arrival, and those who did took it as natural, as though he were a regular visitor.

Lenin answered questions—without answering. He asked no direct questions himself. He sat on the edge of a bench in the corner of the room and took off his bowler. Sat and listened, as only he could: picking up the nuances which others did not even hear.

No one, as it turned out, knew more than was in the same old dispatches, except for this one thing: victory had come "after three days of struggle"—"after three days" was a bit of fresh news brought by someone. This "three days" gave it the stamp of authenticity, did it not?—they gasped, and no longer doubted. Lenin found it unnecessary to voice his objection: why, in that case, had there been no report during those three days? All in all, no one knew more than was in the dispatches, but they filled every last gap in their information with a multitude of words.

One man (he had never seen him before), with his tie tugged awry, kept rushing at person after person, waving his arms like a cock flapping its wings, leaving his incoherent sentences unfinished and moving on. A woman, a tall woman, sniff-sniffed at a little nosegay of snowdrops: whatever anyone said to her set her sniffing and rocking in amazement.

Contempt was all that Lenin felt for the mouthings of these would-be revolutionaries, eloquently discoursing on *freedom* and *revolution,* with no understanding at all that events might fall into patterns as varied as the combinations on a chessboard, knowing nothing of the enemy or of his skill in intercepting a movement under way or even forestalling it. They might have been talking about a day of general rejoicing, as though it was all decided, had already happened. (But what had happened, and what was needed to make it happen—which of them understood that?) What was the Tsar doing? What counterrevolutionary armies were advancing on Petersburg? Would not the Duma most probably panic and quickly make a deal with the reactionaries? Were not the proletarian forces still weak and unorganized? These were things they did not think about, questions which they did not attempt to answer. Suddenly, it seemed, they were all reconciled to each other, forgetful of party differences, these animated ladies with ribbons around their hats who filled each other's ears with jubilant twaddle, and lo and behold, now that for an hour or two they had felt themselves no longer involuntary inhabitants of Switzerland but "all just Russians," they indulged in just Russian and typically groundless speculation as to how all of them could most quickly make their way home together.

I ask you!

Lenin, too, was buttonholed by effusive bores with chimerical projects. People came and sat next to him —some of them knew him, and some did not, for not all those present were politically minded. He looked through screwed-up eyes at these arm wavers, drunk without wine, these twittering ladies, and gave no one a sharp answer, or for that matter any answer at all.

The plan they were working on was this: All émigrés must now unite, irrespective of party (petit-bourgeois heads, rotten through and through!), and form a General Committee for the Return of Russian Émigrés to Their Homeland. And then . . . and then . . . and then they would somehow return—just how, nobody knew, though all sorts of suggestions were made. And they were convening a preparatory commission that very evening!

Return, without knowing what was going on there. Perhaps revolutionaries were already being shot against every wall.

There was an influx of fresh people—but not of fresh ideas. Once again, everybody compared his news with everybody else's, and once again no one knew anything more. Lenin left these vacuous chatterers as he had come, almost unnoticed.

Outside, not only had the rain stopped, but the clouds had thinned and it was lighter. The damp was lifting, but it was as cold as ever.

His legs wanted to take him downhill, to the library, then home.

The right thing was to go straight home.

He no longer knew where he should go.

He stood still.

Only two hours ago, at lunchtime, everything had been so clear: he had known that he must split the Swedish party, known what he must read, write, and do for this purpose. Then an unauthenticated, improbable, and unwanted event had crept up on him, seemed at first not to have impinged on him, not to have pushed him off course—but it was doing so now. Diverting his energies, and wrecking his routine.

Suddenly it was impossible to go back to the library.

Nor did he want to go home. In the past year, talking everything over with Nadya had somehow begun to bore him: her replies, delivered with long-winded solemnity, were so obvious as to be superfluous. Never a fresh and original response, no help from her in testing his ideas.

His legs were impatient for motion.

Yes, but not through the streets, he was sick of them, couldn't stand the sight of them. Why not climb the Zürichberg, which was close by?

A wind was blowing, cold but not too strong. There would be no rain, and indeed the sky was growing lighter, the sun might break through any minute.

In his overcoat, which had almost dried in the reading room, Lenin turned sharply uphill. Your legs are less tense in the mountains, and your thoughts more settled; you begin to understand things.

The steeper and shorter the street, the more quickly he would be there, on top. His legs were as strong as a young man's. Boys with satchels on their backs were hurrying from school in the same direction, and Ilyich kept up with them. He wasn't even out of breath, and his heartbeat was healthy.

So far, so good. But—his head . . . His head Lenin carried like some precious and stricken thing. This apparatus for instantly making unerring decisions, for discovering unanswerable arguments, was, through nature's mean vindictiveness, afflicted, and the disease, so it seemed, had ramified, making itself felt in new places all the time. It was probably like mold germinating in a massive lump of living matter—bread, meat, fungus—a thin greenish film with fibers penetrating deep inside: the whole was at once apparently sound and yet ineradicably infected, and when his head ached, he felt the pain not all over but in patches and filaments. You could tell yourself that it was just an ordinary headache, the kind everyone has, and that if you took some kind of powder it would go away. But when at other times you found yourself thinking that it ached in a special way, irremediably, and that the powder would give only illusory relief for a few hours, you were gripped by a dread like that you had felt in the cell at Nowy Targ: you would never break free of it! There was no escaping that head. The whole world awaits your judgment and your decisions! The whole world can be steered by your will. But you yourself are gripped fast, and cannot break loose.

Heart, lungs, liver, stomach, arms, legs, teeth, eyes, ears, all healthy—an inventory to be proud of. But with nature watching like a sharp-eyed and pitiless examiner, you had omitted something from the list—you couldn't include everything—and the disease had immediately noticed your omission and crept and crept through the secret passages of destruction. Just one wormhole is enough to bring the whole statue of health down in ruins.

This weakened his regret for their disagreements and misunderstandings. It makes things so much worse when you try too hard to be friends again. In a year you can learn to do without someone. He needed her. Needed her. But did she need him as much?

Such a short way away, and she hadn't come to see him in a year?

Yes, of course. She was with somebody else . . .

But a protective cover of half-dead resignation settled around him.

From the cantonal hospital he wound his way up the slopes where the more prosperous Swiss burghers had clambered high above the city, closer to forest and sky, with a view far over the lake, and built their houses, the miniature palaces of the bourgeoisie. Every one of them had thought of new ways to beautify his home—whether with patterned brickwork, ornamental tiles, a spire, big gates, a veranda, a coach house, a fountain, or by calling the house "Mountain Rose," "Gordevia," "Nisetta." Wisps of smoke were rising from the chimneys—the fires, of course, were lit for comfort.

This carefully contrived combination of beauty and comfort, shut off from the world by fences, railings, title deeds, and convenient Swiss laws, remote from the herd down below, filled him with seething irritation. Oh, how splendid it would be to swarm up here and destroy these garden gates, windows, doors, flowerbeds, with stones, sticks, heels, rifle butts—what could be finer, what could be more fun? Were the deprived masses so demoralized, had they sunk so deep into the mire that they never would rise in rebellion? Never remember Marat's burning words: *Man has a right to wrest from his fellow man not only superfluous possessions but bare necessities. So as not to perish himself, he has a right to cut his neighbor's throat and devour his still quivering body!*

This splendid Jacobin attitude toward life would never awaken in the proletariat of the lackeys' republic, because it was fattened on scraps which fell from its masters' tables. And opportunists like Grimm entangled it in their spiderwebs.

But in Sweden perhaps?

And what was going on in Russia now? . . .

A great deal could happen in Russia, but there was no one to give it direction. Probably all was lost by now, and drowned in blood—but they would learn about it from dispatches two days late.

It was getting lighter all the time, not because he

was climbing higher, but because the sky was clearing. The smooth, close-packed cobbles on footpaths and carriageways, never sullied by dust or mud, were dry underfoot. Should a passing carriage splash you from a puddle, the water would be clean. There were many trees along the hilly streets, thicker woodland higher up, and higher still the forest.

Here you met people simply taking a stroll, not going about any business. First one, then another slow, sedate bourgeois couple went by, with furled umbrellas and dogs on leashes. Next came two old ladies, conversing in loud, complacent Swiss voices. Then somebody else. All enjoying the luxury of living in such a district. Then passers-by, and signs of life generally, became fewer and farther between.

On the very edge of the forest a level street ran across the mountainside, neither rising nor falling. It led to a railed-in observation platform, where you were supposed—as far as the foliage of trees lower down allowed—to admire the distant view of an inlet, and the whole city under the blue-gray haze in the hollow—the spires, the chimneys, the dark-blue double trolleys as they crossed the bridges. Here, too, the cold, mechanical, metallic clangor of bells floated up from the monotonous gray churches.

There was also a little avenue of tall trees, graveled, with benches, only a dozen paces in length, made to lead to one solitary grave. When Nadya and he had been on the great oval face of the Zürichberg, they had always climbed by other streets and to different places, and had never wandered this way. Now he went up to this grave on its high vantage point.

Breast-high from the ground stood a rough, uneven gray gravestone, and on a smooth metal plate set in the stone these words were engraved: "Georg Büchner. Died in Zurich, leaving his play 'Danton's Death' unfinished . . ."

He didn't at first understand why this name, Georg Büchner, seemed familiar . . . The names he knew best were all those of Social Democrats, politicians. But a writer? . . .

Suddenly he realized. It was his neighbor. Used to live at No. 12, Spiegelgasse, right alongside, their walls adjoined, their doors were three steps apart. An émigré. Lived in the neighborhood. And died there. Leaving "Danton's Death" unfinished.

Diabolical nonsense. Danton was an opportunist, Danton was no Marat—who cared about Danton?— but never mind him, here lay a neighbor. He too, no doubt, had yearned to go home from this accursed, stifling, narrow little country. But had died in Zurich. In the cantonal hospital, or perhaps at 12, Spiegelgasse. The inscription did not say what he died of. Perhaps his head had ached like this, ached and ached . . .

What was he to do about his head? His sleeplessness? His nerves?

And what was going to happen in general? One man was not strong enough to fight all the rest, to correct and direct everyone.

Somehow not a very pleasant encounter.

All Zurich, probably a quarter of a million people, locals or from other parts of Europe, thronged there below, working, making deals, changing currency, selling, buying, eating in restaurants, attending meetings, walking or riding through the streets, all going their separate ways, every head full of thoughts without discipline or direction. And he stood there on the mountain knowing how well he could direct them all, and unite their wills.

Except that he lacked the necessary power. He could stand here up above Zurich, or lie in that grave, but he could not change Zurich. He had been living here for more than a year, and all his efforts had been in vain, nothing had been done.

Three weeks ago this city had been reveling in its tomfool carnival: bands barging through the streets in clownish costumes, squads of zealous drummers and ear-splitting trumpeters, characters on stilts, others with oakum hair a yard long, beak-nosed witches and bedouins on camels, carts carrying merry-go-rounds, shops, dead giants, cannons shooting soot, tubes spitting confetti—how many thousands of idlers had sat up nights preparing for this, making costumes, rehearsing, what an abundance of well-nourished manpower, released from the threat of war, they had squandered on it. If only half as much manpower could be thrown into a general strike!

In a month's time, after Easter, there would be the "farewell to winter" festival (there were more holidays than you could count in this country), and yet another procession, this time without masks and makeup, the craftsmen of Zurich on parade, just like last year: outsize sacks of outsize grain, outsize workbenches, bookbinders' benches, grinding wheels, tailors' irons, a brick-roofed forge on a float with smiths plying the bellows and hammering as it went along; hammers, axes, pitchforks, flails (stirring up unpleasant memories of how his mother had once tried to make a farmer of him, at Alakayevka—he loathed those pitchforks and flails); oars carried over the shoulder, fish strung on poles, shoes on banners, children with baked loaves and pretzels—yes, indeed, they might well boast of all this labor, if they had not lapsed into bourgeois degeneracy, if only they did not so doggedly proclaim their conservatism, if it were all something more than a defiant clinging to the past, which must be destroyed without trace. If behind the craftsmen in leather aprons there were no horsemen in red, white, blue, and silver tunics, violet tailcoats, and cocked hats of all colors; no marching columns of old men in old-fashioned frock coats carrying red umbrellas, no learned judges with outsize gold medals, not to mention marchionesses and countesses in velvet dresses and white wigs—the guillotine of the great French Revolution had left them for later! And once again trumpeters by the hundred and bands by the dozen, and mounted brass bands, and horsemen in helmets and breastplates, halberdiers and infantry of the Napoleonic period (the last time the Swiss had been at war)—how merrily they played at war, since there was no need to march to the slaughterhouse, and the traitorous social patriots would not call on them to turn about and start a civil war!

What sort of working class was it, anyway? When their landlady in Bern, a proletarian who took in ironing, learned that they had cremated Nadya's mother instead of burying her, that they were not Christians—she had turned them out. Another landlady had turned them out simply for switching on the electric light in the daytime, to show the Shklovskys how bright it was.

No, there was no hope of raising them in rebellion.

What could a handful of foreigners do, however sound their ideas might be?

He turned away from the avenue, and took a steep path up toward the forest.

The clouds were thinning to a tender primrose color, so that you could guess where the evening sun was.

Now he was in the forest. It was untended, but there were little avenues here and there. Interspersed with the firs were trees with grayish-white trunks, but not birches or aspens. The damp earth was thickly carpeted with dead leaves. It was muddy and slippery, but in the mountain boots which were so ridiculous on city streets he was quite at home here.

He climbed steeply, working his legs hard. He was alone. No neatly dressed couples took their walks in this damp, muddy place.

He stopped to get his breath.

On the bare trees the damp-blackened bird boxes were still empty.

There is no harder climb than that from illegality to legality. *Underground* means just what it says: you keep out of sight, do everything anonymously, and suddenly you must climb up to a high place and say: Yes, here I am! Take up your arms, I will lead you! Which was why 1905 had proved so difficult for him, while Trotsky and Parvus had seized complete control of the Russian revolution. How important it is to reach the scene of revolution in good time! If you are one week late, you lose everything.

What would Parvus do now? I should have given a more friendly answer!

Shall I go, then? If the news is fully confirmed, shall I go?

Just like that? Abandon everything? And fly through the air?

Beyond the first ridge the ground fell away to a dark damp grove of firs, and the road there was churned-up mud. But you needed no path to walk along the ridge itself—it was dry, with grass and scattered pines growing on it.

Up another hillock.

From here, the view opened out again more spaciously than ever. You could see a large stretch of unruffled leaden-gray lake and all Zurich under the inverted basin of a sky never shattered by shell bursts, never rent by the cries of a revolutionary crowd. And there was the sun, already setting, not down below but almost at eye level, beyond the gently sloping line of the Uetliberg.

As though he were awakening from healing oblivion, the thing which had driven him out into the damp air on the mountain at such an inopportune time, in the middle of a working day, surfaced again in his mind:

the unease and agitation he had experienced in the Russian reading room, the chorus of sheep bleating that the revolution had started.

How credulous they were, all these professional revolutionaries, they would fall for any fairy tale.

This was just the time to show the greatest distrust and caution.

He moved on along the dry pathless ridge, over brown grass and dry twigs. Here on the mountain, squirrels often ran up the trees, and sometimes young mountain goats, the size of dogs, could be glimpsed in the distance, darting across the road.

High up in the silence and the clear air, the pressure in his head eased, the cramping iron band was removed. All irritations, all irritating people—were canceled, forgotten, left down below.

Last winter had been a hard one, and had thoroughly exhausted him. It was impossible to live under such strain, he must take care of himself.

But what was the point? If he was to do nothing, why take care?

In any case, he would not live long. Something was wrong with his head. Seriously wrong.

The ridge along which he was walking ended abruptly where a gravel road ran across it. Here was a place he recognized—the obelisk. A path led down to it. It commemorated the two battles of 1799 in which the revolutionary French and the reactionary Austrians and Russians had fought for Zurich.

Lenin sat down on a damp bench facing the obelisk. He was tired.

Yes, indeed, there had been shooting here, too. It was a frightening thought that Russian troops had been here! That even this place had been within reach of the Tsar's paw.

The clop-clop of hoofs on the hard ground reached him from above, from beyond the brow of the road. Out of the dark wood in the fading afterglow appeared first a woman's hat held by a ribbon, then the woman herself, dressed in red, then a chestnut horse. The horse was walking, the woman sitting erect in the saddle, and there was something in her bearing, in the carriage of her head, which made him think . . . Inessa?!

He shuddered, saw, believed!—although it was quite impossible.

She came nearer—no, of course it wasn't—but there was a certain resemblance. That self-awareness, that way of carrying herself like a rare and precious object.

She came out of the dark thicket, all in red, and rode by in the damp, clean, noiseless evening.

Of the two, the horse was the more conscious of its beauty. Its glossy hide was a light chestnut, almost yellow, it wore an ornate bridle, and it stepped daintily on its neat little hoofs.

The horsewoman seemed apathetic or perhaps sad as she sat looking straight ahead down the sloping road, without a sideways glance either at the obelisk or at the shabby man (or mushroom?) squat on the bench in a round black hat.

He sat very still, studying her face and the hair like a black wing peeping under her hat.

If he could suddenly liberate his mind from all the work that needed to be, that must be done—how beautiful this would seem. A beautiful woman!

Her only movement was the swaying of shoulders and hips as the sway of the horse lifted her toe caps in the stirrups.

She rode on downhill to a turn in the road—and only the rhythm of hoofs was heard for a little while longer.

She rode on, carrying a little part of him away with her.

# [2]

Lenin had made a close study of many earlier revolutions and attempted revolutions (since revolution was what he was born for and had lived for, he naturally knew more about it than anything else), and had his favorite personalities, episodes, methods, and ideas. He had seen for himself only one revolution, and not from the beginning, not all of it, nor had he been in the main centers of action. He had indeed taken no part in it, had through no wish of his own merely observed it, drawn his conclusions, and later amended them.

But there was another revolution, in another country, while he was still a baby, one which he felt a fateful affinity with, which made his heart beat faster like the sound of a beloved name, like an ineluctable passion, which was both love and pain: he suffered for its mistakes more than for his own, he anxiously studied each of its seventy-one days as though they were the most sublime, decisive days of his own life, its name was forever on his lips: the Paris Commune!

In the West, the one thing on which people wanted his views, and considered his opinion important, was the Russian revolution of 1905, and he gave regular talks on it, particularly on January 22, the most notable date in Western minds. (He had done so this year, too, in the Zurich Volkshaus, warning his audience that "Europe is pregnant with revolution!"—with Switzerland mainly in mind.) But it was boring for him to talk about a revolution which had been stolen from him (and the jealous conclusions he had drawn in his rivalry with Parvus and Trotsky were best kept to himself for the time being). No one ever asked him about the Paris Commune, there were many people who could talk about it with greater authority, but he yearned toward it, as if pressing one lacerated breast, one wound, against another might help both to heal. And when one by one all the participants and nonparticipants in the 1905 Revolution were forced to flee secretly, surreptitiously, from a Russia where all was lost, in the damp Geneva winter of 1908, despondent, at loggerheads with all his old comrades, exasperated to the point of nervous collapse, he had sought relief in his lonely work on *the lessons of the Paris Commune*.

In the course of this last anxious winter the cliquish whispering of the Skittle Club had worn him down, and he felt a physical dread of speaking in a large, crowded hall, but he accepted with the greatest alacrity a sudden invitation, arranged by Abramovich, to lecture on the Paris Commune at La Chaux-de-Fonds on March 18, the anniversary of the rising. (Since Huguenot times, many French refugees had lived around La Chaux-de-Fonds. Refugee communards had joined their fellow countrymen, and descendants of both groups still lived there.)

Then the news of revolution in Russia had dropped from the sky and filled out from day to day.

It was less than three days since that first unconfirmed report from Russia (three twenty-four-hour days, since he had not slept for three nights; but most surprisingly his head no longer ached, he no longer felt ill at all after this powerful injection of fresh energy), yet in those seventy hours now many feelings and thoughts had rushed and blazed and roared through his breast and his head, as though through the flue of a great furnace! Knowing so little, piecing the fragments together, he had made picture after picture of what was happening t h e r e . And had found decisions to suit every possibility. Experienced as he now was, his decisions were all impeccably correct, but the picture itself was always deceptive, and subsequent dispatches refuted or modified earlier ones. He had no reliable information *of his own* from Russia, had never had any, and could have none.

As times goes by, you get to know yourself. Even without intellectual soul-searching, you cannot help noticing certain characteristics in yourself. Inertia, for instance. At forty-seven, you aren't quite so nimble. Even when you see the right political steps to take, you cannot get speed up all at once. And when you do, it's just as difficult to stop.

The tremendous news from Russia had not immediately diverted him from his previous course, not instantly taken possession of him—but it was obsessing him more and more powerfully now. The first night had passed in a torment of regret: why, oh, why hadn't he moved to Sweden a year ago, as Shliapnikov had urged him to do, as Parvus had suggested? Why had he stayed in desperately stupid, bourgeois Switzerland? All through the war years it had seemed so obvious that he must not leave Switzerland at any price, that he must sit it out here to the end. But now it was just as obvious that he should have left in time! Whether to split the Swedish party or just to be close to events in Russia— Stockholm was the place. From Stockholm, too, it would be possible to send for someone from Russia, one of the Bolshevik members of the Duma, for instance, if they came back from Siberia.

Earlier it would have been possible to do it quite inconspicuously, through Germany of course, the only sensible way. But now, with everybody alert, in a fever of excitement, endlessly discussing—it was no longer possible to slip away. Damn it all!

It was, however, equally impossible to postpone action a minute longer: whatever the prospects of success, he must begin to act at once. So, as soon as he awoke on the morning of the sixteenth, he exerted himself and by a well-tried route sent off a photograph for a transit visa—to Hanecki. (Poor old Kuba had also been having a hard time: he had been arrested in January for illegal trading and deported from Denmark.) He followed it with a telegram explicitly stating (in case they didn't think of it themselves—he shouldn't have been so careless and impatient) that *Uncle's* photograph should be forwarded at once to Sklarz in Berlin, at No. 9, Tiergartenstrasse.

He must make peace with the whole gang immediately. Nobody else could help to get him out.

The morning of the sixteenth also brought fresh dispatches. The Tsar was supposed to have abdicated!!! (Could he have done so in such a hurry? Without putting up a fight at all?? What could possibly make him do it??? No, this was a trap of some sort. Who was replacing him? That was the thing. If there was no Nicholas, there would be somebody else, somebody cleverer.) And apparently a Provisional Government had been formed (but were the Tsar's ministers in safe custody?), including Guchkov, Miliukov, and even Kerensky. (Shades of the contemptible Louis Blanc! How eagerly your pseudo-socialist rams his behind into a bourgeois ministerial chair.)

The émigré windbags would be in ecstasy: not one among them would shut his pink bleating mouth from morning to night. But when you thought of it: Petersburg was awash with the blood of workers for a whole week, and then, as always in European history, as in 1830, as in 1848, the eternally credulous masses had surrendered power, pure and unalloyed, to that bourgeois scum, to all those Shingarevs and Miliukovs. The old hackneyed pattern!

Let the crowd in the émigré library babble, but a true revolutionary must prick up his ears, strain every nerve, keep a sharp lookout! Back *there* they would make such a mess of things, surrender everything in a spirit of maudlin Christian charity, because there wasn't a real tactical mind among them. It rankled that he was not there himself, that it was impossible to intervene, impossible to direct them.

He hadn't thought of Kollontai all winter, but in the last few days she had become one of his most important correspondents. The center of events had shifted to where she was. As soon as he had mailed the photograph to Hanecki, he sat down to write to Alexandra Mikhailovna: to explain to her what *we* must do now. Our slogans, of course, remain the same: Convert imperialist war into civil war! That the Kadets are now in power, that the fatheads have leaped into the middle of it—is simply too marvelous. Let's see how the darling boys will provide the freedom, bread, and peace they've promised the people. While we wait and see. While we—arm ourselves and wait. Arm ourselves and prepare for the higher stage of the revolution. No confidence in Chkheidze and the socialists of the center! No merger with them! We will act *independently* of all others! Always i n d e p e n d e n t l y ! We will not allow anyone to involve us in attempts at unification. In fact, it will be extremely unfortunate if the Kadet government permits a legal workers' party at all. That would greatly weaken us. It is to be hoped that we will remain illegal. But if legality is thrust upon us, we must preserve an underground section: the underground is where our strength lies, we must never completely abandon the underground! We must wrest *all* power from the swindling Kadets. Only then will we have the "great and glorious" revolution! I am furious, absolutely furious that I cannot come to Scandinavia immediately!

But, early on the morning of the seventeenth, new information put things in a different light: the Kadet government's victory was far from assured, the Tsar hadn't abdicated at all, only run away, and no one knew where he was, but from the usual pattern of European revolutions it was perfectly obvious: he was gathering a counterrevolutionary force, preparing his Koblenz. Even if he did not succeed in this, he could try some other trick—yes, that's it—he might, for instance, flee abroad and issue a manifesto about a *separate peace* with Germany! Nothing could be simpler! They were so very cunning, the Romanovs. (In *his* place that would be the best thing to do, a brilliant step: become the peasants' Tsar-Peacemaker!) He would immediately win the sympathy of the Russian people, the Kadet government would totter and take flight, and Germany —Germany would cease to be the ally of the revolutionary party because it would be of no more use to them . . . (Oh, we have quite a while to wait before we go to Russia, there's nothing for us to do there yet. So why did I send that telegram to Hanecki? How stupid of me to leave a trail.)

Alexandra Mikhailovna, we're afraid that we won't manage to leave this wretched country very soon, it's a very complicated business. We can best help by advising you from Switzerland.

Well then, the comrades who are going from Stockholm to Russia must be given a precise tactical program. It could be presented in the form of theses . . . his hand was already writing them . . . The most important thing for the proletariat to do is to arm itself, that will help, whatever happens: first they must crush the monarchy, and then the predatory imperialist Kadets . . . Ah, Grigory! Sit down and help me . . . The new government won't be able to give the people bread, and without bread, freedom is no use to anybody. The only way to get bread is to *take it by force* from the landlords and capitalists. And this can only be done by a workers' government (by us) . . . Oh, yes! I must write a postscript to Kollontai telling her to acquaint Piatakov and Yevgenia Bosch with these theses. (The time had come when he could no longer scorn even the piglets. Nobody was to be scorned at a time like this. The really useful person to have around just now would be Malinovsky! What a shame they had blackened the man beyond hope of rehabilitation. He was doing very positive work in the prisoner-of-war camps. They had issued another statement in his defense in January. He must be saved, must be brought back.) . . . Next . . . and this is important: we must not neglect to *stir up* the benighted domestic servants against their employers—this will be a great help in establishing the power of the Soviets. What does genuine freedom mean today? First of all, the election of new officers by the soldiers. And in all contexts, general assemblies and elections, elections to every office in the land. The complete abolition of bureaucratic interference in everyday life, in the schools, in . . . Russia's present freedom is very relative. But we must know how to use it for the transition to the higher stage of revolution. Neither Kerensky nor Gvozdev can offer the working class a way out . . . Enough, the post office will be closing soon, I must get the letter off now.

But look at this, Grigory, they've proclaimed an amnesty. A general amnesty must mean freedom for all the parties of the left. Can they really have brought themselves to do it? This is bad. Very bad. Now that he's legitimate, Chkheidze and his Mensheviks will spread themselves and occupy every position before we have a chance. Will they leave us behind yet again?

No, no, we mustn't sit idly by, we must be ready with something. And quickly! We won't go, of course, the revolution may still be rolled back, it's happened so often before, you can never be sure of anything—but we must prepare the way just in case. I tell you what . . . Yes, that's it . . . Is today Saturday? That's bad. Never mind, you hurry off back to Bern, yes, you must go back immediately, there's nobody else: try and catch Weiss at home, late this evening would be best, he always goes off somewhere on Sundays. And tell him to go straight to the German Embassy. On Monday! We must break out of this vicious circle. Why is Romberg silent, why doesn't he send somebody? It's surprising. They ought to be even more interested than we are. We can at least consider traveling via England, whereas they have no other way out. Make Weiss understand that he must in no circumstances mention you and me in particular, but must say that a lot of people, including us, would like to go. In that way we can sound them out, and see what the chances are. What should we ask for? Suppose Germany publicly announces that it is prepared to let through all those who . . . all those whose love of freedom draws them home to Russia. That's it. As far as we're concerned, such a declaration would be a fully acceptable basis.

Another thing! All these diplomats are blockheads, they don't begin to understand who's who and what's what in the revolutionary movement. So let Weiss build us up a bit. Let him hint that the revolutionary movement in Russia is c o m p l e t e l y controlled from Switzerland. That every important action has to be decided on, first of all, in Switzerland. That in Russia, quite literally, not a single important step is taken without instructions from us. So that in present circumstances . . . Got it? Right, get going, I too have an early train to catch tomorrow, to La Chaux-de-Fonds, for my lecture.

All the enthusiasm he had felt for the Paris Commune three days ago had turned to dust.

Next morning, in his haste and absentmindedness, he put on a completely worn-out cap, and at La

Chaux-de-Fonds the chairman of the trade union took him for a tramp and wouldn't believe that he was the expected lecturer.

On Sunday afternoon in the Watchmakers' Club he gave a lecture in German, entitled "Will the Russian Revolution Go the Same Way as the Paris Commune?"—without a written text, improvising from brief notes, before a gathering of two hundred people. He had no real feel for his listeners, no idea what interested them and what they expected. He seemed to have lost his sensitivity, he no longer saw the auditorium or felt the paper in his hand, he let slip all sense of time. What was more, his affection for his early love, the Commune, deserted him, he was imperceptibly drawn further and further afield, and instead of precise comparison, as his thoughts and feelings ran away with him he began confusing two revolutionary experiences—the Commune, and t h i s o t h e r which had flowered so suddenly: is it fraudulent, or the greatest event which life has in store? We must not repeat the Commune's two fundamental mistakes: it failed to seize the banks, and it was too magnanimous: instead of shooting the hostile classes wholesale, it spared their lives, imagining that it could reeducate them. This is the greatest danger which threatens the proletariat—this magnanimity in the middle of a revolution. It must be taught not to be afraid of ruthless mass methods!

He didn't know what the La Chaux-de-Fonds watchmakers made of it all, but he himself was in the grip of a growing anxiety: time was running out! While this lecture was going on here in La Chaux-de-Fonds, there in Petersburg opportunities were slipping away irrevocably, and some pathetic and unworthy person was steadily tightening his hold on power.

A French lecturer replaced him on the platform.

Abramovich had assembled all the local Russians, and since there were still twenty-five minutes or so to wait for the train, Lenin gave them, too, a sort of lecture, and of course on the same subject, but this time without analogies, speaking straightforwardly about things which preoccupied them as much as himself, and ending with this straightforward statement: "If need be, we will not be afraid to hang eight hundred bourgeois and landlords on lampposts!"

Rocked by the train, he thought and thought. There was no real *power* in Petersburg. Power meant the Tsar and his bureaucratic machine, but they had been thrown out. Power meant the army, but it was shackled to the front. The Kadets had no power at all. The Soviet of Deputies carried little weight. What could it do? And there was a great danger, in fact it was almost certain, that Chkheidze's Mensheviks would presently seize control of it. In Petersburg, and in the Soviet, there was a vacuum, and he felt its suctional pull demanding that he fill it with his own power. If he succeeded in taking Petersburg, he could challenge both the army and the Tsar.

Should he go, then? Should he make up his mind at last and go? . . .

Shaken by the speed of the train, Lenin sat by a window in second class, his image reflected in the darkness outside, together with the bright interior of the carriage, fixedly staring, absently surrendering his ticket for a first and a second inspection, not hearing the passers-by or the names of stations—thinking.

Should he go? . . .

He was in that state of mind when you neither see nor hear whether there is anyone else in the carriage. Because he was alone at the window, alone in the train, Inessa was not at Clarens but traveling at his side. How good it was—they hadn't talked like this for a long time.

It's like this, you see—it's quite impossible for me to go. And just as impossible not to. I tell you what—perhaps you should go on ahead for the time being. There's no risk in it for you. And nobody will bar your way. (This was quite sincere, there was no contradiction in it: the person you love is the one to send ahead, because if you feel concern for her you naturally share with her your concern for the cause. That was always the way of it, and how could it be otherwise? And if she didn't refuse outright, it meant that she agreed.)

It was nearly a year since they had seen each other. And their relationship was gradually breaking down . . . But on this auspicious, this happy Commune anniversary, rocked by the train side by side with Inessa, he had the old warm and joyous feeling of closeness, the same urgent need for her, yearned to say a couple of words to her in reality here and now, tomorrow would be too late!

He jumped out at one station to buy a postcard, and mailed it at another.

. . . Dear Friend! . . . I have read about the amnesty . . . We are all dreaming of going home . . .

Yes, dreaming—that defines it exactly! A dream is precisely what it is.

. . . If you want to go, come and see me. We'll have a talk about it . . . No, really, we must see each other . . . If only for a second! Do come!

. . . I would like you to do something for me—find out on the quiet in England whether they would let me go through . . .

England, of course, wouldn't want to let him through: he was an enemy of the war, an enemy of the Entente. But perhaps there was some way of deceiving the English?

Anyway, going via France, England, and Norway might take as much as a month. In that time the new regime would become firmer, find its feet, get into its stride, and there would be no hope of shaking it, of diverting it. He must hurry, before it hardened.

It was the same with the war. People would get used to the war continuing in spite of the revolution, and think that it must be so.

Then there were the German submarines. Now that the long awaited moment had arrived, how could he take risks? Only a fool would do so.

That night, at home in the Spiegelgasse, he slept only fitfully. Sleeping or waking, he was more and more tormented by the nagging question: Should he go? Go at once?

Morning brought dispatches which all said the same thing, without contradictions. The Tsar had indeed a b d i c a t e d! No doubt about it! And not only he, but Mikhail too, the whole dynasty, the whole gang of them had r e n o u n c e d t h e t h r o n e.

There would be no restoration!!

The only burning question now was how to return. By what route? By what means? It must be quick! There mustn't be an hour's delay now! He must get there at once! Before it was too late! Must seize the helm! Correct the course, set a new one, immediately!

Weiss is seeing Romberg today. Good. But for the moment that is . . . just exploring the ground, a tentative inquiry . . . My hasty remark three days ago to Hanecki, about the *"Swedish deaf-mute,"* is of no importance. More important is the passport photograph. (A good thing I sent it.) Could it possibly reach Sklarz today? No, of course not. The day after tomorrow. Then the matter will be considered by the Ministry, and by the General Staff. *They* surely won't delay, they should have thought of it for themselves, should have been quick off the mark, and sent somebody to suggest it. Not a word from them. Blockheads. Everything has to go up the bureaucratic ladder.

Or perhaps they are holding out for a higher price. If so, they are politically beneath contempt. For some distance along the road they can look forward to a solid alliance and a separate peace. (Though later on . . . The Prussian Junker brain cannot of course follow the spiral paths of the dialectic. How can they see beyond today's trenches? What do they know of the world proletarian revolution? Later on, of course, we shall outsmart them, because we are cleverer. But for the time being, all they need think of is making a separate peace, and detaching the Baltic provinces, Poland, the Ukraine, and the Caucasus. All that, we'll readily give them—we've said so right along.)

Siefeldt hasn't turned up, either. Not a sign of life from Moor.

But what about Parvus? The unfailingly clever Parvus! What can he be doing? Israel Lazarevich! Here I sit in this wretched Switzerland as if in a corked bottle! No one knows better than *you* how important it is to be in time for a revolution! Why is nobody offering me a chance to go? Is anything at all being done?

The room in the Spiegelgasse was a rathole. The sun never shone through the window.

Where was I, then? . . . There's no time to think properly, you're bound to miss something. What are they doing there in Petersburg—Kamenev and Shliapnikov? Kamenev bears a great historical responsibility. The *theses* have filtered through to them, but that was before . . . Yes, that's it: I must summarize them again in a telegram. A telegram to Stockholm won't break the party bank. Nadya, Moisei, will one of you go and send a telegram: our tactics: *no confidence in the new government! no rapprochement with any other party!* your sole duty to *arm,* repeat *arm,* yourselves! . . . Put your head scarf on, you've got bronchitis! . . .

All the same, just in case the Germans are too slow, we must also make preparations to travel through England. Tell Karpinsky, for instance, to get a transit visa in his own name, and we can put my photograph on it. Me in a wig, though, or else they'll recognize me by my baldness. Must write to him at once. An express letter to Geneva. Who'll mail it? Very well, I'll run down myself.

The wind was blowing harder and colder along the narrow back streets, and whenever a stronger gust met him head on, it stopped him in his tracks. But it's good to walk in the teeth of the wind, to fight your way against it. It's a lifelong habit, I've always walked against the wind—and I don't regret it. I wouldn't want a different life!

The same wind carried him up the steep street and home—just in time: he was called to the telephone on another floor. Who could it be? Hardly anyone knew this number, he used it only in exceptional circumstances.

Up the dark stairs.

It was Inessa!! All the way from Clarens! Her voice was like the modulations of the piano under her fingers.

"Inessa, it's so long since I heard from you! . . . My dearest! . . . Only yesterday, while I was on a journey, I sent you a postcard . . . We must go at once, we must all go! I'm working on a number of possibilities, one of them is bound to come through! Apart from everything else, we must reconnoiter the English route. Perhaps the most convenient thing would be for you to . . . What? It isn't convenient?

. . . Well, I never insist, you know that . . . You're not sure whether you'll go at all? Not go at all?? Can't make up your mind?" (They were out of tune, at cross-purposes. When you don't meet for a long time it's always the same, you are never attuned to each other—and the telephone doesn't help.) . . . "Why not? How can you bear not to go! . . . I was absolutely certain! It never entered my head . . . Yes, of course, it's your nerves . . . I know, I know" (Let's not discuss our nerves over the telephone, at a franc a minute.) . . . "Well, all right . . . I'll try something else . . ."

She would have done better not to call, it had only depressed him . . . spoiled his mood and his plans . . .

He couldn't guess where their relationship had gone wrong. Or why. What was there to spoil it? When had he ever tried so hard to please, when had he deferred to anybody as he did to her? . . .

He had been surprised that, with the three of them, it had held together so long. But now it had collapsed . . .

The memory of this telephone call rankled, and he couldn't force himself to work. He sat down to write by the window, where it was lighter, with the action program for the Petersburg comrades on his knees—left to themselves, they would never . . . The wind was simply roaring outside and blowing through cracks he had never noticed before. It was March, but maybe he should light the stove? The landlady and her husband would say they were wasting coal. He draped his overcoat over his shoulders.

He must begin by analyzing the situation. What precisely the situation was, he did not know, and he could not reconstitute it from the meager scraps in the papers, but in a general theoretical way he understood it well enough and knew that things could not have gone otherwise in Petersburg . . . Is what has happened in Russia a miracle? There are no miracles, in nature or in history, they are just a philistine illusion . . . the corruption of the Tsarist gang, the brutality of the Romanov family, those organizers of pogroms who have soaked Russia with the blood of Jews and workers . . . An eight-day revolution . . . But it was rehearsed in 1905 . . . Awash in blood and mud, the cart of the Romanov monarchy is overturned . . . This is in effect the beginning of that great universal civil war to which we have long summoned you . . .

The things left unsaid in his conversation with Inessa prevented him from working. Her telephone call had excited him—and left him unsatisfied. They had misunderstood each other, irked each other again.

It is *only natural* that revolution has broken out in Russia first. That was to be expected. We did expect it. Our proletariat is the most revolutionary in the world . . . Apart from that, the whole course of events shows clearly that the British and French embassies and their agents were the immediate organizers of the conspiracy, together with the Octobrists and the Kadets . . .

Are we to go, then, while she stays behind? Stays behind for good? Events could separate people, part them forever . . .

Miliukov is in the new government merely to make honeyed professorial speeches, while the decisions are made by henchmen of hangman Stolypin . . . The Soviet must try to ally itself not with the peasantry at large but first and foremost with the agricultural laborers and the poorest peasants, separating them from the more prosperous. It is important to split the peasantry right now and set the poor against the rich. That is the crux of the matter.

What a hurricane! And there seems to be snow

with it. It's dark even by the window now, I need the lamp again.

No, I shall have no peace until I've written to Inessa . . . Why don't I do it at once?

. . . I cannot conceal my deep disappointment from you. We should be hurrying home, but people keep "waiting" for something . . . If I go via England under my own name, they will simply arrest me . . . I was certain that you would rush off there! . . . Perhaps your health won't let you? . . . At least let Krylenko try, so that we can find out what the procedure is.

Now that his ache had eased, he was seized and carried away by the sudden thought that he could use this letter for another purpose.

. . . Here's something just to think about: so many social patriots and Russian patriots without a party live near you, some of them rich! Why shouldn't the obvious idea of going home via Germany occur to *them*? *They* could easily ask for a carriage to Copenhagen. *I* can't do it—I'm a "defeatist." But they can. If only I could teach that scum, those idiots, some sense. Perhaps you can put them up to it? You think the Germans won't give them a carriage? I'm willing to bet that they *will*! I'm certain of it! Of course, if it came from *me* or from *you*, it would immediately spoil the whole thing . . . But there must be fools in Geneva who would serve the purpose? . . .

The whole problem has come down to this: there is no point in reconnoitering the route through France and England—Germany is the only way to go, of course, but it must look as though the idea originates not with *us* but with somebody else.

If anyone doubts it, we must argue along these lines: Your misgivings would make a cat laugh! Can you see the Russian workers believing for a minute that old and tried revolutionaries are on the side of the German imperialists? Are you afraid they'll say that we've "sold ourselves to the Germans"? People have always said this sort of thing about us internationalists anyway, simply because we don't support the war. We shall prove by our deeds that we are not German agents. In the meantime, all we must think about is going home, if necessary with the help of the devil himself!

But someone—who?—must be induced to take the initiative? Otherwise, even if there's an opportunity, I won't be able to go. We cannot be the only ones or the first to suggest it, as *our own idea*—that would cause difficulties in Russia.

So the day rolled by, bringing no decision, offering no way out.

So much might have happened in Russia, so many blunders could have been made in that one day!

Press your head to the dark windowpane and stare out into the roaring darkness—and you could imagine that those were bullets flying! It must be just like this in Petersburg now. There was a furious howling in the chimney, and that banging somewhere on the roof was new—the wind must have torn something loose. What a blizzard!

I feel as though we're missing our very last chance. Must write, and keep writing.

"Miliukov and Guchkov are puppets in the hands of the Entente . . . It is not for the workers to support the new government, but for the government to support the workers . . . Help the workers to arm, and freedom in Russia will be invincible! Teach the people *not to believe mere words!* . . . The people will not want to go hungry, and will soon realize that there *is* bread in Russia and that it can be *taken by force* . . . And so we shall win through to a democratic republic, and after that to socialism . . ."

He felt wound down and his arms and legs

ached for exercise. That's it—he would go out into the storm and walk till he could walk no more! If he didn't, he wouldn't get to sleep, anyway. Let the wind buffet him, blow right through him.

At the foot of the stairs he buttoned himself up to the chin and rammed his old cap on firmly. (The chairman of the La Chaux-de-Fonds trade union had asked, "Who's the pilot?")

Once outside, he was buffeted and bowled along —a real hurricane! But it was dry underfoot, with only a little snow. The streetlamps were all visible, but the sky was dark. There was a crash and tinkle of glass from a shattered lamp. A rattle of loose tiles— something might fall on your head here.

The narrow, narrow, narrow streets of the old city; turn where you would, it was a labyrinth. You could wander like a lost mouse, and never break through to the spaciousness of Petersburg squares.

Russia used to be governed by forty thousand landlords. Surely we can muster as many supporters and govern better?

On the Niederhofstrasse, the street for nocturnal pleasure seekers, there were hardly any passers-by. They had all taken refuge behind the bright-lit windows. And there, floundering helplessly in the great wind, huddled, bent double, came a familiar limp and flabby figure . . . Grigory!

From the station? Back again already?

"Vladimir Ilyich, there's a lot to tell you, so I decided to come instead of writing."

"What about Weiss? Did he see Romberg?"

"Yes, today. I'll tell you right away."

They staggered this way and that, fighting off the wind with their arms, clutching at their caps. They started trudging back. Talking was difficult, but they could not wait.

At Bern the émigré Committee for Return to

the Homeland had been in session all day long, with Grigory representing the Bolsheviks. Come on, then, how did it go?

"Talk, talk, talk, they discussed every possible way of going—via the Allied countries or via Scandinavia. Then Martov suggested going via Germany!"

"Martov??"

"Yes—via Germany!!"

"Martov did???"

He could not get his breath to shout.

"Yes! In exchange for German prisoners of war in Russia!"

"Ma-artov???"

"Said we should get the consent of the Provisional Government—and negotiate with the Swiss authorities through Grimm . . ."

What success! What a stroke of luck! The suggestion has come from good old Yuli, not from us. So that's what we'll call it—t h e M a r t o v p l a n. As for us, we are merely going along with it.

The first word has been spoken.

# DOCUMENTS*

**March 23**
(*Baron Romberg, German ambassador in Bern, to the Ministry of Foreign Affairs. In cipher. Top secret*)

Prominent revolutionaries here wish to return to Russia via Germany, since they are afraid to go via France because of U-boats.

**March 23**
(*Zimmermann, Secretary of State, German Ministry of Foreign Affairs, to the Staff of the Supreme High Command*)

Since it is in our interests that the influence of the radical wing of revolutionaries should prevail in Russia, it seems appropriate to authorize transit.

**March 25**
(*Staff of the Supreme High Command to Ministry of Foreign Affairs*)

No objections to transit of Russian revolutionaries traveling as a group and reliably escorted.

**March 26**
(*German Ministry of Foreign Affairs to Ambassador Romberg. In cipher*)

Group transport under military surveil-

---

*Documents no. 18, 19, 20, 22, from Werner Hahlweg's Lenins Rückkehr nach Russland, 1917.

lance. Date of departure and list of
names must be submitted four days
in advance. Objections on part of
General Staff to particular individuals
unlikely.

## March 27
(*Ambassador Romberg to Imperial Chancellor Beth-
mann-Hollweg. Top secret*)

From a thorough discussion with our
Russian confidential agent Weiss I
have ascertained how we can support
the revolution in Russia . . . We must
avoid anything which might be ex-
ploited by the warmongers in Russia
and the countries of the Entente. The
partisans of peace in Russia will prevail . . . I replied that if Germany had
clung above all to the ruling dynasty,
it was because in earlier times she had
met with understanding and support
for her peace-loving policy only in
this quarter. If we now meet with the
same good will on the extreme left,
this will suit us just as well.

As regards peace terms, he said
that his party would not go to war for
Courland and agreed to the detach-
ment and neutralization of Poland.

He explained to me that the Kadets, in alliance with the Entente,
possess unlimited means for propaganda, whereas the revolutionaries have
great difficulties in this matter. Weiss
has hitherto claimed only very small
sums, fearing that it would arouse
suspicion in his own party if he was

seen in possession of larger funds. But these objections are no longer valid. The larger the funds we can make available to him, the more active he will be in the cause of peace. I should like to recommend very emphatically that in any case we put 30,000 francs at Herr Weiss's disposal for the month of April, which he wants to use in the first place to enable his most important party comrades to travel to Russia. I believe that it would be unwise at this decisive moment to restrict him too much and so antagonize him. May I also promise him further subsidies?

Since that evening of March 19, when the storm had hit Zurich and battered the old city all night long, then at dawn had brought a heavy fall of snow, shortly followed by rain, then sleet, then snow again, then more rain, then toward evening more snow, and only in the course of the following night, when it had whitened the whole city, had it blown itself out—ever since that night and day of storm, pacing and racing about the cramped cell-like little room from dining table to half-dark window, imprisoned in his Swiss cage, confined to his room by bad weather, his leaping passion to enter the fray almost bursting his rib cage, Lenin had decided, or rather it was decided for him, that since he was detained he must without delay write and send to the Petersburg Bolsheviks a program of action, write and send letters and half-written apologies for letters, and as soon as he had finished get someone to run to the post office with what he had to show for that day, while he plunged into the newspapers (he bought them all now, the whole room was littered with them), and picked out scrap by scrap whatever myopic Western correspondents had spotted and seized on and feeble bourgeois minds had selected as suitable for their press—pick it out, snap it up, bring the searching light of his Bolshevik intellect to bear on it, unravel it, explain it to the uncomprehending, the bewildered, the stupid. "Defend the new Russian republic"? A fraud, deception of the workers. "Now overthrow your Wilhelm!"—a fallacious slogan, all efforts must be concentrated on overthrowing the bourgeois government in Russia. The Provisional Government is a government aiming at restoration of the monarchy, an agent of British capital! Better a split with any of our own comrades than collaboration with Kerensky or Chkheidze, or the slightest concession to them.

In this process of analysis and elucidation he discovered for himself missing links and forged for the party new plans of organization. In response to the magnificent manifesto of the Bolshevik Central Committee (Kamenev's work for sure, he had a head on his shoulders), which was issued in Petersburg on March 13 and reached him much abbreviated in a newspaper he happened to read ten days later, he must suggest and explain how they should organize *now* (his advice was different from that he had given in 1905). This time the whole mass of the people must be armed. The people's militia must take in every single member of the population from fifteen (to draw adolescents into political life!) to sixty-five, both sexes (to pluck women from the stultifying kitchen atmosphere!), and this militia must become *the basic organ of state administration!* Only thus, *with weapons in everyone's hands,* could they insure perfect order, the speedy distribution of bread, and, shortly thereafter, peace and socialism!

Between Tuesday the 20th and Sunday the 25th four such "letters from afar" were dashed off and immediately mailed (once written, they become more and more urgent, you can't hold them up, can't hold them back) to Hanecki—who else?—to that splendid, clever, efficient Kuba, who would make arrangements to send them on to Petersburg. (Copies went immediately to Inessa, who wrote to Usievich, who wrote to the Karpinskys, who wrote back to Lenin. All this was extremely important for synchronizing tactics.) Somebody was always tripping up, which meant another dash to the post office, then a hunt around the kiosks and reading rooms for unread newspapers, and then once again analysis and conjecture, projecting new points in the program like rays of light into the future. First Lunacharsky tries to wriggle out of attacking Chkheidze—let him feel an admonitory chill. Next Gorky, the half-wit, comes poking his nose into politics: with his greetings to the Provisional Government, and his bedtime stories about "an honorable peace," a terribly damaging statement, he must be rapped on the knuckles. (If you can't stick to the party line, don't interfere, get on with your pretty pictures.) Then there's all that unpleasantness with Chernomazov in Petersburg: not satisfied with Malinovsky, they are out to swamp the whole party with buckets of filth. Kollontai is on her way to Russia, lucky thing! While we're stuck here, there might be time to get the five hundred pages of my "Agrarian Program" retyped—who'll take it on? Another thing, I absolutely must write some leaflets for Russian prisoners of war, there are two million of them: "Loudly declare that you will return to Russia not as the Tsar's army but as the army of the revolution" (they could very easily be used against it!), and we will hurry home and send you food and money from Russia . . . Oh yes, as I leave, I simply must write a farewell letter to the Swiss proletariat, brand the chauvinists once again, point the way once again (that's dangerous, though, it might hinder my departure. I know—I'll write it and leave it behind, then set off the fuse with a telegram from Russia telling them to print it). Meanwhile . . .

Meanwhile, I'm not happy about Inessa. She is hurt. Angry. She's staying on in Clarens. (Or perhaps she was no longer there? Their correspondence had broken down, so perhaps she wasn't there?) She was angry with him, but, as women always do, she had twisted it into something different, irrelevant, pretending that there were "theoretical disagreements," capriciously raising objections to things which a child would find obvious. How badly he needed her there, at his side! What a time she had chosen! Surely this was no time for female sulking? There was nobody to collect and systematize all the reports from Russia, he could easily miss something enormously important. Not only was she unwilling to try out the English return route, she wouldn't even come to Zurich for one little day. In 1914 she had abandoned her children and traveled from the Adriatic to Brussels for him, yet now that she was only in Clarens and had no children on her hands, she hadn't once come over.

There was no knowing whether she would go home with them at all.

But all these things, even his troubles with Inessa, were eddies on the surface of the water, while the larger events were silently gliding like great fat dark fish near the bottom.

A cryptic message from Hanecki: "It's *coming!*" But waiting was torture. Counting the days, you would think the passport could have been prepared in Berlin and sent—but it hadn't arrived.

And the all-powerful Parvus said nothing.

Of course, he had every right to be offended. And it was quite possible that he was testing Lenin's nerves, and holding out to strengthen his own position.

But they had no escape from each other: events were forcing them together.

The Germans had paid him millions for a mirage, but now there was something worth paying for.

And there would be someone to receive money now. Now at last it was needed.

Meanwhile, the noisy Return Committees, even

where Zimmerwaldists predominated, were all clinging to *legality,* waiting for permission from the venal Guchkov government, which had sent 180,000 francs privately collected for the return of their dear compatriots, only of course through Allied countries (with German submarines sinking the convoy of fools on the way), and this money was already the center of intrigue: the Bolsheviks might be denied their share, and the meetings almost came to blows.

Ilyich, of course, did not attend, but he was told about these sessions in detail. As these quarrels became more and more heated (and the mood of the émigrés in Switzerland was only a pale reflection of what was to come in Russia), he realized that in his haste he had slipped up badly: it was impossible to obtain an individual passport and travel alone.

So on the twenty-third, a week after sending the photograph, he telegraphed Hanecki to call it off: "Official travel arrangements for individuals unacceptable."

That was that. They refused.

However, Tsivin-Weiss had called several times on Romberg, who assured him that urgent letters were being exchanged with Berlin, some of them by special messenger. Gradually, out of the darkness, out of the future, out of the unknown emerged the contours of the great design—like a mighty locomotive out of the mists, but as yet its wheels were turning very, very slowly, if indeed it was moving at all.

Behind it there was a carriage.

Emerging from the darkness—a carriage.

Not at all bad. Acceptable.

But for the time being, I hope that as far as those windbags in the Return Committees are concerned . . . these conditions are not public knowledge!

No, no. Oh, no. That's all at the official level, our business with you is confidential.

Good, good. So gradually, putting a few heads together, by our joint efforts, we're getting things a bit clearer, finding our way. It's a little less vague. (But how it dragged on! Not like the Germans, this! They should be feeling the heat more now that the Provisional Government had announced that it was continuing the war.)

They began preparing a list of those who would go. They asked their own supporters all over Switzerland, but *secretly,* that was important, they didn't want any outsiders. At the same time (this, too, was important) they told everyone the opposite: England won't let us in, and it can't be done through Germany. And loudly discussed anecdotes of other attempts: Valya Safarova had petitioned the British Consulate, somebody had wired a protest to Miliukov, and Sarah Ravich had had the idea of a fictitious marriage with a Swiss citizen, which would give her the right to travel directly. Lenin laughed, and recommended an "eligible old man"—Axelrod, who could no longer be of use to the revolution in any other way.

With the Germans things dragged on slowly, though sometimes the wheels seemed to turn too fast. Or rather, one machine ground away independently of another. On the evening of March 27, just a week after he had sent the photograph, he gave the Swiss in the Volkshaus a two-and-a-half-hour lecture on the Russian revolution, telling them that the second, the true revolution was still to come, that a suitable form for the revolutionary state already existed in the Soviets, and that it was necessary to prepare immediately for an uprising against the bourgeoisie. The lecture refreshed him by diverting his thoughts from all those exasperatingly inconclusive plans for departure. He was quite happy to walk home in the pleasant evening air. When he got up to his room he exclaimed in surprise: a thin little man with gray wavy hair and a corner of handkerchief sticking out of his pocket sat there smiling, as though expecting a joyous reunion, and was self-importantly slow to rise and shake hands.

Sklarz!!!

Without a word of reproach—or of praise—Lenin advanced with a piercing quizzical look (the look which always frightened people) on Sklarz, who lost his self-assurance and rose, whereupon Lenin wrung his hand as though he wanted to tear it off.

"Well? What have you brought?"

No traveler's tales, no preambles, no sentimental gush—just tell me what you've brought.

This businessman who was becoming more and more at home in the high politics of great Germany, who was received with respect by prominent generals and in ministries, and whose mission today was to bestow generosity, was nonetheless taken aback by that cutting gaze from slit eyes, by the unfriendly curve of eyebrows and moustache, taken aback as though a football had bounced in his face, forgot his smile, the amiably verbose prelude with which he had intended to amuse, even his carefully prepared jokes, and immediately told his big news.

He did not sit down.

Lenin did not sit down.

Only Zinoviev sat and snuffled.

It was like this. Sklarz had come not just from Parvus, although Hippo-head had begun the whole thing (of his own accord, before Lenin's request reached him, as soon as he heard of the Petersburg revolution, believing that he knew what to do quite as well as Lenin). Sklarz had brought all the necessary documents from the General Staff authorizing transit through Germany, together with assurances that the German consul in Zurich, and if necessary the German ambassador in Bern, would assist their departure. Sklarz had brought the documents all signed and sealed, and there they lay—a miracle, except that miracles never happen—on the faded oilcloth in the circle of yellow light from the kerosene lamp.

Here you are. Herr Ulyanov. Frau Ulyanov. All in order.

And Zinoviev? ...

Of course. And Frau Lilina. All in order.

Yes, well . . . and what of . . . ?

Yes, there's one more, five altogether, yes, here it is: Frau Armand.

The genius Parvus had not lost his touch, he had thought of everything.

Inessa, too . . .

That was it, then! All problems solved! Not another hour of waiting: no more maneuvers, diplomatic play-acting, fretting, dispatching messengers, waiting for news, being at everyone's mercy, all he need do was to pack his belongings (and a revolutionary has none!) and go, tomorrow evening if he felt like it! It's only twelve days since the Tsar abdicated, and in three days' time we will be in Petersburg and switch the Russian revolution in the right direction! Could things have gone more quickly, in the middle of a world war? Nobody could possibly spoil things now— he would burst upon the first great meeting in Petersburg before anyone else, beating even the Siberian exiles to it, he would turn the Soviet of Deputies against the squalid Guchkov government, he would create a people's militia encompassing all citizens of both sexes from fifteen to sixty-five, he would do whatever he pleased!

The documents lay where they were. With their Gothic flourishes, with the German eagle stamped all over them, and with Lenin's photograph, which had come in handy after all, already gummed onto them— those precious documents, in the light of the kerosene lamp, on the cheap oilcloth with threadbare patches.

Documents which could not be drawn up until the Chancellor himself said yes.

Parvus had made up for his old misdemeanors.

The lumpish Zinoviev smirked and reached for the documents. Lenin turned on him like an enemy, and he froze.

Alas, the lesson had been learned long ago: the hand carelessly thrust into the flame of revolution gets burned.

Nervously rubbing his almost scorched palms above the documents, Lenin snatched them away and clasped them behind his back.

A deal like this could not remain hidden. It would be impossible to make it look respectable. The threads would be relentlessly unraveled until they led right back to Parvus, and it would be no good trying to hide behind his glorious revolutionary past, he would be daubed with the same mud, and the rudder of revolution wrested from his hands.

Perhaps that was it: perhaps Parvus was going to so much trouble simply so that Lenin would be tarred with the same brush? Perhaps Parvus had arranged this individual and family journey to slip a noose on him and then take him in hand? Dictate conditions, tell him how to conduct the revolution?

But Lenin had spotted the trap in time!

"But you put in the order yourself, Herr Ulyanov! Nothing is more insulting to a businessman than to hear good merchandise called inferior."

"I ordered it, yes. But it was a mistake. Circumstances have corrected it." Lenin spoke gloomily, still on his feet, his voice betraying none of the tension in his mind, dictating like a ventriloquist. "There must be a large group. About forty people. A whole carriage. A sealed carriage with extraterritorial status."

He raised his eyes, and scrutinized Sklarz very closely, and this time there was a gleam of sympathy, and even of good humor. (He had remembered that this man could get through to the German government within twenty-four hours. It was an excellent thing that he had come. Thank you, Parvus! We'll just modify the plan a bit, it'll only take a few days.)

Sensing that Lenin was a little more friendly, Sklarz relaxed and smiled. He was unaccustomed to such treatment even in the most exalted circles, and had done nothing to deserve it.

"Israel Lazarevich asks us to hurry," he reminded Lenin. "In case this *government enjoying the people's confidence* makes peace!"

"It won't, it won't." Lenin's slit eyes twinkled merrily.

He made Sklarz sit down and sat facing him across the table, and not so much with his words as with his eyes hypnotically instilled his instructions so that he would remember and carry them out exactly.

"Go and tell them straight. We've been working along other lines for a very long time. They must clearly understand that we cannot compromise ourselves, and they must not put us in a compromising position. They must not restrict the right to go, exclude people fit for military service, and so on."

(Lenin, for one, was fit, but had never been called up because he was the oldest son in the family: he owed his exemption to his brother's execution.)

"Nor must they inquire into attitudes toward the war. They must not arrange any individual checking of passports. We go out as we came in—not a crack in the eggshell, you understand? And not a word in the press."

It must all be done suddenly. The carriage must

be let through like an artillery shell. The public must have no time to hear of it and discuss it.

"There's another thing." Sklarz had just remembered the most delightful bit. "The German government will meet all the expenses of the journey."

"What next!" Lenin's eyes flashed angrily. "It would look very strange if we traveled on those terms. How stupid your people are. We absolutely must pay for ourselves!" More calmly, he added: "Third class."

He hadn't finished yet. "You come to see me, and you can't manage to dress discreetly. You may have been noticed by some of the comrades. You will, therefore, stay on for a day, and keep to your hotel, while Dora comes here. Without any documents, of course. She can tell some cock-and-bull story, and I will say no. Only then can you leave. And as soon as the government agrees, you must let us know immediately."

When Sklarz had got the message, collected the documents, shaken hands with deferential gratitude, and gone away, the feeble Zinoviev put his surprise into words. "How can *we* put conditions to *them?*" he asked, his flabby shoulders shifting uneasily.

Lenin gave him a sharp squint. "They can't get out of it. It's more important to them than to us."

"We'd better conceal Sklarz's visit."

"No, we'll tell Platten. It will be worse if he finds out for himself. We must not lose Platten and Münzenberg."

Also, for safety's sake—an immediate letter to Hanecki (who might show it around): "I cannot, of course, use the services of people connected in any way with *The Bell"* . . . Not forgetting to mention "your plan for traveling via England . . ."

The more erratic his movements, the more false trails he laid, the safer his burrow.

Take Romberg's offer of a *carriage*. This carriage

must be talked out into the open, helped to emerge into the mind of the public like a chicken from an egg. They must mention it casually in speech and in writing.

"Perhaps the *Swiss* government will get us a carriage . . ."

"Maybe the *British* government will let a carriage through?"

"How do you mean?"

"From port to port, of course. Why shouldn't the British let a sealed *carriage* go through? With Comrade Platten, for instance, and a few others, it doesn't matter who or how many, irrespective of their views on war and peace."

"What do you mean? Britain's an island, and we're talking about a railway carriage!"

"Yes, well, it would go by a neutral ship. With the right to inform all, repeat all, countries of its sailing schedule." (In case a German submarine unwittingly sank its friends.)

No one could talk of anything but the journey. Several émigré committees and all the party directorates had asked Grimm to negotiate with the German ambassador. (Since Martov's proposal to release one German prisoner of war for every émigré repatriated.) Excellent, excellent. The Martov plan was working.

And Grimm had taken it on. (Better still.) But he was not just the Zimmerwald leader, he was also a member of the Swiss Parliament, and it would have been unwise for him to take such a step without the sympathy of the government, of Foreign Minister Hoffmann, for instance. (This meant that there must have been consultations. Why should Switzerland be against it, anyway? The Swiss themselves wouldn't mind sending that rowdy bunch packing. Switzerland itself was in an uncomfortable position, with the war on every side.) Grimm went to see Romberg again and again, negotiating *in absolute secrecy;* not a word must filter through to the press, there must be no stain on Swiss neutrality—but he didn't mind reporting to the main representatives of each party (Natanson, Martov, Zinoviev). "We're all in the know."

It was going at a snail's pace. But never mind, never mind.

Romberg said yes to everybody, and Grimm considered that he had made light work of it. If he says yes, it's yes. All that remains is for you, comrades, to request permission from your Provisional Government.

Oh, thank you! Excuse us for not taking off our caps to you! And after that we spend our lives kowtowing to Louis Blanc–Kerensky?

Through all these anxious days the rogue Radek was missed terribly: they summoned him by telephone from the Davos sanatorium where he was recuperating, but even for the Russian revolution he wouldn't come immediately. Before he arrived, though, he had understood the situation, and thought up yet another diversionary maneuver—through a German correspondent in Bern.

Romberg had given him the same answer as all the others: yes, yes, of course we will let through all those who wish to go.

Still the German frontier would not open, and all those *desirous* of traveling got no further than making inquiries, comparing notes, asking the Provisional Government's permission in telegrams to Kerensky, and mostly just dithering.

Everyone agreed—and nothing had begun to happen. These old-fashioned diplomatic methods were so clumsy.

Nothing could begin to happen until the great dark fish in the depths had finished their run.

Until Sklarz had reported Lenin's counterproposals in Berlin.

Until the German General Staff said its final yes.

Until the German Ministry of Foreign Affairs took fright: by now there had been much public discussion of their return and Prince Lvov had told the Swiss minister frankly that the speedy departure of the émigrés from Switzerland was undesirable. So that they must hurry (who could be causing the delay?). Germany would never have another chance like this.

On Saturday, March 31, Ambassador Romberg in Bern at last received instructions to inform Lenin as quickly as possible that his proposals concerning extraterritoriality had been accepted, and that there would be no individual checks or discriminatory conditions.

On Saturday—and "immediately"! So that there was no question of lazily putting it off over Sunday. Breaking all the laws of discretion, and using the emergency line, the German ambassador started calling around, and finally found the German socialist Paul Levi in the Volkshaus: "Please inform Lenin as quickly as possible that . . ."

Another ring called Ulyanov to the neighbors' telephone at home in the Spiegelgasse, and he went along in some agitation, thinking it might be Inessa.

But no—it was his answer!!!

At long last the way was open! At last they could fix the departure of a group of forty for the day after tomorrow, giving the comrades just time enough to pack, return their library books, put their financial affairs in order, assemble from Geneva, Clarens, Bern, Lucerne, and buy provisions for the journey. They could be away by Tuesday, and the following Saturday—a week later than if he had accepted Sklarz's first proposal—take a hand in the Russian revolution.

While he was still in the gloom of the musty staircase, and then in the dim daylight of his cell-like room (heavy snow with intervals of sleet had been falling all day long), gripping the lapels of his vest to prevent his hands from flinging themselves prematurely into action, soothed by the greatcoat-like weight of his greasy old jacket—Lenin forced himself not to rush off and announce the news to someone but to think. Think. Think, rapidly pacing.

A strong man never loses his head in defeat and despondency. But losing your head in moments of success is easy, and for a politician this is the greatest of dangers.

The way was wide open—and still it was impossible to make use of it: there would be no explaining afterward by whom and how it had been arranged that the leading Bolsheviks alone should suddenly be provided with a carriage, and why they had taken it.

A few more baffling and misleading moves must be made first.

There was no room here to stretch his legs, he couldn't go out in such weather (and reading rooms were long since forgotten). His restless pacing made him dizzy, and fiery spirals bored into his brain.

The way was open—but w h e r e  t o? To a forced wait on the Finnish frontier? Or to one of the Provisional Government's prisons? It was easy to imagine how the gales of chauvinism were howling in Russia by now! In the petit-bourgeois way of thinking, what he was doing was "treason." Even here in Switzerland the Mensheviks, the S.R.'s, and the rest of the spineless émigré riffraff would cry treason.

No!

No . . .

No . . .

It was one thing to be restrained by circumstances—but how difficult it was to restrain *yourself* when you were set free and longing to go.

The next thing to do was to . . . was to . . .

The events which had glided like heavy dark fish near the seabed must now be seen passing over the surface like little white sailing boats.

The negotiations are *concluded?* So now's the time to *begin* them! Let's make it appear that we're only beginning today!

What more suitable personage for this task than guileless, trustful Platten?

Obviously, a group must be got ready. And a list already exists.

(Inessa! Won't you go even now? It's monstrous! You won't go with us? To Russia! To the great day we have waited for for so long? You want to stay in this putrid place? . . .)

Forty people can hardly be accused of treason. If there are forty the blame will be spread too thin to matter. We could, of course, pick up a few Maximalists and a mixed bunch of desperate characters, and it would all look a little more innocent. But . . . it is better not to take outsiders along, not to have unnecessary witnesses to every move we make—and who knows what may happen? Anyway, what profit is there in transporting our enemies by our own efforts, in our own carriage, to Petersburg, just to fight them there? No! Every detail, including the date and time of departure, must be kept secret until the last moment.

Only the fact that negotiations are going on must be public.

Without an agreement already in your pocket, you couldn't possibly begin such negotiations. What a humiliation it would be if they failed! But now that we have an agreement, we can go ahead.

Like all proletarian business, like every step in the proletarian cause, this journey needs to be highly organized. Bind them with hoops of iron. Can't have some turd slithering out of it afterward. We must all be in the same boat. No one must be able to evade responsibility, no one must be able to say: "I had no part in it! I never suspected what was going on!"

Every one of them, then, must sign his name to it. As though he is taking a solemn oath. Like bandits kissing the knife. So that no one can break ranks later on and rush to expose us. It's a very serious responsibility and all forty of us must share it.

(Surely Inessa will come? . . .)

He sat down at once to draw up such a pledge. On his chair by the window, in the half darkness, with a snowstorm outside, he balanced the paper on his knees and wrote—his slanting handwriting, bigger than usual in these days of agitation, tumbling over itself as it pursued his thoughts obliquely across the page—sketching out points which might be included. "I confirm that I have been informed of the conditions proposed by the German Embassy to Comrade Platten . . . and that in agreeing to conform to them I accept full political responsibility for the possible consequences . . ."

Suddenly out in the corridor he heard Radek's pleasantly sharp, mocking voice. He had come, then! No guest or assistant could be more welcome just then. Karl, Karl, how are you, take your coat off, oh, the snow's got under your collar. You'll never guess what news we have for you!

The little yelps, the flashing teeth which his upper lip could not cover, the crop of curls, the halo of whiskers—Radek the mischievous chuckling school-boy.

Come on, then, let's draft it together. And draw up equally firm conditions for Romberg.

"*You* make conditions for *them?*"

"Yes. What of it?"

"That's delightful!"

Radek was just the man for this sort of prank. His advice was as good as his jokes, he was inspired and yet circumspect.

Only, smoking wasn't allowed in this room, he had to suck an empty pipe. And . . . oh, no . . .

"Vladimir Ilyich! What do we do about *me!* Surely you wouldn't think of not taking me?"

"Why shouldn't we take you?"

"Well, if we say here 'Russian émigrés'—I'm an Austrian subject."

So he was, damn it! Damn it all! They'd got used to thinking of him as one of themselves—he was a "Polish comrade" only for form's sake. But how could they not take him? A Radek couldn't be left behind.

Radek had already seen a way out. If Platten made a written agreement with Romberg (and if there was only a verbal understanding it would be still easier to confuse the issue), he must leave out the word "Russian" and put in "political émigrés." Since only they were under discussion, the Germans would put their fist to it without a second thought.

Normally, tricks would be impermissible at such an enormously important juncture, in such an extremely serious matter, and the German General Staff was not a partner to joke with. But for Radek—that irreplaceable, that incomparable fount of ingenuity—for sharp, caustic, impudent Radek, perhaps he should risk it?

"But will Platten agree to handle the negotiations? Will he want to go?"

"There's nobody else. So he will agree."

"What if Münzenberg were to go? He's a bit firmer."

"Willi? No, he counts as a German deserter. How can he deal with the ambassador? Or travel through Germany?"

"Even so"—Radek rattled his pipe stem against his teeth—"even so, Platten is party secretary here, how can he travel with émigrés? Besides, he will be worried to death that it may somehow harm his Switzerland."

"How can it? Switzerland can only benefit."

No, Lenin had no doubts on this score. Platten as a rule sheepishly deferred to Grimm, but in the most important things he would go along, once he saw the point. He was a workingman, a proletarian to the marrow. Of the discussions with Parvus he knew and would know nothing.

Whereas Radek knew it all, whether you told him about Parvus or not. Radek had an almost indecent admiration for Parvus: in the taverns of Bern he might revile Parvus, as his international duty obliged him to, for his rash step toward the chauvinists, his wealth, his shady deals, his dishonesty, his love life—but he gaped and drooled so that you could see he thought Parvus a fine fellow and longed to be like him! . . .

"As for Sklarz, I've told Platten that he's a two-bit errand boy of the German government, and that I threw him out! I shall say about Grimm that there's something suspicious in his behavior, he's holding up our departure, seeing what's in it for himself. But we can wait no longer, the revolution calls! Let's act like proletarians, openly, without secrets—and apply directly to the German Embassy! And he'll do it!" Lenin spoke with assurance.

What should they instruct him to say to Romberg? A completely new text was required. "In Russia things are taking a turn which endangers the cause of *peace*. Russia must be wrested from the British and French warmongers. We shall of course endeavor in return to liberate the German prisoners of war." (Hold us to it if you can! . . .) "But we must be insured against embarrassment, and have guarantees that we shall not be pestered on the journey . . . We are prepared to travel in locked compartments, with the blinds down if necessary. But we must be sure that the carriage will not be stopped . . ."

Lenin dominated the room, pacing rapidly along its diagonal, three paces this way, three paces that, with one hand behind his back, and flourishing the other, while Radek wrote, steadying the page with his empty pipe.

Radek always stirred in new ideas: If we're taking a step like this, it might help to collect supporting signatures from Western socialists . . . Socialists, of course, but why not some eminently respectable people, too? Where can we find them? . . .

"Romain Rolland, for instance?"

What a brainy fellow! Just the thing!

They must cast the hook at once. Who would dangle it in front of Rolland for them?

Since Radek's arrival, Lenin had ceased to feel as though his head were bursting with a searing eddy of thoughts. He had an outlet for his ideas, he could express them and receive an answer. Here was another: If they demonstratively started fresh negotiations through Platten, shouldn't they just as demonstratively break with Grimm?

Break with a loud snap!

"Taking care to shift all the blame onto him."

"And giving the blackguard a bit extra for what we owe him. Make him regret postponing the Swiss congress."

The way to do it was first of all to publish all the confidential information on his secret negotiations.

That hurts every time—the sudden publication of confidential matters. Leaves the enemy simply stunned.

So why not immediately, without further ado, prepare such a publication?

"Dotting all the *i*'s . . ."

"And publish it tomorrow!"

Yes, with Radek the most strenuous work turned into a merry game. That was what he particularly liked about Radek—the way he entered into the spirit of things.

They were both sitting now—Radek writing, worrying his empty pipe with his teeth—no time for a smoke in the corridor—occasionally laughing and bobbing up and down on his chair as he thought of a neat phrase, while Lenin sat beside him and gave advice.

Radek was the only person to whom Lenin could completely surrender his pen, and sit by with nothing to do but laugh. There had never been a cleverer pen in the whole Bolshevik Party. Bogdanov, Lunacharsky, Bukharin were all weaker writers.

"Another important thing is that it will look as though it's the Swiss who are negotiating, because they want to get rid of us. It's none of our doing."

He was so clever, so quick, simply priceless.

"We'll get it published right away, tomorrow, by Nobs or . . ."

"Tomorrow's Sunday. But I tell you what!" Sparks danced behind Radek's glasses. "As it's Sunday tomorrow, we'll send Grimm a telegram immediately. Right now, on Saturday evening." Radek grinned and bobbed up and down as though there were splinters in his chair.

Lenin, too, bounced happily in his seat.

They talked and talked, interrupting each other, correcting each other, and Radek wrote it all down:

"Our party has decided . . . to accept unconditionally . . . the proposal to travel through Germany . . . and to organize this journey at once . . . We are *absolutely* unable to take responsibility . . . for further delay . . . emphatically protest . . . and are leaving on our own initiative!"

"Beautiful," said Radek, scratching behind his ear. "We'll coat it with chocolate for him. 'We *earnestly* request you to reach an immediate agreement . . .' Reach agreement tomorrow, on a Swiss Sunday! What's more, tomorrow is also April 1, Western-style!"

"April 1?!!" Lenin hadn't laughed so much in a long time. All the tension of the last few weeks burst from his breast in loud, harsh, liberating spasms of laughter. "This will be a nice box of chocolates for the centrist swine!"

" 'Reach immediate agreement . . . and *if possible* t o m o r r o w .' "

"While all Switzerland is snoozing!"

" 'Inform us of the decision! . . . Gratefully yours . . .' "

It was like in a game of chess when you make a well-thought-out move and then see that it is even more effective and promising than you had calculated. This bit of fun—Grimm's Sunday chore on April Fool's Day—was typical of Radek the jester.

"And if he doesn't do it on Sunday—on Monday we shall be free to act ourselves!"

"On Tuesday, anyway . . ."

Ah, but Radek had an even better idea. "Vladimir Ilyich! What about Martov? We must write to Martov, particularly as he's the initiator of the *plan!?*" Radek was choking with laughter.

"Write what to Martov?" Even Lenin's mind couldn't work quite so quickly.

"To tell him that we accept immediately *Grimm's proposal for us to travel via Germany!* That way we can make a fool of Grimm by making it look like his proposal!!! Tell the whole world it comes from him. That the Swiss socialists are shoving us out. A member of the Swiss Parliament!"

Now, this really was a stroke of genius! Bravo, Radek! Grimm would set up a howl! Make frantic excuses! But it's always easier to spit than to wipe it off—you have to learn to spit first and at the right moment.

"The scoundrel will wish he'd printed my pamphlet after all."

"It's getting late, though. We'll have to mail it at the Fraumünster."

"I can run down, Vladimir Ilyich."

"Let's go together since we're in the mood."

In that case they must look around and think what else needed to be done. Of course, a letter to Hanecki in Stockholm—"Urgent that you wire three thousand crowns for travel expenses!"

(Must also write to Inessa: "Don't worry about money . . . we have more than we thought . . . The comrades in Stockholm are giving us a lot of help . . . I hope that we will have you t r a v e l i n g  w i t h  u s ? ")

Another thing—he must draw out the hundred francs he had deposited in the cantonal bank as a condition of residence in Switzerland. No point in pampering the lackeys' republic.

Lenin put on his iron-heavy quilted greatcoat, and Radek the thin summer coat in which he ran around all through the winter, his pockets crammed with books.

He filled his pipe, and had his matches ready.

Lenin said aloud: "That's fine. What can Platten's negotiations with Romberg amount to? Romberg will just take the documents out of his desk drawer. But we had to fling those few days in the chauvinists' ugly faces."

Radek, light-footed and pleased with himself, danced about like an adolescent.

"My hands itch, my tongue itches! I can't wait for the wide-open Russian spaces, can't wait to start agitating!"

And, letting Lenin go first, holding a match ready to strike in the corridor, he said: "It comes to this, Vladimir Ilyich: six months from now we will either be ministers or we will be hanged."

# DOCUMENTS*

**March 31.** *Berlin*
*(Memo by an official of the Foreign Ministry with the General Staff)*

> ... Above all, we must avoid compromising the travelers by excessive attentiveness on our part. It would be very desirable to have some sort of declaration from the Swiss government. If we suddenly send these restless elements to Sweden without such a declaration, it may be used against us.

**March 31**
*(Assistant Secretary of State to Ambassador Romberg in Bern. In cipher)*

> Urgent! The journey of the Russian émigrés through Germany should take place very quickly, since the Entente has already started countermeasures in Switzerland. Speed up the negotiations as much as possible.

**April 2**
*(Count Brockdorff-Rantzau, German ambassador in Copenhagen, to the Ministry of Foreign Affairs. Top secret)*

> ... We must now definitely try to create the utmost chaos in Russia. To

---

*Documents no. 30, 31, from Werner Hahlweg's Lenins Rückkehr nach Russland, 1917.*

this end we must avoid any discernible interference in the course of the Russian revolution. But we must secretly do all we can to aggravate the contradictions between the moderate and the extreme parties, since we are extremely interested in the victory of the latter, for another upheaval will then be inevitable, and will take forms which will shake the Russian state to its foundations.

Support by us of the extreme elements is preferable, because in this way the work is done more thoroughly and achieves its results more quickly. According to all forecasts, we may count on the disintegration being so far advanced in three months or so that military intervention by us will guarantee the collapse of Russian power.

# 'Author's Note

Those who are surprised by V. I. Lenin's choice of words, his way of thinking and acting, may read more carefully those of his works which have been used here.

*V boevoy komitet pri Sankt-Peterburgskom komitete* (To the Combat Committee of the St. Petersburg Committee). *Sobranie Sochinenii*, 4th edition, vol. 9, p. 315.

*Zadachi otryadov revolyutsionnoi armii* (Tasks of units of the revolutionary army). *Op. cit.*, vol. 9, p. 389.

*O lozunge "razoruzheniya"* (On the slogan "Disarmament"). *Op. cit.*, vol. 23, p. 83.

*Rech' na s'yezde shveitsarskoy s-d partii 4.11.1916* (Speech at the Congress of the Swiss Social Democratic Party). *Op. cit.*, vol. 23, p. 110.

*Zadachi levykh tsimmerval'distov v shveitsarskoy s-d partii* (Tasks of the left Zimmerwaldists in the Swiss Social Democratic Party). *Op. cit.*, vol. 23, p. 126.

*Tezisy ob otnoshenii shveitsarskoy s-d partii k voine* (Theses on the attitude of the Swiss Social Democratic Party toward the war). *Op. cit.*, vol. 23, p. 138.

*Printsipial'nye polozheniya k voprosu o voine* (The war question: statements of principle). *Op. cit.*, vol. 23, p. 141.

*Otkrytoye pis'mo k Sharlyu Nenu* (Open letter to Charles Naine). *Op. cit.*, vol. 23, p. 212.

*Dvenadtsat' kratkikh tezisov o zachchite G. Greilikhom zashchity otechestva* (Twelve short theses on H. Greulich's defense of the fatherland). *Op. cit.*, vol. 23, p. 247.

*Nabrosok tezisov 4 (17) Marta 1917* (Draft theses of March 4 [17], 1917). *Op. cit.*, vol. 23, p. 282.

*Pis'ma iz daleka* (Letters from afar). *Op. cit.*, vol. 23, p. 289.

*Pis'ma Lenina voennykh let (1914–1917)* (Lenin's wartime letters). *Sobranie Sochinenii*, 5th edition, vols. 48, 49.

I consider it my duty to mention four recent studies which have particularly helped me in writing these chapters:

Werner Hahlweg: *Lenins Rückkehr nach Russland 1917*. Leiden, 1957.

Z. A. B. Zeman and W. B. Scharlau: *Freibeuter der Revolution*. Cologne, 1964 (*The Merchant of Revolution*. London and New York, 1965).

Willi Gautschi: *Lenin als Emigrant in der Schweiz*. Cologne, 1973.

Fritz N. Platten, Jr.: *"Von der Spiegelgasse in den Kreml,"* *Volksrecht*, March 13–April 17, 1967.

I must express my gratitude to these writers for their close attention to events which determined the course of the twentieth century, but which have been carefully concealed from history, and which, because of the direction taken by the development of the West, have received little attention.

Moscow, 1971
Zurich, 1975

## Author's Glossary of Names

*Abramovich, Alexander E.* (*b.* 1893)   Native of Odessa. Member of the R.S.D.R.P. from 1908. In Switzerland from 1911: studied in Geneva, worked in La Chaux-de-Fonds watch factory. Returned to Russia with Lenin's group. Some indications that he was a Soviet agent in the Bavarian Republic in 1918. On the staff of the Comintern.

*Armand, Inessa Teodorovna* (1874–1920)   Born in Paris, into a French theatrical family. Brought up in Russia by an aunt who was employed there as a governess. Married the factory owner Armand, by whom she had four children, then left him for his younger brother and gave birth to another son (in Switzerland). During the 1905 Revolution was connected with the S.R. group in Moscow, was subsequently exiled, then emigrated. After her second husband's death, studied at the Sorbonne, met Lenin in 1909, and thereafter supported the Bolsheviks. Was Lenin's intimate friend, with short breaks, until her death, and was throughout this period one of his closest collaborators. Visited Russia in 1912, was imprisoned for a short time, but released thanks to her first husband's intercession. Took part in the Kienthal Conference with the Bolshevik delegation. Returned to Russia with Lenin's group. After the October Revolution, was for a time chairman of the Moscow Provincial Economic Council, later head of the Women's Department of the Central Committee of the party.

*Bagocki, Sergei Yustinovich* (1879–1953)   A Pole from Russia; a doctor. Was in Cracow with Lenin, followed him to Switzerland. At that time, was Lenin's assistant in practical and financial matters, and in maintaining conspiratorial contacts through intermediaries with the Germans. An an émigré in Switzerland, lived in style and spent freely (Nobs's testimony). From 1918, representative of the Russian Red Cross in Switzerland.

*Bogdanov (Malinovsky), Alexander Alexandrovich* (1873–1928)   Son of a physics teacher, educated at the Tula high school, in 1899 entered the medical school of Kharkov University. "Parted company" with the local group of Social Democratic intellectuals "over the question of morals, to which they attached unconditional importance." Doctor, sociologist, and philosopher. Light sentences of banishment on various occasions (Tula, Kaluga, Vologda). Sided with Lenin in 1904 and became a member of the first Bolshevik leadership. Theoretician of armed uprising, organizer of tactical assaults, expropriations, schemes for raising party funds. Arrested together with the whole Petersburg Soviet in 1905, but soon released. During the revolutionary years 1906–1907, lived with Lenin at Kuokkala. Consistently adhered to the Bolshevik line of boycotting parliamentary and legal activity, which Lenin abandoned in 1907. Finding Bogdanov's presence in the leadership a nuisance, Lenin attacked his philosophical ideas (in *Materialism and Empirico-Criticism*, 1909) and drove him out of the party. After that, Bogdanov never held an important party or Soviet post. Called up during the war, served as a doctor at the front. Published many works on political economy, philosophy, the organization of science and of the economy, as well as two novels of fantasy. Died as the result of a dangerous experiment in blood transfusion.

*Bosch, Yevgenia Gotlibovna* (1879–1924)   Native of Ochakov. Married at sixteen to the son of a factory owner, left her husband when she was twenty-one, and plunged into Social Democratic politics (in Kiev). Bolshevik; mistress of Piatakov. Exiled to Irkutsk province in 1913, escaped with Piatakov via Vladivostok. Was in Switzerland for a short time, then in Scandinavia. After the February Revolution, chairman of the Kiev Provincial Party Committee, urged the Guards Corps to advance on Kiev and overthrow the Rada, the Ukranian nationalist government. Member of Kiev War Revolutionary Committee. In the first Communist government of the Ukraine (Kharkov, 1918), as People's Secretary for Internal Affairs. During the civil war, assigned to punitive operations at provincial level (Penza, Astrakhan, Gomel), commissar of the Caspian-Caucasian Front. Accused of Trotskyism in 1923. Committed suicide in 1924.

*Brilliant* See *Sokolnikov.*

*Bronski (Warszawski), Moisei* (1882–1941) Native of Lodz; Polish Social Democrat, then Bolshevik. Emigrated to Switzerland in 1907. Close assistant of Lenin, who brought him into the Kienthal Conference. After the October Revolution, worked for a time on the editorial staff of *Pravda;* Deputy People's Commissar of Trade and Industry; 1920–1922, political representative (ambassador) in Austria. Held no important post after Lenin's death.

*Bukharin, Nikolai Ivanovich* (1888–1938) Notable theoretician who once seemed destined to lead the Bolshevik Party. Born into the family of a schoolteacher. Had a mixed upbringing—among intellectuals and ordinary people. Educated at Moscow High School No. 1, joined the Bolshevik Party at eighteen, coopted to the Moscow Committee of the party as a twenty-year-old student. Briefly detained on various occasions. Escaped abroad from exile. Emigré from 1911, studied intensively, began writing. Returned to Russia in 1917 by way of America, Japan, and Siberia. From summer 1917, member of the Central Committee. Led the left Communist opposition to the peace of Brest-Litovsk—instead of reinforcing Germany through a separate peace, Russia should aim at world revolution. Published a great deal in the Soviet period (on economics, on politics, works of popularization). Was a member of the seven-man leadership (Politburo) after Lenin's death and was used by Stalin to destroy it. Trotsky, Kamenev, and Zinoviev were routed with his help, after which he and his supporters Rykov and Tomsky were eliminated. On the threshold of the thirties, seems to have understood the criminality of Stalin's policies, which he believed spelled ruin for the peasantry and for the general health of the nation's economy, but was unable to oppose them firmly and effectively. Shot after a show trial with the usual "confessions."

*Burtsev, Vladimir Lvovich* (1862–1942) Revolutionary, member of the People's Will Party in the eighties, terrorist at the end of the nineteenth century. Arrested, escaped. In the British press, called for the assassination of Alexander III—and even under English law, incurred a prison sentence of eighteen months. Also expelled from Switzerland for terrorist propaganda. Specialized in exposing police spies in the Russian revolutionary movement. During the 1905 and 1917 revolutions, edited the journal *Byloe (The Past)*; from 1911 to 1914, the newspaper *Budushchee (The Future)*, which he sent from abroad to the Tsar, to grand dukes, ministers, and the library of the State Duma. At the beginning of the First World War became a patriot, gave himself up at the Russian frontier, was tried, exiled, and amnestied (1915). Under the Bolsheviks, arrested on various occasions, resumed publication of *Byloe*, then published *Obshchee Delo (Common Cause)* under the Whites. Reemigrated.

*Chudnovsky, Grigory Isaakovich* (1871–1918) Social Democrat; Menshevik. Spent many years abroad. Returned to Russia with Trotsky, joined the Inter-District group, then the Bolsheviks. He and Antonov-Ovseenko were in charge of the assault on the Winter Palace. Military Commissar of Kiev. Killed in the Ukraine.

*Greulich, Hermann* (1842–1925)   Native of Breslau, bookbinder. One of the founders of the Swiss Social Democratic Party and its newspaper *Berner Tagwacht*. Most popular of Swiss working-class leaders ("Papa Greulich"). Member of the Swiss Parliament from 1902 until his death.

*Grimm, Robert* (1881–1958)   Printer, mechanic. One of the leaders of the Swiss Social Democratic Party. From 1905, trade-union secretary in Basel. From 1919, secretary of the party and editor in chief of the *Berner Tagwacht*. From 1911, member of the Swiss Parliament; from 1946, its chairman. Initiator and chairman of the Zimmerwald and Kienthal conferences. One of the organizers of the "2½ International" (to the left of the socialist International, but more moderate than the Comintern).

*Guilbeaux, Henri* (1885–1938)   French Social Democrat, internationalist. Opposed to the war, came to Geneva in 1915, published the journal *Demain* from 1916. Took part in the Kienthal Conference. On the staff of the Comintern, but lost sympathy with the U.S.S.R. in the thirties.

*Hanecki* (sometimes spelled *Ganetsky*) (*Fürstenberg*), *Jacob* (1879–1937)   From a wealthy Warsaw family. Joined the Social Democrats at the end of the nineteenth century. Attended the Second Congress of the R.S.D.R.P. as a member of the Polish socialist delegation. Was for many years simultaneously a member of the Polish and the Russian parties. Briefly detained on various occasions, never sentenced for a long term. As a conscript, abused his regimental commander, but was excused because of his "excitability." Twice escaped from exile. Before the war, joined Radek in splitting the Polish Social Democratic Party (in opposition to Rosa Luxemburg). From 1912, an intimate collaborator of Lenin, with him in Cracow, then in Switzerland, whence he moved in 1915 to work with Parvus in Scandinavia as director of his agency. In March 1917 he, Radek, and Vorovsky were left in Stockholm by Lenin in what they called the Foreign Bureau of the Central Committee, to insure the uninterrupted transfer of funds from Parvus for the reinforcement of Bolshevik organizations and the Bolshevik press in Russia, and also to carry on Bolshevik propaganda directed at the West. After the October Revolution, was in the People's Commissariat of Finance (as Chief Commissar for Banks). Took part in negotiating the "Supplementary Agreement" with Germany in August 1918, by which Russia's obligations under the Brest-Litovsk treaty were expanded to include increased supplies of foodstuffs and *matériel* to Germany on the eve of that country's defeat. Took part in important diplomatic discussions in 1920–1925. Many dark patches in his biography. After Lenin's death, People's Commissar for Foreign Trade, various minor posts. Arrested and shot in 1937 together with his wife and son.

*Inessa* See *Armand.*

*Kamenev (Rosenfeld), Lev Borisovich* (1883–1936) Educated at Tiflis high school and Moscow University (Law Faculty), where he began his revolutionary career and from which he was expelled. After a brief period of detention, went abroad, where he joined the Bolsheviks in 1903. Returned to Russia several times, was briefly detained twice. Active as propagandist in the revolutionary years, prolonged residence abroad from 1908, became a member of Lenin's new entourage. Posted to Russia after Malinovsky's exposure in 1914, to lead the Bolshevik group in the State Duma from outside (when war broke out—from Finland). In November, arrested while secretly conferring with them near Petersburg, tried in 1915, made things easier for himself by rejecting Lenin's defeatist line, which the Bolshevik faction in the Duma had accepted. Returned to Petrograd after the February Revolution, and since he enjoyed Lenin's confidence more than others there, led the party until his return. The only member of the party who spoke out against the *April Theses*. When the Bolsheviks seized control of the Second Congress of Soviets on the night of their coup, he became chairman of that body and of the new Central Executive Committee. Took part in the negotiations with Germany at Brest-Litovsk. He was one of the ailing Lenin's three deputies—the others being Rykov and Tsiurupa—in 1922. He and Zinoviev were constant companions in failure in the struggle against Stalin. Already doomed, he demanded at the 1934 congress that the party should not engage in ideological debate with the Kulak opposition group led by Riutin but should shoot them instead. He was shot himself after the 1936 trial.

*Kamo (Ter-Petrosian), Semyon Arshakovich* (1882–1922) Native of Gori in Georgia, son of a wealthy contractor. Expelled from school for expressing freethinking views in Scripture lessons. Influenced by his older compatriot Dzhugashvili (Stalin). Resourceful and skillful in illegal activities under arms, successfully carried out expropriation operations on Stalin's instructions, including the famous Treasury raid (Tiflis, June 1907). While traveling to Berlin to carry out his next raid, was arrested by the German police with a case full of explosives. Avoided being handed over to the Russian government by successfully pretending for years to be violently insane. Was, however, finally handed over, but saved from execution by a German press campaign in defense of "a man well known to be sick." Escaped from prison hospital to join Lenin abroad. Returned to the Caucasus in 1912, was wounded and arrested during another interrupted mailbag robbery, and sentenced to death. A liberal public prosecutor, however, delayed implementation of the sentence until promulgation of the amnesty on the tercentenary of the Romanov dynasty, and so saved his life. Released from prison by the February Revolution. Sent by Lenin to a mountain resort in the Caucasus for his health. Served in the Cheka in Baku. Carried on underground activity after the establishment of the Menshevik government in Georgia. Rejected Lenin's suggestion that he should enroll in the General Staff Academy. Died after being run over by a car.

*Karpinsky, Viacheslav Alexeevich* (1880–1965) Social Democrat from 1898; Bolshevik from the time of the split. In Geneva as an émigré from 1904. Lenin used him for minor editorial and practical tasks. In the Soviet period, doctor of economic sciences.

*Keskula, Alexander Eduard* (1882–1963) An Estonian from Tartu. Took part in the 1905 Revolution. Arrested, but amnestied; emigrated. Before the war, studied unsystematically in Switzerland. In 1914, put himself at the disposal of the German ambassador in Switzerland, Baron Romberg; tried to obtain German support for the Estonian liberation movement. Romberg used him for liaison with Russian revolutionary émigrés of various factions, including Lenin. To give him greater scope, he was transferred by the Germans to Scandinavia. There he sent agents to Russia and financed Bolshevik publications (Bukharin, Piatakov, etc.), without disclosing the source of his funds. Acted as channel of communication between the Bolsheviks in Scandinavia and in Switzerland.

*Kharitonov, Moisei M.* (1887–1948) Social Democrat from 1905. Studied law in Switzerland from 1912.

Close to Lenin, returned to Russia with his group. After the October Revolution, head of the Petrograd militia. In the twenties, secretary of provincial party committees, first in the Urals, then at Perm, then at Saratov. Supported the Zinoviev-Kamenev opposition in 1925, then their bloc with Trotsky. Occupied no important post after this.

*Kollontai, Alexandra Mikhailovna* (1872–1952) Daughter of a Ukrainian general and a Finnish peasant woman. Brought up in a rich landowning milieu, not allowed to attend high school or Bestuzhev courses, where she might come into contact with revolutionary elements. Studied privately with professors of history and literature. An early marriage to escape parental control did not last long. Joined cultural and educational societies, all concerned with aid to revolutionaries. Studied economics abroad. Social Democrat from the end of the nineteenth century. Witnessed the shooting on the palace square on January 9 (22), 1905. Wrote proclamations for both Social Democratic factions. "I felt a greater affinity for Bolshevism, with its intransigence"—but until 1915 she was a Menshevik, favored general reconciliation in 1914, and was only gradually converted to Lenin's "civil war" and so to Bolshevism. Before and during the war, Shliapnikov's mistress. People's Commissar for Social Insurance in the first Bolshevik government. Then for many years Soviet ambassador to Norway and Sweden.

*Kozlovsky, M. Yu.* (1876–1929) Social Democrat, Petersburg lawyer, had clandestine links with Parvus's agency. Member of the Executive Committee of the Petrograd Soviet in 1917. Arrested in July, together with some leading Bolsheviks, after the revelations about Bolshevik dealings with the Germans. (They were all released at the time of the Kornilov mutiny.) After the October Revolution, chairman of the Extraordinary Commission of Investigation in Petrograd and chairman of the Little Sovnarkom. Later, People's Commissar of Justice for Lithuania and Byelorussia.

*Krassin, Leonid Borisovich* (1870–1926) Native of Tobolsk province, revolutionary from student days (influenced by political exiles). Received a technical education, periodically interrupted by arrest and exile; became an engineer. This decided his future role in the party: as its expert on conspiratorial techniques, the making of explosives, armed attacks. It was Krassin, too, who established contact with the factory owner Savva Morozov, and arranged regular financial help for the party from this source. From 1903, a Bolshevik, and even became a member of the Central Committee. At the height of his revolutionary career he was also in charge of the whole Petersburg lighting grid. Emigrated in 1908, ousted from the Bolshevik leadership in 1909, gave up politics. Worked as an engineer in Berlin, returned to Russia, where he held managerial jobs. Rejoined the party in 1917. Took part in the Brest-Litovsk negotiations and in the "Supplementary" talks in Berlin (August 1918; see *Hanecki*). Went to see Ludendorff at Staff Headquarters in a vain effort to persuade the Germans not to detach the Caucasus and Turkestan (Ludendorff's plan was frustrated by the arrival of the American expeditionary force in France). Held several important economic posts; was People's Commissar for Foreign Trade, then for Roads and Railways; from 1920, ambassador in London; took part in other diplomatic negotiations, including the Genoa and Hague conferences.

*Krupskaya, Nadezhda Konstantinovna (Nadya)* (1869–1939) Daughter of a court official. From 1897, Lenin's wife (the marriage was formalized in church so that she could go to Siberia with him). Shared his whole life, performed routine tasks for the party. Tried to write original works on education, but achieved nothing of significance. After the October Revolution, was among those in charge of the People's Commissariat for Education. In 1925, joined Zinoviev and Kamenev in their unsuccessful opposition to Stalin. Thereafter, during Stalin's dictatorship, kept silent.

*Levi (Hartstein), Paul* (1883–1930)   German Social Democrat, lawyer. As an émigré in Switzerland, member of the Zimmerwald left, later in Germany a Communist. Reverted to the Social Democratic Party in the twenties.

*Litvinov, Maxim Maximovich* (1876–1951)   From a well-to-do family in Poland. Attracted to Marxism while doing military service as a volunteer. Arrested with the Kiev Committee of the R.S.D.R.P. in 1901, escaped from imprisonment in Kiev in 1902, and fled abroad. A Bolshevik from 1903. In 1905 made an unsuccessful attempt to transport arms from Britain to Russia. Continuously in emigration except for short trips to Russia. In London from 1907. Represented the Bolsheviks in the International Socialist Bureau (Second International). After the October Revolution, was the first Soviet political representative (ambassador) in London, was arrested in retaliation for Lockhart's arrest in Moscow and exchanged for him. Successful diplomatic career, Deputy People's Commissar, then from 1930 to 1939—i.e., in the peak years of the Stalin terror—People's Commissar for Foreign Affairs and herald of P e a c e in the West; his speeches flooded the pages of Soviet newspapers and were popular. Demoted during the years of Soviet friendship with Hitler's Germany. Ambassador to the United States, 1941–1943. Again Deputy People's Commissar for Foreign Affairs, 1943–1946.

*Lunacharsky, Anatoly Vasilievich* (1875–1933)   Prolific journalist and lecturer, feeble dramatist and writer (his choice of pen name—Voinov, from *voin,* "warri-

or"—indicates the level of his talent). Native of Poltava, from the family of a civil servant with radical leanings. Studied Marxism from the age of fifteen, agitator among workers at the age of seventeen. When he left high school, went to Zurich University. Returned to Russia in 1899, engaged in propaganda. Three short periods of imprisonment—a few months at a time; banished to Kaluga, Vologda; studied intensively, published first works. Emigrated in 1903, joined Bolsheviks, and visited all émigré groups to popularize their position, agreed to speak on the principles of armed uprising at the Third Congress of the party. During the 1905 Revolution, active as journalist, underwent one month's detention, and emigrated until the next revolution. Contributed to many Bolshevik publications. Pupil of Avenarius, differed with Lenin on philosophical questions in 1908–1909. Made an unsuccessful attempt to found a distinct party, the *Vperyod (Forward)* group. In the Trotsky-Martov group during the war. Returned to Russia via Germany with the second émigré party, was for a few months a member of the Inter-District group until they merged with the Bolsheviks in July 1917. In this way he came back to Lenin. Imprisoned for a short time by the Provisional Government, together with certain leading Bolsheviks, on a charge of treason—collaboration with the Germans. "Both before I went to prison and while I was there, my life was in extreme danger on various occasions." Released a month later. After the October Revolution, People's Commissar for Education until 1929. During the civil war, paid many visits to the fronts and to forward areas, incessantly haranguing the troops. Equally well known in Moscow as an irrepressible lecturer. In 1923 published a book on the leaders of the Revolution without mentioning Stalin. This mistake earned him many years of disfavor and brought him into real danger.

Died en route to Spain to take up his appointment as ambassador.

*Malinovsky, Roman Vatslavovich* (1876–1918)　Pole, native of Plock. Tailor, then metalworker. Three convictions for larceny. While performing military service, became an informer for the secret police. Originally a Menshevik, went over to the Bolsheviks in 1910. Coopted to the Central Committee by Lenin, appointed chairman of the Russian Bureau (i.e., director of the party on Russian soil). Split the Social Democratic group in the Duma on Lenin's instructions and became leader of the Bolshevik faction. Conducted its work and composed his speeches under the simultaneous guidance of Lenin and the Police Department. But in 1914 a new head of the Police Department decided that it was self-defeating for the state to use a prominent member of the Duma as an informer, discharged Malinovsky, and ordered him to give up his work in the Duma. (The situation is reminiscent of the way in which the police themselves exposed Azev.) Malinovsky resigned his parliamentary position without explanation and vanished. Rumors that he was a provocateur began to circulate, but Lenin, Zinoviev, and Hanecki exonerated him in 1914 and again in 1917: "The leading organs of the party are absolutely sure of Malinovsky's political honesty. The accusations are absolute nonsense." During the war, was in the army and taken prisoner by the Germans. In 1918, decided to return to Russia after Lenin had promised him personal safety. (According to rumors, a written guarantee signed by Lenin was taken from Malinovsky at the frontier.) He was tried by a tribunal on November 5, 1918, in Lenin's presence. Malinovsky defended himself in a six-hour speech. He was shot immediately.

*Martov (Tsederbaum), Yuli Osipovich* (1873–1923)　Began revolutionary career as a student, was expelled and arrested on various occasions. In Vilna in the 1890's he formulated the ideology of the Jewish Bund, but he soon became an opponent of that party. Arrested together with Lenin in Petersburg in 1896, exiled for three years. Unlike Lenin, he had no influence and so served his sentence in the Turukhan Territory. Emigré from 1901. Leader of the Mensheviks. Could not tolerate Bolshevik unscrupulousness. Favored the development of Social Democracy by legal means. At the beginning of the war, was against defense of the fatherland, but also against converting the war into civil war. Returned to Russia via Germany with the second émigré party in May 1917. Was for a socialist coalition government and against the seizure of power. At the Congress of Soviets in October, spoke against the assault on the Winter Palace. Protested strongly against the dissolution of the Constituent Assembly, and while the Red Terror was raging, against the death penalty. In 1920, with Lenin's permission, left for Germany, where he published *Sozialisticheskii Vestnik (Socialist Herald)*. One of the founders of the "2½ International" ("for dictatorship of the proletariat, but without terror"). Died of tuberculosis of the throat.

*Moor, Karl* (1852–1932) Swiss Social Democrat. In 1892–1906, member of the editoral team of the *Berner Tagwacht*. Well-to-do. During the war a double agent for German and Austrian secret services (code name, Baier). Was very helpful to Lenin. Took care of Münzenberg while he was in prison in Switzerland, and of Platten in prison in Lithuania, rescued Radek from prison in Berlin (1919). Carried out secret diplomatic missions for the Soviet government. After the October Revolution, an honorary citizen of the Soviet Union, and lived there most of the time until 1927. Spent his last years in Berlin.

*Münzenberg, Wilhelm (Willi)* (1889–1940) Native of Erfurt. Emigrated to Switzerland in 1910. There he became secretary of the Socialist Youth International and editor of its organ *Jugend Internationale*. Organized workers' demonstrations in Zurich during the war. Took part in Kienthal Conference. From 1916, among the leaders of the Swiss Social Democratic Party. In 1917, the German authorities gave him travel privileges (although he was a deserter from the German army). Also in 1917 was responsible for bloody street fighting in Zurich. Arrested as a result, and again in 1918. Deported to Germany at the end of the war. Secretary of the Communist Youth International, 1919–1921. Visited Lenin in Moscow in 1920. In 1924, set up as a publisher of left-wing newspapers. Communist deputy in the Reichstag till 1933, when he emigrated to France. Summoned to the U.S.S.R. by Stalin, but refused to go. Found hanged in the forest near Grenoble in the summer of 1940.

*Nobs, Ernst* (1886–1957)  Son of a tailor. Teacher. From 1915, editor in chief of the party organ *Volksrecht* and other socialist publications. From 1916, chairman of the party organization in Zurich. From 1917, one of the leaders of the Swiss party. From 1919, member of the Swiss Parliament; from 1943 to 1951, member of the government; in 1948, President of Switzerland.

*Parvus (Helphand), Alexander (Israel) Lazarevich* (1867–1924)  Native of Minsk province (Berezino); spent his childhood in Odessa. Completed course at Odessa high school in 1885, Basel University in 1891. Began successful career as a journalist in the German left-wing press ("the journalistic revolution"), intermediary between the German and Russian Social Democrats (Plekhanov, Potresov). Organized the publication of *Iskra (The Spark)* in Leipzig and contributed articles to it. Expelled from various German *Länder* for his journalistic activities, moved to others. Real leader of the Petersburg Soviet in 1905, spent some months in the Kresty and Petropavlovsk prisons, administrative exile for three years in Siberia, escaped en route, returned to Petersburg, went abroad. Sharply attacked the "Russian course" (policy of rapprochement) adopted by the German government from 1907. From 1910 to 1915, was in Turkey and the Balkans, where he became extremely rich. Acted as financial adviser to the Turkish and Bulgarian governments when they came into the world war. From February 1915, entered into negotiations with the German Ministry of Foreign Affairs. Undertook to bring Russia out of the war by starting a revolution there. Under cover of trading operations, sent German money to Russian revolutionaries—after the February Revolution, exclusively to the Bolsheviks, enabling them quickly to reinforce their press and their membership, which were ineffectual and low in February 1917. After the revelations of July 1917, which were not followed up, he fiercely attacked Kerensky in the German press. In 1917 he obstructed concerted socialist efforts to end the war and influenced the German government to await the collapse of Russia into anarchy and then neutralize it. Wanted to return to Russia after the October Revolution (he had no confidence in Bolshevik organizing abilities, and condemned Lenin's "concessions" to the peasants). Lenin refused to accept him. Parvus began attacking Lenin only when the Soviet government assigned two million rubles to "support revolution in Europe." He thought that it would be very dangerous if the Bolsheviks made Russia a great military power. Left for Switzerland after the German revolution of November 1918, settled in a villa by the lake at Zurich. His orgies there, together with the scandals involving Sklarz in Berlin (he had bribed members of the Social Democratic government), led to Parvus's expulsion from Switzer-

land. He built himself an opulent residence on the
island of Schwanenwerder in Germany and lived there
for the rest of his life.

*Piatakov, Georgi Leonidovich* (1890–1937)  Son of an
engineer. As a fifteen-year-old pupil of a technical
school, took part in street meetings, and was expelled.
At sixteen, conducted anarchist propaganda, took
part in an expropriation, trained himself for terrorist
activity. Social Democrat from the age of twenty. In
1913, exiled to Siberia; from there went via Japan to
Europe (Switzerland, Sweden). After the February
Revolution, chairman of the Kiev Committee of the
Bolshevik Party, then also of the Kiev Soviet of
Workers' Deputies. Took an active part in the October
rising in Kiev; underground work in the Ukraine;
from the end of 1918, first head of the Soviet government in the Ukraine. For most of the civil war was a
commissar; did not shrink from punitive operations.
In 1920, joined Trotsky's attempt to create a Labor
Army (prototype of the labor camps) in the Urals. In
1922, chairman of the tribunal which tried the S.R.'s
in Moscow. From 1923, member of the Central Committee. He was concerned throughout with the administration of the economy, and by 1930 was the real
overlord of heavy industry. Arrested, tortured, shot
after a show trial.

*Platten, Fritz* (1883–1942)  Metalworker, then draftsman.
Secretary of Swiss Social Democratic Party, took part
in Zimmerwald and Kienthal conferences, where he
sided with Lenin. When Lenin's group went home he
was not allowed into Russia by British frontier con-
trols. Returned to Switzerland, established contact
with Baron Romberg to arrange further émigré
echelons. ("We must increase the number of firm
partisans of peace in Petersburg by bringing them in
from abroad.") Member of Swiss Parliament from
1917, founded the Swiss Communist Party in 1918.

At this time made a number of visits to Moscow, was one of the prominent figures at the inaugural meetings of the Comintern (1919), was a member of the Bureau of the Comintern. Secretary of the Swiss Communist Party until 1923; from then until his death, lived in the U.S.S.R. Died in exile.

*Plekhanov, Georgi Valentinovich* (1856–1918) The first important Russian Marxist. Founded the Marxist Liberation of Labor group in Geneva in 1883. For many years, leader of the Russian Social Democratic movement—until the split with Lenin in 1903. At the Second Congress, where the split took place, he still declared himself in favor of revolutionary dictatorship. Later he again allied himself with Lenin in a futile attempt to regain the leadership of the party. In 1914 he took up a patriotic position, to which he clung more and more fervently in his remaining years. In 1917 he returned to Russia via England, arriving a few days before Lenin. Because of the fragmentation of the Social Democratic Party he had long ceased to lead the Mensheviks, and controlled only the Edinstvo (Unity—i.e., *national* unity) group, which tried to ally itself with the Kadets and was smashed as a result of the October Revolution.

*Potresov, Alexander Nikolaevich* (1869–1934) Gentleman, son of an artillery colonel. Inherited compassion for the people from his mother. Graduated in science, began studying law, but succumbed to the lure of politics. First visited Switzerland in 1892 and made contact with Plekhanov and the Liberation of Labor group. Became Plekhanov's publisher in Russia. Exiled to Vyatka province, 1898–1900: produced the plan for *Iskra* together with Lenin and Martov—the three of them exchanged letters from their places of exile—and in 1900 went to Switzerland to carry it out. Withdrew because of illness in 1901–1903. One of the first to return to Petersburg in 1905 to take part in the revolution, cooperated with Parvus and Trotsky in publications. After the suppression of the revolution, refused on principle to emigrate. Plekhanov attacked Potresov from abroad in reply to his critical articles and Lenin took advantage of this. (The term "liquidator" originated in this polemic.) Potresov believed that the underground could not express the interests of the workers and that socialists should concentrate on legal organizations. He felt that the 1914 war was the beginning of the end for Russia. Supported Guchkov's War Industrial Committee. Acknowledged leader of the Menshevik Defensists. Strongly opposed to a separate peace, lived underground after the Bolsheviks came to power, arrested by the Cheka, released thanks to the efforts of old acquaintances. In February 1925, suffering from spinal tuberculosis, allowed to leave for treatment in Berlin. Bedridden until his death.

*Radek (Sobelsohn), Karl Bernhardovich* (1885–1939)   A brilliant journalist and an audacious and resourceful politician. Native of Galicia; Polish Social Democrat. Emigrated, returned to Warsaw for the 1905 Revolution, again emigrated to Berlin. Opponent of Rosa Luxemburg in the Polish Social Democratic Party, expelled from the German Social Democratic Party for unseemly behavior. At the beginning of the war, left Germany for Switzerland to avoid the draft. Attended Zimmerwald and Kienthal conferences, was sometimes at odds with Lenin, sometimes his ally and favorite. Traveled through Germany with Lenin's group, stayed behind in the Bolshevik Foreign Bureau in Stockholm for the rest of 1917 (see *Hanecki*). Took part in the Brest-Litovsk negotiations. At the end of 1918, went to Germany to help start a proletarian revolution, was arrested; visited in prison by prominent politicians. Released. Was in Germany on various secret missions (seeking an alliance against

Poland, etc.). In 1923, sent there again to foment revolution; did not succeed. Member of the Central Committee, member of the Executive Committee of the Comintern. In 1923–1925, shared the discomfiture of the opposition leaders and ceased to hold prominent party posts. For many years the most effective writer in the Soviet press. At the show trial of January 1937, made incriminating statements about others. He was not shot, but died in confinement shortly afterward in unknown circumstances.

*Rakovsky, Christian Georgievich* (1873–1941) Son of well-to-do Bulgarian parents, and member of a family which played a considerable part in the fight for independence from Turkey. Involved in political disturbances as a fourteen-year-old schoolboy; emigrated at the age of seventeen to Geneva, where he came under Plekhanov's influence and made the acquaintance of the international Social Democratic movement. Connected with Russia by marriage, traveled there. Published articles in the left-wing press (pen name, Insarov). An émigré for many years in Western Europe, persistent revolutionary activity in Roumania and Bulgaria. Took part in Zimmerwald Conference. Liberated from prison in Roumania by the February Revolution, went to Petersburg, joined the Bolsheviks. After the October Revolution, a commissar in southern Russia (of a naval unit, the Odessa Extraordinary Collegium, etc.). On instructions from the Soviet government, discussed with Skoropadsky and the Germans the separation of the Ukraine from Russia and a peace treaty between the two. Nonetheless, when the Bolsheviks occupied and reoccupied the Ukraine, it was always Rakovsky who became chairman of its Council of People's Commissars, and in fact he governed the Republic until 1923 (combining this office with many military-political and economic-administrative posts). Went to Britain as political representatve in 1923, to France in 1925. From 1919, in the Central Committee of the party and a member of the supreme leadership. Fell, together with the leaders of the first anti-Stalin oppositions. Condemned at the 1937 show trial. Died in prison in unknown circumstances.

*Ravich, Sarah Naumovna* (1879–1957) Social Democrat from 1903; in Geneva from 1907. Was arrested in Munich while changing money stolen from the Russian Treasury in Tiflis. Returned to Russia with Lenin's group, became a member of the Petrograd Committee of the Bolshevik Party. Apparently arrested in 1938, but survived the camps. Wrote a novel about the Decembrists.

*Riazanov (Goldendakh), David Borisovich* (1870–1938) In the revolutionary movement from the age of seventeen, "almost the first to become a Marxist in Odessa." Following his theoretical and bookish inclinations, became a historian of Marxism. Arrested several times, made several trips abroad. From 1907, an émigré, writing a history of the First International, published certain works of Marx and Engels for the first time, became the leading expert on their literary legacy. Attended Zimmerwald Conference. Returned to Russia via Germany with the second party of Russian émigrés. In 1917, joined the Bolsheviks. Lecturer, founder and director of the Marx-Engels Institute. Expelled from the party in 1931. Died in exile.

*Safarov, Georgi Ivanovich* (1891–1942) Social Democrat from 1908, émigré in Switzerland from 1912, sided with Lenin and left for Russia with him. Chief editor of *Leningradskaya Pravda,* active member of the Zinoviev-Kamenev opposition in 1928. Expelled from the party as a Trotskyist in 1927. Arrested in 1935.

*Semashko, Nikolai Alexandrovich* (1874–1949) Son of a gentleman in Orel province; nephew of Plekhanov; educated at Yelets high school, and (with interruptions when he was in detention, or confined to his native country) in the Faculty of Medicine at Kazan University. During the 1905 Revolution, was conspicuous at meetings in Nizhny Novgorod, was arrested, released on bail, emigrated. Close to Lenin in Geneva and Paris. After the October Revolution, People's Commissar for Health. (Many hospitals in the U.S.S.R. and many streets with hospitals on them, are named after him, just as many streets with post offices are named after Podbelsky.)

*Shklovsky, Georgi Lvovich* (1875–1937) Social Democrat from 1898, emigrated to Switzerland in 1909. Chemist. Helped Lenin in routine matters (treasurer, etc.). Returned to Russia in summer 1917 with the third party of émigrés. In 1918, in charge of the Soviet office in Bern, then held other diplomatic posts. In 1927, demoted as a Trotskyist. Committed suicide during the Great Purge.

*Shliapnikov, Alexander Gavrilovich* (1885–1937) From a family of Old Believers in Murom. His father, an artisan, died young, leaving a wife and four children. He had three years of elementary education, dreamed of becoming a skilled workman, and eventually became a highly qualified fitter and turner. Originally a stanch adherent of the Old Belief, he succumbed to the spirit of the time and was converted to Social Democracy. Worked in Sormovo, then in Petersburg. Arrested on various occasions, never held for more than a year, but either amnestied or released against guarantees. From 1905, a Bolshevik. Emigrated in 1908, worked in several Western European factories. During the war, crossed the Russian frontier from Scandinavia several times, and was the only one in the Bolshevik Party to provide a real channel of communication between the emigration and the homeland: he delivered literature to Russia, and strengthened the party organizations in the capital and the provinces (of which he made a clandestine tour). From 1915, chairman of the Russian Bureau of the Central Committee; i.e., formally and in fact in charge of the whole party on Russian soil, while all other well-known leaders were lying low during the war years and the majority of party committees did nothing. The February Revolution found Shliapnikov in Petersburg. He became one of the Bolshevik members of the Executive Committee of the Soviet, created the Red Guards, made the arrangements to welcome Lenin on his return. But he was soon pushed into the background as former émigrés began arriving in large numbers. Was chairman of the Metalworkers' Union for many years, People's Commissar for Labor in the first Soviet government. When the government fled to Moscow, was given the job of organizing an orderly evacuation of Petersburg. Led the Workers' Opposition (1921), which accused the party leaders of forgetting the interests of the workers and of political degeneracy. Furiously attacked by Trotsky, Lenin, and the majority of the Central Committee: he was never forgiven for his role in this opposition. Thereafter, held only secondary posts. He was hemmed in by informers, and in 1929 Stalin used to telephone Shliapnikov at night and demand that he incriminate himself. Expelled from the party in 1933, exiled, arrested a year later. Under investigation for three years, would not give an inch, so that it was impossible to bring him into court in a show trial. Shot in September 1937. Rehabilitated by the Public Prosecutor's office in 1956, but still denied posthumous reinstatement in the party: a *workers' opposition* is unforgivable.

*Siefeldt, Artur Rudolf* (1889–1938) An Estonian from Tallinn. Sampled nearly all revolutionary factions, finally joined the Bolsheviks in Zurich from 1913 to 1917. Helped Lenin in his communications with

Kesküla. Left Switzerland in 1917 with the second émigré group to travel through Germany.

*Sklarz, Georg* (*b.* 1878) Businessman, expressed no political opinions. From the beginning of the war in 1914, an agent of German Intelligence and the Naval General Staff. Worked in Parvus's agency, then made big deals on his own, in war supplies to begin with, and continued his operations in ruined Germany after the war. Accused at a scandalous trial of bribing certain leading German socialist politicians—Scheidemann, Noske, Ebert—and high-ranking officers.

*Sokolnikov (Brilliant), Grigory Yakovlevich* (1888–1939) Son of a doctor; high-school education in Moscow. Bolshevik from 1905, member of Military Technical Bureau which organized armed raids. Emigrated in 1909 from exile on the Yenisei. Graduated from Faculty of Law in Paris. During the war vacillated between the *Nashe Slovo* group (Martov–Trotsky) and the Bolsheviks. Returned to Russia with Lenin's group. From July 1917, in the Bolshevik Central Committee, editor of *Pravda,* member of the Politburo when the October Revolution took place. Organized the seizure of the banks, became their commissar general. Signed the Brest-Litovsk Treaty as head of the Soviet delegation, took part in the supplementary discussions in Berlin. In charge on the political side of operations to put down the workers' risings at Izhevsk and Votkinsk and the peasant risings in Vyatka province. Then in charge of punitive operations on the Don which provoked the Don rising. Army commander during capture of Rostov and evacuation of Whites from Novorossisk. In 1920 he, Safarov, Kaganovich, and Peters were in charge of operations to subdue Turkestan. Occupied an unfortunate position in the party discussion on trade unions. From 1921 to 1926, People's Commissar for Finance. From 1929, ambassador in London; from 1934, Deputy People's Commissar for Foreign Affairs. A defendant at one of the Moscow show trials. Died in confinement.

*Tsivin, Yevgeny* (known to German and Austrian Intelligence services as *Weiss,* and *Ernst Kohler*) Russian revolutionary who worked in Switzerland during the war in contact with the Austrian and later also with the German Intelligence services.

*Uritsky, Moisei Solomonovich* (1873–1918) From a merchant family in the town of Cherkassy. Educated in Belaya Tserkov high school, Law Faculty of Kiev University. Took part in Social Democratic movement, had no difficulty in escaping from exile and going abroad. A Menshevik. During the war, with Trotsky in the *Nashe Slovo* group, was Parvus's channel of communication with the Inter-District group in Petersburg. Went with them when they merged with the Bolsheviks, and immediately became a member of the Central Committee. Member of the Military Revolutionary Committee, which directed the uprising in October 1917. Commissar of the Constituent Assembly —and dispersed it. Head of the Cheka in Petrograd, organized the Red Terror in the former capital. Killed by the student Kanegiesser.

*Weiss* See *Tsivin.*

*Zinoviev (Apfelbaum), Grigory Yevseyevich* (1883–1936) Native of Yelizavetgrad. Uneducated. In his youth, an office boy. Joined the Social Democrats at eighteen, emigrated at nineteen without having been arrested. Met Lenin in 1903 and joined him for good. Tried studying at Bern University, first in the Faculty of Chemistry, then in the Law Faculty, but abandoned the attempt. During the 1905 Revolution, complained of heart trouble (at the age of twenty-two), was forbidden by a specialist to "take any part in politics," and went abroad again. Once the major revolutionary events were past, he recovered and returned to Russia.

In 1908 he was arrested for the first time, was released after a few months as a result of intervention on his behalf, and this time went abroad to stay. From 1907, he was a permanent member of the Bolshevik Central Committee. When Lenin changed his entourage in 1908, Zinoviev became his closest assistant, and co-editor of all his publications. He followed Lenin to Galicia, and back to Switzerland, was taken by him to the Zimmerwald and Kienthal conferences. Throughout the war years the "Central Committee" meant Lenin, Zinoviev, and anyone they cared to coopt. He returned to Russia via Germany in Lenin's group, was fully informed on the connections with Parvus and the question of German aid. After the press revelations in July 1917 he went into hiding with Lenin (on the Finnish Gulf) to escape possible trial. Remained in hiding until the October Revolution. After the Revolution, chairman of the Petrograd Soviet of Workers' Deputies, chairman of the Council of People's Commissars of the Union of Communes of the Northern Region—i.e., after the flight of the Soviet government to Moscow in March 1918, he was virtual dictator of Petrograd and northwestern Russia. The terrorist operations of 1918–1919 were carried out under his direction. From 1919, head of Comintern. In 1923–1924 he helped Stalin to defeat Trotsky and entrench himself as Secretary General. In 1925 he and Kamenev led the Leningrad Opposition, which tried to seize power in the party but was defeated by Stalin in alliance with Bukharin. After this he tried acting in alliance with Trotsky, but they could not recover lost ground. After 1926, lost all his main posts, and all importance. Tried twice—in 1935 and 1936—before he was shot. Is said to have kissed the boots of the Chekists who led him out to be shot, pleading for mercy.

## Translator's Notes

**KNOT I,** *Chapter 22*

1  July 16–17, 1914.

2  The letterspaced words throughout the text follow the Russian edition. This special spacing is used by the author for emphasis.

3  "Very truly" is in English in the original.

4  "One shot for every Russian!"

**KNOT II,** *Chapter 47*

1  That is to say, January 22 by the Western European, Gregorian calendar. At this point, the Julian calendar was still in use in Russia.

**KNOT III,** *Chapter 1*

1  The dates used throughout this and subsequent chapters are those of the Western, Gregorian calendar.

# Translator's Glossary of Names

*Alakayevka*   A village in Samara province. Lenin's mother bought a house at Alakayevka in 1889, and Lenin spent the summers there with his family until 1893.

*Axelrod, Paul Borisovich* (1850–1928)   A co-founder with Plekhanov of the first Russian Marxist party, the Liberation of Labor group, formed in Switzerland in 1883. Influential as a theorist. One of the leaders of the Menshevik wing of Russian Social Democracy from 1903. A "liquidator" after 1905. A centrist in the First World War. Stanch supporter of the Provisional Government. Left Russia after the October Revolution; died in Berlin.

*Black Hundreds*   Extreme right-wing monarchist organizations which sprang up during the 1905 Revolution, the most important being the Union of the Russian People and the Union of the Archangel Michael. With the encouragement and sometimes the assistance of police, their rank-and-file members sought to stamp out revolution by counterviolence. Their targets included not only members of revolutionary parties but, on occasion, liberal politicians. Their anti-Semitic outrages seriously damaged the reputation of the Tsarist government in Western Europe.

*Bloody Sunday:* January 9, 1905 (January 22 in the Western calendar)   On this day a procession of workers 150,000 strong, led by a priest, Father Gapon, attempted to present a petition to the Tsar at the Winter Palace (he was not, in fact, in residence). The Governor General of St. Petersburg, Grand Duke Vladimir, ordered troops to open fire on the demonstrators;

285

more than a thousand were killed and several thousand
wounded. This was the signal for the general strike
which grew into the 1905 Revolution.

*Clara*   See *Zetkin*.

*Duma*   Representative legislative assembly established by
the Tsar after the 1905 Revolution. There were four
successive Dumas between April 1906 and October
1917:

1st Duma: April 27 to July 8, 1906: 18 S.D. delegates;
Bolsheviks boycotted the elections

2nd Duma: February 20 to June 2, 1907: 65 S.D.'s,
including 18 Bolsheviks

3rd Duma: November 1, 1907, to June 9, 1912: 19
S.D.'s, including 6 Bolsheviks

4th Duma: November 15, 1912, to October 6, 1917
(dissolved by the Provisional Government)

*Economists*   Russian Social Democrats in the 1890's who
held that, considering present Russian conditions,
Marxists should not attempt to form a socialist political
party but should support the liberal opposition to the
autocratic system, while simultaneously assisting the
proletariat in its economic struggle for higher wages
and better conditions.

*Expropriations*   Euphemism for robbery with violence as
a means of raising party funds, practiced during and
immediately after the 1905 Revolution both by the
Bolsheviks and by the Maximalists. (Even the biggest
Bolshevik coup—the Tiflis Treasury raid—was less
spectacular and lucrative than the Maximalist raids
on the Moscow Merchant Mutual Credit Bank and the
Petersburg Treasury in 1906.) Lenin regarded such
raids as a form of "partisan warfare," and the Stockholm congress of the Bolshevik Party (April 1906),
while condemning expropriation of "private capital"
approved raids on government agencies. Hostile publicity in the socialist press abroad—including criticism
from the Mensheviks and from Trotsky—and the

Stolypin government's success in repressing revolutionary activity forced the Bolsheviks to abandon this
practice.

*God Builders*   Literary-philosophical group which sought
to endow Marxism with religious appeal. In their
teaching, God did not exist but would be created by
the collective self-perfection of the human species.
Through its most important members (Lunacharsky,
Bazarov, and Gorky), the group had personal and
ideological links with the Machists. Lenin held that
any form of religion was incompatible with Marxism,
and saw this jejune mystification as an attempt to win
back "petit-bourgeois intellectuals" disillusioned by
the abortive 1905 Revolution.

*Gorky, Maxim (A. M. Peshkov) (1868–1936)*   The only
major Russian writer in the Social Démocratic camp.
Joined the Bolshevik Party in 1905. His ideological
instability (i.e., receptivity to new ideas) troubled his
relations with Lenin, who, however, showed unusual
patience in his efforts to win the errant writer over:
he was not only an ornament to the movement but
useful in spreading its influence and swelling its funds.
Gorky was an associate of Bogdanov and a God
Builder in the years immediately before the war. He
returned from emigration to Russia in 1913, and
founded the journal *Letopis* in 1915. In 1917–1918
his articles in *Novaya Zhizn (New Life)*, highly critical
of the Bolshevik Party and the new regime's policies,
greatly annoyed Lenin. From 1918 to 1921 he occupied himself mainly in attempting to resuscitate Russian cultural life. In 1921 he left Russia, revisited the
country in 1928 and 1929, and returned in 1931.

*Grigory*   See *Zinoviev*, in Author's Glossary.

*Grishka*   See *Zinoviev*, in Author's Glossary.

*Ilyich*   See *Vladimir Ilyich*.

*Imperialism (Imperialism As the Highest Stage of Capi-
talism)*   An ambitious attempt by Lenin, completed

in 1916, to provide a theoretical foundation for his views on war and revolution. Among other things, it purports to explain why reformist Social Democracy is based on illusions, and why the first proletarian revolution may occur in one of the less highly developed capitalist countries.

*Inter-District group* (Russian, *Mezhrayontsy*)   A Social Democratic group formed in St. Petersburg in 1913, consisting, to begin with, of adherents of Trotsky or Plekhanov who wanted the party to rise above the Bolshevik-Menshevik squabble. During the war, conducted anti-war propaganda in the Russian army. Played an important part after the February Revolution, when several prominent returning Social Democrats, including Trotsky and Lunacharsky, joined them. Incorporated in the Bolshevik Party in August 1917.

*International*   The Second International, established in 1889, was long divided over socialist attitudes toward war and did not survive the First World War. After the war, the following were formed: the Bern International, uniting the right wing (1919); the Communist International, or Comintern (1919–1943); the Vienna International, or "2½ International," uniting the center with the anti-Bolshevik left. In 1923 the Second International was reborn out of the merger of the Bern and Vienna internationals.

*Iskra (The Spark)*   Russian Marxist journal and organization established by Lenin in Munich, December 24, 1900, in collaboration with Plekhanov, Axelrod, Vera Zasulich, Potresov, and Martov. Lenin's attempts to gain control of *Iskra*, which he wanted to become the party's organizational center, led to a split of the Bolsheviks and the Mensheviks at the Second Congress (Brussels, July 30, 1903). The bone of contention between the two factions of the R.S.D.R.P., *Iskra* passed out of Bolshevik control in November 1903.

It continued to appear, with a Menshevik slant, until October 1905.

*Kadets* ("Kadety," a name composed of the initial letters in Russian of their original party title: Constitutional Democrats) The most important Russian liberal group, which established itself as a political party in 1905, to participate in elections to the first Duma. Also known as the Party of People's Freedom.

*Kienthal Conference* International socialist conference, April 24–30, 1916, to discuss views on war and peace. Though the Zimmerwald left failed to carry the vote on any of the major issues discussed, the conference was in Lenin's view a further step toward the creation of a new, revolutionary socialist International.

*Koba* A romantic Caucasian outlaw, hero of the Georgian novelist Kazbegi's *The Patricide*. Joseph Dzhugashvili used this *nom de guerre* until in 1912 he began styling himself Stalin, and old Caucasian cronies were allowed to call him Koba even after he became dictator.

*Kommunist* Short-lived journal published by Lenin in Geneva. One double number appeared in September 1915, including three of his articles. He hoped to make this the international journal of the Social Democratic left, but his disagreements with other editorial contributors (Bukharin and Piatakov) precipitated its collapse.

*Kuba* See *Hanecki,* in Author's Glossary.

*Letopis* A literary, scientific, and political journal founded by Gorky and published in St. Petersburg from December 1915 to December 1917. Its eminent contributors included Blok, Mayakovsky, and Pavlov. Lenin disapproved of its editorial policy, set by Mensheviks and members of the *Vperyod* group, but Bolsheviks, including Krupskaya, used it as a vehicle for legal publication.

*Lilina, Zinka* Zinoviev's mistress.

*Liquidators* Name given by their enemies to those—

mainly Mensheviks—who, after the revolutionary wave of 1905–1907 had receded, urged Russian socialists to concentrate on the battle for reforms within the Duma and for the legalization of the workers' movement; in effect, to abandon revolutionary activity. Lenin succeeded in fusing in his own mind this hostile trend to his right with his foes on the left: Recallists and Ultimatists.

*Luxemburg, Rosa* (1871–1919)   Born in Zamosc, Poland, emigrated to Switzerland, 1889; graduated from Zurich University. Outstanding leader of the left wing of Polish Social Democracy (the Social Democratic Party of the Kingdom of Poland and Lithuania), which through her friend and one-time lover Leon Jogiches (Tyszka) she continued to dominate even after 1898, when she made Germany her main sphere of activity. Her major theoretical works, particularly *The Accumulation of Capital*, were unacceptable to Lenin. In spite of her misgivings about Bolshevik elitism, and her awareness that Bolshevik organizational principles might lead to the establishment of a personal dictatorship, she sided with Lenin on various occasions, most notably at the Fifth Congress of the R.S.D.R.P. in 1907, and at the Stuttgart Congress of the Second International in the same year, when their joint amendment to a resolution seemed to have committed international Social Democracy to the use of an eventual European war as the occasion for revolutionary "overthrow of the bourgeoisie."

During the First World War, together with Karl Liebknecht and Klara Zetkin, she led a left-wing group in the German Social Democratic Party which became known as the Spartacus League. Her anti-war policy ("struggle for peace without annexations," "war on war") fell short of the radical demands of Lenin and the left minority at the Zimmerwald Conference. Whereas Lenin thrived on splits, she strove to pre-

serve the unity of the massive German Social Democratic Party, while working for its ideological conver-
sion from within: it was the party majority which in
the end expelled her left-wing group from its ranks. In
prison at the time of the Bolshevik Revolution, she
hailed it with enthusiasm, though Lenin's opportunist
agrarian policy and the summary dismissal of the Constituent Asembly disturbed her. One of the founders
of the German Communist Party in December 1918.
During the rioting in Berlin in January 1919 she was
murdered while under arrest.

*Machists* Followers of the Austrian physicist and philosopher Ernst Mach (1838–1916). His reexamination of
Newtonian physics prepared the ground for Einstein's
work, and his influence as a philosopher can be seen
in the development of twentieth-century neo-positivism.
He sought to replace explanatory with purely descrip-
tive procedures, in which only empirically verifiable
data were admissible, and rejected as metaphysical
such concepts as absolute space and time, substance,
"thing." Lenin regarded Mach's teaching as subjectivist
and idealist, and as incompatible with traditional Marxist materialism. In his only extended philosophical
monograph (*Materialism and Empirico-Criticism*),
Lenin attacked Bogdanov and others who wished to
reconcile Machism with Marxism.

*Maximalists* An extremist group which broke from the
socialist revolutionaries in 1904. Distinguished by its
fanatical belief in "propaganda by deed"—i.e., political assassination and robbery ("expropriations"). A
majority of the group, by then much reduced, decided
in 1920 to dissolve itself and seek membership in the
Bolshevik Party.

*Moisei* See *Bronski,* in Author's Glossary.

*Nadya* See *Krupskaya,* in Author's Glossary.

*Nashe Slovo (Our Word)* A newspaper published in Paris
from January 1915, on the initiative of Antonov-

Ovseenko, then a Menshevik, but in 1917 and afterward one of the outstanding Bolshevik military leaders. *Nashe Slovo* opposed the war and denounced "social patriotism," but was less narrow and dogmatic in its editorial policy than Lenin's *Sozialdemokrat*. Its contributors included Radek, Rakovsky, Kollontai, Uritsky, the future Soviet Commissar for Foreign Affairs Chicherin, and above all Trotsky, who represented the paper at the Zimmerwald Conference.

*Octobrists*  A moderate Russian conservative party founded in 1905, which, unlike the liberals and all parties to the left, regarded the concessions made by the Tsar in his manifesto of October 17, 1905, as a satisfactory basis for cooperation between government and Duma in the reconstruction of Russia after the 1905 Revolution.

*Recallists* (Russian, *Otzovisty*)  Dissident group within the Bolshevik Party which in 1908 opposed Lenin's tactics of "temporary retreat" and of "using all legal possibilities," including participation in the Duma, to reinforce the party's political position. The Recallists, whose members included Bogdanov and Lunacharsky, demanded the recall of Bolshevik deputies from the Duma, and total withdrawal underground by the party to prepare the next armed uprising.

*Rosa*  See *Luxemburg*.

*R.S.D.R.P.* (Russian Social Democratic Workers' Party) Founded in March 1898 at the First Congress at Minsk. At the Second Congress (Brussels–London, 1903, split into two factions—Bolsheviks and Mensheviks; and at the Sixth Pan-Russian Conference (Prague, 1912), broke up. From March 1918, the Bolshevik faction took the name of Russian Communist Party.

*Rütlian reformists*  Members of the Rütliverein, a Swiss educational society for workers and artisans which existed from 1838 to 1925. (According to tradition, the three cantons sealed their alliance against the

Hapsburgs on the field of Rütli in 1307.) Attacked by Lenin as disseminators of petit-bourgeois reformist illusions among workers. Merged with the Swiss Social Democratic Party in 1925.

*Schmidt, Nikolai Pavlovich*  Nephew of Morozov; wealthy student who committed suicide in prison, 1906, bequeathing his fortune to the R.S.D.R.P. His younger sister, Yelisabet Pavlovna, made a fictitious marriage with a Bolshevik, which gave her legal authority to turn her inheritance over to the Bolsheviks.

*Shushenskoye*  See *Yenisei.*

*Sozialdemokrat*  Bolshevik newspaper. After the police confiscated its first number, brought out in Russia in 1908, it was published in Paris until 1914, and then in Geneva. It provided Lenin with a platform for his campaigns against Bolshevik deviationists and for his propaganda during the war.

*S.R.*  Socialist Revolutionary Party, formed at the end of 1901 out of the merging of the Populist groups. Adept at terrorism. In 1917, supported the Provisional Government (Kerensky and Chernov were S.R.'s). Fought against the Bolsheviks during the civil war, and did not survive the Bolshevik victory.

*Stolypin, Peter Arkadievich* (1862–1911)  Prime Minister of Russia from 1906 until his assassination in 1911. Believed that with two decades of peace, Russia could become stable and prosperous. Tried to reinforce the government by an understanding with the Duma, and create a class of loyal and contented smallholders through agrarian reform. Had more success with his stern measures to repress revolutionary activities by summary trial and execution. Was scarcely less unpopular with the court clique than with revolutionaries. His assassin was loosely connected both with the S.R. and with the secret police.

*Tyszka (Tyszko) (Leon Jogiches), Jan* (1867–1919)  Born in Vilna, member of revolutionary organizations from the age of eighteen. Co-founder of the Social Democratic Party of the Kingdom of Poland and Lithuania. Close collaborator with Rosa Luxemburg, and for some years her lover. Took part in the revolutionary events of 1905 in Warsaw; arrested in 1906 and sentenced to eight years' imprisonment. Escaped, and after 1907 controlled the S.D.K.P.L. from Berlin. Internationalist during the First World War; prominent member of the German socialist left. Led the Spartacus group while Rosa Luxemburg was in prison, and until his own arrest in March 1918. Secretary of the Central Committee of the German Communist Party at its establishment in December 1918. Arrested in March 1919, murdered in prison.

*Ultimatists* Dissident Bolshevik group which shared the general views of the Recallists, differing only on minor questions of tactics.

*Ulyanov* Lenin's real name.

*Vladimir Ilyich* Lenin's forename and patronymic. The patronymic Ilyich, used alone, indicates affectionate respect.

*Volodya* Affectionate diminutive of Lenin's forename.

*Vorbote* Theoretical journal published by the Bureau of the Zimmerwald Left, of which only two numbers appeared (in January and May 1916). The first included Lenin's article "Opportunism and the Collapse of the Second International," and the second his thesis "Socialist Revolution and the Right of Nations to Self-Determination."

*Vperyod (Forward) group* Extreme leftist Bolshevik schismatics, whose views Lenin considered a "caricature of Bolshevism." This alliance of Recallists, Ultimatists, and Machists attracted (sometimes, as in the case of Krassin and Gorky, only briefly) many past and future luminaries of Bolshevism who in the years 1909–1917 found Lenin's policies timid, opportunistic, and unrevolutionary, and his behavior within the party intolerably highhanded. Among its members were Bogdanov, Lunacharsky, Liadov, Alexinsky, Manuilsky. Loosely held together by common disapproval of participation in the Duma and other legal organizations, by eagerness to precipitate a fresh armed uprising in Russia (which Lenin in 1908–1914 rightly thought had no chance of success), and by its demands for complete freedom of thought within the party. Its numbers were steadily reduced by internal quarrels and defections. In 1917 its remnants fused with the Inter-District group and so were brought back into the Bolshevik Party in August of that year.

*Yenisei* One of the great Siberian rivers. The Yenisei region, remote and primitive, was used as a place of exile since the seventeenth century. Lenin spent the years 1897–1900 in exile there (at Shushenskoye); Krupskaya joined him in May 1898.

*Zetkin, Klara (Clara) (nee Eisner) (1857–1933)* Prominent in the German Social Democratic Party, the Second International, and the international women's movement. Close friend of Rosa Luxemburg, whom she supported in the First World War. Perhaps influenced by her Russian émigré husband, she was less inclined than Rosa to criticize Russian comrades. Joined the infant German Communist Party early in 1919. Took active part in the Communist International, where, in spite of occasional vacillations, she supported Soviet leadership. As the oldest serving deputy, made the opening speech in the Reichstag in August 1932, calling for a united front against Fascism. Died near Moscow; her remains are immured in the Kremlin wall, near the Lenin Mausoleum.

*Zimmerwald Conference* International socialist conference, September 5–8, 1915, intended to reestablish international socialist links after the collapse of the Second International. The right, most effectively represented by Axelrod and Ledebour, dominated the conference. From Lenin's point of view, its value was that it enabled him to identify and attach to himself a stanch leftist minority. "The development of the international socialist movement is moving slowly . . . but definitely in the direction of 'a break' with opportunism and social chauvinism."

# ABOUT THE AUTHOR

ALEXANDER SOLZHENITSYN, Nobel Prize laureate and Russia's finest living writer, was born December 11, 1918, in Kislovodsk, Russia. In February 1945, as a young captain in the Russian Army, he was arrested by SMERSH, the Soviet armed forces counterintelligence agency, and charged with making derogatory remarks about Stalin in correspondence with a school friend. Solzhenitsyn spent eight years in concentration camps and three years in exile for his offense—an experience which provided the raw material for *One Day in the Life of Ivan Denisovich* and *The First Circle*. During the mid-1950s he was a patient in a cancer ward, but later recovered. In 1962, with Nikita Khrushchev serving as patron, *One Day in the Life of Ivan Denisovich* was published in the Soviet Union, but the printing was stopped almost immediately. This is the only one of Solzhenitsyn's novels to have been permitted publication in his native land. Solzhenitsyn was awarded the Nobel Prize for Literature in 1970, but was unable at first to leave the Soviet Union to receive the Nobel medal and prize money of $80,000 for fear Soviet authorities might not let him return to his family. At a time when Solzhenitsyn was being ostracized by Soviet officialdom, expelled from the U.S.S.R.'s Union of Writers, and denied the use of state archives and libraries, he nevertheless produced *August 1914*, a masterful account of World War I. In late 1973, he authorized the publication in the West of his *The Gulag Archipelago, 1918–1956*, a historical account of the Soviet Secret Police, prison camps, and terror system. *From Under the Rubble* was undertaken by Solzhenitsyn and other Soviet dissidents to reinstitute a climate of intellectual debate on the fundamental direction the Soviet Union should take. The project was begun while Solzhenitsyn was still in Moscow, but was completed after his expulsion from the Soviet Union in 1974. Following his expulsion, Solzhenitsyn became the center of international controversy. His campaign against détente elicited a broad spectrum of response from his American audience, but on one point both his supporters and critics have agreed: his integrity and commitment to the cause of freedom are unshakable. *Lenin in Zurich* is his most recent book.

# THE NAMES THAT SPELL GREAT LITERATURE

Choose from today's most renowned world authors—every one an important addition to your personal library.

**Hermann Hesse**

| | | | |
|---|---|---|---|
| ☐ | MAGISTER LUDI | 2645 • | $1.75 |
| ☐ | DEMIAN | 2944 • | $1.75 |
| ☐ | ROSSHALDE | 7370 • | $1.50 |
| ☐ | STEPPENWOLF | 7979 • | $1.50 |
| ☐ | GERTRUDE | 10060 • | $1.95 |
| ☐ | THE JOURNEY TO THE EAST | 10136 • | $1.75 |
| ☐ | SIDDHARTHA | 10266 • | $1.75 |
| ☐ | BENEATH THE WHEEL | 10352 • | $1.95 |
| ☐ | NARCISSUS AND GOLDMUND | 10466 • | $1.95 |

**Alexander Solzhenitsyn**

| | | | |
|---|---|---|---|
| ☐ | AUGUST 1914 | 2997 • | $2.50 |
| ☐ | ONE DAY IN THE LIFE OF IVAN DENISOVICH | 2949 • | $1.50 |
| ☐ | STORIES AND PROSE POEMS | 7409 • | $1.50 |
| ☐ | CANCER WARD | 10151 • | $2.25 |
| ☐ | THE LOVE-GIRL AND THE INNOCENT | 10246 • | $1.50 |

**Jerzy Kosinski**

| | | | |
|---|---|---|---|
| ☐ | STEPS | 2597 • | $1.50 |
| ☐ | THE DEVIL TREE | 7865 • | $1.50 |
| ☐ | THE PAINTED BIRD | 8257 • | $1.75 |
| ☐ | BEING THERE | 10625 • | $1.75 |

**Doris Lessing**

| | | | |
|---|---|---|---|
| ☐ | THE SUMMER BEFORE THE DARK | 2640 • | $1.95 |
| ☐ | THE GOLDEN NOTEBOOK | 7747 • | $1.95 |
| ☐ | THE FOUR-GATED CITY | 7937 • | $1.95 |

**André Schwarz-Bart**

| | | | |
|---|---|---|---|
| ☐ | A WOMAN NAMED SOLITUDE | 7880 • | $1.75 |
| ☐ | THE LAST OF THE JUST | 10469 • | $1.95 |

Buy them at your local bookstore or use this handy coupon for ordering:

---

**Bantam Books, Inc., Dept. EDG, 414 East Golf Road, Des Plaines, Ill. 60016**

Please send me the books I have checked above. I am enclosing $_____ (please add 35¢ to cover postage and handling). Send check or money order —no cash or C.O.D.'s please.

Mr/Mrs/Miss_____

Address_____

City_____State/Zip_____

EDG—3/77

Please allow three weeks for delivery. This offer expires 3/78.